THE EINSTEIN PAPERS

THE EINSTEIN PAPERS

CRAIG DIRGO

POCKET BOOKS

NEW YORK LONDON TORONTO SYDNEY TOKYO SINGAPORE

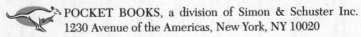POCKET BOOKS, a division of Simon & Schuster Inc.
1230 Avenue of the Americas, New York, NY 10020

ISBN: 0-671-03489-8

First Pocket Books hardcover printing May 1999

10 9 8 7 6 5 4 3 2 1

POCKET and colophon are registered trademarks of
Simon & Schuster Inc.

Printed in the U.S.A.

*For my father, Lt. Colonel Earl Dirgo—an atomic warrior
who died too soon*

THE EINSTEIN PAPERS

PROLOGUE

"It can't . . . ," Albert Einstein started to say, "it's so . . ."

Then he lowered his arm and his fingers relaxed.

The noise of the chalk shattering as it struck the worn green linoleum was not loud. Still, the sound in the otherwise silent laboratory had the same effect on Einstein as snapping a leather belt on a dog's rump. He jumped. Stepping forward, closer to the blackboard, his left shoe ground a piece of the chalk into dust as he stared at the final equation in shock.

All at once the shock faded away and he felt instantly euphoric. It was the same sensation felt by a gambler hitting the grand prize jackpot after a lifetime of losing. He grinned and stared up at the heavens. He felt a welcome peace he had never felt before.

The feeling was electrifying, instantaneous, and completely unexpected.

The hair on the back of Einstein's neck stood straight out. This was immediately followed by a tingling sensation that grew quickly until his entire scalp felt as if it were on fire. Einstein shook his head, then turned it slightly sideways and stared at his final notation once again.

The last symbol jumped from the blackboard as if lit by a huge spotlight.

Several minutes passed as Einstein's mind fought to accept the reality of what had finally been accomplished. He blinked and continued staring at the equation on the blackboard.

Almost without thought, he reached in his pocket, removed a box of wooden kitchen matches, and struck one against the side of the box. It flared instantly, tingeing the air with a sulphur smell as the flame grew larger. He held the burning match poised in the air in his right hand. With his left he removed his ancient meerschaum pipe from the pocket of his trousers.

Frozen in place, the match burned slowly down as Einstein stood mesmerized, staring at the blackboard. Seconds passed until the last remnant of the flame licked the tip of his finger, breaking his concentration. Flicking the match back and forth to extinguish what little flame remained, he tossed it over his shoulder toward an ashtray already overflowing with spent pipe tobacco that sat on a long wooden table parallel to the blackboard.

Opening the box and lighting a second match, Einstein touched this to the top of the pipe, then drew deeply through the stem. Blowing the smoke through his mouth, he took a few steps, then sat down behind the long table and leaned back in an old leather chair.

And then he smiled again.

The final and most difficult part of the puzzle that Einstein called the Unified Field Theory was discovered on the second day of August, during the last month of World War II. The solution he had sought for decades surrendered itself to him at just past three in the afternoon.

Just prior to the eve of the Great Depression, in 1929, Einstein had delivered his first paper on the theory. Now, sixteen long years later, the physicist was a rapidly aging man of sixty-six. The last few years, as the aches and pains of old age grew stronger, he began to fear he might leave this earth without ever solving the theory. The last four years had passed without Einstein making any noticeable progress, and he had become discouraged. But he had forged ahead—somehow confident he was on the right track.

He was nothing if not patient.

And then, like an epiphany revealed to the faithful, the answer had made itself clear.

His face remained in a smile of triumph as he stared at the

solution again. Einstein laughed, at first to himself, a chuckle really, but this was soon followed by a loud, raucous belly laugh. He wiped a tear of joy from his eye.

It was all so uniquely obvious.

Rubbing the side of his nose with the tip of his finger, he stared again at the blackboard. Just at that instant a shaft of sunlight burst from behind the clouds outside. A single beam shot through the window of his laboratory as if it were a beacon from the heavens. The beam lit the dust hanging in the air, a visible legacy to Einstein's refusal to allow the cleaning people to violate his inner sanctuary. His pipe smoke rose toward the beam, mixing with the dust and deflecting the light.

For a moment Einstein experienced complete clarity of thought as he stared at the fruit of his years of labor etched in chalk on the blackboard. Then, placing his pipe in a briar rack on the table, he rose from the chair. He walked the few steps to the couch in his office and lay down, pulling a light blanket folded on the edge of the couch across his body. In seconds he was sound asleep.

He dreamed no dreams that afternoon.

When he awoke from his nap he walked home and ate dinner. He told no one, not even those closest to him, of the discovery he had just made.

Einstein spent the following day locked in his laboratory carefully rewriting the complete series of equations onto three fresh blackboards. Then, without pausing for even a moment of rest, he spent the next forty-eight hours testing and retesting his complex formulas and equations, attempting to find a flaw. By the third day the exact same conclusion had been reached.

Shaking his head in amazement, Einstein sat in his worn leather chair once again. The physicist felt ecstatic that the Unified Field Theory was at long last solved. His knowledge that the theory had at last been proven, that his years of work were not in vain, was a defining moment of personal triumph.

In the rarefied world in which Einstein worked, the answers he sought never revealed themselves easily. Even so, the Unified Field Theory had consumed a great deal of his life, more than any other problem he had sought to solve. Rising from his chair, he committed the solution to memory, then began erasing the secret from the blackboards.

"I shall go sailing now," he said under his breath as the last equation disappeared from the board.

Satisfied the grand puzzle to the universe was at last completed, he decided to reward himself with a rare day away from his laboratory. When he reached the door he paused and stared back at the now blank blackboards.

"Yes," he said to himself again, "a sailing trip is in order."

The sixth of August, 1945, dawned warm, with bright clear skies, in Princeton, New Jersey. The sun creeping over the horizon signaled the beginning of what promised to be an idyllic summer day. Waking without the benefit of an alarm clock, Einstein rose slowly from his bed. He rubbed his hands across his wrinkled face, a face that was easily one of the most recognizable in the world. It was graced with a bushy white mustache, a bulbous nose, and eyes that looked upon the world with a curiosity that age had not diminished. His hair was long, straight, and stood away from the scalp as if electrified. A distinct lack of physical exercise had given him a thickness in the midsection, as is often the case with older men, but overall his health was still quite good. Other than smoking a pipe, his only unhealthy habit was a propensity to overwork himself.

Dressed only in tattered boxer shorts, Einstein looked out the small dormer window of his upstairs bedroom. The rising sun shot across his lawn, the golden rays forming a blinding arc across the dew-dampened grass. The beams of sunlight broken by the shrubbery surrounding his yard looked to Einstein like the fingers of God himself. He smiled at the thought, then slowly stepped from the window.

Caring little about fashion, he donned the same clothing he had left on the floor at the foot of his antique wooden bed the night before. He pulled on the same pair of wrinkled tan pants, with the same worn black suspenders hanging down, then zipped up his fly and snapped the pants closed. Donning yesterday's shirt, once white but now a yellowish color from repeated washings, he absentmindedly fastened the buttons crookedly, one hole too high, then pulled the suspenders across his shoulders. He tucked his shirt in, but carelessly left one of the tails partially out. Sitting on a worn chair, he pulled on a pair of dingy socks and laced up his worn brogans. Rising slowly from the chair, he stretched his arms to the ceiling and took several deep breaths.

Morning exercise completed, and dressed to his satisfaction, he shuffled downstairs.

His housekeeper, Helen Dukas, was already awake. Bustling about the kitchen, she poured a cup of coffee from the stainless steel percolator as Einstein sat down at the cluttered kitchen table. After the cup was placed in front of him, he sipped the steaming liquid slowly, all the while curiously examining a flower Dukas had placed in a glass on the table.

As she had every morning for the last seventeen years, Dukas prodded him to eat a good breakfast, begged him in fact, but the old man just wanted a slice of toast. Finishing the toasted bread, Einstein began arranging the crumbs into intricate patterns on the smooth Formica of the table. As he sipped his coffee, he stared at the crumbs. Slowly reaching for a scrap of paper, which happened to be one of his paychecks that lay atop a jumbled pile of mail on the table, he quickly began scribbling equations on the back.

For his celebratory day off, Einstein had requested a car and driver from the Princeton University motor pool. Though he possessed one of the greatest analytical minds of all time, he had yet to operate a motor vehicle. The driver, a student named Mike Scaramelli, arrived promptly at seven. He slid the car to a stop in Einstein's driveway. After pausing to wipe a handprint from the passenger window with his handkerchief, he walked up the steps and knocked on the front door of Einstein's home at 112 Mercer Street. Hearing the knock, Einstein rose from the table and stuffed the check, the back now covered with equations, into the pile of letters on the counter.

"I will be back before dark," he said to Dukas as he walked from the kitchen.

"Be sure to take a light jacket, Albert," Dukas said as she began to wash Einstein's breakfast dishes in the sink. "One can never tell how the weather may turn."

Walking across the hardwood floors of his living room, Einstein paused at the coat rack and removed a jacket. Placing the thin cloth coat under his arm, he opened his front door, then smiled at Scaramelli. As he walked out the door, he paused to tuck the newspaper lying on his porch under his other arm. In the driveway, he climbed into the rear seat of the automobile.

"Is the fuel tank full?" Einstein asked once he was settled.

"I topped it off this morning, Dr. Einstein," Scaramelli noted.

"Good, gasoline is scarce, what with the war and all."

"Yes it is, Dr. Einstein," Scaramelli said. "The director of the motor pool was unsure where you wanted to be driven."

Einstein reached across the front seat and pointed out his destination on the map Scaramelli held. Tracing the best route to take with his fingertip, Scaramelli placed the map next to him on the front seat, then put the 1939 Packard into gear and began driving east, toward the ocean. Einstein settled back again in the rear compartment and began to read the comics in the newspaper.

It was 7:12 A.M. The pair would reach their destination, a marina on the New Jersey coast, in just over an hour.

❖ ❖ ❖

Einstein was a man tied to his work. He had few hobbies, but he truly loved to sail. He would often struggle mentally with his formulas while at sea, claiming that he could think more clearly in the salt air. Today's voyage, however, was to be strictly recreational; the Unified Field Theory was left locked in a far part of his mind, the solution a secret he was not ready to share. He had yet to tell a soul that the theory was now complete. There was time enough for that.

Einstein treasured his sailboat as he did few physical possessions. The vessel allowed him the opportunity and freedom of being truly alone. Away from the closed classrooms and laboratories where he had spent most of his life. Alone with the deep thoughts that clouded his every waking moment.

Ernest Hartley, the owner of the marina where Einstein moored his boat, kept the physicist's twenty-seven-foot-long mahogany sloop perfectly maintained. He understood that his genius friend was not always comfortable with simple mechanics and was easily puzzled by things others might consider commonplace.

At eleven minutes before eight, the car carrying Einstein was still fifteen miles from the marina. Although Einstein was not due for another half-hour, his sailboat's heavily varnished wood was already gleaming in the morning sun, awaiting its owner's arrival. Hartley finished hosing the vessel off with fresh water and rubbed the last of the brightwork to a dull glow. Hoisting the sails, he gave them a quick visual inspection, then checked the sailboat's lines for frayed ends. He tested the rudder and found it moving smoothly. Hartley wiped his hands on a towel and walked back inside to await Einstein's imminent arrival.

Rolling down the tree-lined road leading to Hartley's Marina, Einstein folded the newspaper in half and placed it on the leather-covered seat next to him. Nowadays the newspaper only depressed him. The news was only of death and dying, of a long war he hoped would soon end. Instead, he listened to the mechanical sounds coming from the Packard as he stared out the window at the farmers' fields just inside the border of trees. Cranking down the window he listened as the flock of Bob White's in the bushes near the trees chirped the song that gave them their name.

With World War II sapping most of the industrial production of Detroit, it was very difficult, even for prestigious Princeton University, to purchase any new automobiles. That was fine with Einstein. The dark gray Packard had long been his favorite, and the man who ran the motor pool was well aware of that fact. When Einstein requested a car, it was usually the Packard that arrived.

Elegant yet understated, the Packard-designed coachwork was finished in a lacquer color the factory called mourning dove gray. The entire length of the body sported a pair of thin red accent lines that ended on the front fenders in a rolling wave. The hood was long and hinged in the middle, with a chrome strip down the center. To each side of the hood sat fenders, the passenger side featuring a rounded hump where the sidemount spare tire was stored. Huge round headlights, mounted inside the flowing sheet metal of the fenders, pointed the way forward. The vehicle was powered by an eight-cylinder engine that operated so quietly it was nearly impossible to tell when the engine was running. Its power was channeled though a hydro-static transmission that required no shifting of the gears. The seats were finished in red leather, the headliner was made of gray mohair, and the thick felt carpets muffled any road noise. Set inside the massive dashboard of the Packard was a radio that sent the sound to a speaker in the driver's area as well as to a single chrome-covered speaker mounted on the dividing wall to the rear compartment and facing to the rear. On the radio an orchestra performing works by Beethoven was playing lightly as

Scaramelli slowed, then turned off the pavement and started down the dirt road to the marina.

Braking the Packard sedan to a stop on the gravel parking lot of the marina, Scaramelli scurried to open the rear door, then waited as Einstein climbed slowly from the leather-trimmed rear compartment. On the gravel next to the Packard, the physicist stood and breathed deeply of the salt air for a few moments.

"What a glorious day," he noted, his words still thick with his native German accent.

Scaramelli nodded silently. The student was still in awe of the great man and found ordinary conversation with him difficult. He walked respectfully behind as Einstein entered the marina building.

Hartley looked up from the fishing magazine he was reading on the counter as the door swung open. He smiled, folded the magazine closed, and greeted Einstein warmly. "Good to see you, Doctor. Your boat is all ready to sail."

Einstein returned the smile and nodded slowly. "Thank you, Ernie," he said simply, his eyes squinting slightly from the dim light inside the building.

With Hartley leading the way, Einstein and Scaramelli walked through the marina building. The shelves lining the marina's walls were crammed floor to ceiling with dusty chandlery. Boxes of oil were piled next to wooden crates containing bottles of soda. Spools containing the material to sew new sails sat alongside shelves stacked with fresh-cut hardwoods that tinted the air with their scents as they aged. A polished brass antique binnacle with round balancing weights sat off to one side.

Einstein paused to peer at the compass inside. "That is what started me in science," he said to no one in particular.

Hartley smiled at the physicist, having heard the story before.

"I wondered why the needle always pointed north," Einstein said quietly as the men exited through the door leading to the dock.

Walking along a weathered wooden ramp, the trio stopped at Einstein's boat, which rocked gently in the waves lapping at the dock. The floating dock where the sailboat was moored was nearly level with the ramp. The water was at high tide.

"You should catch the outgoing tide nicely," Hartley said, studying the water.

"Ah, an ebb tide," Einstein said as he climbed aboard the vessel whose bow was already pointing seaward. "Excellent."

Checking the boat absentmindedly, he raised one of the sails of the sloop, then settled behind the helm. His hands upon the highly polished wheel, he nodded toward Hartley, who started untying the lines but then stopped.

"I forgot something, Doctor," Hartley said. "I'll just be a second."

Running inside, he quickly returned with a paper sack, its top folded over and fastened with a wooden clothespin. "My wife made you lunch, in case you get hungry."

Einstein, always somewhat embarrassed by the attention he generated, thanked the man humbly. "You're too good to me, Ernie," he said slowly. "Please be sure to thank Katherine for me."

"What time should we expect you back?" Hartley asked as he handed the sack to Einstein.

"Time is but a concept, my good friend," Einstein said. "But since you asked, the latest should be an hour or two before sundown."

With a motion from Hartley, Scaramelli cast off the last of the lines holding the sloop in place. The boat was now free of the dock and Hartley carefully shoved the bow from the dock with his foot. The wind began to carry the vessel to sea. With a slight wave of his hand, Einstein steered toward the open water, a single sail raised to the wind.

Hartley reached in his pocket and removed a pack of Lucky Strikes. He lit one and puffed. Then he and Scaramelli stood watching from the dock until the small boat was safely past the breakwaters and in open water. When only a small white speck of sail remained silhouetted against the horizon the two men walked back inside.

Three-fourths of a mile east and three miles south of Hartley's Marina the dark green water of the Atlantic Ocean relentlessly surged toward land. On the tops of the waves a thin curl of white broke into foam as the seawater slid from its peak and rushed toward land. The troughs between the waves were wide and even spaced. The smell of salt and seaweed hung thickly in the air, as if the winds were being misted by a natural perfume. The sun this morning was bright yellow and radiating heat. It hung above the horizon at one-third of its daily arc. Thin clouds overhead moved on the breeze, racing seaward away from land.

Einstein reveled in a silence broken only by the noise of the wind whipping against the fabric of the sails. The salt spray blown back from the bow as it dipped into the troughs between the waves quickly buffeted his flowing hair until it was a tangled white mess. Breathing deeply of the salty air, Einstein allowed himself a small chuckle of delight. He hooked a rope to the wheel, then tied it to a cleat on the gunwale to make a crude autopilot so that he could go forward to raise another sail. Back at the helm, he unhooked the rope, then steered farther south along the coast of New Jersey, keeping the sailboat just in sight of land.

It wasn't that Einstein was afraid of the deeper water, he wasn't. It was just that the seabirds stayed closer to shore. He loved to watch the birds as they swooped and dived at the sea, in a spontaneous ballet of water and air. He stared off the port bow as a hawk dived to the water, retreating with a small fish in its beak.

Standing at the wheel, he waved his hand at the bird as if to signal hello.

Throughout his life, Einstein had always been a deeply religious man. In a magazine interview, he was quoted as saying that he believed all his best ideas came from God. His religious side also made him cherish the natural world surrounding him. Perhaps more than others he understood the complicated powers at work on the planet. Certainly he appreciated them more than most.

He was a simple man bound to complex thoughts.

Continuing along the coastline, he daydreamed back to a time several years ago. On a day of sailing much like this, a huge blue whale had breached off his sailboat's starboard bow. Running forward to drop the sails, he had waited patiently until the whale breached again, directly alongside his vessel. To this day he could still recall the intense feelings that had washed over him as he gazed into the huge whale's eyes. Einstein clearly remembered that he had seen in the eyes of the whale a great intelligence, wisdom, and knowledge. The experience had filled him with deep emotion.

Warmed by the sun and tickled by a pleasant breeze, the physicist studied the sea carefully as he sailed south. All around his sailboat he witnessed life. Atlantic porpoise slid to the surface like graceful dancers in an underwater tango, while schools of small fish boiled to the surface to be fed upon by dive-bombing gulls and pelicans.

Continuing twenty nautical miles south along the coast, content just to be sailing, he at last grew weary and stopped in a small protected cove he had found on a previous voyage. He dropped the anchor off the bow, then glanced the short distance to land. The shoreline, carpeted by a thick forest of trees leading down to the water's edge, would provide him with a quiet spot to spend his afternoon. From the trees the chirping of birds rolled across the water and brought him peace. A pair of bullfrogs croaked out their calls while a butterfly flitted from shore and landed on the main mast.

Einstein walked back to the stern of the boat, stretched his aching back, then settled on the deck near a coiled pile of rope. Though he usually paid little attention to food, sometimes literally forgetting he needed to eat, he had a robust appetite this afternoon. He took out one of the liverwurst sandwiches Katherine Hartley had packed for him. Unfolding the waxed paper he took a huge bite. A dab of hot German mustard dotted his chin and he wiped it away with a fingertip. Deeper in the brown paper bag he found a tin foil package. Removing a deviled egg, the top dusted with orange paprika, he consumed it with childish delight. For dessert he ate from a paper container of fresh cranberries. He washed it all down with a bottle of tepid homemade beer. Carefully placing the refuse back in the paper sack, he stowed it in a side compartment, then sat on the stern of the boat contented. His stomach was full but his mind, for once, was strangely empty. Slowly he fell into a deep slumber.

Ten thousand miles and ten time zones to the west of New Jersey on an ancient rocky island, an artificial sun was about to burn with all the intensity of a hell come to earth. Sun glinted off the silver fuselage of a lone B-29 as it flew high above the water. On the wings, on either side of the fuselage, the four Wright Cyclone engines that powered huge four-bladed propellers droned in a monotonous beat as the bomber was guided north.

Colonel Paul Tibbet, Jr., was the commander of the bomber *Enola Gay*, the plane assigned to unleash the unnatural sun. Tibbet, operating under a thick cloak of secrecy, had explained the purpose of the mission to his crew only a few hours before.

The crew of the *Enola Gay* was a tight group, honed to perfection through the long hours they had spent training and retraining these last few months. They were as close as men could be, each trusting the other completely. Even so, no one aboard kidded around as usual on the flight north toward Japan. The crew was lost in their own thoughts. They were the chosen warriors for a new age, and they were justifying to themselves the devastation they knew they were about to inflict.

Tibbet signaled the crew they had arrived at the ten-minutes-to-target point. The crew shed their doubts and began to prepare for the bomb run. Trained almost to the point of brainwashing, they were robotic in their movements. The crew would perform their mission exactly as they were trained. They would deliver the payload to the target area.

That was their job.

When the *Enola Gay* crossed above the city of Hiroshima at an altitude of 31,000 feet, the navigator reversed his cap and stared for the hundredth time at his charts. Checking, then rechecking his course settings, he shouted to the bombardier that they were approaching the targeted building.

The bombardier concentrated completely. Ignoring the sweat that dotted his forehead, he sat peering into the Norden bombsight, his breath coming in shallow waves. Positive they were above the same building he had been shown on the aerial photographs earlier that morning, he activated the release mechanism that freed the weapon they had nicknamed "Little Boy." Staring down through the open bomb bay the loadmaster watched as "Little Boy" dropped from the belly of the plane. It twitched to the left and right, then steadied itself.

As if in a race with destiny, the bomb picked up speed and plunged rapidly to earth.

Free of the 10,000-pound weight of "Little Boy," Tibbet wasted no time jamming the *Enola Gay*'s yoke to the right. Steering the bomber in a radical turn away from land, Tibbet advanced the throttles, then watched the instruments that registered the engines' condition with concern. The *Enola Gay* was in a deadly race against time to distance its crew from the unnatural cloud of poisons due to be unleashed by the explosion. The scientists had not released much information about "Little Boy" to Tibbet and his airmen, but one thing they had made clear.

Be as far away as possible when the weapon explodes.

When "Little Boy" detonated in the air 1,850 feet above Shima Hospital in Hiroshima, the *Enola Gay* was racing south at top speed. It was just after 8:15 A.M. As the mushroom cloud carrying thousands of screaming souls raced skyward, several of the crew peered from *Enola Gay*'s windows to witness the fireball of death they had delivered. Few men have seen death—fewer still live to tell about it. Staring in mute horror, their faces lit by the blinding light of fission, the interior of the B-29 fell silent, save for the relentless droning of the engines. Ten minutes after the blast, as the shock of their actions began to abate, the copilot wrote in the pages of his personal journal, "My God, what have we done?"

It is a question as yet unanswered.

At the exact same instant in time 10,000 miles across the globe, the natural sun was turning Einstein's face a dark red as he lay napping on the stern of his sailboat, which was still anchored in the secluded cove. All at once, he awoke with a terrible feeling of dread.

Instantly, he struggled to a sitting position, wide awake. Hoisting himself to his feet, he felt strangely, indefinably, and unnaturally sad. His heart was pounding loudly in his chest. His entire body was clammy, as if swabbed with a horsehair brush dipped in a bucket of sweat. Rivers of sweat formed on his face and ran down, dotting his shirt like rain. He swallowed, a mysterious coppery taste in his mouth. And then he vomited on the deck.

Einstein searched the heavens for an answer but found none. He looked to the shore for a clue but could not locate a single animal. The turtles he'd watched earlier lounging on the rocks at the waterline were now gone. The flocks of birds that had flown overhead were nowhere to be seen. The bullfrogs were silent, the butterfly gone.

As if in a bizarre natural void, the shoreline showed absolutely no sign of life.

Unnerved by the unnatural scene, Einstein quickly weighed anchor. He pulled the rope starter on his tiny Sears outboard motor and waited until the motor caught, then steered the sailboat from the cove. Once free of the cove, he turned off the outboard and hoisted all sails. Steering the sloop north, he sailed toward Hartley's Marina as fast as the winds would take him. The winds, however, had changed since earlier that day and it took a great deal of work to make headway. Einstein continued to study the heavens for some clue to his feeling of dread, yet none was forthcoming. Deep in his heart he feared that he knew the answer to his feelings—he only hoped he was wrong.

Spinning the wheel angrily, Einstein keeled the sailboat over on its side and ran north with the wind. As he steered into deeper water in an attempt to catch the offshore breeze and then angle his way back to land, he noticed a pod of whales in the far distance. One of the huge mammals, as if drawn to the sailboat by some invisible force, broke away from the pod and came alongside. Einstein watched as the whale paced the sailboat's speed, then breached directly amidships.

He jammed the sailboat's rudder toward land.

Ernie Hartley and Mike Scaramelli were sitting on a deck built off the back of the marina. The two men were lounging on red metal chairs shaped like clamshells. They shared the local newspaper, swapping sections across a white, freshly painted metal table as they awaited Einstein's return.

"They're making quick work of rounding up the Nazis," Hartley noted, handing Scaramelli a fresh section.

"Still tough going in the Pacific, though," Scaramelli said and then sipped from a bottle of Bubble-Up.

It was slow at the marina that day. Hartley had been summoned inside only three times to tend the cash register. Twice he had sold live shrimp to fishermen for bait. Once it was to sell someone a wooden float for a crab pot.

From inside, perched on the ledge of an open window, a new Philco radio—which Hartley had recently won as first prize in a contest sponsored by an oil company—played big-band music through its large single speaker. The music suddenly stopped and an announcer's voice broke in with the news.

"News from the war front. The United States Armed Forces announced moments ago that they have dropped a new type of bomb on Imperial Japan. While details are few, the device appears to be a new fission-type weapon quite different and many times more powerful than any bomb yet detonated. Reports from the Japanese city of Hiroshima, the target of the bombing, indicate widespread damage and loss of life. The Supreme Allied Command refused to comment on the device other than to say they hoped it would bring a quick conclusion to the hostilities.

"Now back to the music with recordings from the Glenn Miller Orchestra."

Hartley ran inside. He spun the tuning dial of the Philco in an attempt to find any additional news about the bomb. Unfortunately, the only stations he could reach on the tuner featured either music or sports. Scratching his head, he walked slowly back outside to await Einstein's return.

On the horizon, eight miles distant, a boat under full sail appeared first as a white speck. Hartley trained his binoculars on the speck. The vessel grew larger as it neared and he struggled to make out the image. Still moving at full speed, the sailboat hurtled past the outer breakwaters and the far end of the harbor. From the sailboat's bow curled a wake of white water that signaled its haste.

"It's Einstein," Hartley said when he could finally catch a good view of the man behind the helm.

Hartley and Scaramelli raced to the dock to help with the mooring. Slipping alongside the dock, Einstein lowered the sails at the last moment. The sailboat's forward momentum was strong and Einstein ran to the bow and tossed a line to Hartley to slow the vessel.

"He's coming in too fast," Hartley said to Scaramelli.

Taking the line from Hartley's hand, Scaramelli fastened it around a bit, slowing the sailboat's movement. Just as the boat's stern began to swing around, Einstein threw the stern line. Hartley grabbed the line and quickly cleated it off. The boat lurched, then settled into place.

Einstein jumped from the boat. He looked strangely gaunt, his face lined with tension. His shoulders were sagging and his shirt was soaked with pools of perspiration. He seemed unsteady on his feet and his eyes were bloodshot. He appeared much older than the man who had sailed away only a few hours earlier.

"Did the water turn rough?" Scaramelli asked.

"No, it was smooth," Einstein said, waving his hand and staring unseeing into the distance. "Were you listening to the radio by chance?"

"Yes, we were," Hartley said.

"A bomb," Einstein blurted. "Was there any news reports about a bomb?"

Hartley quickly repeated the news broadcast they had heard. Scaramelli filled in the few points Hartley left out.

Einstein, his face now creased with a frown, turned his head away from the men and gazed across the water. "It is as I feared," he said simply as he turned to leave.

As Einstein made his way toward the ramp, Hartley stared at the physicist. His cheeks were stained with the dried tracks of tears, his hair was disheveled, and his eyes seemed dead. He shuffled up the ramp slowly. Einstein lowered his head and dropped his shoulders, as if weighted with a burden no mortal man should carry. Once at the top of the ramp, he walked solemnly toward the Packard. He settled into the rear compartment and buried his face in his hands.

Scaramelli waved to Hartley as he climbed quietly into the driver's seat. He started the Packard and allowed it to settle into a quiet idle. Then he backed out of his spot, set the gearshift into drive, and pulled slowly away from the marina.

Einstein said nothing on the ride back to Princeton. The sun was setting and the air outside the Packard was heavy. Once, when they were still a few miles from home, Scaramelli peered into the rearview mirror and saw Einstein looking out the window at the summer scenery, lost in thought. He continued to sit quietly until the Packard pulled into Mercer Street.

When Scaramelli drove into the driveway at 112 Mercer Street and shut off the engine, Einstein spoke his first and only words since leaving the marina. "What has happened today is wrong, Mike. Never forget that," he said quietly. "And I will never let it happen again."

Einstein appeared to be trembling as he climbed from the rear compartment of the Packard. He walked with the tottering gait of a much older man. Scaramelli quickly moved to support his elbow and helped him up the steps to the door of his house. Once Einstein was safely inside and settled on a couch in his living room, Scaramelli summoned Dukas, then quietly returned to the Packard and drove slowly back to the university motor pool.

In the years to follow, Scaramelli's life would change greatly. He would graduate from college, marry, and begin a family. Even so, as the years passed, Scaramelli often thought back to that August day at the marina. The event remained etched in his memory, as if it were only yesterday. And until the day he died, Scaramelli never forgot the look of sadness and remorse that had been so visible in Albert Einstein's eyes.

The next day, at the headquarters of the FBI in Washington D.C., J. Edgar Hoover was scanning a thick file. He closed the file, then sipped from a cup of tea.

Motioning for his second-in-command, Clyde Tolson, to refill his cup, he spoke.

"We need to find out why I didn't know more about this atomic bomb. The last report I received from our field agents stated the scientists were still unsure if the thing would even work. Now the military's gone and blown one off. It's going to look like the FBI was caught with our pants down if we don't quickly find some role for this agency in the atomic age. We *need* to have the FBI some- how involved with nuclear power. It's quite obvious now the impact will be huge."

Tolson stared at his boss and companion and quietly nodded. "A lot of the scientists that worked on the project have radical views. Perhaps that's our entrée to this so-called atomic age."

Hoover reached back and scratched an itch on his ear. "Good idea, Clyde. Let's start with Einstein. We already have an exten- sive file on him."

Tolson rose from his chair. "I'll call and request the file from storage, then pick it up after lunch."

"Good," Hoover said, "and while you're at it, have a couple of field agents begin a covert round-the-clock surveillance of Einstein. One more thing, Clyde," Hoover said. "Bring me the file on his housekeeper. I think her name is Dikus, or Dukas."

"Yes, Edgar," Tolson said, as he walked out of Hoover's office and set out down the hall.

Six days later, when a second atomic bomb was dropped, this time on Nagasaki, Einstein made his decision. The Unified

Field Theory must be kept secret. The power that could result from the improper use of the theory was simply too great a risk for the world at this time. A world populated by men who in the last war had just displayed its cruelest side. A world that seemed bound to wage war and spurn peace.

The bomb the United States had dropped on Hiroshima agonized Einstein. He was a devoted pacifist. Still, he had tried to justify it by imagining to himself the lives that might have been lost in an invasion of Japan, with fighting island-to-island. The bombing, if it caused Japan to surrender, may actually have saved lives.

He almost succeeded.

It was the bomb the United States dropped on Nagasaki that sealed Einstein's decision. The Japanese were already beaten. Japan's supplies of food, fuel, and medicine were at dangerously low levels. The Japanese air force and navy were nearly decimated. The country's infrastructure was in ruins. Japan's surrender was only a matter of time.

Once the bomb was ignited over Nagasaki there was no turning back.

Outside 112 Mercer Street, the black Ford sedan driven by the pair of FBI agents was so nondescript it stood out. Even *with* the availability of automobiles severely limited, no one but a government agency would order a car equipped with blackwall tires and no chrome trim. The FBI agents sitting inside the Ford were dressed in the stark black suits and white shirts that conformed to the agency's approved dress code. It was only the sweat rings under their arms that might draw them a reprimand from Hoover.

FBI agents were not supposed to sweat.

"It has to be ninety degrees in here," Agent Mark Agnews said.

Agent Steve Talbot mopped his brow with a handkerchief. "Even the slightest breeze would help."

Talbot leaned back in the seat and lowered his fedora over his eyes as Agnews continued to watch Einstein's residence.

Inside Einstein's house at 112 Mercer, the ground-floor study was clouded with smoke. "For what reason would the FBI want to investigate *me?*" Einstein asked.

"Are you sure it's the FBI?" Dukas asked.

"Yes, I asked the chief of the campus police to look up the license plate number," Einstein said. "It was registered to the FBI."

"What are you going to do about it?" Dukas asked.

Einstein rose and walked to the window. Parting the curtains slightly, he stared at the Ford sedan parked slightly up the block.

"Well," he said finally, "I know what we should do right now."

"What is that, Doctor?" Dukas asked.

"Let's bring those men in the car some iced tea," Einstein said. "It's sweltering outside."

"We have movement outside the house," Agnews said to Talbot, who was reading a pulp magazine.

Talbot stared out the window. "It's Einstein. And it looks like he has a tray in his hands or something."

"We've been made," Agnews said. "He's coming right toward us."

Einstein crossed the street and walked up to the open window of the Ford with the tray balanced in front of him. "I thought you men might be thirsty. It seems the FBI does not believe in giving their agents breaks."

He filled a glass and handed it to Agnews in the driver's seat. "Pass it over," Einstein said.

After filling a glass for Talbot, he motioned to the pitcher.

"I'll leave what's left, in case you get thirsty later. When you're finished, just leave the pitcher and the glasses on my front porch."

Agnews stared at the scientist through the open window of the Ford, then smiled. "Thanks, Dr. Einstein," he said.

"It's no trouble," Einstein said. "I just have one question."

"What is it?" Agnews asked.

"Do I notify you before I plan to go anywhere?"

"No, Dr. Einstein," Talbot said, leaning out the window. "The way it works is you're not supposed to know we're here."

"I shall attempt to hide from you then," Einstein said as he walked away.

"That would be fine," Agnews shouted after the retreating scientist.

Over the last week Einstein had studied the FBI agents and their habits. The surveillance consisted of three separate teams. Each team was comprised of two agents. A total of six agents in all. The teams seemed to rotate their shifts around so that each team worked both night and day shifts.

Einstein noted that as the days passed the agents had become lax in their surveillance. They no longer observed his home through binoculars. Frequently one agent would leave the car to fetch lunch or to use the restroom in a university building a block away.

It was time for Einstein to put his plan in motion.

Einstein's gardener was a cranky old Irishman named Jack O'Toole. O'Toole had cared for Einstein's grounds for too many years to remember, and the men had grown quite close. In the summer, when O'Toole finished with the yard work he would share a cold drink with Einstein and talk baseball. In the winter, when O'Toole performed snow removal duties, the men would enjoy a hot toddy and discuss weather and politics.

Still, as close as the two men were, O'Toole opposed Einstein's plan.

"Al," O'Toole said slowly, "I didn't think you knew how to drive a car."

"I have never actually driven a car," Einstein pleaded, "but I am quite good on the bumper cars at the amusement park."

"Very funny," O'Toole said, "my truck has a four-speed gearbox. Do you think you could learn how to shift gears?"

"No problem, you just push the pedal on the left to the floor then select the gear you wish. Next you engage the gear by using the hand shifter that is located on the floor."

"This is rich," O'Toole said, laughing. "How far do you need to drive?"

"Not far," Einstein lied.

O'Toole stared at his friend for a moment. "I must be crazy. But, sure, you can use my truck. But I want you to know you have to have it fixed if you bang it up."

"Thank you, Jack," Einstein said, touching his friend's shoulder. "Now let me explain the rest of my plan."

Twenty minutes later, Einstein and O'Toole stood in the living room in their costumes. Atop O'Toole's head was Einstein's felt slouch hat. Tufts of gray hair tumbled down from the sides and rear.

"This itches," O'Toole noted, "and these pants feel like they're going to fall off."

"Helen brought the hair back from a dog-grooming parlor yesterday—I think she said it was from an Afghan hound."

"And the false mustache," O'Toole said, feeling like he was about to sneeze.

"From the same four-legged donor," Einstein said, smiling. "Now pay attention to how I shuffle when I walk."

Einstein demonstrated his walk. He was dressed in a set of work clothes similar to the ones O'Toole customarily wore. Helen Dukas had purchased the clothes from a nearby Sears Roebuck store only yesterday upon learning of the plan. O'Toole trailed along with Einstein until he had mastered the walk.

"Good, good, you have it perfectly," Einstein said finally. "Now we go outside."

Helen Dukas watched the men from a chair in the living room. "I think you two are starting to enjoy this cloak-and-dagger stuff."

Einstein said nothing. Hooking his thumbs into his pants pockets he bowed his legs and swung his hips from side to side.

"I don't walk like that," O'Toole said, shuffling along behind him.

"But you do, my friend," Einstein said.

"This is never going to work, Dr. Einstein," Dukas said quietly.

"There's Einstein," Talbot said as the men walked onto the porch.

O'Toole shielded Einstein as they walked toward the driveway. Leading Einstein to the driver's door of the truck he opened the door and waited as Einstein climbed into the seat. Once Einstein was in place, he spoke.

"Here's the key, Al," O'Toole said, "just please try not to wreck the old girl."

"How about you?" Einstein asked. "Will you be all right?"

"No problem," O'Toole said. "I'll just shuffle down to your office and take a nap on your office couch for a few hours."

With a wink at Einstein, O'Toole walked away from the truck. As he shuffled up the street toward Einstein's office, Agent Talbot turned the Ford sedan around. Keeping a respectful distance, the Ford sedan carrying the FBI agents followed O'Toole.

Neither Talbot nor Agnews was watching in the rearview mirror as Einstein backed the truck from the driveway and slowly pulled away.

*　*　*

Grinding the gears, Einstein forced O'Toole's 1939 Chevrolet pickup into first gear and set off for Hartley's Marina. It was a hot summer day and the air hung over the land like a burning blanket.

Inside the dark-green Chevy truck Einstein clutched the wheel in a death grip. At the stop sign down the street from his house Einstein managed to stop the truck in time. Restarting the engine, which had stalled when Einstein had slammed on the brakes while forgetting to push down on the clutch, he lurched from the stop in second gear. A thin trickle of sweat ran down the side of Einstein's face as he reached for third gear.

Appearing like some bizarre circus parade, the procession of the fake Einstein followed by the FBI agents in the black sedan was nearing its end. O'Toole was less than 125 yards from the outer door to Einstein's laboratory and was already savoring the pride from a job well done.

O'Toole slowed as a perky young female student approached from the opposite direction. Her head was down, staring toward the pavement, but she raised her face to smile at O'Toole as they got closer. Two steps later the toe of her left shoe hooked on a piece of uneven sidewalk and sent her tumbling to the ground.

"Are you okay?" O'Toole asked excitedly.

"Fine, fine," said the student. "I just need to be fitted for glasses and I've been too vain to follow through with it."

Agnews and Talbot had stopped the Ford sedan and were watching the scene.

"Here, let me help you up," O'Toole said.

The female student raised her arm to O'Toole, who bent at the waist to help lift the girl to her feet. At that instant, the hat O'Toole was wearing fell from his head, flipped over once, then landed, crown down, on the cement. From the passenger side of the Ford sedan Agnews stared at O'Toole in shock.

"We've been had," he said to Talbot as he stared at O'Toole.

"That looks like the gardener," Talbot said.

"Then Einstein must be driving his truck," Agnews said.

Talbot swung the Ford in a half-circle and raced off after the truck. But the FBI agents were too late to catch the fleeing scientist.

Princeton Police Patrolman Duke Tanner was stopped at a filling station four blocks from Einstein's house when the pickup rolled past. Tanner listened as the driver of the truck ground the gears. He watched as the driver swerved to avoid a metal trash can on the side of the road. Tanner decided to follow the Chevrolet. After following the truck for several miles he pulled abreast of the pickup at a stoplight.

Tanner stared at the driver in amazement before shouting out his open window. "Is that you, Dr. Einstein?"

Einstein glanced at the light nervously before turning to Tanner. Einstein was still having trouble coordinating the clutch and gas pedals when pulling from a dead stop and he feared he was going to stall out the engine again when the light changed. "Hello, Officer, it's me."

"I didn't know you could drive," Tanner said.

"Just learning," Einstein said as he stared again at the light. "You're never too old to learn new skills."

"Let me follow behind you to make sure you get safely out of town," Tanner said.

Einstein said nothing, he just gave Tanner a thumbs-up sign. When the light changed he lurched from the stop in the wrong gear. Tanner followed Einstein several miles, then tooted his horn and turned back toward Princeton as the truck made its way into the New Jersey countryside.

❋   ❋   ❋

By the time Einstein had an hour of driving under his belt he became cocky. Flicking on the AM radio, he began to sing along with the songs. Even though Einstein had become more confident, the drive to Hartley's Marina would take him twice the time it took Scaramelli. Halfway through the trip the physicist got lost on a series of back roads and had considered turning back. But he continued to press on.

Flicking on the windshield wipers to clear the glass, Einstein merely succeeded in smearing the bugs on the glass into streaks. He pulled to the side of the road and checked a map until he was convinced he was driving in the correct direction. Pulling the truck back onto the road, he drove a few miles, then stopped at a four-way stop. He sniffed the air for the smell of salt and took the fork to the east. Einstein began to feel a sense of relief when the surroundings started to look familiar. When he reached the marina, he slid O'Toole's truck to a stop in the parking lot.

Hartley was surprised to see Einstein. He always called ahead for Hartley to ready his sailboat. Even so, the marina owner prepared the vessel for sailing without comment. Once the boat was ready, Einstein left it tied to the dock and returned to the pickup, where he removed a weathered satchel, which he carried belowdecks and stashed in a compartment beneath the table.

"Will you be working today, Dr. Einstein?" Hartley asked as he untied the line holding the bow of Einstein's sailboat to the dock.

"Lately it seems I'm always working," Einstein said easily.

Hartley nodded and, with nothing more forthcoming from Einstein, pushed the sailboat from the dock. Einstein steered away from the dock out toward the ocean.

"What time should I expect you back?" Hartley yelled as the sailboat neared the breakwater.

Just at the edge of his hearing, Einstein heard the question and shouted a reply.

"When I'm finished," he said. With that, he waved goodbye to

Hartley, hoisted all sails, and set a course for the deserted cove he had visited on his last voyage. Just over an hour later, anchored stern to shore in the shallows, Einstein removed his shoes and socks and rolled up his pants. Wading through the water, he made his way through the brush and climbed up a small rise. He scanned the terrain, finally selecting a fine oak tree. From a flask of Holland gin he took a large swallow of the peppermint liquor.

After finding a comfortable seat at the base of the oak, he removed a sharp wood chisel from a canvas bag he had carried ashore and began carving on a board. It was late in the afternoon, the sun almost at the horizon when he finished.

Ten Years Later

Einstein suffered stoically through what had become almost unbearable pain. In the last several days, the hardened aorta he steadfastly refused to have operated on had begun to slowly leak blood. This day in April 1955 brought an air of approaching parting, of a journey nearing its end.

The attendant in the passenger seat was daydreaming as the ambulance raced toward Einstein's home. As the driver braked to a stop in front of 112 Mercer, the sound of skidding tires brought the attendant back to the present. Jumping from his seat, he ran to the rear and helped the driver unload the gurney. They wheeled the gurney to the front of the house and the driver rapped on the door. Helen Dukas flung it open at the first sound of the knock. From inside the house the ambulance driver could hear that an argument was still raging.

"The end comes sometimes. Does it matter when, or where?" Einstein said to Dukas.

The two attendants listened in silence as the housekeeper tried valiantly to reason with the stubborn physicist. "The nursing field is one I simply do not understand, Herr Professor," Dukas said finally. "It would make me more comfortable if you went to the hospital."

The attendants watched as Einstein considered this. "Very well, then," Einstein said, "I will go to the hospital, but I'll need to send a telegram to Niels Bohr in Denmark. Can we stop on the way to the hospital?"

"I will take care of the telegram after you are in bed in the hospital," Dukas said in a firm voice. "Now it is time to go."

With that, Einstein rose to his feet unsteadily.

After loading Einstein on the gurney and strapping him down, the ambulance attendants carried him down the steps and carefully slid the cart in the back of the Cadillac ambulance for the trip to the hospital. Once Einstein was safely in the rear, the driver ran forward and climbed behind the wheel while the attendant closed the door from inside and kneeled on the floor next to the old physicist.

"What is your name?" Einstein croaked.

"Gunther," the young attendant said, "Gunther Ackerman."

"Do you speak German?" the physicist asked.

"Yes, my father was German."

"Good," Einstein said, coughing.

As the ambulance pulled away from the curb, Einstein began speaking rapidly in German. The attendant sat quietly, listening. Einstein continued a nonstop monologue until the ambulance pulled into the hospital's emergency entrance. As the rear doors were yanked open, Einstein motioned the attendant still closer.

Gasping for breath, he whispered in German, "The force will be in the wind."

The young attendant, by now quite puzzled by what he had heard, merely nodded at the gravely ill scientist.

The next day was Sunday, for most a day of rest. Einstein, though still in extreme pain, continued relentlessly with his work, drawing and making notations on a pad of paper. The telegram was sent to his fellow physicist Niels Bohr, but as yet Einstein had received no reply. Shortly after midnight, Monday morning, Einstein began muttering loudly in German. His frail body, the physical shell that merely housed his incredible mind, was fast failing him. Twelve minutes later, at last succumbing to intense pain he could no longer endure, he took two deep breaths and left this planet. He traveled upward, secure in knowing his body of work lived on. He hoped only that the clue he had left behind would fall into the right hands.

Helen Dukas, who had worked for Einstein the last twenty-seven years, was deeply saddened by his death. She returned to 112 Mercer from the hospital later that same morning, intending to straighten up Einstein's home one last time. As the cab that had brought her from the hospital pulled away, she could see several military vehicles parked outside.

She walked up the steps, then opened the front door to find the house full of strangers. Agents from both the Atomic Energy Commission and Naval Intelligence were conducting a meticulous search of the small frame house. A tall, thin man sporting a pencil mustache and wearing a brown felt fedora stared as she entered the living room.

"Who are you?" he asked Dukas quietly.

"I work," Dukas blurted, "or did work, anyway, for the doctor."

The man simply nodded, then ordered her to remain in the kitchen until the search was completed. She was led away by the arm by a bulky sailor.

Lost in her grief, Dukas could only comply.

Dukas sat sobbing quietly at the Formica table in the breakfast nook, watched by a guard in a United States Navy uniform. She dabbed at the corners of her eyes with a wadded-up tissue. Sipping a cup of hot tea, she listened as the uninvited guests stomped up and down the stairs of the house. When the noise died down, she bullied her way past the sailor and entered the formerly neat and tidy living room.

Boxes containing Einstein's documents as well as his personal journals sat on the hardwood floor near the door. Watching quietly for a moment, Dukas heard the man in the fedora issue the order to load the truck that had pulled up outside. Soldiers immediately began carrying out the boxes.

Dukas looked at the man in the fedora suspiciously. "Where are you taking the professor's papers?" she asked forcefully.

The man barely looked at her as he spoke. "They are property of the United States government now," he said in a cold voice.

With a wave of his hands to the remaining soldiers to clear the room, the man in the fedora walked from Einstein's home into the early-morning fog. Dukas collapsed on the couch, sobs wracking her body, alone with her grief.

At almost the exact same time, a second group scoured Einstein's hospital room, looking for any papers that might pertain to the Unified Field Theory.

These, and all subsequent searches, turned up nothing.

CHAPTER 1

Two miles south of Hampton Bay, New York, three miles east of land in the Atlantic Ocean, Ivar Halversen turned his head slightly in the brisk wind and glanced over the sailboat's gunwale. He watched a harbor seal who was floating on his back dive down as the boat passed. Shifting position to relieve the pressure on his back, he spit into the saltwater to his side. To the north, a wall of clouds had formed and was slowly advancing southward. Halversen was already chilled—the temperature had dropped sharply and was becoming colder by the minute. The dingy yellow wax-treated canvas slicker and rain pants he wore provided little insulation against the increasingly harsh wind. Wiping his dripping nose on the back of his wool glove, Halversen stared at the sea. Salt spray, blown from the sailboat's wake and whipped by the wind, cut into his cheeks, the only part of his skin still exposed beneath his tightly secured hood. He adjusted the wheel of the boat slightly and continued north.

Though usually at home and at ease on the water, Halversen was tense and apprehensive. His feeling of fear was undefined, but real nonetheless. The feeling of dread began the first instant he heard mention of the vessel named *Windforce*. A visual inspection of the decrepit sloop at the marina in New Jersey did little to alleviate his unnatural concern. From when he had first climbed on her decks to the instant he had stepped off and foolishly accepted the job of transporting her north, the vessel seemed to be mocking him. The spooky feeling the vessel exuded at the dock was just as palpable now. He found himself peering fore and aft as if expecting the grim reaper to suddenly appear. The result of not finding anything amiss only heightened his sense of unease.

Halversen felt as if he were being watched.

Old, weathered, and poorly maintained, the *Windforce* was a boat past its prime. She had been constructed in Connecticut of hand-selected white Florida cypress and fine New England oak at the turn of the century. Twenty-seven feet in length, with her decks carefully trimmed in teakwood, she had been an expensive boat in her day. Her brass fittings were now covered with verdigris, her sails bleached by the sun and frayed at the edges. The vessel had most recently been stored out of water and the planking in her hull was loose, allowing water to slowly seep into the lower cabin area. The fabrics that covered the cushions on the benches belowdecks were torn and tattered, and when Halversen had inspected the insides of the cabinets he found so many spiderwebs that it looked like they were filled with thin cotton candy.

During the *Windforce*'s long life at sea the United States had experienced the conversion to electricity, the growth of both automobile and plane travel, and the assassination of two presidents while in office. Now, as 1965 drew to a close, yet another war was claiming the youth of the nation. *Windforce* was a vessel from another age, an antique whose time had passed.

Recently purchased by a new owner who was unfamiliar with boats, *Windforce* was found to be rotting out from under herself. When the cost of needed repairs appeared to exceed her value when completed, the decision was simple. After a long and fruitful life, the boat was due to be scrapped in Providence.

The *Windforce* was on her final voyage.

As Halversen continued sailing north he tried to visualize the *Windforce* when she was new. He tried to imagine the fun times people had shared aboard her decks. Unfortunately his mind drew a blank. The only thoughts he felt were troubled ones, and his imagination was sadly lacking.

"Just a tired old tub now," he muttered to the distant wind.

Halversen was thankful he had sailed the waters off the East Coast for nearly thirty years. A voyage north can be treacherous in good weather. Even with a new boat and modern navigation aids it was tricky, the winds and currents constantly changing. Single-handedly sailing a decrepit old boat, with only a compass to navigate, was two degrees short of suicide. If he didn't need the money he'd be home in bed right now.

He took his position and sailed on.

The *Windforce* was under full sail and racing toward the cloud bank as Halversen passed Long Island and rounded Montauk Point. The dark wall forming the squall line was now directly ahead. He steered into the blackness. Visibility was quickly diminishing in the tossing tempest. As the troughs between waves grew deeper and more erratic, Halversen stood as tall as he could on the stern, straining to see through the wind-whipped spray over the bow. More than once, the wheel was jarred from his hands by the waves and he struggled to keep *Windforce* on course.

The sound of the foghorn broke through the storm. It was from the car ferry just leaving New London, Connecticut, on its return passage to Long Island. At the sound of the horn he braced his feet on the deck and struggled to mark his position on his soggy chart.

He was just south of Block Island.

Twelve nautical miles from New London, aboard the ferry *Pawcatuck*, Captain Ira Blanchard stared at the radar set intently. The dim green screen showed a few flecks as the wand swept side to side in a half-circle. This weather is not fit for man or beast, Blanchard thought to himself. No one would be out here unless he was an idiot—or had no other choice.

The view from the window of the pilothouse on the *Pawcatuck* was a gray void. Blanchard wiped off the mist inside the windshield with his handkerchief, then flicked on the outside wipers to dissipate the rain splattering on the glass. After warming his boots for a second over the heater vent on the floor, he reached over and refilled his coffee mug from the pot on the bridge.

"Real bitch of a storm," Blanchard said, staring straight ahead out the window.

Second Officer James Conner, who was standing with a clipboard in his hand monitoring a bank of gauges on the pilothouse wall, turned to reply. "We've seen worse, Captain," Conner noted casually.

"It's early in the year," Blanchard said quietly.

"You know the fickle ways of the Atlantic, sir," Conner replied.

"Double-check the radar," Blanchard ordered.

Conner scanned the set quickly. "All clear, Captain," he said.

"Then maintain present speed, Mr. Conner," Blanchard ordered. "I'd like to get home for dinner."

Aboard the sloop *Windforce* Ivar Halversen had his hands full. The aged sailboat groaned in agony as wave after wave rolled across her bow, each one stronger than the last. Struggling to maintain his northerly heading, Halversen continued to navigate with the compass and the now quite soggy marine chart. The storm intensified every second that passed, and visibility was now measured in mere feet. Any noise was swallowed by the wind whistling around his hood.

Unknown to Halversen, the giant car ferry *Pawcatuck* continued at full speed, the wooden sloop *Windforce* an almost undetectable speck on its radar set.

Halversen felt but did not hear the main sail rip. He raced to the bow and lashed down the shredded sail with a dirty piece of sisal rope. He was starting back to the helm when he first noticed the *Pawcatuck* steering straight for the *Windforce*. The ferry was less than fifty feet from his starboard bow and advancing fast.

Halversen raced back to the wheel, slipping hard on the drenched decks and wrenching his knee. Reaching his hand up from his place on the deck, he cranked the wheel left to the stops in a futile effort to steer the *Windforce* out of the path of the *Pawcatuck*.

The *Windforce* strained to turn but the winds were strong against her. Barely responding to the rudder, the sailboat was turned sideways by a wave. It moved directly in front of the path of the advancing car ferry.

Halversen glanced in horror at the massive black metal hull of the *Pawcatuck* towering above him, looking for all the world like the wall of a giant skyscraper. Before he could leap over the side, the red Plimsoll mark on the *Pawcatuck*'s hull struck him savagely in the chest. He was thrown behind the helm as the sharp edge of the metal hull broke the main mast with a shower of slivers.

On board the *Pawcatuck* they never saw nor felt the collision with the sailboat. The ferry tore into the *Windforce* and plowed through the aged boat with barely a shudder. The *Pawcatuck*'s steel hull and giant diesel-powered propellers split the *Windforce*'s wooden hull in two, then quickly ground the planks into pieces, spitting them to the side like pencil shavings in a hurricane.

His spine shattered and wedged tightly behind the sailboat's wheel, Halversen was unable to move his limbs as the *Windforce* plunged downward. At first he fought the impending death trying in vain to force his brain to move his paralyzed limbs. Acceptance of his fate came quickly. Pinned fast to the remains of a boat he had been only hired to deliver, Halversen accepted the inevitable and opened his mouth to the seawater. As the remains of the shattered boat descended into the inky black abyss, his muscles relaxed against the pressure of the water. Arms flapping eerily, he sank into the depths.

The *Windforce* and sailor Ivar Halversen were no more.

Twelve days after the mishap, a life ring with the name *Windforce* stenciled on the side was found on the beach at Block Island. Two years later the ring was donated to the maritime museum at Montauk, Long Island, along with a load of salvaged marine parts for a display entitled: Flotsam and Jetsam of the Seas. After the exhibit ended, it was hung on the fence leading to the museum along with hundreds of others. The sun and salt air wreaked havoc on the painted letters until finally they were hardly visible at all.

CHAPTER 2

Belowground in the northeast corner of the basement of the sprawling Commerce Department Building located between Fourteenth and Fifteenth streets in Washington, D.C., Burt Lipshiski dipped a corn chip into a crock pot filled with melted Velveeta cheese and salsa. The building was completely deserted. The only sounds came from a small black-and-white television and the shouts of Lipshiski and his partner, Carl Lincoln, as the game unfolded.

"As long as you're getting up, make me a dog," Lincoln said.

"Chili and cheese and onion?" Lipshiski asked.

"Whoa!" Lincoln said before answering his partner. "Those damn Broncos are going to pull this off. Yeah," he said finally, "the works."

It was in that instant, while Lincoln and Lipshiski were busy eating hot dogs and watching the Super Bowl, that the intruder slipped past their office. Working quickly, he overrode the security system protecting the laboratory at the far end of the hall. The intruder, one of the members of an elite Chinese intelligence apparatus tasked with stealing Western technology, had planned for his entry and escape carefully.

Since early 1997, when the Chinese first learned of the laboratory, until now, Super Bowl Sunday 1998, the agent had prepared his action carefully. He selected the date with purpose—believing Americans to be both dumb and lazy, he felt sure the Commerce Building would be only lightly guarded during the game. The agent hated Americans, finding them unmotivated and concerned only with the most petty of details.

He had lived in Washington, D.C., for almost a year now, posing as an employee of the Chinese Embassy, and he had seen little to change his opinion. He had grown up in a thatch-roofed shack with pigs living in a pen next door, and now he discovered that for most Americans an automobile without air conditioning was an unbearable hardship.

The agent had also found that the average American citizen cared little for the politics of the world. Americans seemed content if they were able to pay their bills, own a home, watch cable television, and screw their spouses on weekends.

The agent believed America's role as leader of the world would soon be ending.

It seemed fitting the burglary was planned for the most American of days, Super Bowl Sunday. Slipping into the laboratory during the first quarter, he copied what he needed from the computers, then rifled through desks for the next two quarters before slipping out in the middle of the fourth.

He waited in his car on the street outside, listening to the end of the game on his radio. A pair of bumper stickers sat on the seat next to him. As soon as he confirmed that the team called the

Broncos had won, he got out and slapped the winner's bumper sticker onto the rear of his car.

Once that was done, he drove into traffic, madly honking his horn, as if the Bronco's winning the game was the greatest event of his life. The horn honked until he was but a block away from the embassy.

It was the perfect touch to end a successful operation.

CHAPTER 3

Li Choi was seeing an apparition.

Closing his eyes, he rubbed them with his fingertips, then opened them again. Strangely enough, he could still see the blond-haired man. It must be my mind playing tricks, Choi thought to himself. Some residual memory from American tele-vision perhaps, dredged from the depths of my subconscious and brought about by the torture of the past few weeks. It was a logical assumption and it brought Choi some degree of comfort.

The ghost who had appeared inside his cell looked vaguely like the star of a detective show he had enjoyed when he was in the United States. What was the name of the show? Choi thought to himself. It was about a detective in Florida, the city of Palm Beach. Oh well, no matter, he thought; the show will come to me after the ghost disappears.

Or perhaps I'm actually asleep, Choi thought.

Since being abducted in the parking lot of a Chinese grocery store in San Francisco seventy-one days before, the thoughts that ran through Choi's mind were a jumbled mass of bizarre images, seemingly unlinked. The shock of his kidnapping, combined with his being transported to the remote laboratory and weapons facility at the foot of the Qilian Mountains on the dividing line between Gansu and Qinghai provinces on the edge of the Gobi Desert in China, and his worry for his family's safety in the United States, had combined to bring Choi to the edge of madness.

None of this was happening and he knew he would soon awake.

He rubbed his eyes again. The apparition remained.

And then the blond haired man framed in the door spoke. "Li Choi, I presume?"

Choi stared from the metal cot bolted to the wall of the cell where he had spent the last several months under armed guard. Each evening, after a full day in the laboratory, he was brought to the cell and locked inside for the night. He was so conditioned to the door being closed and locked, his mind could not comprehend the door now being wide open without a guard present.

"Where is the guard?" Li managed to stammer.

"He met with an unfortunate accident. His neck snapped," the blond man said quietly as he stared at a photograph. "It must have been when I twisted it."

Choi swallowed, rubbed his eyes, and stared again at the man. The man's accent was obviously American. He stood tall, a shade over six feet. If Choi had to guess his weight, he would place him at just over two hundred pounds. Judging from his biceps, which thrusted from the sleeves of his shirt, very little of that weight was fat. The glacial blue eyes beneath his thick blond hair stared at Choi with a barely concealed danger. The blond man's lips were sculptured and his strong chin had a thin scar that ran along the left side like an exclamation mark. He was dressed in khaki pants with a multipocketed shirt that matched. The buttons on the clothes were made from a sharp-edged metal of dull finish. His feet were covered with paratrooper boots. The clothing bore no insignias, and other than a watch, the man wore no jewelry. Like a caged tiger, he seemed to be emitting waves of heat and impending motion from the aura surrounding his body.

"Index finger, please," the man said.

"But I just . . ." Choi stuttered.

"I'd love to stand here and chat, but I think someone might be along soon to check on the guard. Since he's dead, and I have no intention of joining you for eternity in this cell," the man said easily, "let me print you and see if we have a match. If we do, the time has come for you to leave."

"My family, they said they'd kill my family," Choi said, sitting upright on the cot, wondering why the unreal aspect of this encounter was barely diminishing.

The man nodded, then pressed Choi's finger to an ink pad, then a slip of paper. He fed the paper into a black plastic box roughly the size of a sandwich and waited until a light flashed green.

"Who would have thought?" the man said as he pushed a series of buttons on his wristwatch. "It *is* you."

Less than a minute later, the numerical code Taft had entered into his wristwatch was beamed through space to an orbiting satellite and then back down to an NSA facility in Maryland.

"Confirmed as a valid transmission," the intelligence officer said to his partner, who was standing with a telephone in his hand. "Contact General Benson. His man is inside and has verified the target's identity."

Without another word the man removed the black nylon pack from his back and began to dig around. From a zippered pocket he extracted a single photo and handed it to Choi. The picture showed Choi's wife, Chun, and his son, Li Jr. They were standing next to the blond-haired man in front of Disneyland. Mrs. Choi held a copy of a newspaper in her hands.

"What is today's date?" Choi asked, squinting to read the newspaper's date.

"September 21st, 1999," the man answered.

The picture had been taken less than a week before.

"How did you . . ." Choi began.

"Listen, I'll explain later. Right now we've got to get out of here," the blond-haired man said as he repacked his equipment, then walked over and helped Choi off the cot to his feet. "What's your physical condition?"

"I'm weak and one of my eyes is blurry from being beaten," Choi said. "My kidnappers wanted me to renounce the United States. They said since China paid for my education I became no more than a common thief the minute I filed my immigration papers."

The man nodded and reached back into his pack. He took out a thermometer and placed it under Choi's tongue, then set two fingers on Choi's wrist. He stared at his watch as he took Choi's pulse, then removed and read the thermometer.

"You'll live, I expect," the blond-haired man said.

Choi watched as the man placed the pack on his back; then he followed him into the hallway outside the cell.

The man turned to Choi and whispered, "So did you . . . did you withdraw your citizen papers?"

"No damn way," Choi said proudly.

"Good," the blond-haired man said. "Now, if you'll just remain quiet and let me do my job, I'll get you out of here and back to the States."

Stepping over the body of the guard, whose head was twisted at a grotesque angle, the two men walked to the far end of the hallway and stopped at an outer security door. Beyond the door rose a stairway that led to the ground above and freedom. The blond-haired man removed a suction cup sporting wires from one of the pockets on his shirt and stuck it to the door. Placing a small speaker in his ear he listened for a second.

"All clear," the man said. "Get ready."

"One question," Choi said. "What is your name?"

"John Taft," the man said, peering through the glass in the door. "My name is John Taft."

Opening the door, he led Choi outside.

CHAPTER 4

Although the remoteness of the Qinghai Advanced Weapons Facility afforded it a natural defense against infiltration, the Chinese had taken no chances. The grounds were peppered with buried motion detectors, and detailed radar scanned the grounds for anything out of place. Trained guard dogs patrolled the perimeter on regular intervals and the fence was electrified to an intensity that caused it to hum as if a series of hornets' nests lay just to the other side.

Taft glanced down at his watch.

"This is going to get hairy," he whispered to Choi.

"What do . . ." Choi began to say.

Twenty miles to the southwest, along an ancient but still active fault line, the last of a series of carefully measured explosive charges Taft had set in place ignited. An earthen dike along the Qargan River blew, flooding the ugly scar in the land with millions of gallons of water. The plates in the earth bordering the fault line, loosened by the explosions and now lubricated by the water, shifted.

With help from man the forces deep in the earth were unleashed.

At that instant the ground began to shake lightly. The tremors increased their intensity until undulating waves shook the building Taft and Choi stood alongside.

And then, like a series of giant Christmas lights run amok, the electrical transformers at the corners of the facility exploded with blinding blue flashes and the grounds were plunged into darkness and chaos.

Taft was slipping on a pair of goggles as the ground first shook. He stared out on the darkness through a comforting green glow.

"I guess what they say is true," he said as he reached out to a trembling Choi. "It's not nice to fool with Mother Nature."

Tugging at Choi's shoulder, he motioned for him to follow. One hundred yards north of the building that housed Choi's cell the pair paused and crouched in a ditch.

"I'm sure they have an emergency generator, so watch for a spotlight any second," Taft said.

As if Taft had willed it, a beam of light bobbled on the ground, then began to sweep the grounds.

"When the light sweeps east in a few seconds, you're going to follow me to the fence," Taft said.

Choi watched the searchlight begin its swing to the east. The spotlight passed over the top of the ditch and continued on its path. Taft grabbed Choi's arm, yanking him easily to his feet.

"Now," Taft whispered, pulling the scientist along by his arm.

At the edge of the fence Taft spit on the wires. Finding it dead, he motioned to Choi. "Go under, I'm right behind you."

Choi squirmed into the depression Taft had dug through the sand under the fence on the way into the compound. He watched from the other side as Taft picked up an electric jammer hung on the fence. Designed to temporarily defeat the motion sensors on his way into the facility, the box had served its crude purpose.

Quickly collecting several tumbleweeds from the ground, he slipped into the hole, covering the entrance behind. Taft climbed out the other side just as the light began to sweep back to where they crouched.

"Quick, follow me," Taft whispered.

He grabbed Choi by his jacket and pushed him into a washed-out gully several feet away. Taft hit the ground seconds before the light swept across them. He sat upright just as soon as the light passed overhead.

"So far so good. The quake was designed to give us some time to undertake our escape," Taft noted as an aftershock rippled through the earth. "With their electronics systems barely functioning, it should be some time before they think to check on you."

Choi watched in stunned silence as Taft quickly withdrew a global positioning system, or GPS, from his pack. He scanned the numbers, checking their exact location. Staring briefly at a plastic-covered map, Taft next glanced at the small compass on his wristwatch, then stuffed the GPS and map back in the pack.

"This way," he said quietly to Choi.

Choi struggled to keep pace with Taft, who made his way quickly down the gully. After a twenty-minute jog, Taft stopped and checked their location once again. Glancing at the moon, he took a northern fork of the gully. Two hundred yards later, the pair sighted the Shule River. The river was flooded with recent rains and the muddy water surged quickly past. Taft stopped and took his bearings again. After staring around for a second, he walked a few feet to the left then reached beneath a pile of brush at the water's edge and removed a metal folding shovel.

"Eureka," Taft said quietly.

Choi watched in amazement as Taft unfolded the shovel and began quickly digging in the sand of the riverbank. After removing two feet of sand overburden, Taft uncovered a four-foot-by-six-foot wooden crate. He dragged the box out of the hole and pried open the top with the shovel. Moving quickly now, he removed a package from the box and tossed it on the ground. Next he pulled a nylon cord lanyard. With a loud hiss a black rubber raft began to inflate. When the raft was partially inflated he pulled a strip running down the center. This released a catalyst into the bottom compartment, and he waited as the chemicals mixed and the floor became rigid.

"So far so good," Taft said, as he dug farther into the crate and removed a compact four-stroke outboard motor and an auxiliary fuel tank.

Taft looked at Choi, then into the box. "You want a cold beer?"

Seeing the look of shock on Choi's face, Taft smiled. "Just having fun with you, pal," he said quietly.

Moving rapidly, Taft dragged the raft into the water. Wading in, he attached the motor to the stern, then placed the extra fuel tank in the rear. Taft climbed back onto the shore and threw the wooden crate in the hole and shoveled sand over the top. After smoothing the sand with the shovel, he brushed over the area with a tree limb to blend it in with the surrounding shoreline. Hoisting the shovel to his shoulder like an ax, he turned to the thoroughly stunned Choi. "How do you feel about boat rides?"

"They're okay," Choi stammered, still somewhat in shock.

"Good. Climb in," Taft said, wading in the river. Then he tossed the shovel inside and pulled the stern farther into the current.

"You ride in front," he said to Choi.

Choi settled into the bow as Taft, dripping water, climbed over the side at the stern. He settled into the seat and pulled the rope start for the motor. Firing on the first pull, it quietly settled into a low rumble.

Taft flicked the reverse gear on the motor body and backed the raft into the current. As the force of the current flipped the bow around and downstream, he flipped the gear box into forward and began to steer the raft downstream. In a matter of three minutes' time the raft was approaching speeds of thirty miles an hour.

Wrapping his arm around the tiller, Taft pushed a series of buttons on his watch again. When he finished, he throttled the outboard to full speed. The wind from the raft shooting downstream was whipping Choi's hair as he turned in his bow seat and glanced back at Taft. The American was staring straight downriver. A dull glow was emanating from his icy blue eyes as he steered the raft carefully through the narrow rock canyons.

Although Choi could not hear over the muffled roar of the engine and the sound of the water slapping against the hull, Taft's lips were pursed.

It appeared he was whistling.

CHAPTER 5

In the nerve center of the Qinghai facility it was absolute chaos. The portable radios carried by the guards were powered by batteries, so they could still communicate with each other, but the power surge that occurred when the transformers exploded had fried the main radio terminal. Those in command were having a tough time making their wishes heard.

It was nearly an hour before the guards could be organized.

One hour and twenty minutes after the explosion, as Taft and Choi were speeding down the Shule River in the outboard-powered raft, a guard finally made his way to Choi's cell.

"Zhou, wake up," the relief guard, Ping Chowluk, said, shaking the lifeless guard who lay on the concrete.

Rolling Zhou to his back caused the dead guard's head to flop to one side. Ping noticed the purple bruise on the side of Zhou's face where his blood had settled after death. Zhou's tongue was thrust through his teeth in a death grimace. The body was already cooling.

When Ping approached Choi's cell, he found the door slightly ajar. He pushed it open and peered inside.

The cell was empty. Choi was nowhere to be seen.

Running down the hall, Ping swooped his hand down and picked up a piece of paper. He dashed up the stairs leading outside and sprinted across the courtyard to the main security office for the Qinghai Advanced Weapons Facility. Bursting inside the office, he shouted to Hu Jimn, the officer in charge.

"Zhou is dead," Ping said, panting from the run, "and Choi has escaped."

"That bastard," Jimn grunted. "The power surge from the earthquake must have unlocked his cell door. Let's just hope he didn't get far."

Jimn rolled his chair across the tile floor to the back-up communications radio and began to issue orders into a microphone. "All guards outside. Begin a sweep of the fence perimeter, we have a missing prisoner." Jimn then switched channels and spoke again. "Chang!" he shouted into the microphone.

Jimn's second-in-command, Chang Yibo, answered instantly. "Yes sir."

"Where are you right now?"

"Enrichment facility one," Yibo said into his hand-held radio.

"Go to the barracks and wake all the off-duty guards. I want you to divide the men into groups of two to search all the buildings from top to bottom," Jimn shouted.

"What are we looking for?" Yibo asked.

"The scientist Choi has escaped," Jimn said.

"Do you think he's still on the property?" Yibo asked.

"We have no way of knowing until we search," Jimn said loudly.

Turning back to Ping, he asked, "Did you notice anything unusual in Choi's cell?"

"Only this, but it was in the hallway outside," Ping said.

He handed Jimn the British five-pound note he had picked up from the hallway outside the cell.

"Odd," Jimn said quietly as he pocketed the note. Then he returned to radioing instructions to the search teams.

Half of the buildings at the Qinghai Advanced Weapons Facility had been searched when one of the guards walking the fence perimeter radioed Jimn that he had found a hole scooped out under the outer fence.

"Do you see tracks?" Jimn asked.

"Yes sir," the guard quickly replied.

Jimn ran from the security office, arriving at the hole in a matter of minutes.

"There were tumbleweeds placed over the opening. Our dog dug them out," the guard told Jimn.

Jimn slipped under the fence and followed the footprints for a few yards to the east. Shining his flashlight on the larger footprints, he examined the sole markings carefully.

"Get someone to make a plaster mold of these immediately," Jimn shouted back across the fence to the guard.

Jimn stood staring into the distance as the guard, dragging the dog along, ran toward the security office.

Chang Yibo had left the office building he was searching when he heard of the discovery of the hole over his radio. He slipped under the fence and joined Jimn, who was staring down at the prints.

"What do you make of it, sir?" Yibo asked.

"The smaller prints must be Choi's," Jimn said. "They are of the type made by the slippers we give prisoners. The larger set appears to be made by a pair of British paratrooper boots. I can make out the words 'Clark's-London' and the size."

"What is the size?" Yibo asked.

"Size twelve," Jimn said. "There can't be many Chinese people with that size near here. Assemble a group of trucks, dogs, and trackers. I want you to follow these prints and recapture Choi."

"What shall we do if he's with the Brit?" Yibo asked.

"Bring them both to me," Jimn said quietly. "I will deal with the Brit."

Taft glanced at the GPS. The unit's screen cast a faint green glow in the black night and he held it close to his face to read the numbers. Once he had established their position, he steered the inflatable a few miles farther downstream, then pulled to the shore.

In the last few hours, the pair had traveled nearly a hundred and twenty miles west. The sky to the east was starting to lighten with the coming sunrise as Taft grounded the raft on shore.

"Time to get out," he said to Choi.

Climbing onto the riverbank, Taft unscrewed the engine from the transom and placed it in the middle of the raft. He slit the sides of the raft with a black carbon composite knife and pushed it back into the water. It drifted a short distance, then began to sink.

Brushing the sand from his hands, he turned to Choi. "Feel like a crisp morning jog?"

"Not particularly," Choi said wearily.

Taft scrutinized the tiny scientist carefully. "How much do you weigh?"

"Fifty kilos," Choi said.

"What's that, about a hundred and ten pounds?"

"Exactly," Choi said.

Taft reached into the pack and removed a small tin of pills and a canteen of water. "Take one of these."

Choi took the pill and stared at it in the dim light. "What is it?"

"Good old American amphetamines. Swallow that little pill and you'll be able to *run* to the western border," Taft said, smiling faintly.

Choi washed the pill down with a sip from the canteen. "What next, Mr. Taft?"

"My friends call me John," Taft said.

"You consider me your friend?"

"As long as you don't get me captured or killed," Taft said. "Now follow me, we have to catch the morning train."

Without another word Taft trotted down the river a distance to throw off any trackers, then climbed the riverbank and began walking quickly toward the north. Choi followed close behind— like a lemming following the pack off a cliff.

"The tracks end at the Shule River about two kilometers from the fence," Yibo said to Jimn over the portable radio.

"Have your men wade across the water and search the opposite side for footprints. They might be trying to throw off the scent of the dogs," Jimn said. "I have a helicopter coming. Signal the pilot with your flashlight when you hear the rotor blades."

"Very good, sir," Yibo said.

Choi stood next to Taft in the shadow of a rusting metal trestle bridge. They watched in the distance as an old steam locomotive approached from the west. Far to the rear of the locomotive, like a string to the heavens, trailed a thick cloud of black coal smoke.

The wagon path running across the trestle bridge was thankfully deserted. Taft and Choi were now so deep in the vast wasteland of the Gobi Desert that goats outnumbered people by two hundred to one. It was very doubtful they would be spotted by any Chinese citizens.

"Stay out of sight until I tell you to move," Taft said, staring into Choi's eyes. "When I signal you, we will climb to the top of the bridge then leap off onto the top of the train."

Most of Choi's life had been spent sitting at a desk staring at equations. His idea of an adventure was ordering take-out pizza. Still, the amphetamines were coursing through his blood, and he grinned at Taft in the morning cold. "Okay, whatever you say," he said loudly.

Taft stared at the tiny scientist. "I may have miscalculated the dosage of the amphetamines. Are you okay?"

"Sure," Choi answered quickly.

"Rock and roll, my little scientist friend," Taft said with a chuckle.

The locomotive was passing under the bridge. Taft waited for a few seconds until a third of the train had passed, then motioned for Choi to climb the bunk and get into position to jump. Choi watched as the ancient cargo train thundered past, then turned to Taft. "Just *who* do you work for?"

"I work for the United States government. And believe it or not, I'm here to help," Taft said as he wrapped his arms around the tiny scientist. Holding Choi tight, he leapt from the bridge. The pair slammed onto the roof of the cargo car with a dull thud. Checking Choi and finding him uninjured, Taft motioned to the ladder that would take them inside the car.

The sound of rotor blades broke the quiet of the morning outside Qinghai. The approaching Chinese-built SA 365 Dauphin helicopter was as advanced in its design as those built in the

West. Constructed under a French license, the craft featured a completely enclosed Fenestron tail rotor and streamlined front glass bubble. The twin-engined SA 365 was fast and smooth flying.

At the sound of the approaching helicopter, Yibo signaled the pilot with his flashlight. The Dauphin turned and slowed, landing in a cloud of dust. Yibo ran over to the helicopter while the rotors were still spinning.

"Which way?" the pilot shouted over the noise of the engines.

"Up the river fifty miles first," Yibo answered over the increasing noise as the pilot prepared to lift off.

Eighteen minutes later, just as the sun began to rise over the line of mountains in the distance, Yibo was scanning the ground through a pair of West German binoculars.

"We're just crossing the fifty-mile point!" the pilot shouted.

"Then turn around and fly downstream from where we started," Yibo shouted across the cockpit.

"How far?" the pilot asked.

"Until we find something," Yibo replied, continuing to scan the ground.

Over an hour later, nearly two hundred miles downstream, Yibo called to the pilot, "Hover over the river, I see something in the water to the left."

The pilot lowered the helicopter until it was hovering over a black object stuck on a log wedged at a bend in the river.

"Drop me on the bank. I need to examine that object," Yibo shouted to the pilot.

As soon as the helicopter touched down, Yibo ran to the water and waded in. Lifting the edge of the object, he saw it was a raft. From inside he removed the small outboard engine. After reading the brand name he carried the motor to shore. Wading back into the water, he dragged the raft from the log and arranged raft and motor together on the riverbank. Then he returned to the helicopter.

"Fly directly down the river at a slow speed. We are searching for a pair of footprints," he shouted to the pilot.

Six minutes later the pilot spotted the tracks.

CHAPTER 6

To anyone driving past on the road, the three-story office building on the outskirts of Bethesda, Maryland, appeared innocuous, bland, uninspiring. An eight-by-six-foot sign set atop a brick planter that read CAPCO MINING was the only indication as to the nature of the business inside. Anyone stopping and wandering into the building would never notice the advanced security measures the building featured.

Visitors were under surveillance by video cameras hidden in the trees from the time they turned off the main road until they reached the parking lot. The video surveillance continued once they left their car and approached the building. Once inside the lobby, few would notice the tinted, bulletproof glass, and no one but an expert in security would recognize that the entire lobby had reinforced walls and support beams that could withstand all but the most powerful bomb blast.

If a threat were detected, the security guards stationed at the lobby desk could seal off the lobby with a push of a button. A few seconds later, after the guards had placed gas masks over their faces, the entire lobby would be misted with a gas that rendered anyone in the lobby unconscious in less than three seconds.

There was little that could be done to the outside of the building to defend against a suicide bomber driving a vehicle loaded with explosives. However, the grounds outside the building, numerous locations on the street, as well as the parking lot were outfitted with hidden barriers that rose hydraulically when activated. Designed to shred the tires and hook the rims of any vehicle that posed a threat, it made the building impervious to anything short of an assault by tank.

The security measures might seem extreme for an ordinary business concern, but Capco Mining was a mining company in name only. The Capco building outside Bethesda housed the National Intelligence Agency, the smallest of the United States intelligence organizations. The NIA reported directly to the National Security Council, and its primary mandate was antiterrorist activities.

The NIA was comprised of several autonomous divisions, including the Technology Department, the Transportation Division, the Infrastructure Division, the Foreign Terrorism Division, and the Special Security Service, which handled operations requiring the use of human agents.

The large budget for the NIA was buried inside the budget of the National Security Agency to hide the agency from the prying eyes of congressmen and reporters. The agency had remained small and discreet since its founding in the early nineteen-eighties.

On the third floor of the NIA building Larry Martinez was scanning a computer database when his telephone rang. Martinez was of medium height, just over five feet ten inches, and lean from his weekly regime of running. His face was classically handsome, with the high, well-defined cheekbones, strong chin, and jet black hair that indicated the influence of Spanish blood in his native Mexican race. But it was his eyes that most people noticed—they were a pale brown dotted with flecks of gold and green, and when he spoke, they looked directly into your soul.

Martinez was a man at peace with himself and the world, and little over the years had changed that.

"Just thought you'd like an update," Deputy Director Richard Allbright announced to Martinez over the phone. "Your partner got inside and has the subject in his custody."

"That's good news, but he still has a long way to go," Martinez noted, his voice showing the concern he felt.

"That's true—we can only hope for the best," Allbright noted. "But as luck would have it, Taft's plan to trigger a seismic disturbance seemed to have worked. The Earthquake Center in Colorado reports it as a five on the Richter scale. Our satellites report communications into Qinghai as limited, but that could change at any moment."

"You'll keep me posted?" Martinez asked.

"You can be assured of it," Allbright said. And then, changing the subject, he asked, "How are you coming on the Einstein-Choi connection?"

"I've compiled a list of items to investigate. I'll be out in the field today doing research. Do you want field reports as I progress or just a standard daily log?"

"Call if you're onto something big," Allbright said. "Otherwise, a standard report."

"Very good, sir," Martinez said.

"That's all, then, Larry. Know that we're all pulling for your partner and his safe return," Allbright said as the telephone went dead.

Martinez entered a command into his computer, then waited as the information printed. Swallowing the last of his coffee, he gathered the papers, slid them into a file folder, and then called down to the security desk to inform them he would be leaving the building.

CHAPTER 7

Rumbling through the barren wasteland of the Gobi Desert, the cargo train maintained a speed of just over fifty miles an hour. The trip to Urumqi, 375 miles from China's border with Kazakhstan—in the former Soviet Union—would take just over twelve hours. Taft had little to do except stare at the land as it rolled past the open door of the cargo car. In the distance Taft could see gusts of wind blowing the sandy soil, forming clouds of dust. Other than a single instance when he spotted a man leading an ox far in the distance, Taft had yet to see another living thing. Choi was sleeping, sprawled out in the far corner of the railcar. Taft could see him occasionally twitch and mutter in his sleep. Finally, with little else to do, Taft settled down to rest. Placing his pack under his head, he concentrated on relaxing his muscles. Breathing deeply and regularly he began to drift off. It would be the last chance for sleep until he and Choi crossed the border—or died trying.

"Bring the dogs!" Yibo shouted into the radio.

The helicopter was parked on the edge of the stream, its engines shut down.

"Do you think you have them?" Jimn asked over the radio.

"The pilot spotted a set of tracks leading from the water. We are approximately one hundred twenty miles downstream of the facility. It appears the tracks match the set found near the fence, but the wind has been gusting and the tracks are already becoming obscured. They are disappearing as we speak."

"Can you search from the air until the dogs arrive?" Jimn asked.

"Not enough fuel. We didn't start out with a full tank," Yibo noted.

"I understand," Jimn said. "I'll bring a spare fuel pod and the dogs in another chopper. It will take me two hours to fuel, load the dogs, and fly out there. You'll just have to wait until I arrive."

"Very well, Mr. Jimn," Yibo said as he replaced the microphone, then settled in his seat to doze.

In the executive dining room of the Chinese government offices in Beijing at eleven minutes past noon, the prime minister's lunch was interrupted with the news that Choi had disappeared.

The executive dining room was as ornate as the palace of a feudal lord. Finely detailed brass statues of horsemen, each standing seven feet tall, stood to each side of the carved ebony doors leading to the hallway. Rich tapestries hung from the walls, their beauty highlighted by hidden golden spotlights, while thick Persian carpets muffled the sounds of the servants as they set out the elegant repast.

A large sandalwood dining table stood in the center of the room with a brass incense burner spouting thin tendrils of smoke. Delicate, nearly translucent vases were set to each side of the incense burner, and each one contained a visually perfect flower arrangement. The lunch for the leaders of China was artfully arranged on a separate side table and was kept warm in silver chafing dishes. There were dumplings filled with tiny bits of shrimp and crab and marinated beef, two kinds of fish, a noodle dish, and a marinated cabbage, scallion, leek, and seaweed dish the prime minister particularly enjoyed.

After reading the report on Choi's escape, along with an update on the progress of the search, the prime minister sat back, raised his hands to have his plates taken away, sipped his tea, then lit a Chinese Panda cigarette.

"I expect the boots and the pound note are but a crude ploy," he said slowly to the vice-minister while at the same time lightly stroking his chin. "Even so, have the secret police give me an update on the location of all British citizens currently in the western desert. I may be wrong in my thinking, but I believe it's not the British who want Choi—it's the Americans. Ever since we liberated Choi they have been seeking his return through diplomatic channels. When that got them nowhere they must have decided to take action." He paused and sipped the tea again, then turned to the army general at his left. "I would like a report on the placement of any American forces near our borders," he said. Then he motioned to his aide that the meal was over and the man quickly began to clear the plates. "One must think wherever there are American troops stationed, that's where these two will head," he said to all present.

Sliding his chair back from the table, he rose and walked from the room.

Thirty minutes later, Sun Tao, head of the Social Protection Department, or SPD, China's secret police, entered the prime minister's outer office.

He waited as the male secretary rang the inner office, then motioned to Tao.

"You may enter, sir."

Tao proceeded to the inner office, then across the room to the prime minister's desk near the window and placed the two reports on the desk. He waited until a young Chinese girl, no more than twelve years of age, finished polishing the prime minister's nails and packed her manicure tools into a leather case. She left the office soundlessly.

"Records showed there were nearly forty British citizens

working or studying in the western desert. Enough, it would seem, that one might be the man helping Choi. There are, strangely, no Americans in the area." Tao paused, waiting to see if the prime minister would ask him to sit.

"Continue," the prime minister said to the still-standing Tao.

"As to the deployment of United States armed forces, the closest to China appear to be in the Philippines and Thailand, which both hold sizable contingents of American troops."

The prime minister nodded. "I think the tracks the security guards spotted going west are designed to mislead our searchers," he said, glancing at his fingernails. "Three men must have infiltrated Qinghai. Two are leading us astray to the west, while one is leading Choi south as we speak. The kidnappers of Choi have no one that can help them to the west." The prime minister reached down and picked up a gold pen and rolled it between his fingers. "Choi and one of the others are probably going toward Hong Kong," the Prime Minister said quietly to Tao. "It would have to be. What single man would be stupid enough, or skilled enough, to infiltrate one of our most secure facilities and then steal off like a thief in the night?" The prime minister paused again. "Have the border with Hong Kong secured. If there are no Americans nearby, it *must* be the British working *for* the Americans. Next have the location of all the Brits verified. Whoever is not where he should be, is either with Choi or knows where he is."

"Immediately, sir," Tao said.

The prime minister's thinking was flawed. His mind was preoccupied with thoughts of a coming war.

By the time Jimn and the tracking dogs arrived and followed the scent to the railroad bridge, it was late afternoon. Climbing back aboard the pair of helicopters, Jimn and Yibo ordered their pilots to fly west along the tracks. They had traveled but a few miles when Jimn radioed Yibo.

"I just received a scrambled call from Beijing," Jimn said. "I've been ordered to move our search south."

"Shall I fly back to Qinghai, refuel, and search to the south?" Yibo asked Jimn.

"No," Jimn said, "you go ahead and follow through on the search west."

A single hound was still on Taft's tail. He would prove hard to shake.

"Li, wake up," Taft said, shaking Choi's arm.

Choi came slowly out of his slumber. "That pill . . ." he said slowly.

"It's not the pill that's affecting you—it's the stress of the escape. Your body is simply not accustomed to so much excitement," said Taft.

Choi struggled to sit upright. He saw Taft staring at the GPS and the plastic-covered map. Taft marked a spot on the map with a grease pencil and put it away. Next he removed two food packages from inside.

"Eat," Taft said as he tossed one of the packages to Choi.

Choi stared at the printed label: Sesame Chicken. Americanized Chinese food.

"My own selection," Taft said. "Mix water in the pouch, it's not too bad."

Choi nodded, took the offered canteen, and began to mix his meal. He would have preferred American food. He developed quite a taste for hamburgers and hot dogs while attending school in California. Still, he knew that his American rescuer had made a gesture of respect toward him and he began eating the mock Chinese food without complaint.

"Where are we now?" Choi asked as he finished the pouch and tossed it from the train.

"We'll soon be in Urumqi. That's where these particular

tracks end," Taft said as he rummaged in the pack. "Pudding?" Taft continued, tossing a tin to Choi, who caught it.

"If we are captured I want you to know I won't talk. They can torture me but it won't work," Choi said as he began spooning the pudding from the tin.

"Mighty white of you, but you've been watching too many spy movies," Taft said as he tossed his empty can of pudding from the open door of the railcar. "Nowadays, we're being trained to tell our captors everything. Torture has just become too advanced. In time they'll get whatever they want out of you, anyway."

"So you just tell them everything you know?" Choi asked incredulously.

"Then we swap agents later. It's considered bad sport to torture the enemy to death. The trick is to know only enough to complete your phase of the mission. Then, if you tell them everything, you jeopardize no one else. At least that's how it works in theory. Just for example, I don't know who else is helping us today—if there even *is* someone," Taft said. "And I wasn't told a whole lot about you or even why I was assigned to liberate you."

"So if we're caught I should tell them everything?" Choi asked.

"Except what I just told you."

Choi stared at Taft in confusion.

"You need to work on your sense of humor," Taft said, smiling. "We're not going to get caught."

"But if we do," Choi said.

"This time the rules are a little different," Taft said, rising and staring out the open door of the railcar at the passing countryside. His back to Choi, his voice suddenly adopted an icy tone. "You can't be taken alive, Li. I'm sorry."

Choi sat silently as the words washed across him. He had been rescued from hell only to stare death in the face.

❊   ❊   ❊

A late afternoon haze lay over the railroad tracks leading to Urumqi as the Chinese helicopter sped west. The sun would soon drop below the horizon, making the search that much more difficult.

"Chang," Jimn shouted into the radio of the helicopter now speeding south.

"Yes sir," Yibo answered.

"I have called ahead to Urumqi. They are assembling men to search the train as soon as it reaches the railyard."

"That should prove if the prime minister is right," Chang said.

"Let's hope," Jimn said as the radio went dead.

CHAPTER 8

A man carrying a British passport bearing the name Malcolm Leeds steered a dark blue Land Rover around an ox partially blocking the dirt road. Four weeks into a scheduled six-week archaeological dig near Xining, the isolation of the remote site appeared to be wearing on Leeds's spirit. He needed a city, needed it badly.

So far, the archaeological work had proved to be extremely important, a crude stone temple from the Yuan dynasty, the time of Kublai Khan, had been located and excavations were slowly proceeding.

Inside the first hallway to be cleared the archaeologists had found indications that the Mongols, who had built the temple, had traveled farther than previously thought. Muslim religious

markings adorned the walls of the hallway, and what the archaeologists now believed was a crude map showing the world as far
away as the Middle East was located on a thick slab of stone
with supports like a table.

"Will the hotel in Lanzhou have television?" Leeds asked
Deng Biao, his Chinese assistant on the dig who was seated in
the passenger seat of the Rover.

"It does, but your Chinese is so poor that you won't be able
to understand what is being said." Biao moved his bony ass on
the seat, trying to find comfort.

"No CNN?" Leeds said. "No SKY TV?"

"Lanzhou is not Beverly Hills."

"Is there hot water so I can at least take a shower?"

"Yes," Biao said, "the hotel has hot water, clean sheets, and
electric lights. All the little luxuries you have been complaining
about for the last few weeks."

Leeds, like the vast majority of Western archaeologists Biao
had met, seemed much more at home in a classroom than in
the field. Most archaeologists chose their discipline because
they had some romantic vision of Indiana Jones playing in their
heads. By the time they finally received a doctorate and came to
the harsh realization that their income rivaled that of a cat food
salesman, most became bitter and resentful. They usually ven-
tured out in the field only enough to publish the minimum
amount of papers to retain their job. Leeds was proving to be
just such a one, Biao thought to himself.

Deng Biao was completely taken in by Leeds's ruse.

"Good, a shower and a newspaper will go a long way toward
changing my mood," said Leeds.

Driving slowly down the rough road, at a spot about seven
miles from Lanzhou, Leeds rolled down the side window as a
Chinese helicopter roared overhead.

"Helicopter. Civilization can't be far now," Leeds noted.

"No, not far. But it will take time to reach," Biao said as he pointed through the windshield down the hill toward the Lanzhou.

Oxcarts, motorcycles, and hundreds of bicycles were blocking the dirt road as far as the eye could see. The line of humanity was being slowly funneled toward a barricade in the road in the far distance. The helicopter touched down near the checkpoint as Leeds watched the scene through the windshield.

"That's funny, I don't remember a checkpoint on this road," Biao said quietly.

"This is going to slow us down considerably," Leeds noted gloomily.

"Do you know the correct way to roll on the ground so you don't get injured?" Taft asked Choi.

"Not really," Choi said honestly.

"We don't have much time. Watch what I do carefully," Taft said as he demonstrated the correct roll on the wooden floor of the train car.

The satellite pictures the NIA had used in planning the escape revealed that the railroad tracks would make an abrupt turn on the outskirts of Urumqi. The photographs, now etched in Taft's memory, showed a small creek to one side, with the area around the creek thick with trees and brush. The planners felt it was the safest place for Taft and Choi to exit the train without being spotted.

And now it was fast approaching.

The railroad engineer in the locomotive applied the brakes to slow the train for the curve. A loud grinding noise ran the length of the train.

"Get ready," Taft said as he stood at the door of the railcar, watching the ground alongside race past.

Sticking his head entirely out the door, Taft spotted a patch of leaves and mud fifty yards ahead. "I've spotted our jump site.

You're first," Taft said as he reached for Choi, leading him by the arm toward the open door. "Ten seconds more."

Choi shivered with fear. The sequence of events in the last twenty hours was overwhelming. It was all too much to comprehend. Yesterday at this time, he was just finishing up working in the laboratory at Qinghai. Now he was being swept along in a wild escape orchestrated by a crazy American working for some organization the man refused to identify.

Choi stared at Taft. The American appeared completely calm. In fact, he appeared to be enjoying himself. The hand squeezing Choi's arm was steady, the eyes staring out at the passing ground intense and unblinking.

"Five, four, three, two, one. Remember to roll—*go*," Taft said, and he pushed Choi from the train.

Choi forgot to roll. He bounced on the ground with a sickening crunch. Three seconds after pushing Choi from the train, Taft leapt from the open door. Rolling in a ball like a gymnast, he popped back to his feet while still being carried forward by the momentum. Quickly grabbing Choi and tucking him under his arm, Taft raced into the trees. They needed to be out of sight before the caboose passed and the conductor noticed them. Choi screamed in agony from his shoulder injury as Taft carried him farther from the tracks into the woods.

Once safely in the brush, Taft stopped and lowered Choi carefully to the ground. "You forgot to roll," Taft said quietly.

"My shoulder," Choi said through the pain now clouding his thoughts.

Taft rolled him carefully over on his back. Pulling Choi's shirt over his head, he inspected the injured shoulder.

"It's pretty bad—it's already showing heavy swelling. My guess is a fractured shoulder blade or a broken bone somewhere in the back. But I'm no doctor, so it's only an educated guess."

"There's no way I can make it to the border like this," Choi said through gritted teeth. "Even the slightest movement is excruciating. You're going to have to leave me and go on alone."

"So you want to die here?"

"Leave me. In time the Chinese will find me. You can escape easier without me to slow you down."

Taft walked a few steps away and stared into the distance. Listening to the quiet sounds of the forest, he stared up at the sun. He walked back to Choi. "I thought we already covered this. There is no way I can allow you to be recaptured. I have my orders."

Choi licked off the sweat forming on his upper lip. "So the savior becomes the executioner?"

"They gave me no choice," Taft said, staring directly into Choi's eyes.

"Do you know what it is that makes me so valuable your boss would risk your life to save me?" Choi said, suddenly frightened by the unblinking gaze.

"No. And I don't want you to tell me," Taft said coldly. He paused and wiped the sweat from Choi's forehead.

"Here are your options. I can make your death painless. I have tablets in my pack you could take that will bring death in under thirty seconds. Two, I could kill you myself. Please don't ask me to do that. I've never killed anyone who wasn't trying to kill me first. Three, I have pills that will render you unconscious. Then it's up to me to get you across the border somehow."

Taft towered over the tiny physicist, peering down.

At last Choi broke the tension. "Unconscious, huh? I think I'd like to give that a try."

"Good choice," Taft said as he reached in the pack and removed his case of pills. "Here's the only downside. It's still three hundred and seventy-five miles to the border. Your shoulder might be further injured by the trip. I have no way to gauge that. I *can* tell you, however, that once we cross the border, my people will have a doctor waiting. As soon as we're safe your shoulder will be set. I give you my word."

"What if we are captured, Mr. Taft?" Choi said as he raised the canteen to his lips to wash down the pill.

"I'm getting you out alive," Taft said in a voice that could freeze water, "or we both go to meet our maker. You see, Mr. Choi, *I* have no choice as well."

Before he could ponder Taft's words, Choi drifted over the edge to blissful unconsciousness. Taft felt for his pulse then prepared to set off for the border.

Rifles locked and loaded, a dozen Chinese soldiers wearing the khaki fatigues of the Chinese army approached the blue Land Rover that was inching its way up to the checkpoint. Leeds watched through the windshield as the soldiers took their positions in the front and to the sides of the vehicle. Several of the soldiers pointed their rifles at the radiator as a Chinese army officer ran to the passenger side and dragged Biao from his seat. After handing Biao over to a soldier to detain, the officer circled around the back of the Land Rover and pulled Leeds from the driver's seat. Hands held over his head, the archaeologist immediately kneeled on the ground.

"Don't shoot, I'm a British citizen. My passport is in my shirt pocket," Leeds shouted.

The Chinese officer pulled Leeds to his feet and pushed him toward another soldier, who began to lead him toward a waiting jeep.

"Wait," the officer shouted in Chinese seconds later.

He walked over to the archaeologist and lifted Leeds's boot as if he were inspecting a horse's hoof. "Clark's-London," he said in English as he slapped his hand against the side of Leeds's head.

Leaving the doors open on the Land Rover, the officer loaded the pair into the back of the jeep, then sped off to the checkpoint.

Hundreds of Chinese peasants, carrying caged ducks, vegetables, and grain to trade, filed around the open doors of the now abandoned truck. They continued on their way to Lanzhou as if nothing had happened.

The helicopters carrying Jimn and Yibo were still 150 miles from Urumqi when the radio call came from the checkpoint near Lanzhou.

"It seems our troops have captured the pair in Lanzhou," Jimn radioed Yibo.

"The raft and set of footprints must have been a decoy after all," Yibo said. "What would you like me to do now?"

"Fly to Anxi and refuel, then return to the weapons laboratory and take over security. I'll go to Lanzhou and make the identification," Jimn answered.

"As you wish, sir," Yibo said quietly.

As the helicopter carrying Yibo turned and headed west, something still weighed heavily on his mind. Somewhere in the deep recesses of his subconscious he had the nagging feeling that he was traveling farther from their prey. Scrunching down to sleep in the noisy helicopter, he banished the unwanted thoughts.

It was only a gut feeling. And besides, Jimn, not he, was in charge.

Hiking three miles west to skirt the town of Urumqi while carrying a Chinese physicist is not as easy as it sounds, Taft thought to himself. As evening turned to night, Taft stopped to catch his breath on a small hill above an abandoned farmer's shed. He checked his coded notes once again, and searched his memory for the aerial photograph he had studied. Comparing the landmarks on the ground with the ones in his head, he concluded he was in the right area. In a grove of trees covered with brush, Taft left Choi and crept carefully down the hill. From outside the shed he heard no sound. He slipped through its ramshackle door, then flicked on a small penlight he carried clipped to his shirt pocket.

There his chariot sat as planned. *Perfect*, Taft thought to himself. *I just might get out of China alive.* He rubbed his hand over the smooth leather of the saddlebags and smiled.

It was time to start the last leg of the trip to freedom.

The sharp sting of the leather glove across Deng Biao's face brought him from his stupor. "Once again you tried to desert your country for the West. You are a traitor and a thief," the interrogator shouted.

"What are you talking about? I'm an archaeologist with Beijing University. I'm working on a dig near Xining," Biao said in Chinese.

"Liar," the interrogator said, again striking Biao across his cheeks.

"You little fucker," Biao said in English.

"What did he say?" the interrogator asked the English interpreter.

"He said he doesn't know what this is all about," the interpreter said, sickened by the sight of violence and beginning to believe Biao was telling the truth.

Two doors down the hall, Malcolm Leeds was being treated with slightly more civility. "Why did you kidnap Li Choi?" the interrogator asked.

"Who's Li Choi?" Leeds asked.

"Please don't play dumb with me, Mr. Leeds," the interrogator said coldly.

"I'd like to see the British consul," Leeds said, his anger rising.

"In time, in time," the interrogator said as he slammed the

door to the cell and walked down the hall to speak with Biao's interrogator.

CHAPTER 9

Martinez wiggled around in the chair to find a comfortable position. The oak armchairs in the Archives Department of the FBI were about as soft as a boulder. The light was dim in the reading room, but at the far end of the twenty-foot-long, thirty-year-old conference table, Martinez could see that the agent assigned to watch him as he searched the files was nodding off.

Martinez was reading the field reports from the FBI agents that followed Einstein. He was trying to determine why China kidnapped Choi, a student applying for asylum who was an expert in obscure Einsteinian physics. The reports spanned ten years, from 1945, when Hoover had first ordered the surveillance, to 1955, when Einstein passed away in a hospital in New Jersey.

The reports contained little of interest. One event, a report of Einstein shaking off his followers in the summer of 1945, shortly after the surveillance began, was interesting. The only other report Martinez found useful was a report of an intercepted telegram destined for physicist Niels Bohr, while Einstein was dying. The surveillance in between those two events seemed to be as worthless as a bowling ball without holes.

Martinez slid the aging oak chair back from the table, creating a clatter in the silent room. "I'll need copies of these two reports," he said to the agent, who had awakened with a start. He handed the agent a sheet of paper with the file numbers written in pencil.

"It usually takes about thirty to forty-five minutes," said the agent, stifling a yawn.

Martinez handed the agent a card that contained only telephone numbers. He circled the correct one with his pencil. "Could you have your people fax the reports to my office? I'm running on a tight schedule."

"Sounds fair," the agent noted, taking the card from Martinez.

"Thanks for your help," Martinez said as he strode from the room.

Black leather helmet and fake Fu Manchu mustache masking his features, Taft nudged the shifter with his toe into fourth gear, then twisted the throttle wide open. The black Chinese-made motorcycle sped up, a staccato popping coming from the exhaust pipe. A cloud of dust trailed behind as Taft drove down the dirt road. To his right, Choi sat in the sidecar, head lolling from side to side. He was still in a deep stupor and, with luck, would remain so for some time.

The night was clear and cool. The dim yellow beam from the cycle's headlight shared illumination duties with the full harvest moon. Taft glanced down at the odometer. Three hundred miles to go. At the current rate of speed they would cross the border around four in the morning. He leaned to one side to bank the motorcycle around a curve.

Two hours later, and 222 miles north-northeast of Alma-Ata, Kazakhstan, a chill wind carrying the cold of a thousand northern nights swept through the open rear cargo door of a U.S. Air Force C-130 Hercules sitting on a dirt field one mile from the Chinese border. A pool of light from inside the plane puddled on the ground outside. Blowing across the steaming cup of coffee, the pilot of the C-130, Dewey Brable, took a sip of the hot liquid, then set it on the rear ramp and lit a Marlboro cigarette.

"Feels strange to be inside the Soviet Union," Brable said to Taft's boss, Retired General Earl Benson, who stood smoking a cigar alongside the ramp.

Benson chose not to answer. Instead he shouted into the plane to the radio operator, "What's their location now?"

Checking his direction-finding set mounted alongside the radar, the air force lieutenant measured the distance with calipers and shouted back, "Under two hundred miles, sir."

"Good," Benson said.

"How did we receive permission to land here?" Brable asked Benson.

"The Commonwealth of Independent States is our ally now," Benson said.

"Any chance of you telling me what agency you work for?"

"No chance in hell," Benson said, smiling. "Now, where did you get that coffee?"

Jumping from the helicopter while its main rotor was still turning, Jimn raced into the security building in Lanzhou. Walking quickly down the hall toward the interrogation room, his polished black boots tapped out a muted staccato. He stopped at the door to the room containing Deng Biao. Motioning to the guard to move, Jimn opened the door. It took him only a second to make the identification. He stared at Biao, then the interrogator, before speaking in a cold voice. "This had better not be the person you think is Choi."

Twitching with fear, the interrogator said in a rush, "I was not the one to make the identification. I'm only handling the questioning."

"And what did you find out?" Jimn asked.

"He claims to be an archaeologist."

"He may be—because he sure as hell isn't Choi, you stupid ass," Jimn screamed.

He walked to a nearby cell and looked at Leeds. "Where were you night before last?"

"I was having dinner with the mayor of the town of Xining. You can call him and verify this," Leeds finished.

"Where did you purchase your boots?"

"I bought them in Hong Kong. The British army swears by them."

Storming from the room Jimn ran to a telephone to check with the mayor of Xining. When Leeds's story checked out, Jimn telephoned the prime minister.

Twelve minutes later two Chinese fighter jets blasted from the runway at the Lop Nur Nuclear Weapons Testing Center and streaked toward Urumqi. At the same instant, refueled and parked in front of the Advanced Weapons Facility, Yibo was unbuckling himself from the passenger seat of the helicopter when the call came through from Jimn.

"We've been had," Jimn said. "Fly west to Urumqi like we'd planned."

The pilot and Yibo immediately lifted off from the base in Qinghai and flew west.

In the confusion that had been generated, the Chinese troops dispatched to search the train in Urumqi were ordered to stand down and return to their barracks. The cargo train Taft and Choi had ridden was already in Urumqi and being unloaded. To search the train for Choi would be pointless—it was, by now, almost empty.

"A transport plane is arriving," Jimn informed the ground commander. "Load the troops aboard."

Flown west to a landing strip near Yining, they were divided into search teams to patrol the border with Kazakhstan.

The Chinese prime minister, angered he had been fooled, ordered two converted cargo planes that were equipped with sophisticated sensors detecting both heat and movement, to fly from their base near Chengdu. With in-air refueling, they could be over the China–Kazakhstan border in two hours. The instruments on board were capable of detecting and cataloguing the presence of life down to the size of a turtle. If the troops somehow missed Choi, the sensors wouldn't.

The net around Taft and Choi was finally being pulled tight.

"I'm picking up a couple of fast movers in the area," the air force radar operator aboard the C-130 said as he adjusted the radar definition. "Twin MIG-29 knock-offs. In addition I have two Chinese cargo planes on a course for the border. They're two hundred miles out," the radar operator said as the blips on his screen became more defined, "and it looks like a lone helicopter as well."

"They've seen through the diversion in Lanzhou. They're on to them," Benson noted.

"General, I'm receiving a secure transmission," the radio operator shouted from the rear of the plane. Benson walked forward and received the slip of folded paper.

Overheads reveal twin Chinese prop planes inbound from Chengdu, ETA two hours maximum. Intelligence suggests they are bloodhounds.

Our satellites have recorded the bloodhounds leaving their base, Benson thought to himself. God help Taft now. Feeding the strip of paper into a shredder, he stood quietly for a moment.

One hour and thirty minutes later, the jet carrying Jimn from Lanzhou touched down at the deserted airport in Yining. A single jeep sat on the runway, awaiting his arrival. Jimn bolted down the ramp from the jet and climbed into the passenger seat.

"What is the status of the search?" he said to the driver without preamble.

"The troops are in position at the border as you ordered. The fighter jets ordered to watch overhead have reported nothing as yet. Sensor-equipped planes are due within thirty minutes," the driver, a captain in the Chinese army, said as he put the jeep in gear and drove away from the jet.

"Take me to the border," Jimn said.

"Right away, sir," the captain said as he shifted through the gears.

Twenty miles from the Chinese border with Kazakhstan, Taft switched off the motorcycle's headlight at the sound of a helicopter passing overhead. Pulling to the side of the road, he waited until the sound of the rotor blades faded in the distance. He was just about to pull back onto the road when a pair of jets roared close overhead.

"When it rains it pours," Taft muttered as the jets flew past.

Checking his map by the light of the moon, he measured the distance to the dry creekbed where he would turn off the road. Less than two miles. Slamming the motorcycle in gear he twisted the throttle and pulled back onto the road.

"In light of what has happened, there's no way I would feel comfortable continuing the dig," Leeds said to Biao outside the police station where the men had just been released.

"I understand how you feel," Biao said quietly.

"I have radioed the Xining site. They will ship my luggage. I'm leaving immediately for Hong Kong, where I'll catch a flight home," Leeds said quickly as he stood by the cab that would take him to the airport.

"I apologize for the trouble." Biao said. "I only hope your university will not completely pull out of this project.

Leeds shrugged—he could care less.

Jimn shouted orders into his hand-held radio as the jeep bumped along the border. Brush and trees grew thickly on the Russian side, obscuring the view. Chain-link fencing, erected by China in years past, ran from the border crossing outside Yining one mile to the north and south. With the current tension between China and the former Soviet Union, the checkpoint crossing was closed up. The road was covered with concrete barricades. On the Chinese side of the border the land was open. The brush and trees were burned off every odd-numbered year to stem the rising tide of smuggling.

"Chang, do you read me?" Jimn said into the radio.

After a pause of almost a minute, Yibo answered. "This is Yibo."

"Watch the fence line closely from the air. I will start driving south."

"Very good, sir," Yibo said. He ordered his pilot to began sweeping back and forth high above the fence.

On orders from their commanding officer, the Chinese troops that had been assembled formed a human wall and began to walk from the fence line east through the burned-out wasteland. They carefully searched the ground for tracks. High overhead, the jets could see little as they passed at two hundred miles an hour. The sensor-equipped planes were still miles away. They would arrive moments too late to help.

Taft stopped the motorcycle and hastily covered it with brush. He walked a short distance away into the woods. Using a pair of infrared binoculars he stared silently at the line of troops to the south of the fence line. His planned crossing point was thick with Chinese troops. Hoisting Choi over his shoulder like a sack of cement, Taft crept close to the border. He would have to alter his plan.

Keying his tiny portable radio unit he gave the signal.

"Three beeps on 750 megahertz, General," the air force radar operator shouted from the cockpit of the C-130.

"Give me an update," Benson said to the radar operator.

"Two cargo jets, one hundred miles out. Two fighters are still loitering above the scene. The helicopter is upwind, near the fenced portion of the crossing. It seems to be patrolling the fence line."

"What's on the radio?" Benson asked.

An air force radio operator, specially selected for this mission because he was fluent in Mandarin answered. "The Chinese troops have been ordered to patrol around the scheduled crossing point."

"How far is our man's signal from the border?"

"Less than five hundred yards," the radar operator answered, his eyes fixed on the flashing light on his display screen.

"Come on, John," Benson said quietly, "you've almost made it."

Creeping to the edge of the burned area, Taft could see the open space to the border was nearly eighty yards wide. He could only hope that the Chinese had burned the line inside their border and not yards inside Kazakhstan. If he could cross the open area and make it into the woods, he believed he would be inside Kazakhstan. The tree line was the key to living. He had to believe that—it was all that kept him going.

❋   ❋   ❋

"The ground troops have just located a motorcycle," Yibo shouted to the pilot of the helicopter. "Fly south about a mile, I wish to check it out."

At the news of the motorcycle, Jimn also ordered his driver to race south. Screaming into his portable radio, he ordered the troops to locate the trail of footprints and follow them. It was time to bring this to an end. Choi was too valuable to lose.

Taft looked through his night-vision binoculars at the mass of humanity clustered around the motorcycle that had brought the pair to the border. Beams from the soldiers' flashlights intersected as the troops massed, each trying to get a peek at the cycle. Then, as Taft watched, the beams of light took order and began to march directly toward where he was hiding. Taft had removed his boots; with Choi on his back there was only a single set of prints. It seemed his brilliant plan had fooled no one.

"There's only one thing to do," Taft said to himself as he clutched Choi tighter. With his plans in ruins, his only prayer was to sprint across the open space. He hoped he could outrun his pursuers. There was no other option. He began to run to the border as fast as his legs would move.

The sound of a whistle reached Taft's ears around the same time a weak beam of light from a flashlight swept past his pounding feet. The soldier who had spotted Taft screamed into the radio to alert the others as he started running after the fleeing pair.

Punching their afterburners in response to the radio call from the soldier, the two Chinese fighters did a 180-degree turn and began to fly south. Yibo's helicopter was above the motorcycle, about to touch down, when he heard the soldier's call. The pilot turned toward the troops chasing Taft without an order being given.

Hyperventilating to fill his lungs with air, his legs aching dully, Taft made a dead run across the open expanse. The weight of Choi seemed nonexistent as a rampant explosion of adrenaline coursed through his blood. Sixty yards across the open space, he began up the slope of the hill that formed the border. Taft's bare feet were pounding the ground with the intensity of a jackhammer in a paint shaker. Nose flared, he screamed a rebel yell.

A Kentucky thoroughbred would have had a hard time keeping pace.

Jimn shouted into the radio. "Fighters, spray the border with your chain guns."

"What if they cross the border?" one of the pilots immediately asked over the radio as he removed the firing lock from the wing mini-cannon.

"They cannot leave the country alive," Jimn said loudly. "Keep firing until you bring them down."

Fifty yards behind Taft the Chinese troops started up the hill. If they had only stopped and taken a shot with their rifles they would have hit him cleanly in the back. Instead, caught up in the heat of the chase, they ran blindly, their rifles held low.

"Go in at an altitude of ten feet," Yibo shouted to the helicopter pilot.

Dropping down, the helicopter flew just above the troops' heads. The helicopter's powerful spotlight illuminated Taft and Choi just as they crested the hill, jumped over the top, and raced into the woods inside Kazakhstan.

"I've got you now," Yibo said quietly.

Streaking low from the north, the two fighters lined up for their firing run. The lead pilot was seconds from squeezing his trigger and tearing Taft and Choi to shreds when his cockpit was lit up with the blinding light of a phosphorescent rocket. Twisting his control stick, the lead fighter pilot broke off his approach. As trained, the second fighter followed his partner. Both fighters executed a ninety-degree turn to the east.

Seconds after Taft entered the forest that signaled the Kaza-khstan border, he was tackled by a man dressed entirely in black. Taft reared his arm back to punch.

"Stop, we're the good guys," the man shouted with a Georgia drawl.

Taft quickly lowered his arm.

Choi was plucked from where he had been dropped by a second man, just as the helicopter carrying Yibo crossed the border, searchlight sweeping like a death ray.

The next few seconds seemed to last forever. Dust and leaves swirled about as a loud whining noise filled the forest. Crouching and placing his hands over his ears, Taft buried his eyes in his shirt.

Like the phoenix rising from the dead, a United States Marine Harrier jump jet hidden behind the hill rose directly into the path of the advancing helicopter. Massive spotlights on the Harrier's wingtips lit night into day, while a second set of white-hot phos-phorescent flares belched from the forward pods. A voice from both the plane's radio and an external loudspeaker overrode the noise of the whining engines. The amplified voice said in Chinese, "Turn now or you will be destroyed."

Eyes blinded by the spotlights and the flares, Yibo's pilot jammed his cyclic to the side. The helicopter turned back from the border and hovered. The troops racing up the hill paused, unsure if they should advance.

The loudspeaker continued. "This is Captain Don Chin, United States Marine Corps. We are on joint exercises with the Republic of Kazakhstan. Any violation of the Republic's sovereign border will be met with force. Retreat immedi-ately and maintain a minimum distance of one mile from the border."

At that instant Taft was grabbed by the shoulder.

"Now," the man dressed in black shouted.

Crashing through the forest, the four men reached an armored

Humvee a short distance away. Taft and Choi were pushed in the backseat. The soldiers dressed in black climbed in front. The driver turned the key and without a moment's hesitation the Humvee raced away, heading west from the border. In less than twenty seconds, the Humvee was doing sixty miles an hour on the narrow dirt road.

The man in the passenger seat turned and spoke to Taft. "It'll take us several minutes to reach the plane. Do you need some water or something?"

"I've got some coffee in a thermos," the driver added.

Taft rubbed his palms across his face. "Force Recon?" he asked.

"How did you guess?" the man in the passenger seat asked.

"No one else would be crazy enough to attempt a stunt like that. You're the only guys in the military that *want* to die for your country."

"Semper fi," the driver laughed.

"I'll take that coffee," Taft said wearily, "plus a cigarette if you have one."

As the Humvee slid around a curve, narrowly missing a grove of trees, the marine in the passenger seat handed back the thermos, a pack of Camels, and a Zippo lighter.

"Kind of hard to believe," Taft said.

"What's that?"

"I quit smoking seven years ago," he said as he lit the Camel and took a drag.

"The shit is really hitting the fan, sir," the radio operator aboard the C-130 said as he continued monitoring the radio transmissions. "The ground commander, an officer named Jimn, is calling to Beijing to receive permission to cross the border," he said, rapidly translating the radio messages.

"Order the Harrier to back away slowly," Benson told the radio operator. "Keep a close eye on the radarscope," Benson said to the radar man. "If the fighters cross the border, alert me immediately."

"Force Recon reports they have both parties. They say they can see the lights of the C-130 now and estimate their arrival time at about four minutes," the radio operator yelled to Benson.

"Warm your engines," Benson said to Brable, who was already in the pilot's seat, waiting for instructions.

"Roger," Brable said as he reached to the overhead panel and flicked the switch to spin the starters.

In a matter of seconds smoke was pouring from the four turboprop engines. They quickly warmed to operating temperature. Brable waited for further orders.

"Is the Harrier away from the border?" Benson asked.

"He's backing up. The pilot estimates he's about two miles west of the border and as yet unchallenged."

"Where's the Humvee?"

"Less than one mile away and closing fast."

"Order the Harrier to turn and retreat at full speed," Benson ordered.

The radio operator shouted the order into the radio. The Marine Harrier turned and began to pick up speed; seconds later it shot past the C-130.

"Here they come!" one of the C-130's riggers screamed from the rear door.

"Start down the runway," Benson shouted to Brable, who immediately advanced the throttles. "Radio the Humvee we're moving; order them to run up the ramp as we taxi," Benson said to the radio operator.

"You're gonna love this," the driver shouted to Taft as soon as the message came over his radio earpiece.

Taft tossed the Camel butt out the window and took a last swig from the cup of coffee. "What now?" he asked.

"We've been ordered to drive up the ramp of the plane while it's taxiing down the runway."

"You guys ever try that before?" Taft asked.

"No, but I saw it in a movie once," the driver said as he floored the throttle and raced after the retreating C-130.

The tension was as thick as mud in the cockpit of the Air Force Hercules as it taxied toward takeoff. Benson wiped the sweat from his brow with his sleeve.

"Jimn just received permission to cross the border. Beijing has ordered him to capture the escapees and return them for trial no matter what it takes," the radio operator shouted to Benson.

"Let's hope our backup plan works," Benson said quietly.

The Humvee lined up behind the rear ramp of the retreating C-130. With a burst of speed the truck shot up the ramp. Tires slipping on the C-130's metal floor, the Humvee screeched to a halt inches from the bulkhead to the cockpit. Taft waved at Benson through his open window.

"Ramp up. Take off," Benson screamed to Brable.

Its throttles pushed to full, the C-130 sped faster down the runway. Brable watched his airspeed, then pulled back on the yoke and climbed into the air. He steered the plane west, away from the border with China.

"I've got a flight of seven jets as yet unidentified. They're in a classic delta wing pattern approaching from the front at a very high rate of speed," the radar operator of the C-130 shouted.

"Our baby-sitters have arrived," said Benson. He began walking back to the cargo area.

"Son of a bitch!" Brable shouted from the pilot's seat as a flight of Russian Mig-31E fighters raced past them heading east toward the border.

Within minutes after the Russian Migs appeared on the Chinese fighter's radarscopes the prime minister quickly changed his mind about a cross-border excursion. Chinese air and ground forces were ordered to immediately retreat from the border.

"I need a heading, sir," the navigator shouted back to Benson.

"First to Volgograd to refuel. Then we're going home," Benson yelled forward.

Leaning against the door of the Humvee, Benson smiled. "So, John, how was your trip?"

"So-so," Taft said quietly.

"As usual you did an excellent job," Benson said to Taft.

"That's why I get the big money," Taft said, turning his attention to Choi, now struggling to wake up. "Where's the doctor on this plane? I made him a promise we'd fix his shoulder."

CHAPTER 10

After leaving the FBI archives, Martinez made his way to a nearby restaurant. Settling into a booth in the rear, he ordered coffee and a fried egg sandwich, then began to study the notes he had compiled about Einstein. He was most curious about Einstein's last days—it was reported that the scientist was working feverishly up until the time of his death.

What did the scientist believe was so important that he would continue his labors even in frightful pain? Was the work simply the demented mathematical rambling of a man near death? Why did Einstein send a telegram to Niels Bohr in Denmark? What were his last words?

Martinez closed the file as the waitress brought over his fried egg sandwich. Returning with a pot of coffee, she topped off his cup, then retreated. Martinez stared at the sandwich. Plain white bread, not toasted and smeared with mayonnaise. He glanced at the egg inside. A round white orb with a yellow yolk that burned like the sun at the center. To the side of the sandwich was a handful of rippled potato chips and a wedge of dill pickle, which Martinez abhorred. Tossing the pickle into the ashtray, he took a bite of the sandwich, then washed it down with a sip of coffee. Then he reached into his pocket for his cellular phone.

"This is Agent Martinez," he told the person that answered. "I'm driving to New Jersey this afternoon pursuant to my investigation. I'll have my cellular phone with me if anybody needs to reach me."

"Very good, Agent Martinez. I have a message for you from the deputy director. Do you want it now?"

"Yeah, go ahead."

"The mission was successful," the operator read. "They're on their way home."

"Thanks. That's good news," Martinez said as he switched off his phone.

Martinez quickly finished the sandwich, tossed a five-dollar bill on the table, and left. Climbing into his NIA-issued sedan, he glanced at a map, then began to drive north. The drive to the hospital in New Jersey where Einstein died would take less than three hours. Plenty of time for him to ponder his questions.

Twenty-three hours and twelve minutes after lifting off the runway in Kazakhstan, Taft twisted the key in the lock of his front door at his home in Virginia. He was aching, fighting jet lag, and had moved beyond merely tired to exhaustion. Stooping on the porch, he picked up several days' supply of newspapers, then swung open the heavy wooden door. Dank air from inside the house washed across Taft's face. It was obvious that sometime during his trip to China his dehumidifier had stopped working. With the Potomac River laying a mere fifty feet from his back door, his house was naturally damp.

Walking to the computer control panel for his house, Taft punched in his burglar alarm code, then scanned the panel to see what was wrong with the dehumidifier. The readout on the panel indicated the problem was a blocked water outlet. Taft unlocked his back door, found the outlet pipe next to his dryer vent, then with a stick removed several acorns stuffed into the opening by a rogue squirrel. A flood of water ran from the pipe, then slowed to a trickle.

Back inside he scanned the panel to find the dehumidifier was now running. Soon enough the air in the house would dry out. He would need to open a few windows to rid the house of the stale smell, but that could come later. Scrolling through the memory on the control panel, he found everything else had functioned properly in his absence.

Leaving his bags on the floor in the entryway, he walked into the kitchen, where he swung open the refrigerator door and reviewed the contents. With nothing else looking good, he decided he would make a sandwich.

He toasted two pieces of slightly stale sourdough bread and spread them with creamy Italian dressing. Next he layered ham, turkey, and roast beef on one half. Slicing an overripe tomato, he laid the juicy pieces on the second slice of bread, which was already layered with cream cheese. Finally, he slammed the two sides together and sliced the sandwich in half with a sharp knife that hung above the sink. In the back of the refrigerator he found a Blenheim's ginger ale and popped off the bottle cap. Carrying sandwich and bottle to the kitchen table, he began to scan through the stack of old newspapers.

Finished with the sandwich, and bored with yesterday's news, he was opening windows and watering his plants in the living room when the phone rang. He answered with a terse hello.

"Welcome back," Martinez said easily. "I heard you were successful."

Taft looked at the number readout on his phone. The readout was scrambled, indicating Martinez was calling from inside their office.

"I see you're hard at work. Anything interesting happen while I was gone?" Taft asked his partner.

"A little. Your decoy's out of China, his feet just went wet over international waters a few minutes ago. Other than that, I was doing an interesting research project that coincides with what you were working on. I'll explain it when you get here."

"Sounds good. You'll forgive my lack of excitement over the decoy, but of course I had no idea of the plan," Taft said as he placed the empty watering can back under the sink.

"Agent 24 was posing as a British archaeologist. The Chinese detained him for a while. We think it aided your escape. Of course he had no idea you were grabbing Choi, so he convinced them to release him without much difficulty."

The total number of NIA operatives was just over fifty. To avoid the use of names, they were often referred to by number. The agent who had posed as Leeds, was 24. Special Agent Taft was number 7. Lucky 7. Taft had been one of the first agents recruited, fresh out of the army, nearly ten years ago.

"Glad to hear that. I'll be sure to thank 24. Is Choi back with his family?" Taft asked, sitting down again in a kitchen chair.

"They're flying him west for a reunion as we speak. We have a high-security compound in Colorado where they'll live for the time being."

"What exactly makes Choi so important?"

"It has to do with advanced physics. Einstein stuff."

"I risked getting killed to kidnap a physicist that specializes in the works of a man who's been dead over forty years?"

"It's more involved than that. I'll explain it to you when you get here."

"Does it say anything in the report about Choi's shoulder?" Taft asked, growing wearier by the minute.

"They have the shoulder in a splint. The doctors say it will be fine in time. Forget about him for now—he's someone else's problem now," Martinez said. "The computer that controls your house called me last night, something with a blocked pipe. I was sending an agent over this morning when I received word you were due back."

The security and physical systems of Taft's home were tied to a computer. If he is away on a mission, which is often, he transfers it to Martinez for monitoring.

"Don't bother. I already took care of it," said Taft.

"What time are you going to report in to the office?" Martinez asked.

Taft glanced at his watch. It was just past nine in the morning.

"Let me get a few hours sleep. How about after lunch?"

"Fair enough," Martinez said.

"I'm glad you approve," Taft said as he hung the phone back on the cradle.

Taft gathered his bags at the front of the house and carried them up the ornate stairway to the second floor. The house was built in 1814. Originally a stage stop, it survived the last 185 years in various incarnations. It had been a boardinghouse, a restaurant, even a store. Long boarded up and abandoned when Taft bought it, the restoration project had taken three years.

Over the years, brick had been laid against the logs that formed the original structure, so that now the exterior walls were several feet thick. The floors were constructed of heavy oak planking. When Taft ripped out old Sheetrock inside, he found ornately carved wooden trim along the walls, as well as an old stone fireplace. He cleaned and painted the woodwork. The fireplace, he found, worked just fine. The house measured around four thousand square feet and although the furnace, air conditioning, plumbing, and electricity were state-of-the-art, Taft made sure it retained the old look on the outside. Most people driving past never gave the house a second glance.

He liked it that way.

Twenty yards to the north of the house was an old stable that he had converted into a garage. Taft even went so far as to have an artist paint the garage doors to make it appear that horses were in stalls inside. With two-hundred-year-old trees on the property and the Potomac River running alongside, the house was quiet and comfortable. It was the one place where Taft could always escape the pressures of his work.

In the bathroom of the master bedroom, he dumped the dirty clothes from his bags into the hamper. He also stripped off the clothes he was wearing and stuffed them on top of the pile. Standing naked, he peered at himself in the mirror inside the bathroom.

The trip to China had cost him a few pounds, and that was not all bad. He had a propensity to gain and lose up to ten pounds in the course of a month, depending on his level of physical activity. He quickly grew bored with any one sport, and his closets and the storage area in the garage were littered with sporting equipment. Skis, tennis rackets, and a kayak shared space with golf clubs, running shoes, and a host of other toys he had purchased over the years. His latest kick was bicycling, a sport he had embraced, then grew bored with several years ago. This time, however, Taft added a twist. He had purchased a cargo cart that attached to the rear of his bicycle and loaded it with bricks to make workouts more effective.

He brushed his teeth; then he contemplated shaving, but decided it would be too much work. Instead, he walked into the bedroom and peeled back the comforter on his antique, king-size brass bed. Slipping naked between the cool cotton sheets, he flicked on a machine that made the sound of the ocean, then stared at the ceiling. In less than five minutes he was sound asleep.

Just before noon, and without the benefit of an alarm clock, Taft opened his eyes. Climbing from bed, he noticed his legs were still aching. The sprint across the border with Choi on his back had stressed his leg muscles and tendons more than he had realized. Now, on the second day, soreness was full-blown.

Reaching into his dresser drawer he removed underwear and socks. Pulling a pair of almost-new athletic shoes from his closet he placed them next to the chest at the foot of his bed. Selecting a white, cotton, button-down shirt and a pair of khaki pants from the closet, he hung them on hangars on the doorknob. Clothes laid out, he walked in the bathroom and climbed into the shower. He adjusted the water first from biting hot to wash to freezing cold to rinse.

After showering, Taft wiped the steam from the mirror and shaved, splashing Bay Rum on his cheeks when finished. Dressing in the clothes he had laid out, he tied the shoelaces of athletic shoes, then walked downstairs.

In the entryway he programmed the security system while calling Martinez on the cordless phone. "I'm leaving. Do you want me to pick you up anything for lunch?"

"Feel like going past Pepito's?"

"That's fine. You want the usual?"

"Oh yeah," Martinez said in anticipation.

"Be there in half an hour," Taft said and hung up the phone.

After a quick call to Pepito's, the Mexican restaurant he favored, to place a takeout order, Taft locked the front door and walked across the yard to the garage. Entering through the side door, he switched on the overhead lights. Several original American muscle cars sat on the white epoxy-painted floor. Near the door sat the new V-10 Dodge Ramcharger Taft had purchased only a few months before. The rest of the garage was filled with nearly thirty motorcycles, the oldest being a 1921 BSA. Pushing the button to raise the garage door, Taft walked back outside and peered out at the sky. It looked clear. The only clouds visible were far to the south, over Prince Georges County, Maryland.

It was a day made for a motorcycle ride.

Decision made, Taft walked toward a row of classics. His eyes came to rest on a 1971 Norton Commando Roadster, and he reached for its key in a lock box on the wall, slid it into the ignition, and twisted. The Norton started immediately, settling into a purr. He walked to a bench and picked up his white Bell helmet, then rolled the motorcycle from the line. At the door he plucked a battered leather jacket off a hook on the wall and zipped it halfway up. As he passed the garage door, Taft pushed a remote control in the jacket's pocket to lower the door behind him. Driving slowly up his blacktop driveway, he listened carefully to the engine. The Norton had recently been missing, and Taft spent most of one afternoon several weeks ago balancing the carburetors. What he had done seemed to be working, as the motorcycle accelerated smoothly.

Twenty minutes later, after stopping to pick up lunch, then tying the boxes on the rear of the seat with a bungee cord, Taft pulled into the parking lot of the National Intelligence Agency and shut off the engine. At the security checkpoint he flashed his badge at the guard.

"What's the good word, Bobby?"

"Good to see you back, John."

"Thanks for noticing I was gone," he said as he made his way toward the elevators.

On the twelfth floor he signed the log, then tracked down Martinez, who was inside the copy room. Seeing Taft with his helmet, he asked, "What did you drive today?"

"The Norton Commando."

"How's the Motto Guzzi coming?" Martinez asked.

"I'm still waiting for parts," Taft said.

Martinez removed his copies from the tray. "Well?"

"Time to eat," Taft said, motioning with his head.

As the pair ate their pork and avocado enchiladas in the break room, Taft filled Martinez in on the trip to China. Following course of habit, Taft would stop speaking when anyone entered the break room. Nearly every task the agents performed was compartmentalized and kept locked inside their heads. It was not unusual to have worked in the same office with another agent for years and never know their tasks.

"The earthquake was a stroke of brilliance," Martinez noted and sipped from a can of soda.

"I can't believe it worked," Taft said, smiling. "Sandra Miles came up with it."

"What if it hadn't gone as planned?" Martinez asked.

"I would have been screwed," Taft said. "I barely made it under the fence on the way into the compound. And Choi was so shaky, I have to believe he probably would have touched the wire. Plus the heat from two bodies would have surely set off the heat sensors."

"Jammer work good on the motion sensors?" Martinez asked.

"I'm here, aren't I," Taft said as an agent entered the room and filled a cup with coffee.

When the break room was clear, Taft finished his story. After the pair finished their meal, he leaned back in his chair and massaged his legs.

"Now let me tell you what I've been working on," Martinez said. "The general assigned me to try to determine if the Chinese kidnaped and imprisoned Choi because of his knowledge of Einsteinian physics, as our side believes."

"Einstein would seem to be old news in the world of physics," Taft noted, "but it's nice to know why the agency decided to risk my life."

"At first I would have agreed with you about Einstein being old news," Martinez said. "But I couldn't find anything else about Choi that would interest the Chinese. I spoke with Choi's professors and fellow students and they told me he was almost obsessed with Einstein."

"I just don't get it," Taft said. "What do we care if the Chinese kidnap a student physicist?"

"That's what's interesting. I just dug something up. I'm not privy to all the information but it seems that for the last forty years the United States has had a small team of physicists employed by the National Institute for Standards and Technology trying to decipher Einstein's last equations—his so-called Unified Field Theory."

"The National Institute of Standards and Technology is under the Commerce Department, right?" Taft asked.

"I know it sounds odd," Martinez said, "but I think they were just looking for an agency that would hide the physicists' salaries in their budget."

"What progress have they made?"

"The first thirty-five years must have been pure tedium for the physicists. They had little success proving anything definitively. About five years ago, however, that began to change. A student named Jeff Scaramelli wrote a paper while he was attending the University of Colorado that set out to prove that Einstein's Unified Field Theory equations were a clever cypher. A coded message, if you please."

"If we have paid physicists working on this theory for the last forty years, why did a student have access to the material?" Taft asked.

"He didn't really. Einstein worked on the theory for decades, publishing snippets of his work. That's what Scaramelli was using. The actual complete theory was never located even after exhausting searches," Martinez said. "By the way, before you ask, Scaramelli is working for us now."

"Good," Taft said, "but that doesn't answer why the Chinese kidnaped Choi."

"The only thing that makes sense is that they have somehow come across information about the Unified Field Theory and need Choi to decipher what they found."

"What makes this theory so important?" Taft asked.

"To be honest, John," Martinez said, "I just don't know. I do know that the FBI watched Einstein for the ten years prior to his death."

"What else did you turn up?"

"I went to the hospital where Einstein died. The nurses and doctors that cared for him are long dead, but I dug around and determined that one of the ambulance drivers was still alive, a man named Gunther Ackerman. He was twenty years old in 1955, when Einstein made his last trip to the hospital. It turns out he stayed in the area, becoming a fireman and later chief. He retired less than a year ago."

"Someone that had met Einstein in his last days—wild," Taft said.

"It gets better," Martinez said. "Einstein was speaking German on the trip to the hospital. Luckily, Ackerman was German and understood him."

"I love coincidences like this," Taft said. "Makes me believe there's a universal plan."

"So true," Martinez agreed.

"So what did Einstein tell Ackerman?"

"This is bizarre. He said: "'The force is in the wind,'" Martinez said.

"What the hell does that mean?" Taft said.

"No idea," Martinez said. "But he said the same thing in a telegram he sent to a Danish physicist named Bohr that the FBI intercepted. I'm trying to figure out what he meant right now."

"Good luck," Taft said. "As for me, I'm going to fill out the paperwork in regards to my mission, then head back home. My legs are hurting from the footrace I did across the Chinese border," Taft said.

"Go spend some time in your hot tub," Martinez noted. "I've still got work to do."

"I don't feel the least bit guilty, Larry. If that *was* your intention. You'll have to save the world without me, at least until after the weekend."

"So you won't be back until Monday?"

"That's the plan. My part of this mission seems finished," Taft said, rising and throwing his and Larry's lunch containers in the trash.

"Don't worry, old buddy, I'll cover for you," Martinez noted, winking at his friend.

"Just don't call me," Taft said. "Maybe this will all go away."

Taft could not have been more wrong.

CHAPTER 11

"Tell them this is not a good time for me," the prime minister of China said wearily. "You might mention the American president visited not two years ago."

The foreign minister nodded his assent. "I think his handlers want a show visit. That makes it appear that he is listening and responding to our Asian neighbors' fearful demands."

"The United States should remain on its side of the world," the prime minister said. "China will worry about Asia."

"I shall make the appropriate excuses," the foreign minister noted as he rose to leave.

Once the foreign minister had closed the door behind himself, General Wai-Leis glanced at the prime minister and smiled. "I think one can safely surmise that by the date the American president wishes to visit, all diplomatic ties will have already been severed."

Wai-Leis was in his late seventies. Though only five-foot-six inches tall, he carried himself like a much taller man. His erect posture came from a lifetime in the Chinese military. His hair was snow white and his hands liver-spotted, but other than that he appeared to be just reaching age sixty. The orbit of one of his eyes sat slightly lower in his face than the other, making one eyelid appear longer, and his teeth were showing the wear of seven decades of use. Still, Wai-Leis was an undeniably handsome man. He was a millionaire many times over, the result of his secret interest in a Chinese weapons firm. And he remained quite active, still managing to visit his mistress once a week.

His friendship with the prime minister spanned five decades.

"Like the days when we began," the prime minister noted.

"A much better time," Wai-Leis agreed.

War was on the minds of the leaders of China. In the last few years their quest toward world-power status had progressed quickly. China had amassed an enviable nuclear arsenal, along with the missiles to launch a strike far outside their own borders. The country had moved to assemble a blue-water navy at a blistering pace. In addition, the influence they enjoyed across Asia was at an all-time high.

These days, when China spoke, Washington listened carefully.

"What do you suppose will happen to Hong Kong once we institute our plan?" the prime minister said casually to Wai-Leis.

"The Americans will call for a trade embargo, but little else will happen," Wai-Leis noted.

"We can withstand that," the prime minister said. "It has proven not to work with both Cuba and Iraq."

When the Chinese had assumed control of Hong Kong in

1997, their economy soared. The first few years saw higher stock market and real estate prices, but the climb had reversed in the fall of 1998 and the Chinese economy was now slowed down by recession.

But even with the worldwide economic slump, the gross national product of China had recently surpassed Japan's and was now second only to that of the United States. This seemingly backward country, a place where its citizens still utilized rickshaws and wagon carts, had, in a few short years, become the second-largest holder of United States Treasury bonds.

With 5 percent of China's GNP devoted to defense spending, the same amount as in the United States, its military was being funded with billions. New high-tech weapons were being amassed at an alarming rate. What China couldn't buy from German or French manufacturers they tried to steal. Whatever was stolen they copied, then built in their own factories. China's arsenal of tanks was now the size of Iraq's in 1991. The Chinese air force now rivaled that of Great Britain.

"Why don't we just use our missiles on Taiwan?" the prime minister asked.

"When I was a young man my first battles for our army were fighting the followers of Chiang Kai-shek. We fought village to village, man to man. We chased him and his followers across the sea to Formosa. Now we should cross the sea and bring Formosa back."

The prime minister smiled. "You are one of the few who still refers to Taiwan as Formosa."

"It shall soon be Formosa again," Wai-Leis said as he puffed on a Chinese cigarette.

As China rushed toward modernization it rapidly increased its imports of oil. Electric lights were showing up increasingly in the most remote villages, with most of the power coming from oil-burning generators. Diesel trains moved goods and people to and from markets. A massive growth in air transportation, as planes and airfields brought the country closer together, used more fuel. More and more frequently, the citizens of China looked forward to owning a motorized vehicle, even if it was only a small motor scooter.

And that required oil.

Although hydroelectric power was a priority for the Chinese leaders, it took oil to fuel the machines to build the dams. Even then, they were short of suitable rivers near population centers. For the foreseeable future they needed to find or import oil, and that required hard currency.

"Once we reunite with Taiwan we can concentrate on our oil problem," the prime minister said.

"It will be child's play if you can give me the superweapon you have spoke of," Wai-Leis said grandly. "With the Soviet Union fractured and everyone in fear of a war between India and Pakistan, we can sweep through Asia like the Japanese before World War II."

The reportedly vast oil reserves that had been located in the Tarim Basin in western China had been greatly touted, but as yet little oil had been pumped. As a result, the last few years had seen China assume a hostile posture in the Far East. First they declared the South China Sea under their domain. The second move for China was to dispute the ownership of the Spratly Islands. Rich oil reserves had been discovered just offshore of this disputed area, and Vietnam, which claimed the area, was bracing for a showdown.

While the Spratley Islands were a prize the Chinese most definitely sought, it was considered by the leaders of China to be the second prize. First the Chinese leaders wanted to reunite Taiwan with the mainland.

"Do not become too cocky, my good friend," the prime minister noted.

"And why is that, esteemed prime minister?"

"Once we have the superweapon, who will need soldiers?"

*   *   *

Less than ten minutes after General Wai-Leis's departure, the Chinese prime minister was shaking his head in disgust as he read the report of Choi's escape. The report had been prepared and delivered by Sun Tao, head of China's secret police. The prime minister finished reading the report then stared at Tao but said nothing. Tao glanced out the window onto Changan Avenue East before speaking.

"Because of his failure to capture Choi we have taken Hu Jimn's family into custody. What do you recommend we do with them?" Tao finally asked.

The prime minister avoided the question. He disliked the messy parts of his job, preferring that those below him make decisions pertaining to life and death.

"How close was Choi to solving the theory for us?" the prime minister asked slowly.

"I'm not a scientist, sir, but the reports I received indicate that a crucial section of the theory was beyond even Choi's reach. The information that was stolen from the U.S. Commerce Department was valuable, but from the start our scientists thought it was incomplete. Once again, with or without Choi, they are at a stand-still."

"This was a long shot to begin with. I had my doubts from the first time our people inside the United States advanced the idea over a year ago."

"According to the intelligence we received we have every reason to believe the theory was completed," Tao noted.

"Have we exhausted all the research that is available on Einstein?"

"Recently we learned Einstein sent a telegram to Niels Bohr, a fellow physicist in Denmark, right around the time he went into the hospital for the last time," Tao said.

"Did we recover a copy of the telegram?" the prime minister asked.

"No copy was found by our spies in Denmark," Tao noted. "However, at that time the American FBI was watching Einstein's every move. The FBI is notorious for stealing telegrams. If it was close to the time Einstein died, who would notice if it was never delivered?"

"Hm . . . what else have we uncovered?" the prime minister asked.

"We have just learned of a series of personal diaries that were recently discovered and stored in the library at Princeton University," Tao said quietly.

"Good—order Jimn to fly there and steal them. Perhaps they hold the key to this puzzle. If Jimn is successful, we will release his family."

"I already have men inside the United States that could do a much better job, sir," Tao said quietly.

"Jimn is an old friend of mine, he must be allowed to redeem himself," the prime minister noted. "Still, just to be safe have another team standing by in case he fails."

"Very good, sir."

"One last thing, Tao," the prime minister said as Tao was walking toward the door. "Bring me the file on Einstein and his theory again."

Nodding his acceptance, Tao walked from the office.

Less than forty-eight hours after being released from a cell in Beijing's Zhoutz Prison, Hu Jimn crept toward the library in Princeton, New Jersey. The university was on midsemester break and the campus was nearly deserted. Jimn had trouble finding a spot to park his rental car where it would not be too noticeable. Finally, a little less than a block away, he found a lot that was not completely empty. Shutting off the car he had locked the doors, then made his way slowly toward the thick foliage. He watched to see if he was being observed.

Once he was sure he had not been seen, he raised himself from the bushes. Snipping the wires on the window to the burglar alarm, Jimn raised the glass and climbed inside. The library was closed for the week of spring break and the air conditioning was off. Superheated air, warmed by the fall sun beating on the roof and tainted by the smell of old papers and musty books, surrounded Jimn like a dusty veil. A thin trickle of sweat started on the back of his neck and ran down his back. His forehead was soon dotted with perspiration.

During a brief planning session Jimn had attended immediately after his release, an agent from SPD had told him their intelligence source in New Jersey had indicated he should try to enter the library at the shift change of the security guards—six in the evening. The guards who normally patrolled the grounds would be in their offices handing over keys and finishing their reports.

The source had been right—Jimn had yet to see a guard.

Standing on the first floor of the library, Jimn scanned a sheet of paper that listed the library's contents. Hacked from the main Princeton computer by experts in China, and converted from English to Chinese to make it easier for Jimn to read, it listed Einstein's diaries as being in a special uncirculating collection. The diaries had only recently been declassified by the Atomic Energy Commission and donated to Princeton. They were still awaiting transcription and were being stored in the Special Collections Department, on the top floor.

Bounding up the stairs, Jimn reached the top and scanned the thick wooden door, which was secured with a hefty padlock. Removing a cloth pouch from his pocket, he unrolled a thin diamond-coated wire and sawed through the clasp of the lock. Once he was finished he twisted the lock and tossed it onto the ground.

As luck would have it, the metal boxes containing the Einstein documents were clearly marked, stacked together in the far corner of the room on a wooden table, and unlocked. Jimn immediately began searching through the safety-deposit–sized boxes like a man possessed. Tossing each box not containing the diaries into a pile in the corner of the floor, he attacked the next in line.

He quickly realized the search would take longer than he had planned.

Two hours of searching passed, and the sun set, leaving the library in darkness. Jimn, who by now was reading with a penlight clenched in his teeth, finally located the first of the diaries. Following a quick review of the remaining inventory, he hoisted the two boxes that contained Einstein's diaries, one under each arm. It was half-past-eight in the evening.

Lugging the pair of boxes downstairs, he was walking toward the window to exit the library when he was startled by a voice from outside.

"Stop. Hold it right there," a security guard said from outside the open window.

The guard was young, barely twenty years old, and he had taken the job to help with his tuition bills at a local community college. Several minutes before, while driving past in his cruiser on his way to buy his older partner a bag of donuts, the young guard had noticed the library window partially open.

In the beam of his spotlight he caught a glimpse of the severed alarm wires. He climbed from the cruiser and fingered the wires in his hand. He was just about to radio the main office to ask for backup when Jimn approached from inside. After issuing his warning the guard fumbled with the flashlight in his hand, securing it in his back pocket. Then he reached for his weapon in a holster on his belt.

He was several seconds too slow.

At the sound of the guard's voice Jimn dropped the boxes containing Einstein's diaries to the floor, then reached into the shoulder holster under his jacket. With a fluid motion he withdrew a .38 caliber Beretta. Before the guard could react, Jimn fired one round, hitting him in the head.

The guard hit the ground in a heap.

Tossing the boxes of diaries through the window, Jimn climbed through the opening. He had to step over the body of the guard, a pool of his blood now staining the dirt, in order to pick up the boxes.

Soon he was back in his rental car, miles from the university, racing north to Newark.

Midnight Eastern Time in the United States was one in the afternoon in China. The prime minister sat in his office, sipping a cup of green tea.

Placing the cup back atop the saucer, he looked up as Tao entered the office. "What do you have to report?"

"Jimn reported in. He managed to steal the diaries—but he shot one of the Princeton guards in the effort," Tao said.

"Where are the diaries now?"

"Jimn scramble-faxed them several hours ago. Since that time a team of physicists has been reading them. One of the scientists found something that makes him believe the key to the theory is aboard Einstein's sailboat. A coded reference mentions leaving a package of great world importance. 'The package that holds the key to the force is in the *Windforce*,' he wrote," Tao noted. "The scientist is an Einstein buff—he claims that was the name of Einstein's sailboat."

"Interesting. Do we know where Einstein's sailboat is now?" the prime minister logically asked.

"Our computer expert inside the United States found records that indicate the vessel disappeared off the east coast of the United States in 1965. The vessel was due at a scrapyard in Providence, Rhode Island, but never arrived."

The prime minister lit a Panda cigarette and blew a cloud of smoke toward the ceiling. "First call the embassy in New York and ask them to hire a marine salvage firm that cannot be traced back to us. We must find and recover Einstein's boat," the prime minister said. "After that, get rid of Jimn. Shooting that guard could bring us unwanted attention. He is no longer of any use to us."

"What of Jimn's family?" Tao asked.

"They can go free," the prime minister said as he rose from the table. "That was the deal we made."

The day after he had stolen the diaries, and less than twenty-four hours after the Chinese prime minister had ordered his death, Jimn sat on the bed in his room at the Newark Motor Lodge. His life was in terrible disarray. After being released from prison he had been ordered aboard the plane that flew him to New York before he had a chance to see his family.

Jimn feared his family would never be released from jail.

His motel room was old and badly in need of remodeling. The Formica on the dresser was chipped, the paint on the walls stained and spotted. The carpeting on the floor was threadbare, the single vinyl chair near the wobbly table torn. A strange smell of stale liquor, cigarette smoke, and fear permeated the room.

Jimn stared bleakly at the television. The picture tube was ancient, the colors bleeding into one another. The noon news anchor, her hair a mysterious shade of orange, was reporting the shooting of the security guard at Princeton University.

Averting his eyes to avoid watching the guard being removed from the scene, Jimn noticed a peculiar dark stain on the ceiling. *Why was I ordered to stay in such a dump,* he thought to himself?

He rubbed his eyes with his fingers.

Jimn was depressed—both by his surroundings and the news broadcast. The last thing he had wanted was to kill someone in the United States. Not that killing was abhorrent to him, he had participated in his share of torture and executions, but he knew that his superiors would see the shooting as another failure by him.

Jimn decided to grab a moment of fresh air. He walked down the hall to the soft-drink machine to buy a soda. He had been ordered by his handlers in Beijing to stay at the motel until he was contacted with further instructions, but that didn't require him to remain inside the room at all times, he thought.

After the soda I will order myself lunch to be delivered. Perhaps an American pizza. I think it's safe to celebrate the acquisition of the diaries at least, Jimn thought.

Jimn walked down the hall to the soda machine. Finding he was short of the change he needed, he went to the office and asked the manager to break a dollar bill. Turning away from an episode of *The People's Court*, the man changed the bill without a word.

As he exited the office, jingling the quarters in his hand, Jimn happened to glance toward his room. A man with his back toward Jimn was opening the door with a key. Jimn stared, not yet registering what he was witnessing.

The sound of an automobile horn in the parking lot broke Jimn's concentration. Now inside the room, the man ran out at the sound of his partner's signal. Jimn, still standing near the office, watched as a second man got out of the car and began to run toward him. Both men held pistols in their hands.

They're here to kill me, Jimn realized instantly. Dropping the change, he turned and sprinted across the parking lot and into the street. Several cars swerved to avoid striking him as he dashed blindly across the roadway. Jimn knew that the killers had been sent by the Chinese government. He knew because he now recognized the man who had entered his room. Jimn had trained him himself.

Across the street from the motel, Jimn ducked as a bullet shattered a neon soft-drink sign on the side of a coffee shop fronting the road. As Jimn ran past the front door of the restaurant, which was filled with lunchtime diners, a second bullet struck and shattered the glass in a newspaper machine directly in front of him.

He raised his arm to cover his face. A spear of glass from the display window cut into his leg. A third bullet entered Jimn's back, nicking his lung. As the sound of the approaching sirens increased, Jimn continued to run. Exiting the restaurant's parking lot, he found himself at the edge of an open field along Newark Bay. He mounted the concrete breakwater that formed a wall along the water's edge and began running south.

The sirens were almost upon them as one of the Chinese assassins stopped and carefully aimed. Squeezing the trigger, he watched as his round hit Jimn, flinging him into the dirty water of the bay.

The police now very near, the assassins disappeared into the shadows. For so blatant a shooting there were few witnesses. Jimn floated facedown in the filthy water, a trail of blood leaking from his body marking the spot, as the first police car pulled into the field next to the coffee shop.

CHAPTER 12

That same day, Taft leaned against the nondescript sedan he had checked out of the NIA motor pool earlier that morning. He was chewing on a stem of grass. They were parked two miles north of Potomac Beach, Virginia, along the Potomac River. The location was forty-seven miles south of the NIA offices. Tossing the stem of grass to the ground, he looked at his partner.

"I always enjoy fall," he said to Martinez.

"A little cooler and not so humid," replied Martinez.

"It always seems to be a time for reflection."

Martinez sat upright and slid off the hood of the sedan. "John Taft trying to be philosophical with me?" he said. "Will wonders never cease?"

"Every time I try to take our conversations to a deeper level you turn me away," Taft said sarcastically.

"Only because I know you so well," Martinez said. He began to walk across the dirt parking lot toward the river. "I'll leave any deep thinking to you. I just want a paycheck."

"What, and you think I'm motivated by a higher calling? I quit believing in this shit we do years ago." Taft kicked an aluminum beer can toward Martinez. "Put on your serious face, partner, it's time to be NIA secret agents," Taft said quietly as a man began walking toward them. "Let's just play along and get this over with. Then we can go grab something to eat."

"I still don't know how we got assigned this detail. This contractor could care less about our being here," Martinez said, watching the man approach.

"Benson has me on light work, remember? He's worried I've been working too hard—claims I might burn out again."

"You must be from the NIA," the contractor said, stopping in front of the men.

His head was crowned with a white hard hat. His lips were spread in a smile. Sticking out a slab-like paw, he shook hands with the pair. "Let's get you some hats and we can start the tour. I think you'll be impressed."

He led them to a construction trailer, where he found hard hats for Taft and Martinez. Stepping around a mud puddle, they walked toward the river's edge. At the edge of a row of trees was a concrete building about the size of a four-car garage.

"The electronics that form the heart of this installation are still being sorted out, but let me give you the ten-dollar tour," the contractor said as he opened the door and led them inside. "It works like this. Sensors are buried underground, pointing toward the water. These, along with the set on the opposite shore, can completely cover the river with ease."

Several screens lit up and began to display readings from the multitude of sensors. The screens featured bar graphs as well as colored displays. A banner ran across the top giving a written assessment of anything that passed either on top of or below the water.

Taft and Martinez watched the display with interest as a school of fish passed downstream.

"Is it fully automatic?" Martinez asked.

"Not yet. Eventually the signals will be sent to the NSA at Fort Meade and recorded on tape. Unless the river is breached by something the system determines to be dangerous, it will work silently and automatically. At start-up, however, we will have technicians here on site in case there's a problem."

"What happens if a submerged object tries to come up the river?" Taft asked.

"Increasing intensity alarms alert the NSA. Then they will immediately contact the Marine base at Quantico," the contractor said proudly.

"Looks like a good system," Martinez said.

"The software will be sorted out over the next few weeks. I'm sure we'll be able to meet the October 15th deadline without a problem," the contractor noted. "So, do we get a positive report?"

"I don't see why not," Taft said. "We'll fill our agency in on your progress. You don't have to follow us out—we can drop off the hard hats on our way."

"Fair enough," the contractor said, returning to his work. "I guess that's about it."

Taft and Martinez returned the hard hats to the hooks on the wall of the trailer. Taft paused in the office long enough to fill a conical paper cup from the water cooler, slurp the cold liquid, then toss the wadded-up cup across the room into a trash can.

"Two points," he said as he opened the door and, followed by Martinez, exited the trailer.

The pair continued across the dirt to their company car. Taft slid behind the wheel and twisted the key as Martinez settled down in the passenger seat.

"Who came up with the idea that terrorists might try to take submarines up United States rivers?"

"Some asshole Senate subcommittee," Martinez answered. "They fear that submarines or pleasure boats with explosives attached or dragged behind could be brought up the Potomac. What will they think of next?"

"It figures," Taft said. "We could accomplish the same outcome with a metal net stretched across the river. Another waste of time and money."

"I think the general is just giving you a break after you made the world safe for scientists," Martinez said smugly.

"You can be a real smart-ass, Larry," Taft said, then changed the subject. "Do you want to stop and eat?"

Martinez nodded, then rolled his window down to spit.

"I sure would like to know the whole story behind that physicist Choi," Taft said as he set the cruise control and leaned back. "The rumor I heard today is that the Chinese have a million-dollar bounty on his head."

"The Chinese are becoming a giant problem for our side," Martinez noted.

Taft began to scan the billboards for a restaurant. "So?" he said to his partner as he pulled into a diner. "So, are you privy to what the theory's all about?"

"I know it's called the Unified Field Theory," Martinez said. "And for something that's been around for decades, it's suddenly very important."

"That's it?"

"That and some people think it could be used to make one hell of a weapon."

"Well," Taft said, "that makes me feel a little better."

"Food would make me feel a lot better," Martinez said as he climbed from the car and began walking toward the door of the diner.

On the top floor of the National Intelligence Agency, General Earl Benson sat in his silent office. The walls, windows, ceiling, and floors were covered with layers of metal, Kevlar cloth, and crushed iron ore to deflect all attempts at monitoring. Computer-controlled heating and air-conditioning kept the office at a constant temperature.

His first few years in this office Benson wanted nothing more than to escape. During his twenty-six years in the army, where he rose in rank to a three-star general before retiring, Benson had always enjoyed commanding his men in the field. He still missed the feeling of being outside.

For someone used to the outdoors, his office felt like a tomb, sterile and unfeeling. At every opportunity he walked the halls of the NIA, checking on his men. In violation of protocol, he also took every opportunity to leave his office door open. Over the last several years, Benson had grown more accustomed to the quiet, and to a sense of containment, but he still didn't like it. He welcomed every interruption.

Benson's secretary, Mrs. Mindio, buzzed his phone and waited for the general to answer. He picked up almost immediately.

"Benson."

"This is Colonel Thompson at the National Security Agency. Your agency filled out a priority scan on a man named Hu Jimn?"

It was standard NIA policy. To keep abreast of mission developments after the fact, all the names of the principles his agents had contact with—or "actors," as the agency referred to them—were delivered by courier to the NSA. If, within the specified period of time, the person was mentioned in any electronic medium, the computers at the NSA would flag it and spit it out.

"That's correct," Benson said.

"The National Crime Information Computer just ran a check on him for the Newark police," said Thompson.

"Are you sure?"

"Positive. Even the description you gave us matches the profile the police filed."

"Thanks for the tip. Are you still monitoring electronic transmissions from the Chinese embassies?" Benson asked.

"We are, but we have nothing to report yet," Thompson said, and then signed off.

Benson raced from behind his desk and opened his office door. Mrs. Mindio, Benson's assistant for the last ten years, sat knitting a pair of baby booties. "Who's on point?"

Mrs. Mindio scanned the list by her telephone. "Rienhart and Gold were just called to investigate a bomb threat at JFK's grave," she said calmly, referring again to the sheet. "That makes the point team . . . Taft and Martinez."

"I sent them down to do a construction inspection on a new intelligence facility south of here," Benson said. "They should be done by now. Please beep them and have them call me back on a secure phone."

"Yes, General," Mrs. Mindio said as she began dialing.

Taft was eating a Reuben sandwich and sipping an iced tea inside a diner that looked like it hadn't been remodeled since it was built thirty years ago. He stuffed a blob of stray sauerkraut back inside the bread with the tip of his finger. "That's some wild stuff about Einstein. So our side thinks the Chinese are making progress on this Unified Field Theory."

"I guess Choi wrote the definitive paper about it. He was in the process of being hired by a United States Government think tank when he was snatched. The idea is . . ." Martinez began.

"Hold that thought. My beeper just went off," Taft interrupted as his watch began vibrating.

He found the diner's pay phone and dialed the number to the NIA.

"The general requests you to call him immediately from a secure phone," Mrs. Mindio said.

"Right away," Taft said as he gestured to Martinez to have the food wrapped to go.

Outside, Taft unlocked the NIA sedan, pushed the button to open the trunk, then walked back and removed a briefcase. He opened the case and switched on the phone. It took several seconds to hook to a satellite with a scrambled signal. Taft waited as the red light switched to green, signaling the phone was ready to use. Climbing into the driver's seat, he dialed Benson's office number. Martinez walked from the restaurant, carrying a sack with their lunch, just as the call went through.

"This is Agent Taft."

"Is Martinez with you?" Benson asked.

"He's right here," Taft said as Martinez slipped into the passenger seat.

"Find out if he remembers a man named Hu Jimn from the report he wrote on the China project," Benson ordered.

Taft repeated the information and Martinez nodded yes.

"He says he does, General," Taft said.

"Good. I want you two to drive to Quantico and board a Marine helicopter to Newark, New Jersey. Keep this phone with you and I'll call you when you land."

"What's this about?" Taft asked.

"Just tell Martinez that the Newark police have Hu Jimn. He's been shot," Benson said and the phone went dead.

"We're going to Quantico to catch a flight to Newark," Taft said as he started the sedan and slammed it into gear. Punching the throttle, Taft squirted out into traffic and began driving to Quantico. "Who's Hu Jimn?"

"That's the guy that chased you through China. He's with the SPD, China's secret police."

"Well, then, I guess we just received some good news."

"What was it?" Martinez asked.

"He's been shot."

CHAPTER 13

Flying over Piscataway, New Jersey, the Sikorsky VH-60A from Quantico was just over an hour into the seventy-five-minute flight. The myriad highways on the ground below looked like strands of licorice being overrun with ants. To the west, several stratocumulus clouds floated past, their fluffy bulk casting a shadow on the towns below. Martinez glanced out the window and tugged at the seat harness. Taft sat comfortably in his passenger seat, scanning a map of New Jersey in the atlas he had removed from the trunk of the NIA sedan.

"No use looking at the map," Martinez said. "We don't know where they've taken the body."

"Just getting a feel for the terrain," Taft said as he closed the atlas.

Glancing out the window, he could see the water of Newark Bay as the helicopter slowed and turned for approach at the

Newark Police Aviation Facility. The flashing lights on the landing pad drew near as the helicopter descended. Taft barely felt the helicopter touch down.

"Smooth landing, Captain," Taft yelled to the front as he rose to a crouch and waited for the door to lower.

"You ever fly one of these, Special Agent Taft?" the pilot asked.

"I wish we had these. The helicopters I was assigned to were an older vintage."

"These Sikorskys practically land themselves," the pilot said modestly.

"I've never flown any type of helicopter that didn't require constant attention," Taft said as the electric motor started the door moving.

When the side door reached the ground, Martinez and Taft climbed out and walked under the main rotor. The Sikorsky immediately lifted off to return to Quantico. To the side of the landing pad a thin, hatchet-faced man stood calmly smoking a cigarette. He waved to Taft and Martinez. They walked across the landing pad to where the man stood.

"I've been ordered to be your liaison," the man said, placing the cigarette in his mouth. Squinting from the smoke, he extended his hand. "Del Wyme."

"I'm John Taft," said Taft, shaking Wyme's hand.

"Larry Martinez," his partner noted, and he also shook with Wyme.

Wyme led the pair through a back door into the police station. Skirting the main reception area, which was already filled with people awaiting the morning release of prisoners from the jail, he paused at a side door and slid a plastic card through a reader. When the door buzzed, Wyme opened it and led Taft and Martinez inside. Walking through the halls crowded with police and civilian technicians, he kept up a nonstop discourse. "We found him floating in the bay," Wyme said as he rounded the corner.

"Hey, Jerry," he said to a passing detective. "Anyway, after we lifted him from the water we found his passport stuck in his shoe," Wyme said, slowing down. "This is my office," he said, pointing to a small office with a glass front. "The coffee is next door in the break room. Go ahead and make any phone calls you need to, have a cup of Joe. Whatever. I'm going to be in the bathroom a few minutes—my stomach's been killing me," Wyme said as he walked off.

"Coffee?" Martinez asked.

"Okay. You fetch the coffee. I'll call the office." Taft walked into Wyme's office and opened his briefcase. When the secure phone had locked on to a satellite and the green light came on, Taft dialed Benson's office.

"This is Agent Taft."

"Hold, please."

Taft waited for a few seconds.

"This is General Benson."

"Martinez and I are now at the Newark Police Department."

"I've received a description and picture of Jimn from the Central Intelligence Agency. Stand by and I'll fax it to you," Benson said.

Taft waited as the picture hurtled through the air down to the briefcase. Martinez walked into the office and handed Taft a Styrofoam cup of black coffee as the page began to print. Taft smiled at his partner and nodded. Tearing off the page, Taft glanced at it, then handed it to Martinez to read.

"It's a clear copy, sir," Taft said.

"Good. What I want you to do first is ascertain that the person in custody is Hu Jimn."

"We'll do the identification, sir," Taft said easily. "What then?"

"Then question him and find out what the hell he was doing in our country," Benson said.

"You mean he's not dead?" Taft asked incredulously.

"No, just wounded. Detective Wyme will take you to the hospital."

"We'll call you back when we know something," Taft said.

"Very good," Benson said as the phone went dead.

Taft replaced the phone and closed the briefcase. Sipping the burning-hot coffee, he stared at Martinez. "For some reason I assumed Jimn was dead."

"Me, too," Martinez said as he sipped his coffee.

"Just our luck," Taft said. "He's at the hospital, merely wounded."

Taft looked up through the glass wall as Del Wyme approached. He was carrying a folded-up newspaper and wearing a smile. "Much better. Let me just get another cup of coffee and I'll take you to Jimn," Wyme said as he picked up a coffee-stained twenty-ounce mug from his desk, walked into the break room, and filled the cup.

Taft and Martinez stood next to the door to Wyme's office. He returned from the break room, set the cup down on his desk, then removed a light jacket from the hook on the back of his door and put it on. Clutching the cup once again, he led them down the corridor to the parking lot. At the front door, he signed the log, then motioned with his head for the pair to follow. Wyme led them to an unmarked Ford sedan that was instantly recognizable as a detective's car.

Taft sat up front with Wyme, Martinez in the back. Driving from the parking lot, the Newark detective made an obscene gesture at the No Smoking sign on the car's dash as he lit a Winston and inhaled deeply. "George Washington grew tobacco," he noted laconically. "This antismoking shit is getting out of hand. Now can you tell me why you feds are interested in Jimn?" he asked.

"Guess what I'm going to tell you," Taft said.

"It's classified," Wyme said, speaking like the cartoon character Deputy Dog.

"Bingo," Martinez said from the rear.

"I can accept that. But just so you know, if this goes past five o'clock, the feds are buying me dinner," Wyme said.

Ten minutes later Wyme pulled into the emergency room driveway and parked at the far end. Flashing his badge at the only person nearby, a laundry attendant who had immigrated from El Salvador, he led the trio inside. Once in the lobby, Wyme motioned with his head toward the elevator and, after a short wait, the men rode up to the fifth floor in silence.

"This way," Wyme said as they exited the elevator.

Leading the way down the hall, Wyme stopped at the door and spoke to a police officer sitting in a chair outside. "These guys are feds. They need to question the prisoner."

The officer grunted and leaned back in his chair. Wyme opened the door and the trio walked inside. A monotonously beeping heart monitor sounded out an endless staccato. Jimn was hooked to several machines, as well as two separate intravenous bags. An oxygen mask covered his mouth and nose. His eyes fluttered as Taft approached.

"Hi," Taft said easily, "we met last week along the Kazakhstan border. I was riding a motorcycle. You were trying to kill me. Remember?"

Jimn's eyes bulged and his face turned beet red.

"I just wanted to formally welcome you to my country and ask you a few questions," Taft said slowly.

Martinez stepped closer and examined Jimn for several distinguishing scars. Finding them, he checked Jimn against the rest of the description—including a picture—that Benson had faxed them, then folded it up and put it in his jacket pocket.

"It's him," he said without hesitation.

Taft looked down at Jimn. "What are you doing in my country?"

"I'm on vacation," Jimn whispered in English.

"Gee," Taft said, "I think you're lying."

"Yeah, well, screw you," Jimn muttered quietly.

"I think you got that backwards, Jimn." Taft smiled down at Jimn, then turned to Martinez. "Larry, could you take Del for a cup of coffee? I'll be fine here alone," Taft said, turning his gaze back to Jimn.

Wyme looked confused as Martinez led him away by the arm. "Five minutes, Del, that's all," Taft said.

Taft grabbed the oxygen hose leading to the mask and kinked it in half. "Screw *me*, huh?"

It only took a few minutes to convince Jimn to talk.

"So you grabbed the diaries, shot the guard, faxed them to China, then delivered the originals to the Chinese Embassy in New York?" Taft said as he watched Jimn gasping to catch his breath.

"Yes," Jimn said weakly.

"Did you happen to find anything interesting in the diaries?"

"I didn't read them. I just delivered them."

"Who tried to kill you?"

"There were Chinese agents, employed by my government," Jimn said.

Taft sat back and thought for a moment. "Guess what, Mr. Jimn?" he said at last.

"What?" Jimn croaked.

"I'm afraid you're going to have to die," Taft said slowly.

The heart monitor began beeping loudly as Jimn passed out.

Taft walked out of the room.

"Don't let anyone but hospital staff enter this room," he said to the guard. "I'll have a couple people from my agency take over within the hour."

The policeman nodded and returned to reading a dog-eared magazine he had taken from a waiting room.

Taft located Martinez and Wyme at the end of the hall. Three minutes later they were back on the road.

❖　❖　❖

"The guard from Princeton is still alive," Martinez said as he replaced the phone in the hotel room they had rented near the Newark Airport two hours later.

"Jimn was sure he killed him," Taft said easily.

"The bullet grazed the side of his head and knocked him unconscious. It also took off the top of his ear, but they sewed it back on. The lucky bastard is going home tomorrow."

"Wild," Taft noted. "I wonder how Wyme's coming along?"

"Let's call him and find out," Martinez said.

Del Wyme was standing outside the coroner's office smoking a cigarette when his cellular phone rang. "Yeah, this is Wyme."

"What have you found for us?" Martinez asked.

"I've found the right man for the job. I'm just waiting for the proper forms," Wyme said.

"Come by the hotel and pick us up."

"Hell, yes," Wyme said, "I'm not doing this alone."

At 5:46 the following morning, Captain Nigel Crofts of the garbage scow *Gartec One* was squinting through the haze as he piloted his ship past Mariner's Harbor.

"Aldean!" he shouted to his deckhand, who was below brewing coffee. "Come up here!"

The deckhand climbed up the stairs from below and stood next to Crofts.

"Look over there in the water," Crofts said.

In the distance, both could see what appeared to be a body floating facedown in the water off the starboard bow.

"Looks like a floater," Aldean noted. "You want me to try and hook it?"

"Nah," Crofts said, "we'll let the police handle it."

Crofts slowed the garbage scow to peer out the side window. It was definitely a body. With his VHF radio he reported the discovery to the police. A boat from the harbor patrol was sent to investigate and retrieve the corpse.

The newspaper machine had not yet been replaced in front of the diner across from the Newark Motor Lodge but the excitement didn't seem to have hurt business.

"Is this stuff normal for you feds?" Wyme asked, sipping coffee.

"All in a day's work," Taft replied.

"With Jimn's passport in the corpse's pocket and the body so badly decomposed, our little caper should fool who we need it to," Martinez noted.

"You tipped off someone at the television station?" Taft asked Wyme as he forked scrambled eggs into his mouth.

"They'll send a film crew to the dock when the boat comes in," Wyme said, stirring more sugar into his coffee.

"Another team from our agency is flying up to take custody of Hu Jimn around ten this morning," Martinez said. "That should end your involvement in all this. You've been a great help, Del," Martinez continued. "Here's a number in Washington you can call if you ever need a favor," he said, handing over a card.

"Does this mean you're leaving?" Wyme asked.

"Yeah," Taft said.

"Boy, am I glad to hear that," Wyme said as he sipped the coffee.

"Now you're making us feel like you don't like us," Taft said.

"Let's just finish breakfast and I'll take you back to the station."

"Golly," Martinez said, "we haven't even had time to see the sights of Newark."

CHAPTER 14

Six days after Jimn was moved from the hospital to a safe house, the Chinese put their plan to recover Einstein's sailboat into motion. First they hired an international private detective agency based in New York City named the Axial Group to look for clues to the location of *Windforce*. The Axial Group was staffed largely by retired—or fired—law-enforcement officials. It hired out to the highest bidders, regardless of affiliation. The agency was well known for their lack of cooperation with legitimate authority.

They were rogues that worked for payment, not ideology.

It took detectives from the agency less than a day to determine when the *Windforce* had left New Jersey for Providence. With a check of the weather records, the detectives understood the conditions Halversen had been forced to sail in.

The fate of the search was sealed when a pair of agents located the life ring from the *Windforce* on the fence outside a maritime museum on Long Island. They photographed the life ring. The name was badly faded but still slightly visible. A day-long search of the museum records resulted in finding a copy of the receipt that had been issued to the person who donated the items. The donor's name was Mack Trimble and his address was listed as a post-office box on Block Island.

Steven Klamn worked for the Los Angeles Police Department until accepting an early retirement. The offer to retire had come after Klamn had pepper-sprayed, then beaten, three

Mexican citizens who had slipped across the border and made their way to Los Angeles in search of work.

Klamn had been in a bad mood that morning. The water ski boat he had bought less than six months before had been repossessed from the driveway of his home. He was two months late on the payments. And when he had stopped at the bank to plead for the boat to be returned, the vice-president he spoke to, a turban-wearing Indian, had also asked for his credit card.

It wasn't as if Klamn was *totally* prejudiced. He liked white people just fine.

After leaving the bank in his cruiser—short a boat and his credit card—Klamn had been livid. When the trio of illegals darted in front of his black-and-white it was a classic case of wrong place, wrong time. He had slammed the car into park while it was still moving forward, then set off after the fleeing aliens on foot. After cornering them in a dead-end alley, he hosed them down with pepper spray. As the illegals writhed on the ground, rubbing their eyes and gasping for breath, he took out his nightstick and set to work.

When one of the men nearly died from brain swelling brought about by the beating it was too much even for the LAPD. Klamn was given a choice—retire or face prosecution.

He moved east and joined the Axial Group.

Klamn stepped off the Block Island Ferry and lit an unfiltered cigarette. He walked up the slight rise toward town. After stopping to get directions from an elderly man sitting on a bench on the street, he made his way to the post office. When he located the specific post-office box he was interested in, he peered through the tiny window of the box and read the address on the mail inside. The mail was not addressed to Mack Trimble.

Making his way to the counter of the post office and finding no one in line, he rang the bell on the desk and waited. From the back, a man in his early forties wearing long hair and a beard approached. He had the appearance of an aging hippie.

"Can I help you?" the man asked politely.

"Maybe," Klamn said.

"You're going to need to put out that cigarette," the man said. "No smoking in government buildings."

Klamn grimaced, then tossed the butt on the floor and ground it out with his heel.

"That better?"

"Not for my floor."

"I'm looking for a customer who has a box here—someone named Mack Trimble."

"We don't have a customer by that name," the man said easily.

"How can you be so sure? You didn't even look it up," Klamn asked.

"Well, to begin with, we couldn't tell you if he did have a box, but I happen to know for a fact that he doesn't."

"Why's that?" Klamn asked logically.

" 'Cause Mack was my father, and he's dead," the man answered.

Klamn stared across the desk. "I'm doing historical research and found a receipt for some items that your father donated to the maritime museum on Long Island. In particular, there was a life ring with the name *Windforce* on the side."

"I remember," John Trimble said. "Dad said he picked it off the beach on the east end of the island. It sat in our garage for a few weeks before he got rid of it."

"You remember anything else?"

"Some planks washed up on shore a few days after he found the ring."

"Anything else?"

"Not really."

"Thanks. That's all I need," Klamn said, turning to leave.

John Trimble watched as the man walked out the door. He felt uneasy about the encounter but he wasn't sure why. He tried to remember if the man had mentioned his name or why he was doing the research but came up blank.

Shrugging his shoulders, Trimble returned to sorting the mail.

With the information that the Axial Group had been able to gather, the Chinese hired a marine salvage firm based in North Carolina named SeaSearch and began their hunt for the *Windforce*.

Luck was on their side.

On the third day of the search the sea off Block Island was smooth. The earlier rain had flattened the ocean waves. The seas were running less than one foot. The sky had cleared after the brief outburst and now it was a deep bright blue.

"One more lane to the north, turn at the mark," one of the salvage technicians said quietly in his North Carolinian drawl.

Captain Gerald Holtz turned his head from the wheel and acknowledged the instructions. "Lane twelve north, fifty-meter swath. Turn at the mark."

Stroking his chin, he glanced at his GPS and carefully timed the approaching turn. The two hired technicians sitting in bucket-seat chairs in the pilothouse of the salvage vessel *Deep Search* watched their screens intently. On the port side of the ship's pilothouse a television screen displayed a picture of the ocean bottom that was beamed from a video camera mounted on a towed, remote-operated vehicle, or ROV. The image was somewhat blurred as the bottom was being stirred by an incoming tide. On the starboard side of the pilothouse a separate television screen displayed images from a Klein color hydroscan sonar. Sound waves bouncing off the ocean floor reflected back to the sensor and then were displayed in graphical form on the monitor. Together the two instruments painted a surprisingly detailed picture of the ocean bottom. The crew were professionals and they had already covered much of the target area.

The swells were diminishing as the *Deep Search* drove back and forth across the ocean surface. The routine was as monotonous and repetitive as mowing a giant field of grass. Holtz sipped from a can of soda.

So far, the crew of the *Deep Search* had found little of importance—various pieces of trash, part of what appeared to be a roof from a boat house, and an oblong sheet-metal box, perhaps blown from a passing ship. But nothing that would indicate a sailboat. The GPS placed them just two miles east of Block Island when the sonar began to reflect a small anomaly deep below the surface.

"Captain, please slow to one knot. Maintain the same heading," the technician manning the sonar said, never turning from the screen as he spoke.

"One knot, same heading," Captain Holtz acknowledged.

Concentrating on his positioning equipment, Holtz moved the wheel slightly to maintain his heading. The course of the *Deep Search* remained steady. Straining to make out the image that was unfolding as the ship passed above it, the sonar operator held his breath.

Quickly measuring the size, the technician screamed, "Just over thirty feet!"

On the port side, a surprisingly clear video image was coming into focus. "I see what looks like a mast," the ROV technician barked.

"Size and shape fit. Mark it," shouted the sonar operator.

Captain Holtz punched the marker button on his navigation computer then turned from the wheel to reply. "Position marked and buoy dropped."

Throughout the remaining hours of daylight, the *Deep Search* passed back and forth over the target. Finally, the remote video camera located and filmed the shattered stern section.

As night fell on the ship they finally received the verification they were seeking. Visible through the murk, lit by the ROV's spotlight, was the target word they had so intently sought.

Written on the stern piece of the sailboat as if by some ghostly hand, and now bleached by long exposure to the sea, was the single word: *Windforce*.

CHAPTER 15

John Taft sat in a lawn chair on the wooden deck behind his house, looking out at the Potomac. It was a clear and sunny day. The faint breeze was scented by the fallen leaves Taft had raked into a pile, then covered with black plastic to build a compost heap. Dressed in only a worn pair of cut-off jeans, he rested his large bare feet on a wooden side table.

Taft had a barrel chest, darkly tanned, and his thick blond hair was bleached light by the sun. Glacial blue eyes stared toward the water with a cool intensity. To his right, reclining on a chaise longue with her face buried in a Clive Cussler novel, lay a stunning and leggy brown-haired beauty.

Taft turned his gaze from the river, reached into his partially empty glass of iced tea, and pulled out a crescent-shaped ice cube. He casually tossed it onto the lady's stomach. She sat idly staring at the ice resting in her navel without moving a muscle. Then, after several seconds, she rose from the lounge chair and flicked the partially melted ice cube back toward Taft. She struck him dead in the middle of the forehead. Just then Taft's cell phone rang.

"John Taft."

"Hey, my friend, how's it going?" Martinez's voice said cheerfully.

"Larry, I'm glad you called. I was thinking I might actually have a day off," Taft said wearily.

"No such luck. A few moments ago the NSA at Fort Meade called General Benson. The Chinese Embassy in New York wired a large sum of money to a marine salvage firm based in North Carolina three days ago. A second large payment was made to the Axial Group."

"I'm listening," Taft said, smiling at the woman, who was arching her back suggestively. "Anytime I hear those shitbags at the Axial Group are involved, it piques my interest."

"We still don't know what it all might mean. Benson thinks it might be tied to Choi's abduction and Jimn's theft of the diaries. Just to be safe, however, we're checking all avenues. The intelligence satellites were positioned to shoot the eastern seaboard and they have observed a salvage vessel named *Deep Search* working a tight grid for the last several hours. It appears that they've found an underwater object and have anchored beside a buoy."

"Do you think the *Deep Search* is connected to the Chinese?" Taft asked slowly.

"No idea. We're attempting to find out who owns the *Deep Search* and if anyone from the firm in North Carolina is on board. No luck yet. Benson doesn't want to raise a red flag just yet, so he ordered you and me to quietly check it out. The powers that be think that to use navy or Coast Guard ships would make us too obvious."

"It sounds like a long shot," Taft noted.

"True, it's probably nothing. Benson also ordered a black-bag team to North Carolina to wire up the company's offices, and I'm running a computer check on the *Deep Search*'s registry, but nothing has turned up yet. This may just be a garden-variety salvage job not even tied to the Chinese, but there's a fishy smell to it. I think we better go ahead and investigate."

"Okay," Taft said easily. "What's my cover?"

"You're being flown from Andrews to Long Island. Pick up a rental car, then drive to the docks—we have a boat waiting there for you to use. You may not know it, but you're quite the serious deep-sea fisherman."

"I think this is more bullshit busywork," Taft said, lowering his voice. "Besides that, I think I was close to getting laid," he whispered into the phone.

"I don't get laid as much as you and I'm married," Martinez said. "Now quit your whining. You're due at Andrews in forty-five minutes."

"All right. Call me back when you have some more information," Taft said in disgust.

"Don't I always?" Martinez said and hung up.

Taft turned to the lady standing on the deck looking out on the water. "I was called into work."

"How long will you be gone this time?" she asked.

"I'm not really sure."

She rose to her feet and planted her hands on her hips. "You play hard-to-get really well, John," she said.

Taft smiled.

"Do you have any moral arguments against quickies?" the lady asked.

"No," Taft said easily.

"Got a spare ten minutes?" she said seductively.

Estimating the distance to Andrews and the time it would take if he broke the speed limit, Taft winked at her. "I've got fifteen."

"Saddle up, cowboy," the lady said as she sprinted for the bedroom.

Twenty minutes later Taft's Ramcharger was doing ninety on the Capitol Beltway.

❖   ❖   ❖

Four hours later, in a fishing boat nearing Block Island, Taft backed off the throttle and the boat slowly settled in the water as it came off plane. Directly ahead lay the salvage ship *Deep Search*. Walking back to the stern of the fishing boat Taft raised the engine hatch cover, then peered for several minutes into the crowded space.

The *Deep Search* bobbed quietly on the surface only seventy-five yards away. Unlocking the boat's communications box, Taft turned on the VHF radio and keyed the microphone.

"Ship off Block Island, this is the fishing boat off your port bow."

The answer came immediately. "Go ahead, this is the ship off Block Island," the radio blared.

Taft noticed the ship did not identify itself by name, strange in itself.

"I'm having fuel problems," Taft lied. "I need another fuel filter. Can you help me out?"

"Hold one minute," the voice on the radio said.

As Taft waited, he found an old package of black licorice in a side compartment of the boat and chomped off a piece. The candy was dry and cracked as he chewed.

On board the *Deep Search*, the captain and first officer held a rushed meeting. They had been ordered to stay on station above the *Windforce* and talk to no one until the recovery could begin. They also knew that to anyone monitoring the radio, a refusal to help a stranded boat was tantamount to burning a church in Rome. It would definitely be noticed.

Taft waited as the next several minutes passed slowly.

Suddenly the radio crackled. "The chief engineer states he has no filters; he suggests you bypass the filter until you reach port," the radio voice advised.

Whoever they are, they're sharp, Taft thought. "Roger that, I will attempt to bypass."

Taft returned to the stern and spent twenty minutes doing nothing to the fuel filter.

Satisfied that he had taken long enough, he straightened up. Returning to the helm, he turned the key and the engine roared to life. Then he closed the hatches, engaged the drives, and set out toward the *Deep Search.* As the fishing boat drew near, several men quickly ran onto the deck of the salvage ship and waved him away. Taft observed the men carefully to see if they were wearing any type of uniform or patches that might identify them. He noticed nothing.

The radio on board the fishing boat barked. "Pull back," the voice ordered.

Taft backed off the throttles and idled the fishing boat alongside the *Deep Search,* looking carefully to see if he could determine what work the crew was performing. He could not. The *Deep Search* appeared to be a catamaran, but no trawl nets or work gear could be seen. After marking the long-range navigation system—or LORAN—coordinates, as well as the GPS numbers, so he could find the site in the future, he reached for the radio.

"Just wanted to thank you. I'm running fine now."

"You are most welcome. We are doing some very precise environmental work that you are disturbing. Could you please leave this area?" the voice on the radio asked politely.

"Roger, Captain, I'm leaving for port," Taft said finally.

Taft cranked the wheel of the fishing boat hard to port and engaged the throttle. He pulled away, leaving the crew of the *Deep Search* slowly shaking their heads. Bringing the boat quickly on plane, he dialed up Martinez on the secure phone.

"I didn't see anything unusual," he said as soon as Martinez answered. "They claimed they were doing environmental work. I didn't see anything to suspect they weren't, but I recorded the position on my charts just in case."

"Sounds good," Martinez agreed. "I'm still working on tracking down the registered owner of *Deep Search*. Once I do I'll get back to you."

"Can I go home yet?" Taft asked.

"Not just yet."

"You're starting to annoy me," Taft said as he hung up the phone, locked the cabinet, and steered the fishing boat back toward Montauk Point.

CHAPTER 16

Later that same night a light drizzle began falling on the salvage ship *Deep Search*. Her twin catamaran hulls allowed the vessel to ride smoothly on rough seas and she barely rocked as she anchored atop the *Windforce*. Inside the recovery bay of the *Deep Search*, a yellow glow from the lights overhead bathed a pair of salvage technicians who were busy checking the slings and winches in preparation for the job ahead.

Captain Holtz paced nervously as he spoke into the satellite telephone. "Yes, we are certain of the identity. Shall we proceed to salvage the wreck?"

Over eight thousand miles across the globe the Chinese prime minister and a small group of men conferred. At last, their spokesman acknowledged Holtz's question.

"Yes, bring it up, then make your way to Boston as quickly as possible."

"We can only recover nine-tenths of the boat easily. What little is left of the stern section is broken into too many pieces to raise."

"It's only a small section of the stern, right?" the spokesman asked.

"Correct, only a few feet. What little there is left is not worth the intense effort necessary to raise it," Captain Holtz answered.

"That's fine. Leave the stern pieces and raise only the main section."

"Very good," Holtz said.

Holtz replaced the phone and turned to First Officer Dietz.

"Let's do it," Holtz said quickly.

In the recovery bay the remote-operated vehicle was dropped down into the water. When it touched bottom, the operators directed jets of water to bore tunnels under the hull.

The ROV's pincer arms held wide canvas straps that trailed behind the jets of water and wrapped around the hull. Maneuvering to the other side of the hull the ROV grabbed the end of the straps poking from beneath the wreck, then propelled to the surface with the straps in its arms. The straps were returned to the recovery bay and the ends were taken by the salvage crewmen and fed into electric winches.

Engaging the motors on the winches the straps were slowly tightened. As Captain Holtz monitored the progress from the pilothouse with the underwater camera, the sailboat was winched upright on the bottom.

Once upright and stabilized, the *Windforce,* a battered hulk containing the greatest scientific discovery of all time, began to make its way slowly to the surface.

Twenty minutes later, the *Windforce* broke through the water in the recovery bay and was winched into the open air. Almost immediately, the doors of the bay slid closed underneath and the sloop sat in slings, above water once again.

In the recovery bay the intercom blared: "Stations please, we will soon be under way."

The noise emanating from the engine room increased as the *Deep Search* set a course for Boston at twelve knots. While the salvage ship made its way north, the salvage technicians immediately began to probe the interior of the old sailboat. The salvagers showed little respect for the skeletal remains of Ivar Halversen. The bones forming his skeleton were yanked free from where they were trapped and tossed into a corner of the bay. They formed a crude pile of what appeared to be bleached driftwood. The barren pile was unceremoniously crowned with the skull, which had been picked clean by crabs.

Like grave robbers in an ancient tomb, the salvagers on the *Deep Search* showed little respect for history. To them, the *Windforce,* a boat that belonged in a museum, was little more than an assemblage of planks. It was merely a rotting, soggy pile of junk sheathing a package they had been paid handsomely to plunder.

First Officer Dietz led the efforts to find the package's clusive hiding place. First, the wooden slats that formed the *Windforce's* berth were ripped out, revealing nothing. Next, crowbars in hand, the technicians began to rip apart the interior panels of the once proud little craft.

The pile of rotting boards mounted on the inside of the sailboat.

As the galley was being disassembled, a technician stopped and motioned to Dietz. The first officer walked over and peered through a crack in the interior wood. His eye caught a glimpse of a black package attached to a side wall below where the alcohol stove had resided. Dietz quickly reached for the crowbar a nearby technician held in his outstretched hand.

Then he stopped himself.

"You better hand me the instant camera," Dietz said flatly.

After shooting a series of photographs, he picked up the crowbar once again and pried the panel carefully away. The slats that formed the wall came apart one by one, the tongue-and-groove work cracking as Dietz bore down on the crowbar. Once the wall was removed, Dietz reached in and wrenched the package from inside.

It came away easily and Dietz retracted his arm with the

package in his hand. Standing up from his crouch, Dietz hefted the package and stared.

Inside the package, wrapped in oilskin and covered in a black rubber wrap, was what felt like a bundle of papers. The outside of the package was covered with numbers and symbols in a distinctive scrawl. Dietz quickly took an instant photo of the outside, then climbed from the *Windforce* and made his way topside to report to the captain.

One of Einstein's legacies had been unearthed.

CHAPTER 17

Early the next morning in a room in a motel on Long Island, Taft's mental alarm clock woke him from a dead sleep. As he rose with a start to his elbows, the digital clock sitting on the nightstand was flashing 4:30 in bright red numerals.

It was time to go fishing.

Taft rose silently. Quietly slipping out the sliding glass door of the room, he made his way in the darkness to the dock. The sky over the Atlantic Ocean was just beginning to show the light of day. The air in the cove was still as Taft started the fishing boat. The smoke from the exhaust at start-up hung low on the surface of the water. After a brief warm-up period, Taft engaged the drive and pulled away from the dock. With winter approaching, the morning was cool and he pulled on a pair of leather work gloves.

Just to be safe, Taft walked fore and aft and checked his running lights to make sure they were working properly. The surface of the ocean was black, reflecting only the red and green from his running lights. He blew his chilled nose into the wind.

Once free of the channel from the marina, Taft pushed the throttle forward to the stop and steered through a cluster of small islands that rose in the darkness from the depths of the sea. Taft navigated the fishing boat up the back of Long Island toward Block Island. His sleep had been uneasy, and as if his actions were on autopilot he was returning to the position for the *Deep Search* he had marked on his chart the day before. As the fishing boat got nearer to Block Island, Taft scanned the sea with his binoculars.

The ocean was a dark placid pool, quiet and lonely. Taft looked for the required navigation lights the *Deep Search* should be displaying. He listened for noise from the ship's horn or engines. No luck. It was as if the *Deep Search* he had seen yesterday had been a mirage, a ghost vessel that had never really existed.

Taft strained his eyes against the darkness, checked his chart again, then put the throttles into neutral and climbed below into the cabin. As the fishing boat bobbed gently on the ocean surface he called Martinez in Maryland.

Though it was just past 5:00 A.M., the phone was answered on the first ring. "You're not going to believe this shit. I'm on the site, the *Deep Search* is gone," Taft said without preamble.

"What are you doing up so early?" Martinez asked sleepily.

"I'm a fisherman, remember. It doesn't matter why I'm awake—*you* kept me from a night of unbridled passion, so don't expect me to worry if you're getting enough beauty sleep."

"Sounds fair," Martinez said with a yawn. "You sure you're at the right site?"

"I have a GPS on the boat. It marks the area to within a few feet."

"That's strange they left during the night," Martinez said. "My last report had them still there at eleven last night. The satellites should have picked up the movement. I'll call and check." Martinez paused as he thought. "Since we're not sure the *Deep Search* was even tied to the Chinese, what do you think we should do now?"

"Call General B. and ask him. Whatever the case is, I'm here now and can find out." Taft paused, staring at the depth gauge on the boat's dashboard. "I'm within dive depth. I think I'll go down and look around."

"Do you have gear?"

"The agency stocked this boat with everything but a Taco Bell," Taft noted.

"You're diving alone? Without a buddy?" Martinez said quietly.

"I've done it before."

"That's not very safe."

"I could cruise back to Long Island and wait for a dive shop to open," Taft said, laughing. "But then I'd be dragging some innocent civilian into this mess if I found anything interesting."

"You've got a point."

"Then we both agree it's just me?"

"Yes. But if I don't hear from you in an hour, I'm sending out the Coast Guard."

"For what?"

"So they can drag for your body."

"Thanks for the pep talk, old buddy, but you'll hear from me within the hour," Taft said as he hung up the phone.

After rechecking the GPS and moving the fishing boat's position slightly, Taft dropped anchor from the bow and made sure it was set and holding. He returned to the stern and donned a wet suit that was a size too small. Next he checked to make sure the tank of air on board was full. Hooking the buoyancy control device and regulator to the tank, he strapped the set to his back, then slipped on fins and a mask.

Satisfied his equipment was ready, he flopped backward over the side into the cold water. He checked his dive light to make sure it was working properly, then swam to the anchor line. After making sure there were no other boats on the water, he slipped below the inky black surface.

The depth gauge on the fishing boat had put the bottom at just over seventy feet. Taft descended slowly through the murky water, stopping often to equalize his ears. It was a strange sensation being alone in the cold void and he fought off the creeping fear of the unknown. As he moved downward in the water, he peered out into the blackness. When he was just feet from the ocean bottom, he checked his compass, then tied a line to the anchor and began to swim around the line in ever-widening circles.

The water that surrounded him was like a shroud, lit only by the portable dive light he clutched firmly in his hand. The bottom was silty and Taft swam just above the murk, careful not to disturb the sediment into blinding clouds. His safe bottom time passed quickly, and after glancing at his dive console for a readout, he realized he would soon have to begin his ascent.

There's nothing down here, Taft thought to himself. Probably never was. But at least now he'd seen for himself. Taft was swimming back to the anchor line to ascend when the dive light caught something to his left. He swam slowly toward it.

Like a wraith materializing in the gloom, the broken wooden stern section of a sailboat grew out of the darkness. He reached out with his gloved hands and touched the wood, rotten now after its long immersion in seawater. The sloop's small diesel motor had detached itself and lay rusting on the ocean floor. A large red snapper seemed to enjoy swimming around it. Kicking back to the transom of the sunken vessel, Taft rubbed the peeling paint with his gloved hand. As the muck cleared he could just make out the boat's name in his dive light.

Windforce.

He swam back to the anchor line and began his ascent.

          ✻   ✻   ✻

When Taft surfaced, the yellow glow of daylight was fast approaching. He switched off the dive light and tossed it inside the boat. Next he climbed onto the rear platform of the boat and removed his tank. Then he stood and peeled off his wet suit. Dressed only in his shorts, he balanced on the platform, unbuttoned his fly, and urinated into the ocean.

After he had stowed the gear in the proper compartments, he went to the cabin below to phone Martinez.

"Are you fully awake yet?" Taft asked.

"Yeah, I took a shower and I'm having a cup of coffee."

"You prick. I'm freezing my ass off out here."

"*You* claimed to be the fisherman," Martinez said, slurping loudly from his cup.

Taft paused to blow his nose into a paper towel. "I found the stern of a sailboat down there. It looked like the ground nearby had been disturbed."

"No forward section? No bow, masts, or cabin?"

"I believe that was just salvaged by the *Deep Search*. That would explain the disturbance. It kind of looked like something had been dug up then dragged a little ways."

"Interesting."

"I know the name of the vessel that was salvaged."

"Let's have it."

"*Windforce,*" Taft said quietly. "Judging by the small engine I saw, it was probably a smaller sailboat, but don't hold me to that."

"Let me check into this at the office," Martinez said. "I'll get back to you shortly."

"It would be nice if you did *some* of the work," Taft said, hanging up on his partner.

Taft closed up the phone, then reached into a compartment under a seat and withdrew a frayed green towel to dry himself. Climbing out of the cabin, he pulled on a blue fleece warm-up suit he had in his bag. He then started the fishing boat's engine and let it idle.

Walking onto the bow, he pulled the anchor line taut then tied it to a cleat. The boat rocked and the anchor came loose. Feeding the line into the rope locker, he hoisted the anchor from the water and secured it.

With a quick final check of the fishing boat to ensure all was in order, he eased the throttle partway forward to cruising speed and began the trip back.

Taft had no way of knowing the impact of the events he had just set into motion.

CHAPTER 18

Less than thirty minutes later, in his office at the NIA, Martinez again looked at the name *Windforce*, which he had written on a pad of paper. He widened his eyes in amazement as he read the ownership records off the computer twice more. Straightening himself in his chair, he rubbed his reddened eyes and reached for the phone.

On a tree-lined street in Alexandria, Virginia, a lone dog barked as a paperboy pedaled his way along the sidewalk, slinging papers from a bag hanging from his handlebars. Most of the houses on the block had at least their porch light on, and the paperboy used the lights as a target.

General Earl Benson had awakened at 5:00 A.M., as was his custom. Sitting in the nook of his kitchen, he had eaten a breakfast of buttered grits. His first wife had passed away just over a year before and Benson still felt strange when he rose from bed and glanced down at his newlywed second wife. His first wife had never risen before 7:00 A.M. She had always awakened with just enough time to pad downstairs in her slippers and kiss him goodbye before he left for work. His second wife followed suit.

After finishing breakfast and placing the dishes in the dishwasher, Benson walked to his wood-lined study and began reading the intelligence reports the night shift had posted on his computer. He had finished reading the reports and writing his comments and now sat lingering over his fourth cup of coffee. He scratched the head of Margaret, his aged cocker spaniel, and was staring into her cataract-clouded eyes when the phone rang.

"General Benson," he answered.

"This is Larry Martinez. Sorry to wake you but it's important," Martinez explained.

"I was awake but it *still* better be important," Benson boomed.

"Taft just came from the site where the *Deep Search* was anchored yesterday afternoon. The ship's gone. There was diving gear on board his boat and Taft dove the area where the ship had been anchored. In a search of the bottom he found the stern section of a sailboat. He feels that most of the rest of what was a sailboat was salvaged."

"You called me at home to tell me that?" Benson asked.

"It's a little more involved than that, sir," Martinez said. "Taft gave me the name off the stern and I checked the past owners' registry on the Coast Guard computer."

"Spit it out. What's the name and who owned it?"

"The name of the vessel was *Windforce*. The original owner was Albert Einstein. The boat was resold then reportedly lost ten years after Einstein died."

"How did it sink?"

"The record notes it was believed lost in a storm."

"That's worth calling me at home," Benson noted. "What do you make of all this?"

Martinez paused before answering. "This is all speculation,

General, but I think the Chinese found out Einstein left something of value on board his sailboat. Now they are trying to recover it. They hired the Axial Group to help locate the area where it sank and paid the company from North Carolina to actually find and salvage the vessel."

"I tend to agree with your theory, as far-fetched as it sounds," Benson said. "If you're right, we need to find the *Deep Search*. I want to assign you and Taft to see if you can find where the salvagers are now. Keep me up to date on your efforts. I'll be in the office within the hour. If that was Einstein's sailboat, whatever the *Deep Search* recovered could prove to be quite interesting."

"Very good, sir. I'll keep you informed as to our progress," Martinez replied and hung up the phone.

Benson immediately phoned his assistant. "Get me the latest file on the Axial Group and try to establish contact with our insider."

"Should I set up a meeting with the insider?"

"If possible, yes," Benson said. "I'll be in the office in less than an hour."

"I'll get on it right away," the assistant said.

Taft was in his motel room on Long Island washing the salt water off his body in a steamy shower when the phone rang. He shut off the water and walked from the bathroom. "Make it quick, I'm dripping wet. What did you find out?" he said to Martinez as he tightened a towel around his waist.

"That boat has quite a history."

"The research ship or the wreck?"

"The wreck," Martinez said. "I'm still working on the history of the *Deep Search*."

"Hit me," Taft said.

"It was formerly owned by Albert Einstein," Martinez answered flatly.

"Wild," Taft said, whistling. "Have you got any idea why some-one is after his sailboat?"

Martinez paused. "Not yet, but I'm still looking into it, you can be sure. I've got a call into the satellite guys at NSA asking them to trace the overnight course of the *Deep Search*. Benson wants us to locate that ship posthaste."

"Let me finish my shower and get dressed and I'll be ready. If I go for breakfast I'll keep the secure phone with me. Call me on that."

"Count on it," Martinez said.

"Einstein," Taft said to himself as he walked back into the bathroom. "What does Einstein's sailboat have aboard that any-one could possibly want?"

Martinez was thinking the same question as his computer signaled he had an E-mail. The message answered the question about ownership of *Deep Search*. Owned by a leasing company based in Wilmington, North Carolina, the vessel was currently being rented to the marine salvage firm of SeaSearch.

Later that same day General Benson sat on a park bench in Lafayette Square. Several pigeons pecked at the popcorn he tossed on the ground from a paper bag. Benson looked like an aging retiree out for a breath of fresh air. He was dressed in a pair of loose-fitting khaki slacks and a flannel shirt. Although it was warm outside he wore a light jacket. His feet were clad in cheap tennis shoes and his head was covered with a ballcap emblazoned with the letters AARP. His face was disguised with a false white beard and when walking to the bench he had dragged one leg as though old age had given him a limp.

Less than ten minutes after Benson sat on the bench a man approached from the south and slid onto the end of the bench. Removing a sandwich from a brown paper sack, he began to chew.

"I don't know much," the man said between bites.

"Tell me what you do know," Benson said as he tossed another handful of popcorn onto the ground.

"They send one of the agents, a man named Klamn, to look into the disappearance of Einstein's sailboat."

"And?" Benson said.

"Apparently he located a life ring on Block Island and that information was used to set up a search for the vessel."

"Is it the Chinese that hired your firm?" Benson asked.

"You wouldn't be asking me that," the man said as he rose from the bench and tossed the lunch sack into a trash barrel, "if you didn't already know."

Benson waited ten minutes after the man had walked away before he rose from the bench and made his way across the park to his car.

Pieces of the puzzle were beginning to link up.

CHAPTER 19

In his office at the NIA, Martinez scanned his computer database and retrieved a biography of Einstein. Reading the biography, he began to form a more complete mental picture of the famous scientist. Einstein's famous work on the theory of relativity, the theoretical foundation for the technology behind the atomic bomb, was published early in the physicist's life, while Einstein was still a young man.

For the remainder of his career as a physicist, both in Europe and later in the United States, Einstein had worked tirelessly to try to prove his Unified Field Theory. It was rumored he was even working on it the day he died.

For decades prior to his death, the Unified Field Theory had consumed all of Einstein's vast mental attention. The theory he was attempting to prove appears simple enough even to a layman. The Unified Field Theory sought to explain all the forces in the universe—how gravitation, electricity, and magnetism might be tied together. There was no way to know the impact it might have on the world if the relationship between these forces could be understood.

Martinez glanced at the clock on the wall of his office. It was now past 7:00 A.M. He walked to the break room and filled his coffee cup, then grabbed a corn muffin from a plate on the counter. Balancing the cup to keep it from spilling, he reentered his office. Placing the cup on his desk, he closed the door and sat behind his desk. He picked up the phone and dialed George Washington University. An operator at the main switchboard answered and asked for an extension.

"Professor Harris, please," Martinez said.

"One moment. May I ask who's calling?" the operator inquired.

"Larry Martinez. I'm a friend of the professor's."

He waited several minutes to be connected. "Larry, you old fart, what's on your mind?" Mel Harris said when he came on the line.

"Still an early riser, I see," Martinez said.

"I've been doing three miles on the running track Monday through Friday. I'm still in the locker room, in fact."

Harris had been attached to the National Security Agency for several years prior to returning to teaching. He and Martinez had worked together often on joint operations. Still in his mid-thirties, Harris didn't fit most people's mental image of a physics teacher. He looked and dressed like a golf pro but his lightning-fast mind was that of a pure physicist.

"What I'm about to tell you is classified or soon will be. Are you still cleared?" Martinez asked seriously.

"I still get occasional assignments from the Crystal Palace, so yes, I have my ticket," Harris said.

The reference to the Crystal Palace, as the NSA was sometimes called, inferred Harris enjoyed a high degree of clearance.

"Tell me what you know about Einstein's Unified Field Theory," Martinez asked without further comment.

Harris ran through the theory, stopping to expound on the details only when Martinez sought clarification. "That's about the basis of it. By the way, everything I told you is in textbooks. It hardly qualifies as top secret. What else do you need to know?"

"Did he ever finish the work?" asked Martinez.

"Who knows? Apparently not, though some of his papers from his final hospital stay are missing. Plus, no one has ever really deciphered his last set of equations," Harris said.

Martinez considered the statement, "Mel, if Einstein *had* completed the theory, could it be used to create a weapon?"

"Yes. That and a thousand other uses I could think of."

"Just theoretically, how much power might such a weapon contain?" Martinez asked carefully.

"Theoretically, Larry? To put it into layman's terms, it would make a hydrogen bomb look like a popgun. Depending on how exactly the theory was utilized, you might be able to produce an object roughly the size of a golf ball that could blow up a land mass the size of Australia."

"Shit," Martinez blurted out without thinking.

"No shit, Larry. If controlled properly, a mass the size of a small car could blow up the world," Harris said. "But who would be dumb enough to want to blow up the world?"

"Maybe not blow it up," Martinez said carefully. "The mere threat might be enough."

"That would be one hell of a threat," Harris agreed.

CHAPTER 20

Later that same morning the daily briefing room for the National Security Council was crowded. The oblong mahogany conference table in the center of the room was surrounded by representatives of the United States intelligence community, officials from the Department of Justice and officers of the air force, army, navy, and Marines.

Over the years the room had been modified and upgraded. Thick, beige, sound-deadening carpet with rubber backing covered the floor. An eight-by-ten-foot video and computer monitor capable of receiving direct satellite feeds covered the north wall. Electronic frequency jammers wired into the corners of the walls foiled any attempt at recording the proceedings. The entire room was protected from anything short of a direct nuclear blast by reinforced walls, ceilings, and floors. A pair of elite Marine guards stood just inside the door, four more in the corridor outside.

Crystal ashtrays and silver water pitchers were arranged in front of each chair along with note pads and pens. A large paper shredder sat discreetly in the corner of the room. Mounted on the wall directly above the shredder was a presidential seal six feet in diameter. The lighting came from brass sconces mounted on the walls and from brass fixtures recessed into the ceiling. The temperature was computer-controlled and kept at a constant level.

When the room was empty it was as silent as a tomb.

The president of the United States and his various advisors, including Robert Lakeland, his national security advisor, grouped around the north end of the massive table. Aides to each participant were seated nearby in chairs along the wall. A light breeze could be felt from the overhead air ducts.

At precisely 9:00 A.M. Robert Lakeland rose from his chair. "Ladies and gentlemen, I will now begin the morning briefing."

The room quieted and all eyes turned in his direction.

"We have three orders of business to discuss today." Lakeland paused and consulted his typed notes. "First, Mr. Lorando has an update on the situation in the Middle East."

Jack Lorando, from the Defense Intelligence Agency, rose to speak.

"It would appear that the fragile peace that has hung over the region is beginning to crack," Lorando began, consulting his typed notes wearily. "The rejectionist group Hamas has apparently stepped up attacks against the Jewish settlers in the West Bank. As you know, the Palestine Liberation Organization has been acting as police in the area for some time. To combat the growing problem one hundred specially trained Fateh Hawks from the militant wing of the PLO's Fateh group have descended on the area to try to restore calm; but the unrest continues to grow. In addition, we are detecting strong signs that Iran is behind the religious fundamentalist movement in Saudi Arabia." He looked up from the paper and continued the briefing. "At the current time, all we can do is monitor these developments; however, I would like to go on record as stating that the situation could explode at any moment. We have no intelligence to indicate why so many bombings in both Israel and Saudi Arabia are suddenly occurring. The peace has always been a fragile one and much more trouble could result in all-out war in the Persian Gulf region," Lorando stated forcefully.

President Harper spoke from the end of the table. "First, we need to get better intelligence. Human intelligence, not the satellites we have come to rely too much upon. Next," and he turned to the chairman of the Joint Chiefs of Staff, "I'll need an update as to our military presence in the area. If anything erupts, I want us to be ready to respond quickly. As you all know, if the flow of oil from the Middle East is cut off, the economy in the West could quickly collapse." Harper looked around the table. "All of you please keep me posted if anything changes."

Jack Lorando leaned back in his chair. His tanned face began to slacken as he relaxed. He could now spend the rest of the meeting listening. His part in today's meeting was completed. He slipped an antacid tablet unobtrusively into his mouth and waited. Lakeland read again from the printed agenda: "Mr. Canter of the Central Intelligence Agency will brief us on the war games scheduled by China near the Taiwan Strait."

Hamilton Canter, an immaculately attired Ivy League bureaucrat, launched into a vague discourse on the possible effects the war games might pose for U.S.–China relations.

"As has been the case for some time now, the Chinese are hastening their movement from a regional power toward superpower status. The policy that we have followed since World War II has been to avoid containing China. We have always felt that could lead to conflict. Our problem now is that the United States has frequently demonstrated a hands-off approach, with the result that the current leadership of China's military believe they have carte blanche to dominate the entire Far East. Japan, Korea, Vietnam, and the Philippines are all concerned about China's recent aggressive posture."

"Do you believe they may attempt to attack one of the countries you mentioned?" President Harper asked.

"The CIA's position it that an aggressive action is only a matter of time."

"And the war games?" Harper asked.

"China has done that before. It could be posturing. Or it could be something more."

Careful not to commit himself on any specific point, Canter assured the chief executive that his agency would remain on top of the situation.

"Thank you for your report, Mr. Canter," Lakeland said.

The National Security Advisor then introduced the last topic for discussion: "General Earl Benson from the National Intelligence Agency's Special Security Service has one of his agents pursuing a case and asked to address the morning briefing."

Benson, a ruddy-faced, medium-height fireplug, rose and squared his shoulders. An infrequent visitor at the daily briefing, his unusual topics and no-nonsense delivery often left those in the inner circle whispering about his comments for days afterward. Benson rose to his full height and began to speak.

"One of the agents of the Special Security Service has come across some disturbing developments regarding Einstein's Unified Field Theory." Benson sipped from a glass of water before continuing. "As some of you are aware, we recently liberated a Chinese physicist who was kidnaped and returned to China after seeking asylum in our country. He specializes in this particular theory. Soon after the physicist was brought back to the United States a Chinese secret police agent was dispatched to the United States to steal Einstein's diaries from Princeton University. He was successful in his mission but later was captured after his own countrymen tried to assassinate him. We questioned him and he claims he dropped the diaries at the Chinese Embassy in New York City. We now believe the contents of the diaries were sent over a scrambled fax line to Beijing. Our agency has also learned that the Chinese government recently hired a shady international detective and private intelligence agency, named the Axial Group"—Benson waited as the grunts elicited by the mention of the Axial Group abated before continuing—"as well as a marine salvage firm, named SeaSearch, based in North Carolina. At about the same time, satellite reconnaissance reported a suspicious and unidentified research vessel off Rhode Island. The agent who liberated the physicist checked out the vessel. On first inspection, he found nothing to indicate any unusual activity, and so left the area where the ship was operating. Returning early this morning, before sunrise, he found the vessel was gone. His suspicions were aroused and he decided to dive the area where the ship had been anchored. At the bottom of the ocean, he came upon a fragment of the stern section of a sailboat that still had the name visible in paint. Ground disturbance seemed to indicate that the rest of the boat had been salvaged. A check of marine records by the agent's partner traced prior ownership to Albert Einstein." Benson paused. "It is only a feeling, as yet unsubstantiated, but we believe the key, or at least part of the puzzle, to Einstein's Unified Field Theory might have been hidden on the part of the sailboat that was salvaged."

Benson paused to watch the group's reaction. All eyes were upon him, and the mood in the room revealed extreme interest. "We are currently attempting to locate the salvage ship."

President Harper spoke next. "Why is this theory so important and what could this key to the theory be used for, General Benson?"

"In preliminary consultations with several university physicists the consensus seems to be that if Einstein had solved his Unified Field Theory, the results might be utilized to create a weapon," Benson replied.

Lakeland asked, "What type of weapon?"

Benson stared down to the end of the table and delivered the punch line. "There are several schools of thought about that very question. The first is that if someone could harness the forces Einstein sought to explain, an explosive weapon of such magnitude could be built that an object the size of a golf ball could blow up at least half of Australia. To quote one scientist, 'It would make an atomic bomb look like a popgun.' The government think tank I consulted before this meeting renders the opinion that, properly contained and directed, this force could be beamed from a satellite, and that this beam would be capable of reducing all matter in its path to a sort of "—he consulted his notes—"primordial, soupy ooze devoid of any life. Hundreds, even thousands of years might pass before even single-cell organisms might flourish. There are several other opinions as to the uses of the theory as well, but most of the scientists agree that it might explain the very fabric of the universe."

Several in the group shifted in their chairs and straightened up upon hearing Benson's words. A soft murmur arose as scattered pairs huddled to confer.

"We currently have scientists at the government think tanks and leading universities trying to reach some sort of agreement on the possibilities, but at this point it is all just speculation," Benson concluded.

President Harper sat quietly back in his chair before speaking. "Could you give us a basic idea of what this theory is all about?"

Benson glanced down at his notes, cleared his throat, and started speaking again. "I can try, Mr. President. Imagine a tree. The branches of this tree are each a universal force. One branch would be electricity, the next gravity, another magnetism, and others what scientists refer to . . ." Benson paused and read from his notes, "as the strong and weak forces. The trunk of the tree is the Unified Field Theory, the common element that binds them all together. Dr. Einstein felt strongly that these forces had to be linked somehow. To possess the key to the Unified Field Theory would give one the key to control motion, power, and force. Maybe even the key to life itself." Benson looked wearily at the now excited crowd. "I'm sorry, Mr. President, but that's the best explanation I can offer. For anything more detailed you will need a physicist." Some members of the group in the briefing room showed signs of shock, their faces drained of color. Each one sank deep in thought.

"What agent is working on the case?" Harper asked softly.

Benson hesitated before answering. "Mr. President, the identity of our agents is never disclosed to anyone outside our agency. Of course, we believe the president has a need to know. I'll be glad to identify the agent by name after the room has cleared."

The others in the room looked at Benson in stunned silence.

Canter, the head of the CIA, spoke quickly. "We disclose our operations completely, General."

Benson raised an eyebrow. "I know, Mr. Canter, I read about them in the newspaper almost daily," he said dryly.

President Harper raised his hands to quell the erupting skirmish. "I understand what you're saying, General Benson. The need to protect your agent's identity is quite reasonable." The president paused, then added, "The rest of you please cull your files for any pertinent information about this theory. That will be all for today. General Benson, will you please remain?"

The room emptied quickly. Benson's personal aide left last, closing the door firmly behind him. President Harper looked over to Benson. The two men had already faced one catastrophe together and were comfortable with one another. Comfortable enough to be direct.

"How bad is it, Earl?" Harper asked plainly.

"Mr. President, it's all hypothetical at this point, but if the key to the theory has been recovered, the United States could lose its place as the dominant force on the planet. If the Chinese can unlock the power behind this theory, they could use it as a lever against us in negotiations—or force us into an all-out war," Benson stated forcefully. He paused, sighed, then continued. "It would seem we have a dire crisis if we cannot recover the papers."

"Which agents do you have assigned to this, Earl?" the president asked.

"The team of John Taft and Larry Martinez. They were the agents in charge of the 'Leaning Tree' incident," Benson replied.

"I remember them, Earl. They're your best agents, aren't they?"

Benson thought back. "They're very good, Mr. President. Very good."

President Harper nodded. "I want those papers, Earl. Do

whatever it takes to recover them intact. If you can't do that, I want them destroyed."

"Yes, Mr. President," Benson said firmly.

The president rose to shake General Benson's hand and in the same instant they both spoke.

"Good luck," they said at the same time.

They both meant it.

CHAPTER 21

Taft tossed an empty bag that had contained two ham-and-cheese biscuits and a hash brown patty at the trash can in the hotel room, then finished his large cola and tossed that in the can as well.

"What is the *H.L. Hunley*," Taft shouted aloud at the television game in reply to the question. "It was the first submarine to sink a ship in battle."

"Yes," he said to his correct answer, "what is the *H.M.S. . . .*" he began to say when his secure phone rang, jarring his thoughts.

"Yeah," Taft said, still watching the television.

"It's me. The satellites traced the *Deep Search* to Boston Harbor. She's currently docked at Pier 53," Martinez said. "There's a small airport at Westhampton, on Long Island. I've arranged for a commercial helicopter charter service to fly you to Boston. The chopper's waiting for you now."

"It'll take me about twenty minutes to drive there," Taft said, staring at a map. "What do you want me to do with the rental car?"

"Leave it there. I'll have it picked up later."

"Fair enough," Taft said.

"I'm coming in on a Navy jet. I should be there shortly after you."

"You're doing field work?" Taft asked. "Will wonders never cease."

"I think this operation will take both of us," Martinez noted.

"What's the plan?" Taft asked, still watching the television.

"We're going to seize the ship and recover whatever they found."

"Are you bringing along the weapons?" Taft asked.

"Yeah. You want the usual package?"

"Sounds about right," Taft said easily. "You know, I always like it when you get out of the office, Larry."

"I know you do, old buddy," Martinez said, "because I'm a better shot than you."

"My doctor told me it's healthy to embrace reality," Taft noted. "You might want to give some thought to that."

Taft hung up the phone before Martinez could answer.

Throwing his clothes into a black duffel bag, Taft placed the keys to the fishing boat into an envelope and left it with the front-desk clerk. He piloted the rental car to the small airport and left it locked with the keys on the driver's side front tire.

Thirty minutes later he was glancing out the side window of the chartered helicopter as it raced across Block Island Sound.

Less than an hour later, a white baseball cap devoid of markings shielding his eyes, Taft steered his second rental car of the day along Boston Harbor. He watched carefully for the signs marking the different piers. Finding Pier 52, he located an empty parking spot nearby and parked.

Slouching low and assuming the casual gait of a vacationing tourist, he walked east toward Pier 53. His blue eyes scanned the water toward the *Deep Search*, tied fast to the pier.

No crewmen were visible and the vessel was quiet.

He walked back to the rental car and placed a call to Martinez over the secure phone.

"I'm looking at the *Deep Search*. Where are you?"

"I'll be there in ten minutes or so. I pulled a blueprint of the *Deep Search* from the Lloyd's insurance computer. The ship was built in Norway in 1985 and has an internal bay that can be used to launch and retrieve mini-subs for exploration work. With that inside bay the crew could easily recover an entire ship up to sixty feet in length if that was their plan."

"We'll talk about that when you get here. Hurry up," Taft said.

"I'm doing seventy miles an hour through traffic," Martinez said as the phone went dead.

Fifteen minutes later Martinez parked next to Taft, climbed from his car, and slipped into Taft's passenger seat. All that remained was to send out for some food and wait until five P.M. when the dock would be clear of any dock workers or tourists who might get in the way of gunfire.

Captain Holtz and First Officer Dietz of the *Deep Search* waited in suite 312 of the Royal Regent Hotel for a phone call giving them further instructions. If they had been looking to the south of the hotel, they would have seen the sun dancing off the blue water in Boston Harbor. But their eyes were not looking out at the panoramic view. They were instead focused on a European soccer game on the television set. Holtz answered the phone on the side table on the second ring.

"I am in the lobby and will be up directly," a cold voice said. "What is your room number?"

The courier hung up as soon as Holtz replied.

Holtz looked at Dietz. "The courier is on his way up."

Several minutes later a soft rap on the door was heard and Holtz rose from the couch to answer. The man at the door stood almost six feet tall; his black hair was cut close to the sides of his head, and his eyes were almond shaped and dark brown. He moved furtively, his motions concealing a certain danger. He did not bother to attempt any small talk.

After an uneasy pause Holtz introduced himself.

"My name's Chou Tsing," he said coldly. "Now where are the documents?"

Holtz walked to the wet bar and retrieved a briefcase that was stored underneath. Returning to the sitting room, he opened the case. The bundle recovered from the *Windforce* was still wrapped in oilskin, covered in black rubber, and sealed in tape.

Dietz handed Tsing another small packet. "These are instant photos we took. They show where we found the papers in the sailboat," he said as he handed over the packet.

"Good," Tsing replied. "You and your crew are to meet at Logan Airport this afternoon at five. You are being flown to Nova Scotia."

Dietz looked surprised. "Who will crew the *Deep Search* if we leave?"

"We have another crew flying in to take care of the ship," Tsing said quietly. "You and your crew are needed in Canada. We have another assignment for you."

"The sailboat is still inside the recovery bay," Holtz said.

"The other crew will handle the removal of the sailboat," Tsing said easily.

Holtz looked at Dietz before speaking. "Will the same wages be paid for this assignment?"

"Yes, the same wages and bonus will be in effect," Tsing said coldly.

Holtz glanced away. For a moment he saw the home on the Outer Banks he had dreamed of so often. This next job would give him the down payment.

"That's fine," Holtz said. "If you have another job for us, my crew will be at the airport at five."

Tsing closed the briefcase, then left the room without a goodbye.

Holtz and Dietz quietly resumed watching the game. They still had a couple of hours to wait before leaving for the airport.

A few hours left to live.

"What do you think we'll be looking for next?" Dietz asked Holtz.

"I don't know, but all this secrecy is a bit unnerving," said Holtz.

Bigger forces were at work, but they had no way of knowing that. They would take their secrets to the grave.

CHAPTER 22

The *Deep Search* remained deathly quiet all afternoon. Taft and Martinez spent the time studying the blueprints, waiting for the dock to clear. Near five in the afternoon Taft and Martinez watched two seamen from the *Deep Search* leave the vessel, lock the hatches, and pull in the gangplank. Jumping down to the dock, the two sailors gave the mooring lines one last check and then walked down the pier toward the city.

Taft tossed Martinez a portable radio and set off after the pair. Ambling slowly along, appearing to be without purpose, he followed the sailors toward the main road outside the port. Near the port terminal the pair stopped. Taft moved closer and noticed the men were standing below a pick-up sign for the local bus service.

The strong smell of fish assailed his nostrils as he crept

behind a rack holding fishing nets to continue his surveillance. The sun was behind Taft as he shooed several cats out of the way and crouched down to radio Martinez. "Yoo-hoo. It's me."

"Yeah?"

"They're waiting for the bus. Can you have them followed?" Taft whispered.

"Affirmative. I'll get someone on it right away," Martinez answered.

Taft placed the radio back in his pocket and sat back on a pile of nets. After a short wait he noticed a bus heading down the hill trailing diesel smoke. The seamen lifted their duffel bags in anticipation and shuffled from foot to foot. Taft walked from behind the nets and started down the sidewalk below the bus stop. He continued down the hill with his back to the bus, listening carefully.

Hearing the bus slow then stop, Taft waited until the sound of the engine grew louder. When he sensed the bus was just behind him, he turned to read the bus destination tag on the sign above the driver then turned back quickly. The glance was too short for anyone to identify him but long enough for him to read the sign on the bus. It read: Airport/Center. As soon as the bus was out of sight, he raced back to the pier.

"The front of the bus said Airport/Center," Taft said to Martinez.

"I have a couple of Boston policemen following in an unmarked car," Martinez said. He looked at Taft with anticipation.

"Shall we get this show on the road?"

"Sounds about right," Taft said as he led the way to Martinez's rental car.

From the trunk of the car, Taft removed a shoulder holster containing a laser-sighted 9 mm Browning and strapped it across his chest. Reaching into a duffel bag, he removed, then zipped up a lightweight bulletproof jacket and grabbed one out of the trunk for Martinez.

"Body armor. How thoughtful of you."

Martinez zipped up the jacket without a word. A dramatic change had come over both men. The intrigue of the chase now past, it was time for the dirty work. The two stood for a few minutes in silence.

Martinez quietly looked over at Taft; his eyes seemed to be burning with a low-intensity glow. Waves of heat were flowing from his body as if his mental and physical functions were supercharged.

"Show time," Taft said.

Racing down the dock followed by Martinez, they came to the *Deep Search* tied fast to the pier.

"Move fast . . . don't get hurt . . . here we go," Taft said.

In a single leap he jumped the short distance from the dock to the deck of the *Deep Search* then shot a hole in the lock on the main cabin door with his pistol. Twisting the broken pieces, he tossed them to the side and opened the door.

Followed closely behind by Martinez, Taft ran up a passageway through the ship. The pair entered the wheelhouse first. Finding it empty, Taft silently signaled for Martinez to follow. Moving cautiously, still expecting to be confronted, the men climbed down a ladder and entered the recovery bay.

Suddenly in the hold there was a loud creaking sound that made both men jump. Taft headed for the bulkhead, which the blueprints had shown housed the light switches. He flicked the breakers on. The bay was instantly illuminated by the bright fluorescent lighting.

And then, frozen in place, both men stared at the center of the recovery bay in stunned silence.

Slung from the ceiling was a sailboat minus its stern. It was dripping water into a small puddle on the deck. As the harbor waves rocked the *Deep Search* in its slip, so it did the sailboat riding in the sling like a joey in a kangaroo's pouch.

"The *Windforce*," Martinez said finally.

"I'd have to agree," Taft said quietly.

Taft and Martinez began to search the recovery bay. They immediately found the skeletal remains of Ivar Halversen stacked like cordwood in a corner. The pile was three feet long and crowned with his skull. The bizarre sight brought a shiver to both men's spines.

"The report said *Windforce* sank on its way to be scrapped. Those bones must belong to the captain hired to deliver her," Martinez said.

"The rear quarter is caved in," Taft noted. "I doubt she sank in a storm."

Taft walked to the winch and began to lower the sailboat. When the *Windforce* dropped to a level at which he could enter, he slammed the lever to stop the winches. Entering the sailboat by leaping over the side, he immediately noticed the spot where the interior planks had been removed and carelessly tossed into a pile on the berth.

It looked as though the searchers had tried several spots before finding what they were looking for. The entire cabin of Einstein's former sailboat was a mess. Taft dug through the boards but could not find anything remotely tied to the theory. Climbing over the side of the *Windforce,* he yelled to Martinez, who was searching through the pile of Halversen's bones for any clues.

"Can you call us in some help? We'll need to search this ship from stem to stern."

Martinez began dialing his cellular phone.

"And find out where in the hell the seamen are who left on the bus earlier," Taft said as he climbed back inside the *Windforce* to continue searching.

Holtz looked down the airport terminal from the gate for his two missing crew members; the rest of the team from the *Deep Search* were already aboard.

"Here they come, here they come," he yelled to the flight attendant, who was closing the door leading to the boarding ramp.

She stopped as the pair ran toward her carrying duffel bags.

"Just about missed it," the flight attendant said grumpily. "I need your boarding passes. You should seat yourselves immediately. The plane's ready to take off."

Holtz, followed by the tardy seamen, stepped aboard the plane.

The pair of Boston policemen assigned to follow the sailors were detained at the terminal security checkpoint because of their service handguns. Once cleared, they sprinted toward the gate.

The plane carrying the crew of the *Deep Search* rolled from the gate, then immediately lined up for takeoff.

The portable radio clipped to one of the policemen's belts went off just as they arrived at the now empty gate. "At the airport," one of the cops said into the radio. "They just got on a plane." He glanced at the sign. "Looks like Nova Scotia. What? You never ordered us to detain them. We were only ordered to follow them," the officer said, rolling his eyes at his partner. "Okay, we'll see if they can call the flight back," the officer replied.

Replacing the radio on his belt he looked at his partner seriously. "I think we're in trouble," he said accurately.

As the two Boston police officers ran toward the airline office, the pilot of the Nova Scotia–bound plane, now airborne, adjusted the plane's control surfaces for the last turn over Deer Island and out to sea. Completing the turn, the plane began climbing. As it passed over open water outside the bay, a sensitive liquid altitude sensor in the bomb that had been placed in the nose of the plane reached its critical level.

It triggered the fuse.

With a deafening explosion and a huge ball of fire, the front of the plane was blown off. The pilot shot out the opening, still strapped in his seat. Unfortunately, he was speared through his chest like a shish kebab with a piece of wreckage and had died instantly. Debris from the blast in the nose flew back along the length of the plane, ripping off what remained of the left wing. The plane opened up like a peeled banana.

The aircraft, or, more correctly, what was left of the fuselage, went spinning into the sea with a fiery splash of metal and fire. It began to sink almost at once.

No one on board the plane complained about the rough landing. They were all dead.

Like a model airplane blown apart by a firecracker the wreckage plunged through the water and spread out across the ocean floor.

Taft and Martinez stood on the upper deck of the *Deep Search*. As the explosion ripped apart the commuter plane, they turned toward the noise and witnessed the explosion of flames in the air. At almost exactly the same time at Logan Airport the two Boston police officers burst into the airport office.

"We need some help here," the policemen shouted at several clerks who were staring out the window.

"It'll be a while," one of the clerks shouted back without turning. "Our flight to Nova Scotia just went down."

"Shit!" the policemen said simultaneously.

When the police at the airport radioed Martinez that the seamen from the *Deep Search* were aboard the plane that had crashed, he immediately phoned the Coast Guard station at Boston Harbor.

"They see an oil slick on the surface, that's about all," he said to Taft after receiving the Coast Guard report. "They have a ship stationed at the crash site and report the depth of the water is under one hundred feet. Why don't I request the navy send down divers to probe the wreckage."

"Go ahead. Have them do a complete and thorough search of the wreckage," Taft said. "I don't want us to be wondering later."

Taft and Martinez continued with the search of the *Deep Search* for the next few hours. The search was methodical and diligent but nothing that could be tied to Albert Einstein was found.

CHAPTER 23

Fatigued and feeling dejected, Taft and Martinez checked into the Four Seasons Hotel around ten that night. Though they were covered in grease and slime from searching the *Deep Search*, the front desk clerk handled their reservation request professionally.

"Would you like me to call a bellman for you?" the clerk asked with only a trace of indifference after handing them their keys.

Taft stared at the battered green carry-on bag at his feet that contained mainly dirty clothes. "I think we can handle our luggage," he said with a straight face.

The men were both silent on the elevator ride up to their rooms. The elevator's arrival at their floor broke Taft's thoughts. "Looks like you're right here," he said to Martinez, pointing at a door. "I'm up the hall."

Martinez slid his key into the lock.

"I'll call you after a shower," Taft said as he made his way down the hall.

Martinez nodded and opened the door to his room.

Taft walked wearily down the hall. Dropping his bag outside the door, he unlocked his room. A blast of cool air drifted over him as he entered. He tossed the bag on the bed and stripped off his filthy clothes, leaving them in a heap on the floor. In the tile bathroom he quickly adjusted the shower to hot and climbed inside. The heat from the water, combined with the steam, began to relax him as he scrubbed himself clean.

The shower was certainly helping, but he felt lonely, tired, and depressed.

They had been so close to recovering whatever it was the Chinese were after he could feel it inside. Now he was unsure which way to proceed.

He tuned out his negative thoughts and concentrated.

Taft was shampooing his hair when it hit him. He rinsed the remaining shampoo from his hair, shut off the shower, and climbed out. Drying himself with the towel, he walked out of the bathroom and picked up the phone.

Surprisingly Martinez answered on the first ring.

"They transferred whatever they found before the crash," Taft said before Martinez had a chance to speak.

"Great minds think alike," Martinez said. "I was just thinking the same thing."

"That means that whatever they recovered is still in Boston," Taft said.

"Let's get some sleep," Martinez said. "We'll hit it early tomorrow. I'll inform Benson."

"Find out if we know anything more about the Axial Group's involvement."

"Talk to you in the morning," Martinez said.

Taft placed the receiver back in its cradle, lay back on the bed, and tried to watch a comedy show on television. After only a few minutes his eyelids grew heavy. Drifting into a fitful sleep brought about by exhaustion, he passed the night tossing and turning on top of the covers.

Taft awoke naturally at five A.M., the television still playing. Standing naked in his room, he looked out the window at the city below. Bathed in the crisp autumn light of the new morning, it looked fresh and clean. No one but he and Martinez knew there was a cancer festering somewhere nearby.

Taft ordered breakfast from room service, then showered again. Dressed in his last set of clean clothes, a pair of khaki pants and a white polo shirt, he sat barefoot at the table, idly watching the morning news on the television.

A soft knock on the door signaled room service. He removed his handgun from the bag and placed it nearby, just to be safe, then let the waiter in. After signing the bill, he asked the waiter to notify the front desk to prepare their bill for checkout.

"Very good, sir," the waiter said as he palmed the ten-dollar bill Taft had handed him.

Sitting at the hotel room table, he removed the stainless-steel covers from the plates, allowing the steam from the hot food to escape. Taft searched for the hot salsa he had ordered. Finding the ceramic cup, he poured the spicy mixture on the eggs. He dipped his toast points into the egg yolks and chewed quickly. He was ravenous and wasted no time downing the sausage, eggs, and home fries. He was spreading jam on the remaining piece of toast when the phone rang.

"It's show time," Martinez said. "Are you ready for the morning report?"

"Yeah, go ahead," Taft said as he worked his way over to the coffee pot and refilled his cup.

"The navy called. The commuter plane had an explosive device placed in the nose cone. It was a very sophisticated type, with an altitude-sensing detonator. That explosion was hardly an accident," Martinez noted. "I just got off the phone with the general.

We are authorized to request assistance from any government agency we deem necessary. The president is in on this one. The powers-that-be want whatever was on that boat recovered, and they want it now." Martinez paused again. "We have to assume the bombing of the plane was their way of removing any witnesses."

"I agree. The Chinese have proved they're playing for high stakes," Taft said.

"Benson sent two guys to talk with one of the Axial Group's agents, some scumbag named Klamn. They shot him up with truth serum and he spilled what he knew, which wasn't much. Apparently he steered the Chinese to the location off Block Island by tracing a life ring. That appears to be the group's only involvement in this affair, at least as far as Klamn knew," Martinez noted.

"What did they do with Klamn when they were finished?" Taft asked.

"They did him at home while he was sleeping," Martinez said. "It all goes well he'll think it was all just a bad dream."

"That entire group is a bad dream," said Taft.

"True, now back to the business at hand. I had Phillips down at the office pull the records for the crew of the *Deep Search* from the airline computers. Next, I asked him to cross-check them with Boston hotel registrations. He found that the captain and first officer of the *Deep Search* stayed at the Royal Regent two nights ago. Let's check that out."

"Have you eaten?" Taft asked.

"We can pick up something on the way to the Royal Regent."

"Meet me at the elevator in five," Taft said.

"You got it," Martinez said.

Forty-one minutes later, Taft and Martinez arrived at the Royal Regent Hotel.

"We need to know if anyone visited the crew while they were staying here," Taft said to Martinez as they walked through the lobby. Walking to the front desk, he summoned the manager and flashed his Special Security Service badge.

"You had a guest by the name of . . ." Taft said, looking at the computer printout Martinez had given him, ". . . Holtz. He was registered through yesterday."

The manager consulted his records and found the registration card. He reviewed the card. "Yes, I remember him now, a ship's captain," the manager stated.

Taft nodded. "Did anyone visit Holtz while he was here?"

"I was gone for a few hours yesterday afternoon, but not while I was behind the desk," the manager replied.

"Could you check with whoever was on duty while you were gone?" Martinez asked.

"Certainly, one moment," the manager answered, walking into the back office.

As they waited, Taft glanced around the hotel. Not part of a giant chain, the lobby was nicely decorated and discreetly furnished. It was the type of hotel someone would have to recommend.

Perfect for an afternoon tryst. Or as a place to hide out.

The manager returned with a desk clerk who smiled at Taft. "I was working the afternoon shift yesterday. A man asked for Holtz. I knew he didn't know the captain because he asked for *Mr.* Holtz. I'm sure you know how captains like to be called Captain," the desk clerk said eagerly. "Anyway, I directed him to the house phone and rang him through. Holtz must have given him the room number because he took the elevator up to the correct floor."

The desk clerk paused. Taft could see he was straining not to ask what this was all about. "A few minutes later he came down, and the doorman hailed him a cab. I remember it was around three because I went on my break right after that," he finished.

"Was the man carrying anything in his hands as he left?" Martinez asked.

"I don't remember, I was just finishing with a check-in." Then the clerk's resolve finally broke: "What is this all about?" he blurted.

Taft smiled. He had known that the man was going to break. He had seen it coming.

"Sorry, I can't disclose that," Taft said seriously.

"What did the man look like?" Martinez asked.

"Around six foot tall. Black hair. He looked Asian," the clerk replied. "Not very friendly-looking—if that helps any."

"Thanks for the information," Taft said. "If you think of anything else, call this number." Taft handed the clerk a card, then he and Martinez walked to the cab stand to question the doorman.

"I wasn't on duty," the doorman said, "but we have a log book. Let me take a look." The doorman flipped through a cardboard-bound journal. "Just after three we had one pickup. The service was provided by Diamond Cab Company," the doorman said, scanning the prior day's log. "Nothing else until ten of four."

Taft and Martinez walked back inside the lobby to find a quiet place to call the cab company. Martinez dialed the number, identified himself, and questioned the dispatcher.

"We can't give out that information without a court order," the dispatcher said.

"That's your choice," Martinez said, "but in thirty minutes I can have fifty agents of the Immigration and Naturalization Service examining your records with a microscope," Martinez said firmly.

There was a short pause.

"Hang on," the dispatcher said, "let me find what you're looking for."

Waiting on the open line, Martinez could clearly hear the cabbies talking sports in the background. He waited for several minutes.

"Okay, just after three there was a pickup at the Royal Regent. The driver dropped the person off at the Four Seasons. I gotta go now—we're real busy," the dispatcher managed to blurt out as he hung up on Martinez.

"Said he took the man to the Four Seasons," Martinez said to Taft.

Taft laughed. "If we'd known that we could've slept in. Let's go."

They drove back to the Four Seasons hotel.

Taft parked under the front awning. Quickly flashing his badge at the valet, he and Martinez strolled into the ornate lobby of the Four Seasons and headed directly for the front desk. The clerk was the same one who had checked them in the night before.

"Hello, Mr. Taft, Mr. Martinez. How may I help you?" the man asked politely.

Martinez flashed his badge and said. "We're looking for a guest you have. Chinese man, six feet or so, black hair. Asian. Doesn't like to smile."

"Let me ask around," the clerk said.

Martinez glanced at the newspaper sitting on the counter as he waited. Taft wandered away from the desk. He watched as a bellman wheeled a cart past and then loaded its contents into a waiting cab. Taft looked around the lobby, slightly annoyed by the wait.

The front desk clerk returned.

"We have a guest fitting that description in room 202, just above the pool deck," the clerk noted.

"Has he come to the desk to check out yet?" Taft asked.

"Check-out can also be done from the room using the television," the clerk noted as he punched commands into the computer. The clerk waited for the information to appear on the screen. "You're not going to believe this, but he's logged on right now."

"Send him a message he needs to come to the front desk," Martinez yelled.

"Give me a pass-card for the door," Taft said. Grabbing the

card from the clerk's hand, he raced away. "Larry, watch the elevator, I'm taking the stairs," Taft shouted over his shoulder.

As soon as the message to come to the front desk popped up on the television screen, Tsing felt uneasy. Paranoia was common to the Asian and giving in to it had so far kept him alive. Sliding open the glass door leading to the balcony, he climbed over the railing, then hanging from the lower rung, dropped to the pool deck.

Three minutes later, when Taft burst into the room, the drapes bordering the sliding glass door were blowing in a slight breeze.

Tsing made his way through the service kitchen and out through a side door leading to the front of the hotel just as Taft came out of the stairway.

"You see anything, Larry?" he asked Martinez, who stood at the bank of elevators.

"Nothing, man," said Martinez.

Taft's eyes swept through the lobby and beyond.

Just outside the lobby, a man came around the building unwrapping a pack of Camel cigarettes. Taft watched as he quickly walked to the lead cab. Black hair, around six feet tall, he paused at the door of the cab and lit a cigarette, pinching the filter between his fingers. He was scowling and seemed to bark his instructions to the cabbie. And he was obviously Asian.

Taft walked through the lobby toward the front doors, still scanning the crowd. He moved slowly at first, then gained speed until he was trotting. He burst through the front doors just as the cab carrying Tsing was pulling away. Martinez stayed at the bank of elevators and lost sight of Taft in the mass of people.

Taft turned to the doorman. "Quick, I need a cab," he shouted.

The doorman signaled one from the line farther down the asphalt drive.

"Tell the Hispanic man at the elevators that I'm following

the target. He'll know what you mean," Taft shouted as he opened the door of the cab.

"Sir, I can't leave my station," the doorman said.

Taft jumped into the cab and yelled back, "Well, find someone else to do it, then. Just get it done."

Inside the cab the turban-clad cab driver swiveled in his seat and looked back.

"Hello, sir, where can I take you today?" he asked.

"You're not going to believe this, but—follow that cab," Taft said.

"You don't know how long I've been waiting to hear those words," the cabbie shouted as he slid the car swiftly into gear and sped out of the hotel's driveway.

Taft's cab followed several blocks behind the cab containing Tsing. They raced through traffic around the side of the harbor. The cab in the lead stayed ahead, but still in sight. As Taft's cab closed to within a block they were caught behind a stopped school bus. For the first time he lost sight of the other cab. Taft sat fuming in the back.

"We're going to lose them," he said angrily.

"Sorry, sir," the Indian said worriedly. But after a second's pause he shouted, "Wait, I have idea," and, grabbing the radio microphone, he said, "All cabs of Patek Cab Company, please follow the Diamond Cab going south on Hancock Road."

The radio erupted with cab drivers' voices.

"Okay, I'll follow," said a voice on the radio.

"Yeah, okay," a second voice shouted.

"I see him, he turned on the road to the train station. I'll follow him," said a third voice.

"Yep, I see him," said a fourth voice.

Nearly half a dozen cabs began trailing the Diamond Cab— so much for the idea of any secrecy. The subject of the chase sat in his cab smoking and looking out the window at the scenery, oblivious to the commotion. Arriving at the station just in time for his departure, he checked his bags with the porter at the rail siding and immediately boarded the waiting train.

The first cab driver arrived at the station and spotted the man leaving the Diamond Cab and getting on the train. He parked his cab and waited on the siding as the train conductor gave the boarding call.

Taft sat in the back of his cab, waiting behind the school bus. "Now," he said to his driver as the school bus retracted its stop sign.

Over the radio in Taft's cab one of the other drivers said, "He is at train station."

The Indian driver grinned at Taft. "Wait until I tell my friends about this. This is like out of a movie." He laughed as he steered the Chevrolet toward the train station.

The Chinese agent, Chou Tsing, was oblivious he was being followed. He settled himself comfortably in his seat on the train and began reading the magazine he had brought with him.

Taft's cab pulled into a parking spot in front of the station, and he jumped from the cab to see the train receding down the tracks. Racing back to his cab, Taft passed out money to the group of cabbies who had trailed the Diamond Cab.

"Do you know where the train tracks lead?" Taft shouted to his driver as the last cabbie was paid.

"Yes," the man said excitedly.

"Then follow the train," Taft said, climbing back into the cab.

"Sounds good," the Indian cab driver said as he roared away from the station.

They were cruising down the road at a high rate of speed when Taft said, "Pull up to a pay phone—I have to make a call."

"Okay," the cabbie said as he slammed on the brakes and pulled into the parking lot of a convenience store.

Taft dialed Martinez's portable phone. "Larry, it's me. I'm

calling from a pay phone. My cell phone is in your car," Taft said. "Did you get my message?"

"I did," Martinez said, still in the lobby of the hotel.

"I think the guy we're looking for is on an Amtrak train heading south."

"I'll try to intercept you with the rental car," Martinez said.

"I'm staying on this guy, no matter what," Taft said quickly.

"Go for it," Martinez agreed. "Listen, I'll try to reach Amtrak and have the train stopped. Be extremely cautious how you approach the suspect—if it's him we want those papers intact if at all possible. What's your plan?"

"I'm not quite sure yet. Find an atlas that lists the train route as well as roads or highways," Taft said.

"Hold on," Martinez said as he spoke to the clerk. "Here we go, the front desk has an atlas. What do you need?" Martinez asked.

"Where does the train go under Highway 3?" Taft asked.

"You planning on jumping, John?" Martinez said, his voice sounding surprised. "That'll be twice in one week."

"Just like 'Perils of Pauline,' " Taft noted.

"There's a spot just outside Milton where the train has to slow for some curves—at least according to this map."

Taft wrote down the directions, reached through the open window of the cab, and marked them on the cabbie's map. "Take me here."

"You got it," the cabbie shouted.

"I'll call you when I can," Taft said to Martinez as he hung up the pay phone.

"I'm headed toward you," Martinez said into a now-dead phone line.

As the cab carrying Taft raced toward Milton, they caught sight of the train. Little by little, the cab began to pull ahead. Racing down Highway 3, the driver began to panic.

"It's going to be close," he worried aloud.

Just outside Milton, Taft looked again at the cab driver's map, then gave him the final directions to the bridge. In the distance, the train was fast approaching.

From his wallet Taft removed a hundred-dollar bill and handed it across the seat to the cabbie. "Good job."

"Thank you, sir," the cabbie said.

The train was starting under the bridge.

Taft leapt from the cab as it slid to a stop. He was standing next to the open side window of the cab, staring at the approaching train. He estimated the train was going no more than twenty-five miles an hour as it came around the curve. Carefully Taft began timing his jump.

"Wait," the cabbie said, "I have a receipt for you."

"That's okay," Taft said, rocking back and forth as he prepared for his jump.

"Okay, but sir, if I may ask—who *are* you?" the cab driver asked politely.

"My name is Pitt. Dirk Pitt," Taft said quickly.

Timing the train's speed one last time, Taft flung himself off the railroad bridge. Arms and legs outstretched, he flew through the air like a flying squirrel. He landed on top of the moving train with a heavy thud that knocked out his wind and brought tears to his eyes. The wind whipped at his clothes. It took several minutes for him to collect his thoughts.

"Twice in a week," Taft thought to himself as he caught his breath. "I might want to consider buying a ticket in the future."

"Dirk Pitt?" the cab driver said to himself as the train passed from sight. "That's an odd name."

CHAPTER 24

The Amtrak train made its way south, gaining speed with each mile. His eyes still tearing from the whipping air, Taft struggled to regain his breath. He lay quiet for several more minutes, breathing deeply, then pulled up his shirt and glanced at his beet-red stomach. The area nearest his ribs was already beginning to bruise.

The burning pain from his belly mixed well with the stabbing pain from where he had landed on his right hip. He felt like he had been kicked by a mule wearing logging boots. Taft coughed several times. Spitting over his head into the wind, he rolled carefully onto his left hip.

The train was passing through the Massachusetts country side, and Taft sat on the roof of the passenger car for a moment, looking at the scenery. He breathed in the smell of fall through his nostrils as he slowly willed the pain away. Looking behind, he noticed the end of the train was only three cars back. He crouched low to minimize his wind resistance as he jumped across the gaps between cars until he reached the last one.

Laying prone again on the roof he peered his head carefully over the edge. It appeared that the last coach was a sleeping car. Since trains no longer featured a rear club car, they placed the sleepers last to allow the higher-paying passengers with cabins greater privacy.

A small, slightly rusted iron railing surrounded the tiny rear platform at the rear of the car. Behind that was only the tracks and the rails sliding rapidly past. Taft swiveled around on his stomach so his feet dangled off the edge of the car, then slid slowly off the roof.

Taft aimed carefully for the tiny platform. Gaining speed faster than he anticipated, he nearly fell backward off the landing when he hit the platform. His body lurched forward and he bumped the door.

Stabilizing himself with his hands against the body of the railcar, he attempted to open the door to the sleeper coach but found it jammed. Rearing back as far as he could go on the small platform, he rammed the door with his shoulder until it burst open. Strangely enough, no one came out of their cabin at the noise.

Closing the battered door behind him, Taft began walking forward through the train until he reached the car nearest the locomotive—the dining car. Groups of tourists and commuters sat tranquilly finishing their breakfast and relaxing over cups of coffee. Taft was scanning the crowd searching for Tsing and did not hear the porter, who approached silently behind him.

"Can I get you anything, sir?" she asked.

Taft turned and looked into the eyes of a very attractive, five-foot-tall female in a form-fitting, red-vested uniform. She smiled at him sweetly.

"No, nothing. Thanks," Taft said, smiling back.

"Well, you let me know if you need anything," she said walking away, her figure rocking with the movement of the train.

Taft slowly continued his search through both the sitting cars and the bar car.

The train was surprisingly full. The tourists were obviously enjoying a final trip while the weather was still clear. The fall foliage lining the tracks was colored with deep reds, yellows, and oranges. It was nature's last burst before the browns and grays of winter came calling.

Taft's search came up empty.

Sitting down in a seat he tried to figure out how to search the private sleeping compartments. The train was now rumbling through the town of Attleboro, Massachusetts. They would soon be entering the outskirts of Providence, Rhode Island, the train's next stopping point.

Martinez slammed his fist against the side of his cellular phone as he raced in the rental car down I-95. Amtrak would be calling him back for confirmation to stop the train and now his phone wasn't working.

"Cheap shit batteries," he said to himself.

Glancing to the side of the road he saw a sign that said: North Attleboro, 12 miles. Stomping his foot on the accelerator, he took the rental car up to a speed of nearly 100 miles an hour

The attractive porter walked up to the seated Taft and stood alongside his seat. "Are you sure you don't need anything?" she said, smiling seductively.

"Well, maybe you *can* help—you see, I'm looking for a Chinese man, about six foot tall, with short black hair," Taft said.

"Great," she said, her voiced edged in sarcasm.

"No, no," Taft said quickly, "I was in the Army. I spent time in Hong Kong, and I think I may have met him there," he blurted. "I thought I saw him earlier in the bar car, but now he's disappeared. He must have a sleeper car."

The woman looked at Taft with renewed interest. Taft, his heterosexuality now reaffirmed, appeared pleased. "Let me ask my friend who is the sleeping car attendant," the porter said helpfully.

Taft sat back down to wait, glancing out the window at the scenery. The train took a fork and entered Rhode Island. He could see Pawtucket ahead in the distance.

Taft glanced up as the porter returned. "My friend found the Chinese man and told him your story. He wants to meet you.

He's in the next to the last car . . . cabin C," she said with a smile.

Damn it, Taft thought, *I hadn't expected she'd go talk to him. So much for surprise.*

"Great," he said miserably. "I'll just walk down there and visit."

Taft rehearsed his plan as he walked between the cars. He would burst into the cabin, subdue the man, then search the compartment for the papers.

Taft found the hall empty outside cabin C.

Taft paused, then shouldered the door open and burst into the tiny cabin. He was concentrating on any danger in front of him. It was a mistake he would never make again. The instant Taft entered cabin C, Tsing burst out of an empty cabin across the hall. Reaching through the open door he chopped at Taft's neck with the edge of his hand—a hard slashing blow to the carotid artery. Taft swiveled, thrusting his elbow into Tsing's chest.

Tsing was knocked back into the hallway.

Taft leapt from cabin C, both feet off the ground, only to be met by a well-placed kick Tsing leveled at his midsection. He flew back into the cabin, his head smashing against the sharp edge of the overhead storage compartment on the far wall. Then, like a burlap sack filled with pennies, he dropped from the air, his head coming to rest in a corner on the floor of the tiny cabin, unconscious.

The sound of Taft's body crashing to the floor brought several people out of their cabins. Clutching his briefcase to his chest, Tsing walked quickly past toward the front of the train. The train was slowing as it neared Providence station, and over the intercom the conductor reminded the passengers to please remember to take all their personal belongings.

"I need a large cherry slush monster, please," the acne-ridden teenager told the clerk at the combination gas-and-convenience store just off the exit to I-95.

Martinez hopped from foot to foot. In his hand he held a dollar bill he needed changed.

The clerk began slowly to fill the cup with cherry slush. The machine began sputtering. "I'm sorry, it looks like we're out . . ."

"I need change here," Martinez said.

"Hey man, you have to wait your turn," the teenager said.

Martinez ignored the teenager.

The clerk handed over the change and Martinez sprinted for the pay phone. He dialed the number to reach Amtrak central security.

"This is Special Agent Martinez. I'm sorry, my cellular phone quit working. Please stop the train from Boston to Providence. Now."

"When we didn't hear from you, Agent Martinez, we just waited. The train has already reached Providence."

"Damn!" Martinez said as he hung up.

He raced for the rental car and steered toward the train station in Providence.

Luckily for Taft, the female porter, fresh from applying new makeup, decided to flirt with him one last time. Folding the mirror in her office back into the wall, she walked through the train to the sleeping cars. Stopping at cabin C, she noticed the door was ajar.

Taft's shoes and part of his legs were sticking out on the floor. The train was barely moving as she pushed the door to the cabin farther open, then helped Taft to struggle upright. Taft was still drifting in and out of consciousness as the porter ran to get help.

The train pulled to a stop at the station. The porter and sleeping-car attendant held an ice pack to Taft's head, trying to revive him. Slowly Taft's head began to clear. Rising unsteadily to his feet, he noticed the throbbing in his neck blended nicely with his various other aches. He stood on wobbly knees.

The anxious faces of the two ladies filled Taft's field of view. "Wrong guy, I guess," he managed to say before he passed out once again.

Taft was sitting in the back of an ambulance, holding an ice pack to his neck. He was arguing loudly with the paramedics.

"Just let us do a quick series of X-rays at the hospital," one paramedic pleaded.

"I have to go call my partner," Taft said as he walked unsteadily to a pay phone.

He dialed the number but got only a busy signal. He stumbled back to the ambulance.

Twenty minutes later, Martinez pulled into the station at Providence and walked through the crowd until he located Taft.

"He got away," Taft told him.

"What happened?"

"He clubbed me when I tried to grab him in his car," Taft said, rising.

"Then I guess we know he has something to do with this, don't we?" Martinez said as he led Taft toward the rental car.

Once Taft was safely in the passenger seat, Martinez slid behind the wheel.

"You look like you've been in a bar brawl," he said, staring at Taft.

Taft stared over at his partner through a swollen eye. "I tell you one thing."

"What's that?" Martinez said as he slid the car into drive.

"The next time I meet that guy he's in trouble," Taft said slowly. "Real big trouble."

CHAPTER 25

Like most stereotypes, the stereotype of the bespectacled physics nerd with buckteeth and a slide rule stuck to his hip was undependable. Jeff Scaramelli was a brilliant six-foot-seven-inch physicist who looked exactly like the athlete he had once been.

Scaramelli had played college basketball, earning a full-ride scholarship to the University of Colorado for his efforts. It was his grades, however, that had gotten him his master's degree and which would soon earn him his doctorate.

The former basketball star was just completing his doctoral thesis on the Unified Field Theory, and that made him uniquely qualified to work with Einstein's much-maligned ideas. Current physics shunned the theory, considering it an antique. Most professors couldn't understand what little was known of the theory, much less teach it. The action now was in quantum theory and radicals and photonic band-gaps, but Scaramelli liked Einstein's theory just fine.

The call from the shadowy government organization was something new for Scaramelli. Usually he worked at his own pace, in his own direction, trying to pry open the covering hiding the clues to the forces in the universe. Now he was being asked to take a specific direction and get results by a certain deadline.

Scaramelli didn't know if he should be flattered or angry.

He stretched his long legs out on the carpeted floor to the side of his computer terminal at the Advanced Physics Laboratory in Boulder, Colorado. Swishing root beer around in his mouth, he looked out the window to the Flatirons, the string of uniquely shaped foothills that extended up from the city of Boulder.

Bouncing a racquetball repeatedly against the window, he began to think back to what his father had told him about Einstein.

He was deep in thought when the NIA agents brought in his new colleague.

"I'm Li Choi," the diminutive physicist said, smiling.

"I was told we'd be working together," Scaramelli said, rising and extending his hand to Choi. "I read one of the papers you published while you were at Berkeley."

"I'm honored," Choi said as he glanced around the laboratory.

Scaramelli motioned to a computer at a desk nearby. "You can set up at that workstation over there."

Choi looked over at the computer then back to Scaramelli. "Where do we start? I haven't been told much."

"Me either," Scaramelli said easily. "Let's first record your formulas and any observations you have about the Unified Field Theory."

"After that?" asked Choi.

"After that we need to design a method to test the theory. The word I got was that the government is trying to recover a copy of the theory as we speak."

Choi smiled, walked over to the computer, and turned it on. "Come on over, Jeff, and I'll show you what I know. If we are going to work together there can be no secrets."

Eleven hours later, just before midnight Colorado time, Choi had completed his labors. "That's the extent of the work I have completed," he said to Scaramelli.

"Interesting," Scaramelli noted. "Are you hungry?"

"Extremely," said Choi.

"Do you like Mexican food?"

"Absolutely."

"I'll ask one of the agents to pick us up some grub," Scaramelli said, reaching for the phone. "While we're waiting for the food I can explain my idea for a test device. I think we can build something ourselves with most of the parts available at a hardware store."

"Sounds good," Choi said cheerfully.

Four hours later, when the pair finished, the laboratory was cluttered with containers of half-eaten take-out Mexican food, wadded up sheets of paper, and a partially finished gallon of chocolate milk.

"That should do it," Scaramelli said at last.

Choi glanced again at the shopping list. "Looks good. When a hardware store opens in the morning we can start building the device."

Scaramelli reached for the telephone and buzzed the outer office. An agent entered the laboratory almost immediately. "You men need something?"

"We have a list of items we'll need someone to pick up for us tomorrow."

The agent glanced at the list briefly. "Is there anything else you can think of that you might need?" he said, scratching his chin.

"Not really. The big hardware store in town is called McGukin's," Scaramelli said. "They open at nine in the morning."

"We'll wake up the owner and have him meet us there. You'll have these items in two hours," the agent said as he walked toward the door.

"Unbelievable," Scaramelli said after the agent had left. "Are you getting the idea what we're working on is more than a little important?"

"Yes I am, Jeff," Choi said as he yawned. "What do you want to do while we wait?"

Scaramelli pointed to a pair of foam pads stacked in a corner of the laboratory.

"I'm going to sleep a couple hours until the agents get back."

Choi nodded. "That's the best idea you've had all evening."

Five minutes later the pair was fast asleep.

CHAPTER 26

Martinez parked the rental car hastily in front of the Amtrak station and ran toward Taft. "How's the neck?" he asked.

"I'm still seeing double, but it's starting to clear," Taft said as he tossed the cold pack to the ambulance attendant.

"I called the Providence police. They're sending down some officers to help us question the passengers."

"I saw a couple of unmarked cars arrive already," Taft noted. "Sorry I lost the guy, Larry."

"Don't beat yourself up, we'll find him," Martinez said.

Taft and Martinez walked toward the detective from the Providence police who was climbing out of an unmarked car and gave him the description of the man they sought. As the police fanned out to question the station employees and what few passengers still remained at the station, Taft used the secure phone to call General Benson. After explaining what had occurred, he waited as Benson mulled it over.

"It's nearly impossible to find a lone man who wants to stay hidden," Benson said at last.

"Why don't you order a computer search of all plane and train reservations along with all rental car agencies, limousine companies, and cab outfits," Taft asked. "We might get lucky."

"Hold on," Benson said. In the background Taft could hear as Benson shouted those orders to his assistant.

"I just thought of something else," Taft said when Benson came back on the line. "Have some agents begin to phone automobile dealers in Providence and check for any recent cash purchases. If this guy is as smart as I think he is, he just might *buy* a car."

"Good idea," Benson agreed.

"I believe if our target does have something removed from Einstein's boat he has orders to deliver it in person to someone in a position of authority. He won't be hiding them in a locker or burying them in the ground for someone else to retrieve later." Taft paused. "That means that he will logically try to make his way to the nearest Chinese Embassy, which is in New York City."

"I'll have the embassy in New York surrounded and the rest across the country placed under observation," Benson said. "We can't violate the sanctity of an embassy's grounds, but we can sure as hell stop everyone that approaches on the street outside."

"Will you arrange a chopper for us at the Providence airport? If the search turns up nothing here, we'll need to go to New York."

"I'll have it done," Benson said. "You two are the best we've got, John. Now go find this guy or our ass is in a sling."

"Got it, boss," Taft said as he shut off the phone and closed the briefcase.

Martinez stood talking to the lead detective as Taft walked over. "I was just telling your partner my men have questioned nearly everyone still here. No one seems to remember seeing the man you describe," the detective said as he crushed a cigarette butt under the heel of his shoe.

"Does your police department have a sketch artist?" Taft asked.

"Sure," the detective said.

"Let's have him draw up a picture while this guy's face is still fresh in my mind."

"Follow me," the detective said.

Near Warwick, Rhode Island, Mike O'Leary burped a gas bubble that smelled like fish and chips. His feet were up on his desk and he was staring through the floor-to-ceiling glass that looked out on the parking lot. He watched as a dark-haired man climbed from a cab, paid the driver, then began to inspect the inventory. Removing his feet from the desk, O'Leary reached in his desk drawer, removed a breath mint, then slipped it in his mouth. Checking his pocket to make sure he had some business cards, he walked out onto the lot and smiled at the man.

"You have good taste, my friend," he said. "That's a finely crafted machine."

"This one," the man said with a slight accent, pointing, "with the storage compartments. How much for this one?"

"You're in luck," O'Leary said. "That went on sale just this morning, only seventy-nine ninety-five."

The man reached into his pocket and withdrew a wad of hundred-dollar bills. "Seventy-five hundred, cash. And I want it ready in half an hour."

"Congratulations," O'Leary said. "It's already been prepped. Let me just write it up.

Within fifteen minutes Tsing was moving again.

After the sketch artist completed the drawing, Martinez faxed a copy to the Special Security Service office. Clutching the master copy, he turned to the detective. "Can you have someone give us a ride to the airport?"

"I'll have a patrolman take you in a black and white."

"Thanks for your help," Taft said.

"It made my morning," the detective said sarcastically.

Twenty minutes later Taft and Martinez arrived at the airport and choked down a sandwich from the lunch counter as the pilot refueled the helicopter.

In the offices of the Special Security Service a dozen agents sat phoning automobile dealers in Providence.

"I'm finished with my list," one of the agents said, anticipating lunch.

"Start on the used-car dealers," the lead agent replied.

Benson entered the room. "Any luck?" he asked the lead agent.

"Nothing so far, sir."

"This may be a dead end, but let's keep trying," Benson said quietly as he walked from the room.

Twenty-seven minutes later the agent wanting lunch hit pay dirt.

"Mercury Yamaha."

"I was trying to reach Mercury Motors Used Cars," the agent said.

"We are one and the same," Mike O'Leary noted cheerfully. He was still on a high from the easy sale he'd concluded within the hour.

The agent explained who he was and what he needed.

"The only cash sale in the last few days was an hour ago," O'Leary said, his fine mood now dissolving. "A new motorcycle."

"Was the man who bought the motorcycle Chinese, standing around six foot tall?" the agent asked.

"Am I in some kind of trouble here?" O'Leary asked.

"No."

O'Leary paused. "Then, yes, he was."

"Do you have a fax machine?" the agent asked.

"Yes," O'Leary said.

"Give me the number, I'm going to fax you a sketch. Keep this line open and get on as soon as you have the picture."

The agent could hear O'Leary slide his chair back, then the sound of footsteps as he walked across the tiled showroom. Three minutes later the agent heard him return and pick up the phone.

"The fax came through clear," O'Leary said.

"Well?"

"That looks like the same guy," O'Leary said glumly.

Taft and Martinez sat in the rear seats of a U.S. Navy Sikorsky H-76N Eagle helicopter. They were near Norwich, Connecticut, and yelling to each other over the noise of the engines. "This is getting old," Taft said. "We need to grab this guy as soon as he nears the embassy and end this little caper. You and I are starting to look like fools."

"Let's hope we're right about New York or we'll soon be unemployed," Martinez said.

Taft started to answer but was interrupted by the ringing of the cellular phone he had retrieved from Martinez's rental car. "This is John Taft."

"This is Mickelson. How's it going?"

"Agent Mickelson," Taft said, "I hope you have some good news."

"Your target bought a new Yamaha motorcycle in Providence just over an hour ago."

"That qualifies," Taft said, smiling. "Have you got a road map handy, Mick?"

"Already checked it out, John. The most direct route for him to take is straight down I-95."

"Damn, you're good," Taft said.

"Ain't that the truth," Mickelson said as the phone went dead.

Taft turned to Martinez and shouted, "Our man bought a Yamaha. Mick thinks he will probably drive straight down I-95."

"There *is* a God," Martinez said, then switched on the helicopter's intercom. "Take us down I-95," he said to the pilot of the Sikorsky. "We're looking for a man on a new Yamaha motorcycle."

"Roger that," the pilot said as he banked the helicopter south.

CHAPTER 27

It would be easy for the average person to dismiss China as a nation of peasants. A huge land mass containing 1.3 billion people, or four times the population of the United States, all struggling to fill their rice bowls.

The country is far from that.

Chinese mathematicians had already calculated pi by the third century before Christ. The country's inventors were the first to produce paper, the magnetic compass, and the clock. They were even the first to manufacture gunpowder.

In the last few years, the Chinese military had built an enormous power base. The military now controlled 15,000 businesses and 50,000 factories. Norinco, as China North Industries Corporation was called, acted as the principle arms manufacturer for China and controlled a great deal of international arms sales. The company was said to own over eighty international companies that generated billions of dollars in sales each year.

Another company, Polytechnologies, worked as a weapons broker and acquisition agent, and it was even rumored they brokered the purchase of a Kuznetson-class aircraft carrier from the Ukraine. The massive vessel was incomplete when the Soviet

Union fell, and after her purchase she was towed to Hong Kong, where work was progressing at breakneck speed to complete her.

In the race to become a world power there was little standing in China's way.

At an office on Changan Avenue East the leaders of China were proving that the Florentine political theorist Machiavelli could have learned much from the Chinese.

"Have we heard from the courier yet?" the Chinese prime minister asked Sun Tao.

"Nothing yet," said Tao. "The witnesses to the recovery of the documents have been eliminated, however. We bombed the plane they were aboard. It is being reported in the American newspapers as being attributed to wind shear, so that secret is safe. Hu Jimn was successfully eliminated. His body was identified by one of our operatives about an hour ago. The agent arranged for Jimn's burial in the United States."

"Once the courier delivers the key to Einstein's formula, how long will it take for the scientists to create a working weapon?" the prime minister asked.

"They don't know," Tao said. "Perhaps hours, perhaps weeks. Truly it is of little concern, Mr. Prime Minister."

"Why do you say that?" the prime minister said, sipping tea from a delicate china cup emblazoned with the Chinese flag.

"Once we have the key in our possession, the United States will respond to a bluff. We need only tell them we have an operational weapon, then deliver a portion of the key as proof."

"To save time can we have Einstein's documents faxed here once the courier arrives at the embassy?"

"I would think the age of the paper itself, combined with the frailty caused by its immersion in the ocean, would eliminate that option, sir."

"Then we must have them hand-delivered?"

"I'm afraid that's the case."

"When are we due to hear from the courier?"

"He has orders not to contact us here until he is safely inside one of our embassies."

"So we wait," the prime minister said quietly. He paused and the room was silent for several minutes. "I think we need to start planning a diversion, something that will make the Americans move their naval battle groups out of our area. I want them far away when we proceed with the attack on Taiwan."

Tao thought for a moment. "I have an idea," he then said. "What is the one thing the United States will always fight to protect?"

"Oil," the prime minister noted.

"Our scientists have alerted us to something that was developed in the United States that should help us divert the American military."

"What is that, Mr. Tao?"

Tao explained.

CHAPTER 28

To someone who was driving past on the highway, the nondescript two-story office building in the free-trade zone near McAllen, Texas, looked like many others. The building might have housed an import-export firm, a small factory, even a warehouse. Instead, the building was the headquarters for a company named Enviorco. The company's business was genetically engineered microbes.

The Rio Grande Valley in Texas had long been a waste dumping ground. The passage of the North American Free Trade Agreement had only accelerated the environmental damage that was commonplace along the Texas border with Mexico. Since incorporation four years before, Enviorco had seen a growth rate that exceeded a thousand percent a year. Enviorco now owned more patents on biological microbes than any other company in the world. The microbes grown in the laboratory in McAllen were designed to be spread on oil slicks, toxic waste spills, or areas of chemical contamination. After they were sprayed in a liquid mist on the area to be decontaminated, the microbes began to eat the poisons. After digesting the toxins and reprocessing them into nontoxic waste products, the microbes would die soon afterward. The area of contamination would now be clean, the decomposing bodies of the microbes becoming a safe soil mulch. The process had proven to be environmentally sound and the bugs from McAllen were now shipped worldwide.

In the hot Texas sun outside Enviorco's building, the temperature just before noon was already over ninety degrees. A hot, dry wind was blowing south from upstate as Gilbert Moscap walked the short distance to the parking lot and his company car. The wind that blew by him smelled of fertilizer, metal, and citrus. Unlocking the door of the car, Moscap was hit by a blast of super-heated air from inside. He sat down gingerly on the sun-baked seat, then turned the key and started the car. Setting the air conditioner to maximum, he pushed the button to lower the windows until the car could cool. He slid the shifter into drive and set out for a restaurant just across the border in Reynosa, Mexico, for lunch. As Moscap drove onto the highway, Enviorco's parking lot began to empty as the rest of the company's scientists and office workers filed out for the noon meal.

Eight minutes later, the parking lot was almost empty. Turning off the highway leading into Enviorco, three men in a Dodge pickup waved to the guard sitting in the checkpoint, then entered the empty lot. Backing the truck up to the loading dock the three men entered the laboratory through a side door. Though the men were wearing Enviorco uniforms, their hats were pulled low to obscure their features. One of the men removed a slip of paper from his wallet and checked the vat numbers on the tanks of microbes, then directed the others to the north side of the building. Finding the control number they were seeking, the men wheeled the vat toward the loading dock. Through the raised garage door they rolled the vat into the bed of the Dodge, then lashed it down with nylon straps. After driving to the checkpoint, they stopped and handed the guard on duty a set of forged paperwork. Once cleared, they drove back onto the highway.

Forty-seven minutes later, Moscap was passing through Mexican customs to return to the United States when his executive assistant, Connie Lauder, called him on his cellular phone.

"Yeah, Connie," Moscap said as he finished passing through customs, then accelerated onto the highway leading to Enviorco.

"Mr. Moscap, I have Hal King in the office. He just returned from lunch. He claims we're missing a vat of Modified 25."

Moscap thought for a moment before speaking. "Are those the rapid reproducing oil-eaters?"

"They're the zero-oxygen, highly modified bugs that were developed from formula 12," Lauder said, reading from her computer.

Moscap instantly knew what Lauder was talking about. "We were ordered by the EPA to destroy those bugs. What happened?"

Over the speakerphone in Lauder's office, Moscap heard shuffling. "Mr. Moscap, this is Hal King. I ordered some Modified 25 retained so I could experiment with it," King said and paused. "I thought that if I could breed in a time-line we would have something valuable."

Moscap pushed down on the accelerator of the car. He was mad and edging toward livid. He fought a constant struggle with the scientists employed by Enviorco. Most had lived a life ignored by society and craved recognition and respect. They all

wanted to be published in the scientific journals—their brilliance then recognized by their peers.

"Have your experiments worked, Mr. King?" Moscap asked,
struggling to remain calm.

"No, not really," King answered slowly.

"That's why the EPA ordered those microbes destroyed,"
Moscap said loudly. "Did you happen to read the data on their
one and only introduction?"

"Yes sir," said King sheepishly.

"Then you remember that after the microbes cleaned up the
spill they migrated down the pipe string and into the oil reservoir. We nearly lost the entire oil field. When we sampled the
formerly rich oil-bearing sands they looked like they had been
run through a giant washing machine."

"But we halted the migration—" King began to say.

"We halted it by flooding the well with natural gas and burning
it out. Had there been any oil left in the sands we would have had
a catastrophe on our hands." Moscap turned onto the road leading to Enviorco. "I'm about two miles away, King. I want you to
wait for me in Connie's office," he said as he pushed the button
and disconnected the phone.

Near Weslaco, Texas, the Dodge truck carrying enough
microbes to wipe out the entire Texas oil industry was rolling
east. Billy Tolbert spit out the window, scratched the scab on a
new tattoo on his arm, then reached into his pocket for his pack
of non-filtered Camels. Tapping one out of the pack, he flicked
a safety match across the dashboard and lit the end.

"It's another hour to Port Isabel," Tolbert said as he rose up
off the seat and passed a foul wind. "We should hit a drive-
through liquor store and buy a twelve-pack."

His two partners, only weeks out of the Texas state prison at
Huntsville, nodded in agreement. Pulling the Dodge off the

highway, Tolbert purchased a twelve-pack of Shiner, then set out driving east again.

Moscap slid the transmission of his company car into park while it was still rolling forward. Switching off the key, he raced inside Enviorco to Lauder's office.

"First get me security, then pull up a list of our current job sites," he said to Lauder.

Moscap lit a cigarette, his first of the day.

"Security's on the way," Lauder said a few minutes later. "Here's the list of job sites."

Moscap scanned the list. Six job sites were oil spills. The rest were toxic waste. Twenty-four sites total. If there was an order mix-up, the Modified 25 could be headed to any one of the sites. He tore the list in half.

"Take this half," he said to Lauder. "Call them and ask for the foreman. If they have ordered any microbes to be delivered today, ask them not to use them until they can be tested."

Two security guards entered the office and stood standing, awaiting instructions. Moscap pointed at King, who was sitting silently in a chair.

"You," he said, pointing at one of the guards. "Walk Dr. King to his office, take his entrance pass, and secure his computer. Then walk him to his car and see him off the property. He is no longer employed here."

King stared at Moscap silently.

"Don't bother to put Enviorco down as a reference in your job hunt," Moscap said. "And if you ever come on the grounds again, for any reason, I will have you arrested."

The guard led King away by the arm.

Moscap pointed to the other guard. "I want you to go to the checkpoint and find out who it was that left with the microbes. As soon as that's done pull the videotapes for the last two hours from the security cameras both inside the plant and outside."

The guard nodded and raced away.

Moscap ran to a phone and began to call the foremen.

Twenty minutes later Lauder walked over. "I've finished my list. Every foreman I've spoken to claims they always order microbes on Monday. That way they are not at the site over the weekend. Since it's Friday, not one was expecting a shipment today."

"Number seven on my list is not answering. Then I have two more to call," Moscap said.

Five minutes later Moscap had reached all but number seven on his list.

The smell of salt air, fish, and diesel fuel lay like gauze over the deteriorating dock that was located on a dead-end road near Port Isabel, Texas. Pulling the truck up to a rusty cargo ship, Tolbert and his partners climbed from the cab.

The man that had hired them to steal the microbes motioned from the deck of the ship. "Bring the container inside," he said quietly.

A flock of seagulls nearby screeched loudly, fighting over the spoils being tossed from the rear of a passing shrimp boat. Tolbert waited until the din grew quiet to answer. "Show us the rest of our money," he shouted up to the man.

Opening a briefcase, the man angled it so Tolbert could see inside. The cash that filled the inside was neatly stacked with the bank wrappers listing denomination clearly visible.

"Let's go, men," Tolbert said, smiling, as he lowered the rear gate of the pickup.

Tolbert and his partners unloaded the stainless-steel vat, then rolled it up the ramp to the deck of the cargo ship. The man on deck walked into the main cabin with the briefcase and motioned for Tolbert to follow. Setting the briefcase on a table, he pointed to the vat. "Put the container over there first," he said, "then you can count your money."

The least senior of Tolbert's partners began to secure the vat against a bulkhead. Tolbert and the other thief raced to the brief-case and began to rifle through it. The young burglar was just fin-ishing placing blocks of wood under the vat of microbes. He rose and turned at the sound of two soft splats. Tolbert and the second of the trio of thieves dropped to the floor, a cloud of misty blood visible in the beam of sunlight coming through the open door. Without a second thought, the only remaining thief leapt through the hatchway leading to the deck as a flurry of bullets struck the wall beside him. Racing down the ramp, he twisted to the right as a bullet fired from the deck pierced his shoulder.

Moscap pushed the speed-dialer again and waited as the phone rang.

The seventh foreman on the list, Bob Bilcher, smiled at the buxom bartender and rose from his stool. "I'm going to get some cigarettes from my truck, Belle. I'll be right back."

Walking through the dirt parking lot, Bilcher could hear the phone in the truck incessantly ringing. He unlocked the truck and picked up the headset.

"Yeah," Bilcher said.

"This is Gilbert Moscap."

Bilcher was stabbed first by a pang of guilt, then by anger. Someone on his crew must have alerted Moscap to his habit of taking off early on Friday. "Yes, sir," Bilcher said.

"Did you order any microbe deliveries today?" Moscap asked.

Bilcher smiled, his brief anger subsiding. "No sir. I almost always order 'robes to be delivered on Monday."

The cellular phone fell silent for a moment. "Thanks. That's all I need," Moscap said after the pause.

Bilcher hung up the phone and exhaled. Reaching in the glove box he removed a pack of cigarettes. Then he returned to the bar to get good and drunk.

At Enviorco, in McAllen, Moscap rubbed his face with his hands.

"The people on the tapes have their hats pulled low. It'll be tough to get any sort of positive identification," the security guard said when Moscap walked from Lauder's office.

Looking at Lauder, Moscap rubbed his hands across his cheeks again. "We've got a hell of a problem here," he said finally.

CHAPTER 29

Chou Tsing had the Yamaha in high gear in the fast lane of I-95. After reaching behind and patting the saddlebag containing the papers, he flicked on the motorcycle's high beam to signal the beer truck in front that he wanted to pass. Checking the motorcycle's fuel gauge he saw that he had used barely a quarter of a tank. He estimated he would arrive at the embassy in New York City in forty minutes. As the beer truck moved into the center lane, he twisted the throttle open wider. Tsing was just past Stamford, Connecticut.

"We're doing this backwards," Taft said to Martinez as they flew west above I-95. "Let's direct the pilot to fly to the Bronx and then east back toward Connecticut."

"I'll tell him," Martinez said, walking forward to the helicopter's cockpit.

Taft continued to scan the highway with binoculars until the helicopter did a 180-degree turn and raced toward the Bronx. "Let me check with the office again and make sure they have the NYPD assisting at the overpasses," Martinez said when he returned. He dialed Benson's number on his secure phone. "This is Martinez. Is the general available?"

"I'll put you through, Agent Martinez," Mrs. Mindio said.

Seconds later the general picked up. "Go ahead, Larry," Benson said.

"We're still searching from the helicopter. Do you have the NYPD watching the overpasses?"

"They're in place already. All the units should have a fax picture of the Yamaha we lifted from a brochure. They have instructions to stop any red Yamaha with temporary tags that looks even close to the picture."

"And the Chinese Embassy is surrounded?"

"We have the embassy covered so tightly a pigeon couldn't land there."

The helicopter was now over the Bronx. The pilot banked and headed back up I-95. Taft placed the binoculars to his eyes.

"I guess we've done all we can," Martinez noted.

"I sure as hell hope so," Benson said in closing.

Near New Rochelle, New York, Tsing slowed as the traffic thickened. He unzipped his jacket to allow the breeze to blow inside and dry his sweat. He didn't notice as a shadow passed overhead.

Taft and Martinez scanned the interstate with binoculars from both side windows of the helicopter.

"Behind that refrigerator truck," Martinez shouted.

Taft scanned the interstate. "That's a Honda," he shouted to Martinez.

The helicopter flew past Split Rock Golf Course. The town of Pelham Manor was just ahead. Continuing to scan the road with the binoculars, Taft began to have trouble focusing his eyes. "I have to take a short break, Larry. I'm starting to get motion sickness," Taft said. He stared into the distance until his stomach and eyes began to settle. Martinez continued scanning the interstate. Once Taft's vertigo had subsided he resumed watching the road. Two minutes later he spotted the motorcycle.

"There, behind that yellow Jeep," Taft shouted.

"I see it," Martinez said, then raced forward and instructed the pilot. Returning to the rear compartment, he said to Taft, "The pilot will come in slowly from the rear. I told him to stay back and let us check out the motorcycle with the binoculars."

The helicopter pivoted and slowly advanced on the motorcycle. The traffic on the interstate was loosening and Tsing accelerated the Yamaha. Taft strained to see the plate through the binoculars. "I can't be positive but the plate *looks* like a paper temporary tag."

"Let me look," Martinez said. The helicopter pulled closer, hovering twenty yards behind the motorcycle. "Red Yamaha, paper tags," Martinez agreed. "It looks good to me, John."

"Give me the phone," Taft said. Martinez handed him the phone and he dialed Benson's office.

"Benson."

"I think we've got him, sir. I think we should stay back and trail him from a distance. Our men have the area around the embassy sealed. If we try to stop him now he could jump from the motorcycle and disappear with the papers."

"You're right. I'll call NYPD. As soon as the motorcycle nears the embassy we'll have unmarked police cars block traffic, then slowly fill the street around him."

"Then what?" Taft asked.

"We'll steer him around a corner directly into a roadblock."

"I like your plan, sir," Taft said.

"Call our agents on the ground, I want you to give them a running commentary on the motorcycle's location while we set this up," Benson said.

"No problem, sir."

"Don't lose the guy this time," Benson said as he broke the connection.

Taft dialed the agent on the ground, then turned to Martinez as the phone rang. "We'll stay back and follow while the general coordinates with NYPD to surround him in unmarked cars. Once he's surrounded the cars will steer him toward a road-block."

"Where's the roa—" Martinez began to say.

Taft waved with his hand for Martinez to quiet and lifted his palm from the phone.

"This is Taft. Can you hear me?"

The agent working the ground detail replied. "This is Jerry Franks, John. You're loud and clear."

"Hey, Jerry," Taft said. "I'll report to you on the motorcycle's progress at regular intervals, just keep the line open."

"Sounds good," Franks said.

"He's still going south on I-95 and just crossed over the River Parkway." Taft put his palm back over the phone. "Sorry, Larry. Were you going to ask where the roadblock will be set up?"

"Yeah."

"They're still working on that. I think somewhere near the embassy."

"Once we're in Manhattan this chopper is worthless. Once he gets between the skyscrapers our advantage is lost."

"Franks is on the ground. He'll handle it."

"I don't like it," Martinez said quietly. "I don't like it at all."

* * *

Tsing weaved through the traffic on I-95, his eyes intent on every road sign until he found the exit he was looking for. He glanced up as the sign passed: Bruckner Expressway, I-278 to Manhattan. Gearing down the motorcycle, he made the turn and headed toward Manhattan.

"He's turning off I-95 toward Manhattan," Taft said into the phone.

Martinez stared at the map.

"That's called the Bruckner Expressway."

"Martinez says it's called the Bruckner Expressway," Taft said into the phone.

"Hold one," Franks said. "We have an unmarked coming on the highway at White Plains Road. Let me call him on the other phone."

Two minutes later, as Tsing passed White Plains Road, a nondescript Ford sedan blended onto the expressway, staying several car lengths behind the motorcycle.

"I think I see the pursuit car," Taft said to Franks as the helicopter continued flying toward Manhattan.

At Hunts Point Avenue a second unmarked car joined the pursuit. Passing Mary's Park, Tsing slowed for the Second Avenue exit.

"That's the Second Avenue exit," Martinez said, glancing through his binoculars at the sign.

"He's taking the Second Avenue exit," Taft said to Franks.

"We have the ground units on a different line," Franks said. "They just reported that too."

Taft put his hand over the phone and spoke to Martinez. "The ground units are following. We're going to run up against the skyscrapers soon. Should we land and make our way to the roadblock?"

"Sounds good."

"Jerry."

"Go ahead."

"It looks like you have it well covered on the ground. We're going to start having trouble seeing anything from up here as soon as we hit the main part of Manhattan. I think it's better if we touch down and join you at the roadblock."

"I have to agree, John. The roadblock's set up at Fourteenth and Fourth. You can land nearby, in Union Square."

"Got it," Taft said as he cut the connection.

"I'll tell the pilot," Martinez said, walking forward.

Tsing rolled south on Second Avenue, oblivious to an ever increasing number of unmarked police cars following close behind. Several blue-and-white cars with overhead lights flashing were sitting just past Fourteenth on Second Avenue. *It must be a car wreck*, Tsing thought to himself. *I'll just take Fourteenth Street to Fifth Avenue.* Turning on Fourteenth Street, he checked his watch. He estimated he could reach the embassy in less than five minutes. Patting the saddlebags containing the papers once again, he weaved around a slow-moving car and continued west.

Lieutenant Michael Laughlin of the NYPD signaled with his hand to a patrolman.

"Place the traffic cones near the cross street where that Con Ed truck is that we're using as a decoy," he said and turned to Franks. "Once the unmarked cars steer him around the corner, we'll place the cones across the street to stop traffic until we can get the blocking cars in place."

"What about the front blockers?" Franks asked.

"That vegetable truck," Laughlin said, pointing, "will move into place and block, and two patrol cars will cover the sidewalks."

"When will the unmarked cars hit their lights and sirens?"

"As soon as the motorcycle rounds the corner."

"Sounds like we're set," Franks said.

"A mouse couldn't squeeze through here," Laughlin said confidently.

Taft and Martinez jumped from the helicopter as soon as it touched down in Union Square Park. They ran across the grass, then down Fourteenth Street. Sprinting toward Fourth Avenue, they watched for the motorcycle that was due in the area in the next few seconds.

Just past Third Avenue on Fourteenth, Tsing glanced in his rearview mirror to change lanes. Three nearly identical sedans formed a rolling roadblock behind him. And then, just as he spotted them, the police cars' sirens started blaring.

Taft and Martinez turned around at the sound of the sirens. The Yamaha carrying Tsing was just behind them. They watched as the Yamaha accelerated past and saw the driver of the motorcycle reaching back to open the rear saddlebags.

Tsing unclipped the chin strap of his helmet and tossed it into the street. It bounced twice and slammed into a parked car. As the vegetable truck moved to block any chance of exit to the front, Tsing swung his head from side to side, searching for a way out.

Taft's feet pounded up the middle of Fourteenth Street as he chased after the motorcycle. Martinez trailed behind. Screaming at the top of his lungs to clear the street, Taft was less than fifty yards behind the slowing motorcycle.

Tsing saw an out. Without a moment's hesitation, he swerved onto the sidewalk and sounded his horn. The commuters climbing up the stairs from the subway at Fourteenth and Fourth noticed the motorcycle heading directly for the entrance, its horn blaring. They began yelling down the stairs to clear a path.

Tsing steered onto the sidewalk and into the entrance for the subway. Jumping to both sides of the stairs, the commuters exiting the subway parted as Tsing steered down the stairs and around the corner. Sliding carefully down the steps, he alternately twisted the throttle then squeezed up the brakes as he maneuvered down the winding steps.

Taft's legs were burning from the headlong run as he entered the subway stairs and took them three at a time.

Tsing reached the lowest level. He rammed his motorcycle into the tollgate which sprung open. Removing the package containing Einstein's papers from the saddlebags, Tsing leapt through the doors of the subway train just as they closed.

Taft leapt over the shattered tollgate just as the subway train pulled out of the station. Bent over from exhaustion, and a sharp pain in his side, he held his badge in the air as the Transit Police arrived. "John Taft, Federal Agent. Stop the train at the next station. It's a matter of national security," he gasped as the rear of the subway train disappeared from view.

CHAPTER 30

As the Chinese cargo ship left Port Isabel, Texas, and steamed through the Brazos Santiago Pass, two seamen wrapped the bodies of Tolbert and his partner in sheets of plastic. Once the two bodies were covered, one of the men grabbed a mop and bucket. Swishing the mop in the soapy water he began to clean the now dried blood from the deck as the cargo ship entered the Gulf of Mexico and veered to the east. Once safely out to sea, the bodies of Tolbert and his partner were unceremoniously tossed from the rear deck.

George Butler, the only one of the three robbers still alive, was sweating uncontrollably. The sweat ran under the wad of paper towels he had taped in place over his shoulder wound. The salt in the sweat stung as it flowed into the open wound, and Butler gritted his teeth as he stood waiting to cross the Mexico–U.S. border at Brownsville. Melting in with the crowd he passed across the bridge and made his way through the streets of Matamoros to a doctor.

"Hunting accident?" the doctor asked in Spanish once Butler was seated in an operating room.

"That's what I said," Butler said wearily.

"That's odd," the doctor said quietly.

"Why?"

"In Mexico we rarely hunt with .38 revolvers," the doctor said as he yanked the slug from Butler's shoulder and began to dress the wound.

When the Chinese cargo ship that was carrying the microbes crossed the Tropic of Cancer at 90 degrees west longitude, the crew began to scan the sky with binoculars for the helicopter they were due to meet. Once the radio in the wheelhouse of the ship alerted the captain the chopper was closing in, he ordered a flare lit.

"To the left," the copilot of the helicopter shouted above the noise of the rotor blades as he spotted the flare.

Banking left, the helicopter came abreast of the cargo ship then hovered over its rear deck. The waves far out in the Gulf of Mexico were causing the Chinese cargo ship to roll from side to side. Matching the roll of the deck, the pilot touched the helicopter down on the deck of the cargo ship. The skids were quickly secured to the deck with chains by the crew and the loading began. Twenty minutes later, with the vat containing the microbes safely tied down in the cargo bay of the helicopter, the pilot lifted off and plotted his return course to Havana.

There the microbes would be transferred to a Chinese jet for the flight to Egypt.

The day had turned hot and sticky. A dog with mange rolled in the dirt, attempting to scratch his fur. In a rusty tin shack with dirt floors, George Butler scored some smack from a Mexican dealer he knew in Matamoros. He was itching to shoot up and make the pain go away. Instead he waited in line to cross back over the bridge into the United States. The loss of blood from the bullet wound was making his head spin. His face was a pasty white. His hand twitched as if he were afflicted by palsy.

A hundred feet away, across the bridge, in the United States, a border patrol agent finished his iced tea and touched his partner on the arm. "Let's detain the next three Americans."

"After that we go to dinner," his partner insisted.

"Standard questions?"

"Sounds fair," the partner agreed.

The first American passed the test with flying colors. A thin trickle of sweat rolled down George Butler's neck as he approached the desk.

"Identification, please."

Butler handed over a Texas driver's license.

"Where are you from?" the border patrol agent inquired.

"Texas," Butler said.

The agent glanced at the first three numbers of Butler's social security number that were on the license. "Where originally?"

Butler had an outstanding warrant from Pueblo, Colorado, the town where he was raised. He decided to lie.

"Born and raised here in South Texas," he said with enthusiasm, hoping a local boy might receive special treatment.

The agent glanced at the numbers again: 522. The card had been issued in Colorado.

"You need to come with me," the agent said, leading Butler away to a private room.

Five minutes later the dog found the drugs.

The next afternoon the Chinese jet carrying the microbes touched down at an abandoned airport outside Al-Jizah, near Cairo. Two hundred American dollars in the hands of the right people was all the bribe it took to insure that the plane would not be disturbed. The vat of microbes was transferred to a waiting six-wheel-drive truck painted with the logo of an international oil field service company. Once the microbes were safely secured in the rear, the truck drove east and crossed the Khalij as-Suways and onto the Sinai Peninsula. On the ground the Chinese jet was refueled and began the long trip back to Beijing, no one the wiser.

At about the same time the truck carrying the microbes crossed near the Suez Canal and began its trek south down the Sinai Peninsula, George Butler was meeting with a public defender in the dank-smelling defendants' room of the Federal Detention Facility in Brownsville, Texas.

"You get the prosecution to agree to a deferred sentence and I'll give them the goods on a double murder," said Butler.

The public defender was a twenty-seven-year-old Mexican-American who had worked in his position nearly three years. The ideological goals that had prompted him to take the job were long gone. The cynicism he felt would last a lifetime.

"The prosecution can't and won't deal on capital crimes," the public defender said wearily.

"You don't understand. I didn't commit the murder," Butler said as he bummed another of the public defender's cigarettes. "Someone tried to kill *me*. I'm pretty sure they got my two partners."

"What were you doing when this all took place?"

"Is anything I tell you confidential?"

"No, I'm an officer of the court," the public defender said, growing wearier by the minute.

"Let's just say something is missing in McAllen," Butler said quietly.

"Let me see what I can find out. Then I'll see what I can do," the public defender said, rising to leave.

"Can you leave me those cigarettes?" Butler asked.

The defender turned from the door as he waited for the guard to come and take Butler back to his cell. "Sure, Georgie boy. Smoke your lungs out."

Two hours later, after he returned to his office, the public defender read a memo that had been sent from the McAllen Police Department. He picked up his phone and placed a call up the river.

The wheels of justice began to spin.

CHAPTER 31

Tsing squeezed through the doors of the subway train as soon as they opened at the Astor Place Station, at Eighth Street. He raced up the stairs leading to ground level, clutching the pouch containing Einstein's papers. Running across Eighth Street, he slipped into the Cooper Union just as a crowd of New York City police officers began pouring down the stairs to the Astor Place subway platform. The first of the officers to reach the platform found the train stopped. The doors were open and the inside of the train was already cleared of passengers.

Tsing walked through the Cooper Union building, then out the back, into Cooper Square. Since the Americans had successfully trailed him from Boston, Tsing reasoned, they would also be smart enough to be watching the Chinese Embassy closely. He would need to make his way to a different embassy, he thought. He searched his mind for a backup plan.

"He got away," Taft explained to Benson over the secure phone as he stood on the Astor Place platform. "Do we have the phones tapped into the Chinese Embassy?"

"They're tapped," Benson noted, "but I doubt he'll try to initiate contact."

"He knows he's being followed. If I were him, I'd make my way to a different embassy. What's the next closest Chinese Embassy?" Taft asked.

"I already checked that out," Benson said. "It's here in Washington."

"Let's hope that's what he decides to do," said Taft.

"That would be my guess," Benson said. "He is definitely not going to escape our net this time. I'm ordering a cocoon of men to cover the area near the embassy. Sharpshooters stationed on the roofs with orders to shoot the man on sight."

"You're going to order him killed?" asked an incredulous Taft.

"No, the sharpshooters will be ordered to shoot for the legs," Benson said quietly. "Just pray he doesn't try to crawl for the entrance."

Taft paused to think. "There's nothing else we can achieve here in New York. Martinez and I should drive south. We'll keep our eyes open for the courier," Taft said wearily. "Maybe we'll get lucky."

"I'll approve that. But when you arrive, if you haven't located the courier, I want you two to take a break," Benson said. "You're not having much luck catching this guy. I think you're too close to the situation."

"Very good, sir," Taft said as he hung up the phone.

Taft turned to Martinez, standing next to him on the platform. "The general's not too happy with us. He wants to pull us from the search once we get back to Washington if we haven't found this guy."

"I guess that leaves us only one choice," Martinez said. "We need to find him and redeem ourselves."

"My idea exactly," Taft said.

They left immediately, following the route they believed the courier would take.

CHAPTER 32

Six hours later, after the fake oil-service truck carrying the microbes left Al-Jizah, Egypt, it passed At-Tur. The road the truck followed paralleled the Gulf of Suez since crossing onto the Sinai Peninsula. Within the next hour the truck would follow the road turning east briefly at the southern tip of the peninsula. Next the truck would head north along the Gulf of Aqaba before continuing on until reaching Dhahab. A scorpion darted onto the road, then retreated. Nervously twitching, it darted back onto the road just as the truck passed. Crushed by the truck's tire, the scorpion was unceremoniously tossed to the side.

Chup Cho-Sing sat in the passenger seat and once again read the timetable Sun Tao had presented him before he left Beijing. "We are right on time," he noted to the driver, who glanced at his watch and nodded.

"Once we round the tip it should take another three hours to reach Dhahab," the driver said as he swerved to avoid a mound of sand that had blown onto the road.

"Then I will try to sleep," Cho-Sing said as he scrunched down in his seat and pulled his hat over his eyes. "Wake me when we are close."

In Beijing the sun was nearly below the horizon. Inside the prime minister's office the light was growing dim. Sun Tao smiled across the desk.

"Just like we planned, our SPD agents inside Israel report

they have the bombs in place. They are standing by to activate them at our command," Tao said to the prime minister.

The prime minister nodded. "These oil-eating bugs, you are sure they will work?"

"We tested a small sample today. The results were horrifying. However, once they are in place two days from now, we'll know for sure they will work on the reservoirs."

"Your plan is outstanding. We blame the microbes in the oil on radical Israelis. Then the bombs we explode in Israel are blamed on Saudi retaliation," the prime minister said quietly.

"Yes," Tao said, "it would seem a flawless plan."

"Quite brilliant. The war that ensues should draw the Americans to the region and allow us the opportunity to liberate Taiwan. After the liberation is complete and we have strengthened our position we can move against Vietnam and the rest of Southeast Asia."

"We can be certain the Americans will rally their troops to protect their precious oil supply," Tao agreed, "and that will leave the Asian region with a limited United States military presence. Our advisors feel they won't try to stop us from liberating Taiwan unless they possess overwhelming force. It seems that for the last few years the Americans' policy is never to fight a war they are not sure they can win."

"All appears to favor our side," the prime minister agreed. "Have we heard from the courier who holds the Einstein papers yet?"

"Not yet. Our embassy in New York reported they were being closely watched by American agents," Tao noted.

"Those papers are the key to our ultimate success."

"I'm sure our courier Tsing realized the New York embassy was being watched and diverted to his alternate plan."

"The alternate location is Washington, D.C.," the prime minister noted. "Do we have a ship in place to facilitate the delivery of the papers and the courier's escape?"

"I have already taken care of it," Tao noted.

"The time will be tight," the prime minister noted. "October 1st is fast approaching."

In the Middle East, three hours and twenty minutes later, the truck carrying the microbes pulled to a stop in front of a large canvas tent that was erected on the sands outside Dhahab. The air was tinder dry. The night sky was a black carpet dotted with the twinkling lights from thousands of stars overhead. From outside the tent the fuel oil lanterns lighting the inside of the tent made it appear to be glowing. On Chou-Sing's orders, several men raised the flaps of the tent and the truck containing the microbes drove inside. Cho-Sing motioned to the man in charge of the operation in Dhahab. "Remove the vat from the rear of the truck, then begin to fill the smaller tanks as planned."

The foreman shouted instructions to his helpers to begin the work then followed Cho-Sing to a cooler of water nearby. He waited as Cho-Sing drank.

"Have you arranged the boat to carry us across the gulf?" Cho-Sing asked when he had finished and wiped the back of his hand across his mouth.

"Yes," the man said and the noise from a generator arose. This was followed by the sound of an air compressor filling its reservoir.

Cho-Sing nodded, then walked over to watch the operation in progress. A pile of stainless-steel tanks lay in one corner of the tent. The tops of the tanks were threaded and contained a valve stem that had been welded in place. After the men unscrewed the tops of the tanks, the microbes, which were suspended in a gray-green viscous fluid, were added until they reached a mark inside the tanks. Next the caps were screwed back on and the mixture pressurized with air from the compressor. As soon as the tanks were filled, they were reloaded in the rear of the six-wheeled truck.

Forty minutes later the flaps of the tent were pulled back and the truck drove to the water to meet the ferry boat that would transport it across the Gulf of Aqaba. Three hours later Cho-Sing and the truck were inside Saudi Arabia, driving toward the oil fields. The deadly cargo of microbes was reaching the end of its long journey.

CHAPTER 33

Benson glanced across his desk at Taft and Martinez. "I have the embassy covered," he reiterated. "You two are to resume doing the system check with the contractor in Potomac Beach. He has scheduled a test for tomorrow afternoon."

"That hardly seems fair," Martinez said. "John has been on this since the beginning. If he hadn't brought Li Choi out of China and then discovered Einstein's boat we'd already be screwed."

"Thanks, Larry," Taft said, smiling. "I had no idea you felt this way about me."

"No problem," Martinez said.

"You two cut the Heckel and Jeckel routine," Benson said. "It's time you took a break. I want you to go home and get some rest. And *you*, Taft, I want you to shave."

"But—" Taft started to say.

"No buts. Get out of my office and go home," Benson said in a voice that defied argument.

With the meeting obviously at an impasse, Taft and Martinez glanced at one another, then rose from their chairs simultaneously. "Very good, sir," Taft said as the pair began walking toward the door.

Closing the door to Benson's office behind them, they walked down the hall to the elevator. Taft rubbed the stubble on his face with the palm of his hand.

"This bites," Taft said to Martinez as they waited for the elevator.

Martinez nodded. He was angry, Taft could tell, but he said nothing. The elevator arrived and carried the men to the ground floor. The two men walked past the security desk silently.

"I'm going home. Give me a call later," Martinez said as they walked into the parking lot.

"I have to return the rental car, then catch a ride over to Andrews to pick up my car. I'll call you when I'm back at my house."

A stiff wind was forming peaked whitecaps on the waters of Chesapeake Bay. Most of the boats on the bay today were work boats. Fishermen, crabbers, Coast Guard, and U.S. Navy vessels. The few birds aloft were buffeted by the winds like kites in a cyclone.

One of the few ships leaving port in Norfolk, Virginia, appeared to casual observation to be simply a rather large crabber. The ship was maintained but far from spotless. The bow paint was stained with rust near the anchor hawser. The diesel engines smoked a little more than necessary. A large crane in the center of the stern deck could be used to hoist the pots filled with crab onto the deck. The proliferation of radio antennas could be explained by the personal need of a captain who craved accurate navigation. The lack of fish smell was harder to explain, but you would have to be aboard to notice that. As to the mini-sub in the center of the crab pots covered in netting, there was no logical explanation why that would be aboard a crab boat.

The explanation was simple: the *Carondelet* was no crab boat.

Two hours later, Taft pulled his car into his garage and shut the door. Walking to his house, he unlocked the door then carried the pile of newspapers on his porch to his kitchen. He snapped off the rubber bands and glanced at the headlines. Finding little of interest, he returned to the front door and walked out to the mail box to retrieve his mail. As he walked back inside he removed the bills and stacked them in a pile on the kitchen table. Then he grubbed around in the refrigerator, and, finding nothing that was less than a few weeks old, took a frozen pizza from the freezer. After the oven had warmed, he slid the pizza onto the rack, set the timer, and walked upstairs to take a shower and shave. He was back downstairs in the kitchen again when the phone rang.

"It's me," Martinez said.

"What time should we meet tomorrow?"

"I'll pick you up. Your house is on the way to Potomac Beach."

"That's fine. What time?" Taft asked again.

"The test doesn't start until late afternoon. How about two P.M.?"

"I can hardly wait," Taft said as he hung up the phone.

Taft thought about calling one of his girlfriends, then decided against it. He desperately needed sleep. Walking wearily up the stairs, he climbed into bed and slept for the next twelve hours. When he awoke his disposition had improved.

Tsing spent the night in a run-down boardinghouse above a Chinese restaurant on the edge of Chinatown. The boardinghouse wasn't linked to a computer and the guests were not required to fill out any registration cards. He rose early and slipped out of the room without being seen. His breakfast was two plums that he bought from a street vendor, and he washed it down with a bottle of water purchased at a neighborhood store. Last night, after checking into the boardinghouse, he had trimmed his hair short. After buying clothes from a rack on the street and changing in a public restroom, his appearance resembled any of the thousands of Chinese who made their home in New York.

Making his way to the main bus terminal he scanned the outside for signs that it was being watched. Several marked police cars were parked in front, but he doubted that was unusual. Entering the terminal he made his way toward the ticket window. Several plainclothes detectives were checking the crowd, but they hardly glanced at Tsing as he purchased his ticket. He waited until his bus was called, then made his way aboard without incident. He sat nervously in his seat and didn't relax until the bus was past Newark and motoring down Interstate 95.

Arriving in Baltimore in early afternoon, Tsing stole a car from the long-term parking lot at Baltimore's airport using a plastic key that molded itself to the ignition tumblers, then drove south on Highway 301 to Lanham, Maryland. There he pulled into a gas station and used the pay phone to call the Chinese Embassy in Washington, D.C., for instructions.

It was his only mistake so far.

CHAPTER 34

It was six minutes past three in the morning when the truck carrying Chup Cho-Sing and his assistant pulled to its final stop, an oil pumping station deep inside Saudi Arabia. Cho-Sing walked among the tangled mess of piping until he found the spot he was looking for, then ordered his assistant to dig down into the soft sand.

Once the hole was sufficiently deep, he motioned for the assistant to help him carry one of the tanks from the back of the truck. Burying the tank in the hole, he connected a hose from the valve stem fitting directly to a pressure release valve, then stood back and admired his work.

"Wellhead number 6. That completes this operation," he said to his assistant. "The light of day will soon be upon us. Do you want to sleep? I can handle the first leg of the drive back to the Gulf of Aqaba."

The assistant nodded wearily. He raised a broom in his hand. "I will erase our footprints as before," he said as he began sweeping.

Cho-Sing walked back to the truck and reached under the seat for a package. Removing the nylon pouch he removed the clip and checked to make sure it was loaded. Cocking the weapon to load a round in the chamber, he placed it in his front pants pocket and walked back toward the wellhead. Cho-Sing felt no remorse for what he was about to do. He calmly waited until the man had finished sweeping.

The assistant's head was bent over, sweeping the last spot of sand when the slug from the silenced pistol pierced the base of his skull, killing him instantly. Cho-Sing dragged the man off a short distance and tossed the body in a gully. Soon the sand crabs would come by land and the vultures by air. In less than a week, the bones would be picked clean. The assistant's body would never be found.

"Well, that about does it," George Butler said.

Though the murders Butler finally disclosed had been committed in Port Isabel, the chief of police, Anthony Hill, knew his small department was ill-equipped to handle the investigation. In the first place, Hill had no bodies. In the second place, he presided over a force of three, not including the dispatcher. He had been less than excited when the assistant district attorney in Brownsville explained the case. Hill decided to call his friend, who was the chief of police in McAllen, for advice.

"I heard about it," the chief in McAllen said after Hill explained. "A deal was cut with the perp. He came clean for a deferred sentence. Your murder is supposedly tied to a theft that occurred here in McAllen. I'll tell you what, Tony. I recommend you do what I did."

"What's that?" Hill asked.

"Turn it over to the Texas Rangers," the chief in McAllen said easily. "One of the rangers is already here. Do you want me to send him down there?"

"Could you?" Hill asked.

"No problem," the chief said as he hung up.

That afternoon, when the ranger filed his first report about the theft of the microbes, a computer copy was forwarded to the Special Security Service as required. The report from Texas ended up in the Terrorist Technology Division.

NIA Special Agent Sandra Miles began to read the report with interest.

❖   ❖   ❖

Jeff McBride shook the rain off his camouflaged rain slicker before entering his hotel room. He hung the dripping coat on a hanger and began to towel off his sopping hair. When McBride had joined the CIA just out of college, he never thought his assignments would be so boring. He had watched the *Carondelet* patiently for three days as it sat in port in Norfolk. Now that the ship had steamed from port, his assignment was finished and he could return home. With a loud sneeze he added the last notations to the ongoing report on his laptop, then plugged it into the phone line and faxed it to the CIA headquarters in Langley.

CHAPTER 35

The monitoring station for the western oil fields of Saudi Arabia sat baking in the desert sun. Clad in green smoked glass, the building seemed to undulate in the hot air. The area surrounding the building was bleak—acres of sand ringed by a chain-link fence. A few scruffy plants growing from the wasteland did little to alleviate the monotony of the endless expanse of desert. A scorpion peered from his hole atop a hill near the building then slid back inside out of the heat. The temperature was 120 degrees Fahrenheit in the shade.

Inside the building the temperature was considerably cooler; the finest air conditioners money could buy were silently attacking the heat. On the second floor of the building Jackson Trumball slid a fishing magazine into his desk drawer, then looked over at his Saudi partner, Nazir Hametz.

"It's my turn to do the readings," he said, rising from his chair.

Hametz nodded and motioned to the clipboard on his desk. "After that we can go to lunch."

Trumball grabbed the clipboard and walked to the bank of gauges and flashing lights that covered the far wall. He began to enter the readings onto the sheet. Ten minutes later, after Trumball had finished, he entered the data into the computer, then brushed his hair in front of a mirror hanging on the wall.

"What's the special today?" Trumball asked Hametz in a light Texas drawl.

Hametz glanced at the lunch menu hanging by the door. "Looks like Italian," he said as he twisted the doorknob and opened the door.

"Has to beat lamb," Trumball said as he followed Hametz to the cafeteria.

Seventy miles to the north of the monitoring building, at King Khalid Well No. 47, a drop in natural gas pressure automatically signaled to the well to cease pumping. As happened several times a day, some gas was expelled from the pressure release valve. As the valve released the gas, the Enviorco microbes were injected into the well pipe. The microbes began to multiply instantly. They continued downward, eating everything in their path. King Khalid Well No. 47 would soon be as dry as the surrounding land.

Returning from the cafeteria, Hametz burped lightly, then, because it was his turn, reached for the clipboard on Trumball's desk. He began to record the readings from the oil wells on the sheet of paper. Six minutes later he noticed the problem.

"Red light on Khalid number 47," he said to Trumball.

"I noticed a low-pressure reading on that well on the last check. She's been doing that a lot lately."

Hametz tapped the light to see if it was jammed, but it remained glowing. "Call the service people to check it out."

"Okay," Trumball said. Reaching for the telephone, he dialed the field supervisor. "This is Jackson Trumball in monitoring. We have a red light on number 47, northeast King Khalid Field. Do you have a crew nearby that can check it out?"

The static over the phone line made the supervisor sound like he was in a shower. "Northeast Khalid 47?"

"That's the one," Trumball shouted.

"Hold on."

Trumball could hear the man talking in Arabic in the background. "It'll be about twenty minutes," the supervisor said when he came back on the line. "My crew has to load some corrosion testing equipment in the truck. Then we'll drive over. Give me your extension, I'll call you back."

Trumball gave him the extension number and the phone went dead.

"Make sure you note that number 47 is out when you fax that report," he said to Hametz.

Hametz grunted in reply, then sat down at his desk and finished the report.

Twenty minutes later the service supervisor of the King Khalid field, Jake Long, slid his Ford truck to a stop in front of King Khalid Well No. 47.

Motioning to his workers for help, he hoisted a remote color camera assembly from the rear and dragged it toward the well. Removing the bolts securing the wellhead with a wrench, he dropped the tiny camera into the casing, then fed out some cable. Next, he switched on the television screen and adjusted the contrast.

"Feed the cable down slowly and stop when I tell you," he said to one of the workers.

As the camera was fed downward, Long stared at the image on the screen. The camera shot a panoramic view, showing the pipe as a tube looking from above. Long stood in shock, trying to comprehend this image from deep inside the earth. The sides of the pipe, normally coated with oil, were devoid of all petroleum. In the place of oil was a gray-green substance that looked like mucus.

Returning to his truck, Long bought back a fishing tool with a scooped cup. Attaching the cup to the end of a flexible metal shaft, he slowly fed the instrument down the well opening. As the cup reached the level of the camera, Long watched the screen carefully.

"Manipulating a joystick that moved the cup, he scooped up a sample of the gray-green liquid and then retracted the shaft. When it reached the top of the well, Long dipped his fingers into the liquid.

"Looks like baby shit," he said to one of the workers standing nearby.

"Smells like it too," the worker noted.

Long walked to the truck and picked up the phone.

CHAPTER 36

Jeff Scaramelli glanced out the window of the laboratory at the Advanced Physics Center in Boulder, Colorado. A lone female robin was yanking a worm from the turf with its sharp beak. The robin slipped one end of the worm inside its mouth, then tilted her head back and swallowed. Bouncing a tennis ball against the glass and catching it in his hand, Scaramelli turned and glanced at Choi.

"Aurora Borealis," Scaramelli stated.

"That's right. High-vacuum, high-power electrical discharges in the upper atmosphere," said Choi.

"The solar wind colliding with the earth's magnetic field."

"So you think that Einstein was trying to use the earth's magnetic field to prove his theory?" Scaramelli asked.

"Maybe. What if the earth's magnetic field altered gravity? It would be almost imperceptible at any given location, yet small variances could add up to big results," Choi said, scratching his head with the eraser on a pencil.

"So we want to amplify the background magnetism and introduce electrical discharges. How do we simulate gravity?"

"That's the problem," Choi agreed.

Scaramelli walked over to a workbench in the laboratory and picked up one of the items from the hardware store. He felt the heft in his hand, then tossed it into the air and caught it. Polishing the orb on his pants leg, he stared at Choi.

"Why don't we drill a hole through the center of this," Scaramelli said.

"For what purpose?"

"We thread the center with a copper wire and introduce electricity."

Choi nodded slowly. "It's worth a try."

"We have a fabrication shop here at the center," Scaramelli noted. "Follow me."

Pausing to lock the laboratory, the two men walked down the hallway to a set of stairs. They took the stairway to the second floor and walked down to the fabrication shop. A man dressed in machinist's clothing switched off a milling machine as they entered and sauntered over.

"Afternoon, Jeff," he said easily.

"Bobby Escerson, Li Choi," Scaramelli said, making the introduction.

Escerson was tall, a shade over six feet three inches in height.

Though his face was slightly weathered, with a world weariness that said he had seen it all, his smile lit up the room. His hair was blond but flecked with gray at the temples. His hands were large slabs of meat with the proud callouses of a man who knew what work was. Escerson was fifty-two years old but looked barely forty.

Choi recovered his hand from Escerson's paw and pointed to his ballcap. "I'm a Broncos fan too."

"Then we'll get along just fine," Escerson said, smiling. "What can I do for you men?"

Scaramelli lifted the orb in his hand and passed it to Escerson. "I need a hole drilled in the center of this."

"What are you planning to do with it?"

"Run copper wire through the hole and electrically charge the wire," Scaramelli said.

Escerson nodded and walked over to a series of drawers above his workbench. Removing a spool of copper wire, he motioned Scaramelli and Choi over.

"You want this thickness?"

"Thicker," Scaramelli said.

Escerson replaced the wire and opened another drawer. "How about this?"

"Do you have one size thicker?" Choi asked.

Escerson nodded and opened a third drawer. He looked at Scaramelli and Choi and raised an eyebrow.

"That should do it," Scaramelli said.

Escerson closed the drawer and placed the spool of wire on his workbench. "Is this going to hang from the wire," he asked, "like a pendant?"

"Not really," Scaramelli said. "It needs to be suspended in place."

Escerson nodded. "So you'll need a stand."

"Something that holds the copper wire taut," Choi said.

"Magnetic or nonmagnetic?" Escerson asked.

"We're going to charge the copper wire with electricity," Scaramelli said.

Escerson nodded then stared into the distance for a second. "I'll weld you a small stand out of iron with two flanges that come from the sides. That will allow you to hook the positive and negative leads to the stand. The copper wire will come over the sides and attach to the flanges. I'll tighten the wire as I attach it, suspending this ball exactly in the center."

Scaramelli looked befuddled.

Escerson reached for a yellow pad on his bench, then grabbed a carpenter's pencil from a slot on his machinist's coat. He quickly sketched out a diagram.

"Like this," he said when he was almost finished.

Choi and Scaramelli stared at the diagram and nodded.

"One more question," Escerson asked. "Do you want the ball to be able to spin freely?"

Scaramelli looked at Choi, who nodded. "Would that be hard to do?"

"Not if you tell me now," Escerson said.

"Yeah, have it spin freely," said Scaramelli.

"No problem," Escerson said. "How soon do you need it?"

"As soon as possible," Choi said.

Escerson glanced at the part he was machining when the pair entered. "Okay, I can put off what I'm working on now and start on this. If I work late I should have it built by six or seven tonight."

Escerson turned and began to remove an iron plate from below his workbench.

"Thanks, Bobby," Scaramelli said as the pair turned to leave. "We'll buy dinner tonight. What are you hungry for?"

Escerson never glanced up from the iron plate he was turning over in his hands. "I like Thai food, Jeff," he said quietly.

As Choi and Scaramelli left the fabrication shop, Escerson was already marking the iron plate to saw.

❋   ❋   ❋

At 6:47 that evening Escerson buzzed Scaramelli in his laboratory. "You can come and pick it up," he said.

Scaramelli was carrying a Styrofoam container of Thai food as the two men entered the fabrication shop, where most of the lights had already been extinguished. A small pile of iron shavings had been carefully broomed into a pile. Escerson was washing his hands at a stainless-steel sink.

"It's there on the bench," he said.

Illuminated in the glow from a fluorescent light above the bench sat a two-foot-tall iron apparatus. Twin wings rose from the base plate, suspending the ball on the copper wire. The piece had been painstakingly machined and welded with precision. The flanges that attached to the sides were devoid of paint and highly polished. The ball itself was exactly level.

Choi walked over to the bench, and touched his finger to the ball. Moving his finger slightly the ball began spinning freely. Escerson walked over and took the Styrofoam contained from Scaramelli's hand.

"If you men don't need anything else, I'm going to take this home and eat it," he said with a satisfied grin.

"This is amazing," Scaramelli said.

Escerson reached behind his bench, removed a cardboard box, and placed the apparatus inside. Handing it to Scaramelli, he flicked off the light over the bench. He motioned for the door and followed the men to the stairs, clutching his bicycle helmet.

"Be careful not to drop that, Jeff," he said easily. "Everything should be aligned just right now."

The men reached the bottom of the stairs and Escerson began to buckle his helmet.

"Buzz me tomorrow and let me know how it worked," he said as he walked through the door to the parking lot.

Scaramelli smiled, and Choi said, "Let's go experiment."

CHAPTER 37

Sandra Miles had the healthy good looks of a Minnesota farm girl. She was beautiful without being cute, witty without being coy. One of thirty female agents employed by the Special Security Service, she had long ago learned that a sense of humor went a long way in dealing with men. It was early morning as she walked from the commercial jet at the Harlingen airport. Spotting the Texas Ranger immediately, she walked over with her carry-on bag draped from her shoulder. "One crisis, one ranger," she said, smiling.

The joke was one that had followed the Texas Rangers for years. It heralded back to a time in history when the Rangers had been called to southern Texas to quell a riot. When a lone ranger arrived and checked in with the local sheriff, the sheriff said, "They only sent one of you?" "One riot, one ranger," the ranger had replied. It turned out that a lone ranger was all that was needed.

"It seems you know our history," the ranger said. "Mark Carlton."

Carlton thrust out his hand and received a firm shake from Miles.

"I like history," Miles said as the pair walked through the airport toward Carlton's Bronco.

"Do you want me to help you with that bag?"

"I'm a big girl," Miles said. "My only question is just who do I have to sleep with to get some information?"

Carlton laughed as Miles tossed her bag in the back of the Bronco. "You're the first fed I think I'm going to enjoy working with," he said as he unlocked the truck and climbed into the driver's seat.

Steering through the Harlingen traffic Carlton got onto Interstate 77 for the short trip to Brownsville. "I originally was called down from Austin about the theft of a vat of microbes from a laboratory in McAllen," Carlton said as he engaged the cruise control and settled in for the drive.

"What about the murders?" Miles said.

"The druggie copping the deal and telling us about the murders was just frosting on the cake. I'm assuming you're more interested in the loss of the microbes."

"That's correct. Our office was concerned what might happen if terrorists got hold of the bugs." Miles glanced at a thermos wedged between the seats. "Mind if I have a cup of that coffee?"

"Help yourself."

"Thanks. Anyway, our thinking was that in the hands of terrorists the microbes could be introduced into things like the lubricating oil in power transformers, commercial jet engines, that sort of thing. Terrorists could definitely raise some havoc if they put those bugs in the right places."

Miles twisted the cap back on the thermos and sipped the steaming coffee.

Carlton stared out the windshield and thought for a few moments. "That's a distinct possibility, Agent Miles."

"Call me Sandra."

"All right, Sandra. Like I said, that's a possibility, but terrorists could do the same thing with metal shavings, or even sand. The particular batch of microbes that was stolen was somewhat unique," Carlton said as they passed over Highway 100 leading east to Port Isabel and Padre Island.

"Your report didn't go into much detail about that. What makes them unique?" Miles asked.

"These microbes need no oxygen. They can be injected deep into the ground, not just used on surface spills."

"Into wells?" Miles asked.

"You got it," Carlton said slowly.

"How much oil could the single vat that was stolen dissolve?"

"All the oil in Texas," Carlton said as they approached Brownsville.

"This is becoming more interesting all the time," Miles said, then finished her coffee and screwed the cap back on the thermos.

"They'll roll the robbery and drug charge into one and I plead guilty to a misdemeanor charge of possession of drug paraphernalia?" Butler asked.

"That's the deal, George," the public defender said.

"And a deferred sentence on the misdemeanor?"

"Stay clean two years and cooperate fully with the authorities and the charge is wiped off your record."

Butler sat back and took a drag on his cigarette. "I'll take it," he said. "Now, when do I get out of here?"

"You can go in front of the judge this afternoon," the public defender said. "Right after you talk to the feds."

"I'll need a ride back home once I'm released."

"You get your own ride home, Georgie boy," the public defender said, rising. "I may be a lot of things, but I ain't a taxi."

Sandra Miles tossed a fresh pack of cigarettes on the table. "Where did the first meeting take place?" she asked Butler.

"I knew Billy Tolbert from Huntsville. We met the buyer at the Texas Topps—that's a strip joint outside McAllen."

"Did the buyer say what he needed the microbes for?"

"I didn't ask," Butler said.

"Did you notice anything unusual about the buyer?"

"He was a slope," Butler noted.

"Excuse me—a what?" Miles asked.

"You know, a slope," Butler said as he took a drag from his cigarette. "An Asian."

"Do you know what country in Asia he was from?"

"I'm not sure. I was in Korea in the army and this guy didn't look Korean. I also worked for some Vietnamese shrimpers for a while. He wasn't cheap enough to be Vietnamese. He paid for a couple of table dances for Billy and me. The one thing I do remember is that the cigarettes I bummed from him tasted like shit." Butler paused and thought back. "And the pack had a weird design on the front."

Miles rose. "You wait here. I'm going to call my office."

"Is it going to take long?"

"Would you rather we return you to your cell," Carlton asked menacingly, "and send for you when we're ready?"

"No, sir," Butler said. "I'll just sit right here. You know, if that's okay."

Miles walked to an office in the Brownsville jail and dialed her partner at the NIA in Maryland.

"Hey, Smoot. I need you to do me a favor," she said when her partner answered. "Log onto the database and pull up a file that contains information about tobacco companies."

"You thinking of joining a class-action suit?" Smoot said, laughing.

"Hardly."

"Hold on a second," Smoot said. Two minutes passed. "Okay, I'm there. What do you need?"

"Can you find a listing of the graphics on cigarette packs?"

"I'm sure we have something," Smoot said. "It's a good way to identify suspects we're trailing."

Minutes passed as Smoot scrolled through the file listings.

"Hold on, I might have something here." The phone was silent as Smoot retrieved the file. "I got it, Sandra, but there's a couple of hundred listings."

"Pull out all the brands from Asia." Miles could hear Smoot at work on the keyboard.

"There's seventy-seven known brands, including those sold in the Philippines."

"They sure like to smoke over there," Miles noted. "Can you fax me pictures of the graphics on the packs?"

"If I reduce them to the size of a regular pack of cigarettes, I can fit six to a page. What's that make it?" Smoot quickly did the math in his head. "Should be thirteen pages, five on the last page. Give me the number you're at and stand by."

Miles read off the number of the jail's fax machine. She waited as the fax phone rang, then began printing. Scanning the first page she returned to the phone. "Looks good, Smooty."

"What else can I do for you?"

"Nothing right now, but I'll call you later," Miles said.

Miles walked back to the fax machine and removed the pages of cigarette-pack graphics.

"You feds are quite high tech," Carlton noted.

"You should see our budget. It's amazing," Miles said, smiling. "I want to begin showing these to Butler. Will you bring the rest of the pages after they print out?"

"I'd be glad to," Carlton said as Miles walked back to the holding cell.

Butler looked through the first pile without success.

"There's more on the way," Miles said. "Let me hear the story again. You deliver the microbes to a ship in Port Isabel, and the same man who met you at the strip club then shoots Tolbert and your other partner. Is that correct?"

"That's about the size of it," Butler said.

"Do you remember the name of the ship?"

"It was a rusty old cargo ship, it might have been called *Silt River*, something like that. Anyway, it was two words."

"Was it flying an American flag?"

"No, that I do remember. I looked back when I was a safe

distance away. I remember the smoke was increasing from the stacks as the ship prepared to pull away from the dock, but I could still see the flag off the fantail. The flag was all red with a star in the corner."

"You're sure the star was in the corner?" Miles said as Carlton opened the door.

"Yeah, pretty sure," Butler said.

Carlton handed the remaining pages to Butler, who slowly glanced at each page.

"There it is," he said, pointing to page nine. "That's the brand."

Miles followed Butler's finger to a picture of a waterfall flanked by two panda bears. She swiveled the sheet around and read the caption below. Panda Giants brand. Country of manufacture was listed as the People's Republic of China.

"Thanks," Miles said, and she stood up.

"Make sure you tell the judge I cooperated," Butler said as Miles and Carlton walked from the interview room.

"It will be duly noted," Carlton said with contempt.

CHAPTER 38

Benson leaned back in his chair opposite his second-in-command, Assistant Special Security Director Richard Allbright.

"The Saudi government received a threat claiming someone was planning to wipe out their oil fields?" Benson said, incredulously.

"The written demand stated they must recognize the Israeli state or their oil reservoirs would be destroyed," Allbright said and then read from his note pad, "The exact quote was, 'A divine wrath will befall your wealth. The curse of oil has provided you a means to oppose the Jewish state. If you do not recognize Israel's right to exist we will remove the curse forever.' End quote."

"What group claimed responsibility?" Benson asked.

"The Jewish Front for Recognition," Allbright said, glancing at his briefing sheet again. "We have no records of such a group."

Benson swiveled in his chair and glanced out the window. His thoughts were broken by the telephone buzzing. "Yes, Mrs. Mindio."

"Sorry to disturb you, sir. I know you left instructions to hold your calls, but this is important."

"That's okay, go ahead and explain," Benson said.

"The duty officer just left a fresh communiqué. There has been a series of explosions in Israel. There was over—" Mrs. Mindio began to say.

"Bring it here, please," Benson said.

Mrs. Mindio entered Benson's office and placed the report on the desk. She quickly retreated back to the outer office. Benson read the papers rapidly, then handed them to Allbright.

"The NIA will be called in on this, Dick. Our agency's primary charter is antiterrorism. Begin a class-one file—I want you to pull out all the stops to gather information. Cull through all the other agencies' files and see what you can find. Next have someone get me a Defense Department reading on our possible military response—I want to know what military units are being moved to the area to counter the threat. We may need to coordinate a joint operation if we send our agents into the area."

Allbright rose from his chair as Benson's phone rang.

"Get me some real-time data, Dick, as fast as possible. We have some decisions to make before the president calls," Benson said as he grabbed the ringing phone.

Allbright scurried from Benson's office.

Benson lifted the telephone receiver to his ear. "This is

Colonel Thompson at the NSA. We just intercepted a telephone call from a pay phone in Maryland to the Chinese Embassy in Washington. The party at the pay phone asked where he should deliver the package. The party at the embassy replied the 'river drop-off.' That was the entire message."

"Where was the pay phone?" Benson asked.

"Near a town named Lanham," Thompson replied.

"Excellent," Benson said.

"We'll keep monitoring for you, sir," Thompson said and hung up.

Benson leaned back in his chair. First China, now the Middle East. He reached in his desk drawer and removed an orange, which he peeled and began eating. It would turn out he would have no time for lunch.

Before he had eaten a slice of the orange he was already dialing his phone. "Get me a 7.5-minute topographic map of Maryland near the town of Lanham," he ordered his research division.

Benson dialed again.

"Dick," Benson said to Allbright, who had just entered his office, "I need an assessment of what countries would enter the fray if Saudi Arabia and Israel go to war."

CHAPTER 39

The call from Long to his supervisor brought swift action. A white-colored Bell Jet Ranger helicopter flew low over the desert to King Khalid Well No. 47. The sun was below the horizon and the remaining light cast a strange orange glow over the sand.

In the rear of the helicopter, Tom Temple, a geologist employed by Aramco, the Saudi-American company that operated the oil field, checked his equipment once again, then tightened his seat belt.

The pilot spoke into the intercom strapped to his head. "We're five minutes out, Mr. Temple."

Temple watched from the window as they approached the well. The tiny dots on the ground became well pumps and trucks as they flew nearer. Temple could see the tracks across the sands the trucks had made as they drove to the well. It looked as if the service workers were a caravan of old, descending on an oasis. But King Khalid Well No. 47 was no oasis; it was the dusty wind that signals a drought is coming.

The helicopter pilot flew straight toward the well and landed twenty yards away.

Shutting off the engines, he turned to Temple. "Do you need help with that equipment?"

Temple glanced at several oil-field hands who were already running toward the helicopter. "I'll get one of the roustabouts to help."

"In that case," the pilot said, "I need to place sand covers over my air intakes. My instructions were to wait on the ground until you finish," he said as he climbed from the pilot's seat.

A light wind blew from the north, stirring the fallen leaves that were scattered around the grounds of the White House. Inside the Oval Office, Robert Lakeland glanced at his notes again, then continued the briefing.

"The Israeli government received a letter from a group calling itself the "Islamic Sword." They claim they are based in Saudi Arabia, and the bombings in Jerusalem were retaliation for, and I quote, 'The poisoning of our God-given source of wealth.' End quote.

"Poisoning of our God-given source of wealth," the president repeated. "What are they talking about?"

"We have a meeting scheduled with our ambassador in Riyadh in an attempt to determine what the Islamic Sword's talking about. However, Mr. President, that is still several hours away. Whatever the case is, we have a more pressing concern."

"What is that, Robert?"

"Both sides have begun to amass troops in preparation for war. The Israeli military is moving an armored column south to Elat, on the Gulf of Aqaba. From there they can initiate an amphibious assault on Saudi Arabia in a matter of hours. Or, if they choose, their troops can drive through the tip of Jordan and attack en masse," Lakeland said.

"What would be the Jordanian response if that happens?" the president asked.

"The analysts believe that Jordan would be drawn into the skirmish," Lakeland said.

"And the Saudis? What steps have they taken?"

"They have moved a battalion of troops north toward the border. They are forming a defense perimeter from Aynunah on the Gulf of Aqaba in an arc to Tabuk, then on to the border with Jordan. They have asked for additional troops from Oman, the United Arab Emirates, Qatar, and Kuwait to assist them."

"What has the other countries' response been?" the president asked.

"It appears every country Saudi Arabia contacted agreed to help," Lakeland said, glancing at his notes. "Not only that, intelligence suggests that Egypt is mobilizing their armed forces without being contacted. It seems the Egyptians are just waiting to be asked to join the fray."

"What about the nuclear and biological capability of each side?" the president asked grimly.

"Our analysts are almost unanimous about that. They seem

to feel both sides possess at least some of each type of weapon," Lakeland answered directly.

"What's the worst-case scenario if this thing explodes into war?" the president asked as he rubbed his temples with his fingertips.

Lakeland removed a sheet from the pile in front of him and read aloud. "The Israelis or the Saudis attack the other side. As the battle rages on, Iraq again moves against Kuwait. Iran, fearing Iraq will grow in power, sends troops across the Strait of Hormuz to attack Oman and the United Arab Emirates, thus securing access to the Persian Gulf."

"The entire Middle East would then be at war," the president said, shaking his head as if wishing he could toss off the problem.

"That's about the size of it," Lakeland agreed.

"Get the chairman of the Joint Chiefs of Staff in here, posthaste," the president said. "I want an immediate redeployment of a sizable contingent of United States troops to the Middle East. Next, call the ambassadors for Israel and Saudi Arabia. Let's see what we can achieve with diplomacy tempered with the implied threat of military intervention."

"Very good, sir," Lakeland said as he rose and raced from the Oval Office.

"One last thing, Robert," the president said as Lakeland paused at the door to the Oval Office. "Get Benson from the NIA to explain to me what this Islamic Sword is. I want to know who we're dealing with."

"Right away, sir," Lakeland said as he rushed off.

Jake Long peered through the microscope Temple had set on a table next to King Khalid Well No. 47. The oil sands under magnification were retrieved from deep inside the ground. They glowed with an eerie incandescence.

"What the hell is this stuff?" Long asked.

"I think it's an oil-eating microbe. And it's reproducing at an alarming rate," Temple said.

"It must have been injected from that tank my crew removed from the wellhead," Long said. "That tank had no business on this well, I can tell you that."

"That would be my guess," Temple said as he walked toward the helicopter. "I'd better contact my office."

Once inside the helicopter, Temple reached his office on the radio. "This is Temple. Get me Farouk Aziz, please," he shouted to the radio dispatcher.

Long's roustabouts had removed the sampling tool from the wellhead and were now running the color camera down the pipe leading from King Khalid Well No. 47 to the main pipeline. Meanwhile, Long had finished his inspection of the tank his crew had removed and was stowing the tank in the rear of his truck.

"This is Farouk, Tom. Did you find out what was wrong with the well?" Aziz said seconds later.

"I believe the well was injected with what I think is an oil-eating microbe. The sands are completely dry, with no oil residue whatsoever. It is as if someone cleaned them in a giant washing machine."

"Could you have made a mistake?" Aziz asked. "Might it be *something* else?"

Temple said quietly, "We'll test to be sure, but time is very critical."

"What do you think we should do?" Aziz asked.

"The microbes were introduced from a tank hooked to the wellhead. The first thing to do is have crews fan out and check all the wells," Temple said.

"That will take days," Aziz noted correctly.

"The design of the tanks is such that the microbes can only be injected when the well is off gas pressure. That means as long as they are pumping, we have time."

"What do you mean?" Aziz said.

Temple watched from the helicopter as Long raced toward him.

"It appears that the tank was designed so that when the wells quit pumping, the gas-pressure relief valve opens and allows the microbes to enter the well."

In his office in Riyadh, Aziz stared at a huge wall that listed the oil field's scheduled maintenance.

"We have a problem, Tom. That entire field is scheduled to come off-line so we can run a cleaning plug through the delivery pipeline."

"When?" Temple asked.

"About fifteen minutes from now."

"You *have* to stop it, Farouk," Temple said.

He heard Aziz shouting hurried instructions across the room at the same instant Long arrived at the helicopter.

"The microbes are in the pipeline," Long said, panting from the exertion of running across the sand.

"Farouk," Temple shouted, "the bugs are in the pipeline. You have to destroy the line."

"How soon?"

"Right now," Temple replied. "Blow that son-of-a-bitch sky high."

In a massive air-conditioned underground hangar at Saudi Military City in the sandy hills outside Taima, a flashing red light and whooping alarm filled the vast space. A hydraulically operated rear vent door opened at the same time two technicians attached an auxiliary power unit to a jet. Off to the side in the ready room, General Sultan Saud stared through the window at the jet preparations as he spoke on a red-colored telephone.

While his mission was still being described to him he punched his choice of armaments into a computer keypad on the wall next to the telephone. He watched through the window as two teams consisting of a pair of men each began pushing carts containing missiles from a weapons locker. Each of the two teams was responsible for one wing of the jet.

"*Inshallah,*" General Saud said when the telephone call ended.

Racing to a dressing room, he quickly got into his Nomex flight suit. Carrying his helmet under his arm, he pulled on his gloves as he walked onto the hangar floor. The two teams of weapons specialists were attaching the last pair of air-to-ground missiles to the far edge of the wings. As General Saud reached the bottom of the ladder to the cockpit he paused. Turning to the specialists, he spoke.

"This is not a drill. We are live fire. Remove pins and arm the weapons."

Silently the specialists saluted and continued their tasks. Saud climbed up the ladder to the cockpit and waited as his crew chief unhooked the ladder. Moving to the front of the jet, where Saud could see him, the crew chief signaled that it was clear to start the plane's engines. A hum was followed by a whirring sound that gave way to buzzing, then a blast as the jet fuel ignited and spun the turbine.

The crew chief motioned for the front door of the hangar to be opened. Set on hydraulic rams, the door shot up and locked in place. At a signal from the crew chief one member of the weapons specialist team pulled the chocks from the wheels of the jet then ran to the far walls to stay clear of the jet blast. With a salute from his crew chief General Saud edged the throttles forward on the jet. The plane rolled across the hangar floor, through the door and down a slight rise. Gaining speed quickly, Saud lifted into the air. The entire process from telephone call to liftoff had lasted but a few minutes.

Once airborne, General Sultan Saud banked his British-made Tornado fighter to the left and dropped low over the desert. Cruising at an altitude of less than one hundred feet, he had to be aware of his terrain. Far off in the distance he could just make out the thin metal ribbon that was the pipeline.

"I have a visual on the pipeline. Go or no go?"

"It's a go," the control tower at the military city said.

Flicking his fire control button, Saud activated his weapons system. He watched as the image of the pipeline appeared in his heads-up display. General Saud carefully aligned the crosshairs until the pipeline was framed in the display. As soon as the light indicator flicked green, showing the missiles had locked on the target, Saud pushed his firing button with his thumb.

Twin Phoenix missiles streaked from his wingtips. On impact they blasted a ten-yard hole in the pipeline. Saud passed over the pipeline and reviewed the damage. Banking again, he observed a replay of the missile strike through film shot from his wingtip cameras. There was no oil visible on the ground.

He banked again, passing over the hole in the pipeline and stared at the ground one last time. No oil was being spilled on the ground from the jagged hole.

"I'm still dry," Saud radioed back to his base. "I'm moving twenty miles farther down the line. I'm down to two missiles. If I don't strike oil this time, alert the ready one plane to lift off."

"Roger that, General," the air traffic controller said. "Ready one to stand by."

Banking again, Saud pushed his throttles forward and flew farther down the pipeline. Once the pipeline was framed in his heads-up display he stared at it for a moment, then climbed straight in the air.

Arcing around in a 7 G-force turn, Saud again lined up perpendicular to the pipeline. Pushing his firing button with his thumb he loosed a single high-explosive missile. Saud broke left to avoid the shower of burning oil and smoke. The charge blew a hole in the pipeline ten yards wide. A cloud of black smoke rose high in the air.

With a single missile remaining, General Sultan had struck oil.

In Israel, defense forces began to search the homes of suspected Palestinian terrorists as the bombings continued. In Tel Aviv, the explosion of a bomb outside a department store killed ten Israeli citizens. In Jerusalem, an Islamic religious service was interrupted by the blast of a bomb. Eighteen Palestinians were killed and wounded. The Israeli prime minister declared a state of emergency and suspended travel between cities.

The mobilization of American forces to the Middle East moved swiftly. U.S. Air Force planes were ferried from Japan, Korea, Diego Garcia, Guam, and Taiwan to bases in the region. Army and Marine units were deployed from Asia, Europe, and the United States. The ready response troops landed at a base in Sudan, just across the Red Sea from the conflict, and began to set up camp. The U.S. Navy ordered the Seventh Fleet redeployed from the South China Sea and the Philippines. The ships of the fleet began racing toward the Persian Gulf and the Red Sea while vessels from Norway, Great Britain, and Italy were ordered to the Mediterranean.

In Beijing, Tao arrived for his meeting with the prime minister.

"Our plan is working perfectly," Tao noted. "The U.S. Navy is steaming toward the Middle East just as we had planned."

"And the Einstein papers?" the prime minister inquired.

"We should have them in our possession in the next twenty-four hours. The courier has made contact and the plans for extraction are in motion."

It would take a miracle now to save Taiwan.

CHAPTER 40

A warm wind blew the fall leaves from the carefully assembled piles the groundskeepers had raked outside the office of the Special Security Service in Maryland. Sandra Miles leaned forward across her desk. She handed the report detailing the theft of Enviorco's microbes to her partner, Chuck Smoot.

"Do me a favor and read through this before I file it with Allbright," Miles said. "And be sure and tell me what you really think." She began to check her E-mail while Smoot read.

Smoot read quickly through the seven-page report, then set it on the desk in front of him. "Reads good," he said, "but you left out any theory about what the people who stole the microbes might try to do with them."

"I did that on purpose. I'm not even sure who's in possession of them now," Miles said, "except that I'm reasonably sure it was the Chinese that had them stolen."

"Chinese government or Chinese gangs?" Smoot asked.

"No idea," Miles said.

"I can't see why the Chinese government would want them," Smoot hypothesized.

"Or the Chinese Triad gangs—unless they had someone who wanted to buy them," said Miles.

"We might as well start finding out," Smoot said. "Somebody's going to be assigned to retrieve or destroy those bugs. You can bet on that. I would also imagine Allbright will want more technical information about the microbes themselves."

"So you think the report is lacking?" Miles asked.

"There's a lot of questions left unanswered," Smoot said, "that's for sure."

"Technical Division can supply those," Miles said, rising. "I'm going to drop this off at Allbright's office."

"I'll go with you," Smoot said.

"But I thought you felt this report sucked," Miles said, smiling.

"It does," Smoot said, "but I know you, Sandra. And I know what you're up to."

"And what might that be?" Miles asked as the pair started off down the hall.

"You want to leave Allbright enough doubt so we have to continue to investigate and are assigned to the case," Smoot said as they rounded the corner.

"Little old *me* do that?" Miles said. "That makes it sound like I planned it."

Smoot paused at the door before knocking.

"Only because you did."

Dick Allbright perused the report that was filed by CIA agent Jeff McBride and forwarded to the NIA. The report described his surveillance of the *Carondelet* and included photographs of the vessel. Allbright finished, then reached for the phone and dialed Benson's extension.

"General Benson's office."

"This is Allbright."

"Hold one minute, Mr. Allbright," Mrs. Mindio said sweetly.

Benson was concentrating on the missing Einstein documents when Allbright telephoned. He was sitting at his desk with a pair of Special Security Service analysts, studying maps of the highways and rivers around Washington, D.C.

"Yeah, Dick, go ahead," Benson said.

"I just read a report from a CIA agent. He was watching a

Chinese spy vessel disguised as a fishing boat. The vessel left Norfolk, Virginia, last night. The agent claims the vessel was steaming north."

"You think the vessel might be coming here?" Benson asked.

"It's worth checking out," Allbright noted.

"Makes sense. Combined with that call to the embassy the NSA intercepted, it's pretty obvious what's happening," Benson noted.

"You must be thinking what I'm thinking," Allbright said. "The ship from Norfolk is being ordered north to pick up the courier who's holding the Einstein papers."

"Just might be. What is the name of the vessel the CIA man was watching?" Benson asked.

"The vessel is named *Carondelet.*"

Benson wrote the name down on a slip of paper. "I'll call you right back, Dick. Let me see what I can find out."

Benson dialed the number for the regional commander of the Coast Guard. His call was put through immediately.

"Commander Wright," the Coast Guard officer said.

"General Earl Benson. I'm the head of the Special Security Service. I have a priority-one request."

"How can the Coast Guard help you, General?" Wright said smoothly.

"I need to locate a ship named *Carondelet*. It left port in Norfolk last night steaming north."

"We can do that for you," Wright said. "Do you want us to detain the vessel after we locate it?"

"Not yet," Benson said. "I just need to know the *Carondelet*'s current location."

"I can have a Coast Guard chopper off the ground from Virginia Beach in twenty minutes to start the search. Luckily, Chesapeake Bay is not the easiest place to hide. What's your number there, General? I'll call you as soon as we have a sighting."

Benson recited his direct number to Wright.

"I should be able to get you an answer within the hour," Wright said.

Tsing slammed on the brakes of the stolen car. Back in the trees, off the road, he'd spotted a tumbledown barn. He waited until there was no traffic, then turned off the main road and drove down a road long overgrown with weeds and underbrush. Tsing stopped at the side of the barn and climbed from the car. Glancing at the barn, he noticed that painted on the faded and flaking red paint of the barn was an advertisement for Mail Pouch Chewing Tobacco. He could smell cut hay from a field nearby and he flicked his hand at a fly that was buzzing around his head.

Tsing pried open a side door to the barn. The barn was mostly empty. Several piles of trash were heaped in the far corner. Along one side, in a grain bin, was piled ears of corn, now almost petrified. He walked to the doors.

Tsing surveyed the main barn doors and found them secured with a cheap lock. Returning to his stolen car, Tsing retrieved a tire iron from the trunk. Back inside the barn, he slid the tire iron under the lock and popped off the rusty clasp. Leaning the full weight of his body against the barn doors, Tsing managed to wedge the doors open far enough. Then he got the car and drove it inside the barn. After closing the barn doors, he wiped his hands on his handkerchief, then made his way back to the road and started hitchhiking.

He caught a ride with a college student in a van, ending up in White Plains, Maryland, where he spent the night in a cheap motel. Near checkout time, he walked to a nearby diner. There Tsing ate a meal of fried chicken, mashed potatoes, and creamed corn. For dessert he enjoyed a slice of chocolate cake and a cup of coffee.

A death-row inmate could not have ordered a better meal.

When he finished the meal Tsing walked out to the side of the road and began hitchhiking south on I-301. A series of rides, the last in the back of a farm truck, brought Tsing to Bel Alton, Maryland, by late afternoon. Checking carefully to see if he was being followed, he slipped into the woods and made his way to a cove on the Potomac River.

Tonight Tsing was due to be extracted.

That same afternoon, Taft and Martinez stopped for coffee in a cafe just off I-95. Ordering their coffees to go, Taft grabbed several sugars and two creamers and tossed them in the sack. Once back inside the car he handed the sack to Martinez.

"There's cream and sugar in the bottom of the sack. Why don't you hand me mine first, though," Taft said as he started the car and drove slowly through the parking lot.

Martinez handed one of the black coffees to Taft, then dug around in the sack. "You didn't get any stirrers."

Taft set his coffee in the cupholder, then reached in his coat pocket and withdrew a folding knife, which he flashed open with a fluid motion. "Here, stir your coffee with my knife."

Exiting I-95 for I-17, Taft reached for his coffee in the cupholder. He snapped off the lid, tossed it in the rear of the car, and sipped the steaming liquid. Taft engaged the cruise control just as they drove past Camp A.P. Hill, then settled down in the driver's seat.

"I have some vacation time coming up. I think I'll put in a request for time off," Taft said as he blew across the cup to cool the coffee.

"Is this your retaliation for being pulled from the Einstein mission?" Martinez asked.

Taft exited onto Interstate 301. The drive would take them through Port Royal north to the turnoff for Potomac Beach. He turned and looked at Martinez.

"Not really, though I am pissed off about that. It just seems stupid to me for us to be assigned to inspect construction projects. What do either of us know about construction or electronics or advanced sonar?"

"Not much," Martinez agreed, "but I do know one thing about this system."

"What's that?"

"It's got to be one of the only times in the history of the United States procurement that a project has been finished ahead of time."

"What is the contract completion date?" Taft asked as he took another sip of coffee.

"October 15th," Martinez noted.

"Two and a half weeks ahead of schedule," Taft said as he turned off toward Potomac Beach and began to look for the dirt road leading to the site. "Will wonders never cease."

Commander Wright telephoned Benson forty-two minutes later. "The *Carondelet* is anchored just north of the middle of the Potomac River near Point Lookout. Do you want me to have a cutter deployed to the area?"

Benson thought for a moment. "Okay. Can you keep your ship out of sight for now?"

"We can bring a cutter down from Baltimore and have it anchor around the point just out of view," Wright answered. "That way, if you need it, it's right there."

"That would be perfect, Commander. I'll order a few of my men down from Washington to observe the *Carondelet* from shore. For now, I just want to play a waiting game."

"It will take a couple of hours to move the cutter into position," Wright explained. "I'll call you back when she's in place."

Benson reached for the phone. "Have three agents drive to Point Lookout and set up surveillance on a ship in the Potomac named the *Carondelet*," Benson said to the deputy chief of operations. "I'm going to fax you pictures of the vessel now."

"You want a secure phone link to the observation team?" the deputy asked.

"Yes, and have them report to me every fifteen minutes," Benson said.

On the lee side of the *Carondelet*, a canvas awning was stretched from the superstructure to an outboard-powered tender in the water ten feet away. Now safe from prying eyes, the Chinese mini-sub was lowered into the water by crane. The crew manning the mini-sub squeezed into the small opening at the top of the vessel. Once safely on board, the submarine pilot ran through a quick systems check. Finding all the systems functioning properly, he lowered the hatch, locked it in place, and began the slow journey upriver to extract Tsing.

Slipping through the water at a speed barely above that of a walking man, the submarine fought its way against a stiff current. Peering from a glass bubble in the bow of the submarine, Chief Pilot Ho Pei saw little of interest. The water in the Potomac was murky. Once, shortly after they left the *Carondelet*, the current had slammed a turtle against the glass dome. And just as quickly, the current swept the reptile away. The small submarine lacked advanced navigation aids, and the route to Tsing had been plotted into a handheld GPS unit. The information as to their location was relayed to Pei by his navigator.

"Way point," the navigator said in Chinese, stirring Pei from his daydream.

Pei glanced at the sheet taped to the wall of the submarine. Checking his compass with great care, he steered another course heading.

The interior of the submarine was cramped. Pei sat upright in a small bucket seat, watching the water pass outside the glass bubble. Behind him, where the body of the submarine widened, were two seats facing to the rear. One held his navigator. The other one was for Tsing. Like a lumbering tortoise trying to find home, the tiny submarine continued upriver.

The setting sun painted the sky a fiery red as the crew of the *Carondelet* settled in to wait for the submarine's return. They had no idea they were being watched from shore.

They had no idea a noose was being closed around the neck of the river.

As the Chinese mini-sub was making the journey up the Potomac River, Dick Allbright, Sandra Miles, and Chuck Smoot sat in chairs across from General Benson's desk. Allbright was briefing Benson.

"I just received this report, General, and thought you should hear it immediately. Yesterday Agent Miles was dispatched to the Rio Grande Valley in Texas. She was investigating the theft of a vat of oil-eating microbes from a laboratory," Allbright said. "Through a roundabout series of circumstances, she believes she has uncovered evidence that indicates the theft of the microbes was a contract job paid for by someone of Chinese nationality. Once she explained her findings, I suspected it might be tied to the Einstein case. I thought it best you hear about it right now."

"What led you to the conclusion the microbes were stolen by the Chinese, Agent Miles?" Benson asked.

"My evidence is spotty, I admit, sir. It comes from one of the burglars, who is an admitted drug user. He identified the man that hired him as Chinese from the type of cigarettes the man smoked."

Benson smiled. "I guess it does pay to quit smoking," he said and leaned forward. "What do you make of all this, Dick?"

"It ties in nicely with the trouble in the Middle East, sir. The

Saudis are keeping a close rein on information about their troubles. However, a few hours ago the NSA intercepted radio transmissions from an oil-field worker to his superiors that seems to support the hypothesis that one of their fields was poisoned by a man-made biological."

"So this entire mess, the Einstein situation as well as the Middle East, could be all tied together," Benson said.

"You could make that argument, sir," Allbright said.

"I need some theories as to why the Chinese might want to poison the Saudi's oil—who stands to gain, strategic impacts, that kind of stuff."

"I'll get some people on it right away," Allbright said.

Benson looked over at Miles and Smoot. "Agent Miles, I want you and Agent Smoot to investigate the bombings that are occurring in Israel. I'll call right now and have one of our jets made ready. I want you to leave for the Middle East immediately. If the bombings in Israel are being caused by the Chinese, maybe we can stop this war before it begins."

The trio rose to leave. "Work fast, you three. I have to brief the president tomorrow morning," Benson said as they left.

CHAPTER 41

Taft parked the NIA sedan just outside the newly constructed monitoring station near the town of Potomac Beach, Maryland. He looked over at his partner. "What's the purpose of scheduling the test after sunset?"

"To demonstrate the 'above-surface night capability,' " Martinez said, reading from the report.

"Splendid," Taft said as he climbed out of the car.

Martinez closed the folder and joined Taft alongside the sedan.

Walking toward the construction trailer, Taft and Martinez noticed new landscaping that had been installed since their last visit. The freshly planted trees and shrubs hid the site from the road. Martinez was about to knock on the door of the trailer when a voice boomed from inside: "Come on in."

"The sensors we placed underneath the road picked up your car and activated a remote camera," the contractor said proudly. "I watched you drive into the compound." He reached for a pair of hard hats and handed them to the pair. "You are Agents Taft and Martinez, if I remember correctly."

"That's correct. You have a good memory," Martinez said, smiling.

The contractor motioned to the door of the trailer. "Our technicians are already starting the system for the test. We can go and watch."

The three men walked across the dirt parking lot and stopped at the monitoring station. The contractor punched in a code on a key pad to release the door, then swung it open.

The inside of the building was dimly lit and the smell of fresh concrete still hung in the air. To the side, mounted on the wall, one of the three floor-to-ceiling, high-resolution screens was already lit. The screen was displaying a green-colored three-dimensional image of the Potomac River. The contractor walked over to a technician who was typing on a computer keyboard.

"How goes it?" he asked the technician.

"Not great," the man admitted. "The software controlling screens two and three has a glitch. We're running a systems check now."

"These are the NIA inspectors," the contractor said, indicating Taft and Martinez. "How long until we're operational and can demonstrate the system?"

THE EINSTEIN PAPERS 257

"No idea," the technician said, returning to his work.

The contractor smiled wanly at the two agents. "Would you care to wait in the trailer? There's a television you could watch."

Taft looked at Martinez and nodded. Both men began to walk for the exit.

"I'll come and get you when we're operational," the contractor shouted as they exited the building.

It would be close to 9 P.M. before the system was working properly.

At about the same time, at NIA headquarters, General Benson telephoned his wife to explain that he would be late and that she shouldn't wait up for him. Then he phoned down for a dinner from the NIA cafeteria. He was reading the latest reports from the Middle East when the orderly from the cafeteria delivered the meal. Benson signed the bill, tucking a five-dollar bill underneath for the orderly, then removed the stainless-steel cover from the largest plate.

A slab of chicken fried steak covered in a white sausage gravy took up over half the plate. The remaining area on the plate was piled with mashed potatoes ladled with more of the gravy. Removing the cover from another plate, Benson found green beans. The last plate held a slice of pecan pie for dessert. A container of iced tea rounded out the order. After liberally covering the meat and potatoes with salt and pepper, Benson began to eat.

His meal was interrupted with several telephone calls.

The NIA agents in position near the *Carondelet* began to phone in to Benson at fifteen-minute intervals. Their reports said the vessel remained anchored in the Potomac River with no sign of movement on deck. Dick Allbright telephoned from his office and explained to Benson the progress they were making in the Middle East. After completing his report, he asked Benson, "How late will you be working tonight?"

"Late," Benson replied. "How about you?"

"Late. I've got that weird feeling like something is going to break soon," Allbright noted.

"Me too," Benson said. "It's about time for something to happen."

As he spoke those words Benson had no way of knowing that the *Carondelet* was the solution to their problems. The ship seemed but one small piece in a larger puzzle.

"If nothing happens by midnight," Benson said to Allbright, "I'm ordering the Coast Guard to board and seize the ship."

"Do you think the papers are already on board?"

"Maybe, or they soon will be," Benson said. "And this time I want them recovered."

The Chinese Kong mini-sub was powered by quiet electric motors that spun a shaft that ran to the stern. The motors made the submarine's operation almost silent, but they offered little in the way of power to the single propeller. Still fighting the river current, the submarine droned on toward its rendezvous. Inside the mini-sub the humidity was already rising, and droplets of moisture fell from the roof of the vessel like a gentle rain. The air inside the cigar-shaped vessel was turning stale, the smell of fear and uncertainty combined with sweat and body odors.

Behind the glass-enclosed bubble, Pilot Ho Pei struggled to keep the submarine on a compass heading. He rubbed his eyes with the back of his hand. He would be glad when this was over and he was safely back in China.

Tsing nervously scanned the Potomac River, then checked his flashlight to make sure it was still working. His extraction was scheduled for 10 P.M. He was glad tonight was the night—he had the nagging suspicion his good luck was running out. Twice already he had nearly been captured. It was time to leave the United States for good. The constant stress of hiding from his pursuers was taking its toll.

Glancing down at his left hand, he saw it was trembling slightly. Pouring the plastic cup of coffee onto the ground he tossed the thermos and cup into the bushes. Soon, once he was aboard the ship, he could sleep. He glanced at his watch again and stared downriver.

Minutes seemed like hours.

In the construction trailer near Potomac Beach, John Taft was rapidly growing bored.

"This show is just plain stupid," Taft said. "How do a coffee shop waitress and an unemployed chef manage to cover the rent on a high-rise apartment in New York?"

"Quit being pissy, it's just a sitcom," Martinez said.

"We should both be home right now," Taft said. "You with your wife, me with somebody warm and cuddly."

"What happened to the last lady you were dating?" Martinez asked.

"The one who looked like Teri Garr?"

"Yeah, that one," said Martinez.

"She got transferred to Salt Lake City."

Just at that instant the perpetually optimistic contractor yanked open the door of the trailer. "The system's up and running," he said enthusiastically.

Taft and Martinez rose from the old couch in the trailer. Walking across the parking lot, the three men entered the building. All three of the screens were now lit. The contractor pointed to the screens and began his spiel.

"This screen on the left displays the river from the Capitol in D.C. one-third of the way downstream. The middle screen continues from there to about where we are. The last screen is the water from here to the border between Maryland and Virginia, out in the Chesapeake Bay."

"Can you operate both above and below water at the same time?" Martinez asked.

"Yes, we just reduce the image and split the screens in two." The contractor gestured to one of the technicians sitting at a keyboard, who punched in commands. The screen split.

Taft wanted to get the demonstration over as quickly as possible. He walked over to the middle screen and pointed to a blip. "What's this object?"

"That's the great thing about our system," the contractor noted. "It's programmed with the dimensions and characteristics of both man-made and natural marine objects. A storage file in the computer lists boats, whales, whatever. In fact, if there is a personal watercraft out there, for example, we could probably tell you the make and engine size by motor noise and dimensions." The contractor turned to the technician. "Zoom in on the target Agent Taft is pointing to."

The technician punched in the commands. Off to one side, a window opened and the make and engine characteristics of the object were displayed.

The three men stared at the screen. "That comes up as a Chinese Kong 16 mini-submarine, powered by electric motors," the contractor said in astonishment.

"Are you sure this thing is working?" Martinez asked.

"System report is normal," the technician said.

"Son of a bitch," Taft muttered. "That little bastard didn't get away after all."

Taft and Martinez sprinted across the parking lot to their sedan. Taft started the engine, revved it up, and dropped it into gear. The tires broke loose from the asphalt as he raced from the parking lot. With his free hand Taft reached for his cellular phone. He glanced at the clock on the dashboard and decided to try General Benson at home.

"He's at the office," Mrs. Benson said to Taft.

Taft speed-dialed the number for Benson's office.

"Benson."

"This is John Taft, sir. Martinez and I are at the demonstration in Potomac Beach. Is there anything new to report on the Einstein papers?"

"We're observing a Chinese spy ship named *Carondelet* at the mouth of the Potomac. We believe the Einstein papers are on board, or soon will be. At midnight the Coast Guard will board the vessel and seize her. Why do you ask?"

"The Potomac River monitoring system in Potomac Beach just located a Chinese-made mini-sub steaming up the Potomac," Taft blurted out.

Punching the gas pedal to the floor, Taft steered around an eighteen wheeler. Martinez placed one hand on the dashboard as he clutched the passenger-assist strap on the door.

"They must have launched the submarine from the *Carondelet* when we weren't watching," Benson said quickly. "Can you and Martinez intercept it?"

"We're driving toward the sub right now. To receive the directions from the monitoring station in Potomac Beach we need to hang up on you and call them back."

"Which way are you headed?" Benson asked.

"The sub just passed under the bridge at Dahlgren, Virginia," Taft said.

"I'll send backup," Benson said as the phone went dead.

Martinez grabbed the cellular phone from Taft and dialed the computer room at Potomac Beach. "Where's the sub now?" he asked.

"It just passed the bridge at Dahlgren and is angling north to a cove nearby," the contractor said.

Martinez repeated the information so there could be no mistake. Taft pushed the accelerator of the sedan to the floor. Their NIA sedan was doing ninety as they roared over the bridge at Dahlgren.

"Tell Potomac Beach to keep the screens split. I need to know when the sub breaks to the surface," Taft said.

Martinez relayed the instructions and waited. Taft watched the road ahead intently. Lines of trees on each side of the road made it seem the men were traveling through a tunnel. Ahead Taft noticed lights. They were entering the town of Bel Alton.

"The sub is turning toward shore. The location is almost directly across from the town of Bel Alton," the contractor noted.

Taft slammed on the brakes in the center of Bel Alton, then swung the car in a high-speed 180-degree turn. "I saw a road back there leading to the water," he shouted to Martinez.

Pulling off the pavement, Taft steered down a dirt road. The road was tree-lined and fallen leaves littered the packed earth. In the rearview mirror, lit by the car's taillights, Taft could see a cloud of leaves being blown in the air.

He reached to the dash and killed his headlights, then continued on with only the parking lights for illumination. The sedan was a wraith in the night racing toward a clash with destiny brought about by dumb luck.

"The sub is rising to the surface," the contractor said over the cellular phone.

Rolling down his window, Taft sniffed at the air. "We're getting close to the water," he said to Martinez.

Taft was watching to the side of the sedan as they sped down the road. He noticed a path leading through the forest toward the water. He slammed on the brakes and brought the car to a sliding stop. Jamming the transmission into reverse, he drove ten yards backward and wrenched the vehicle into park.

Running to the rear of the car, Taft opened the trunk and

rooted around inside. "Here's what I need," he said to Martinez as he pocketed a road flare. "Do you have an extra clip?"

"Yes," Martinez said as he removed his extra clip from a pouch on his belt and handed it to Taft.

"Stay here, Larry. This job is for someone trained in operations. I've got a feeling it might get wet. You made a pact with your wife you'd stay out of operations from now on, and I don't want you to break that. Call Benson and ask him to have the navy block the entrance to the cove. Let me handle the courier." Taft cocked his automatic with a single fluid motion. "Next, get some choppers with lights over the area. Also request some bloodhounds to be put on standby in case this guy somehow escapes and we need to track him. I'll try to capture him before he runs, but who knows."

"Okay, John, whatever you say," Martinez said. "But be careful, this guy's a crafty little shit."

"I know," Taft said as he stuffed his gun into the waistband of his pants and set out from the car.

Taft began running through the forest toward the water. Away from lights his eyes gradually adjusted to the darkness and his night vision began to improve. He listened to the woods and sniffed at the air.

He was a hunter and he knew his prey was nearby.

At the edge of the forest, near the water, Taft stopped and looked across the river. In the waning light of a quarter-moon he could make out the conning tower of the mini-sub as it broke the surface fifty yards downriver. Taft began to make his way silently along the tree line.

He watched carefully for the courier.

As soon as the submarine's conning tower was fully out of the water, Tsing flashed his light three times. He waited for a reply. Seeing the correct signal from shore the submarine's navigator poked from the hatch of the submarine and turned on a single blue light atop the tower.

Tsing's salvation was at hand.

As soon as Tsing saw the answering signal from the submarine he raced for the edge of the Potomac. His thoughts turned to home and family.

Taft was at the edge of the woods, watching the submarine while scanning the shoreline for sign of the courier. The instant Tsing ran from the woods, Taft struck the road flare against a rock and sparked the end.

It burst into flames with a red chemical glow.

Tossing the flare toward the edge of the river he ran from his hiding spot with his pistol drawn. "Stop where you are," he shouted at Tsing, who was clutching the package containing the Einstein papers tightly in his hand.

The thin line between a civilized man and a barbarian was exposed.

Taft should have shot Tsing without a warning, because in the next few seconds everything went very wrong. Using the light from the burning flare as his beacon, the navigator in the conning tower of the mini-sub drew out a pistol.

The navigator took careful aim.

On shore, with the light of the moon glinting off the wet metal deck of the mini-sub, Taft saw the weapon come from the holster. With an instantaneous reaction, fused in his soul by years of training, Taft lined up his shot and fired two rounds in the direction of the submarine.

His would be the opening salvo.

Then, as if in slow motion, Taft watched as the man on the sub flinched as a slug tore into his left side. As if in reaction to his wound, the man thrust the right side of his body forward while at the same time pulling the trigger of the pistol he held in his hand.

His aim was dead on.

The bullet slammed into Taft's shoulder near his heart. Flung on his back by the force of the bullet, Taft instinctively rolled onto his stomach and squeezed off several rounds at Tsing, then fired the remainder of the clip at the submarine.

Then, with an effort born of will, he began to crawl toward Tsing, who was now lying on the ground at the edge of the river. In the sand behind Taft, the trail of blood grew wider with each foot he traveled. Reaching the folder of papers Tsing had dropped, Taft drew them closer, then clutched them against his chest.

And then Taft felt nothing, nothing at all.

At the sound of the gunfire, Martinez immediately ignored his fears, his promise to his wife, as well as his instructions from Taft, and ran toward the water. Sweeping the beam of his flashlight along the ground, he searched for Taft.

Finding Taft lying next to Tsing in a crumpled heap near the water, Martinez reached under him and supported his head. Martinez could see blood bubbling out of the wound in Taft's shoulder. It looked like an artery had been nicked.

Kneeling next to Taft, Martinez glanced out on the river. A small V-shape plowed through the water heading downstream. The water's disruption was the only visual sign of the submarine making its escape.

From the back pocket of his pants Martinez removed a handkerchief and pressed it to the hole in Taft's shoulder. The handkerchief was almost immediately soaked through with blood. It was serious but Martinez didn't hesitate a second. Ripping strips off Taft's shirt, he made a compress bandage, then pressed some of his body weight against the wound to staunch the bleeding.

Placing his knee over the wound to continue the direct pressure, he reached into his pocket and pulled out his cellular phone. Hitting the speed dialer he was connected with the NIA operations center in seconds.

"This is Agent Martinez. My number is 04356. Listen carefully: my partner, Agent Taft, has been shot and the wound appears to be life-threatening. I need a medical evacuation helicopter immediately. Our location is approximately two miles west of Bel Alton, Maryland, on the bank of the Potomac River," Martinez said crisply.

"Affirmative on the helicopter, Agent Martinez, we'll dispatch a medevac immediately. What else do you have to report?"

"Tell Benson the submarine has gone underwater again and is headed downstream."

Martinez glanced down at Taft's wound. Blood was spreading around the edge of the shirt.

"Understand, Agent Martinez," the dispatcher said, "we have the navy standing by to intercept the submarine."

"Taft's wound is bleeding profusely," Martinez said. "It's soaking whatever I put on top of it."

"Keep direct pressure on the wound, just keep adding another layer of cloth as the one below becomes soaked," the dispatcher said. "Now take two fingers and place them on Agent Taft's neck next to the collarbone."

"Okay," Martinez said, "I'm touching his neck."

"Feel for a pulse," the dispatcher said.

Martinez moved his fingers around near Taft's collarbone until he detected a slow steady beating.

"Agent Martinez," the dispatcher said quickly, "I just received word that the medical chopper has lifted off. They estimate they can reach you in five minutes. Can you light the area so they can find you?"

"There's a red road flare that's already lit. It's burning on the ground," said Martinez.

"Did you find the pulse?" the dispatcher asked.

"Yes, it's slow but steady."

"Are the bandages thoroughly soaked?"

"Pretty much," Martinez said.

"Hold on. Let me see what else we can do," the dispatcher said.

The dispatcher rolled from the switchboard and punched a series of commands into a computer terminal. She rolled back to the switchboard and keyed the microphone.

"We had a team of agents observing a ship on the Potomac River. They're headed toward you now as fast as they can travel. In case something happens to the helicopter, they have a first-aid kit in their car and will assist you." The operator paused for a second. "Agent Martinez, I want you to remove your shirt, fold it into a compress bandage, and add it to the top of the bandages already in place. Can you do that?"

"Sure," Martinez said as he shrugged off his jacket and ripped his shirt off.

"Remember, don't remove the bandages already in place. Just add your shirt on top and continue to apply pressure."

"Got it," Martinez said.

The dispatcher glanced at a message on her screen.

"The helicopter reports they can see the Potomac River," the dispatcher said quickly.

"I can hear the chopper now," Martinez said.

"They report they see the flare," the dispatcher said, scanning the screen. "Agent Martinez, you need to keep up the pressure on the wound. Do not take the pressure away until someone can take over. Now I need you to feel for a pulse again."

Martinez placed his fingers on Taft's neck and felt around. It took him longer this time to detect a pulse.

"I've still got a pulse," Martinez told the dispatcher, "but it's not as strong. The helicopter's landing now."

"Hang in there, Agent Martinez, we're going to pull Taft through this," the dispatcher said firmly.

The medevac helicopter touched down on the only open area nearby—a spit of sand some fifty yards downstream. Two attendants jumped from the chopper before the pilot had a chance to throttle back the engine. One carried a plastic box containing medical equipment while the other held a portable stretcher in his hands. Racing up to Martinez and Taft, the pair assessed the situation almost instantly. One of the attendants reached for the radio microphone clipped to his shoulder while the other took over compressing the wound from Martinez.

"Let us do our job now," one of the attendants said as he placed his hand on Martinez's shoulder.

It was only then that Martinez had a chance to look around.

CHAPTER 42

Only five days remained before the fiftieth anniversary of Mao Zedong's announcement of the formation of the People's Republic of China. The Chinese plan to attack Taiwan and bring the island back under Communist rule was moving at a blistering pace.

Seven Chinese fast-attack submarines were already in place in the Strait of Taiwan. Their mission was to cripple the Taiwanese navy when its ships steamed from port to defend against the blitzkrieg naval attack coming from mainland China.

Much work had gone into the amphibious portion of the attack from the mainland. Paratrooper battalions were being assembled in Xiamen, in Quanzhou. The Chinese attack plan called for tens of thousands of troops to be dropped in a massive coordinated air-lift over Taipei, Taichung, and Tainan.

After crossing the Taiwan Strait, the mainland Chinese naval force would split in two, with several battleships supporting the amphibious assault, while the remainder of the fleet would be assigned to the west side of the island, where they would shell Taiwanese military installations and villages from the sea.

After the flotilla made it across the Strait, the Chinese air force would perform a close support role for the amphibious troops as well as a continuous carpet-bombing mission designed to soften up guerrilla resistance in the high mountains that formed Taiwan's backbone.

Inside the command headquarters for the attack, located at the Chinese Combined Military Command Center in Beijing, the Chinese prime minister stared at the ten-by-twenty-foot model of Taiwan, then questioned the head of the army.

"Are you sure you can keep open the supply lines to your troops on the ground?"

"Once the marines have established a beachhead and we have control of the Strait, the navy assures me they can run a continuous convoy of supply ships across the one-hundred-mile stretch of open water," the general replied confidently. "However, it is a somewhat moot point, sir. Taiwan is a rich country. Food for our troops will be readily available on the island. In addition, once we start to capture the Taiwanese military stockpiles, we can use their own weapons against them if we need to."

"What if the Americans show up?" the prime minister asked.

"The key is to move rapidly and decisively, sir. Our analysts assure us that once we are ashore in force, the Americans will not wish to risk an all-out war to stop us."

"So the key is rapid deployment," the prime minister noted.

"The first twelve hours are critical, sir," the general agreed. "Those hours are the key to success."

"Then make those first hours count," the prime minister said.

"We see little chance of difficulties," the head of the navy replied.

"Please continue with your work. I will return again tomorrow." The prime minister turned to his left. "Mr. Tao, if we could now meet in my office, I have several matters to discuss."

Tao followed the prime minister from the planning room. After walking the length of the building, he followed the prime minister into his office.

"I am concerned about the Einstein papers, Sun," the prime minister said as he sat down behind his desk. "Has the courier made any attempt to contact us?"

"Not since the last call he made to the embassy in Washington," Tao noted.

"That was three days ago."

"True. But the courier has instructions to proceed to the embassy in San Francisco if he feels that the drop-off point is not secure. Perhaps he detected the Americans were again on to him and he is traveling to the West Coast."

"The Americans proved they are already wise to our recovery of the papers. They proved that when they surrounded the embassy in New York. If the papers are not in our possession prior to the assault on Taiwan, our intended threats against them will be meaningless, and they will know this."

"Not necessarily, sir," Tao said quietly. "You see, *they* have no way to know we don't possess the papers."

The prime minister leaned back in his chair and sat silently for several minutes. Then he began to chuckle. "That is true, Sun Tao. That is true."

Chief Petty Officer Mark Ramsey stared into the sonar scope, then twisted a knob and adjusted the image. "This is like shooting ducks in a pond," he said over his intercom to the pilot of the Navy P-3 Orion that was flying a circular pattern over the Potomac River.

"Like ducks, huh?" the pilot replied.

"Like ducks that are tied together," Ramsey said.

"Control, this is Spotter. We have a positive identification on the target in the river," the pilot said.

"Affirmative, Spotter. Drop pingers, a dye marker, and a depth charge, ASAP."

"Roger that, control," the pilot said.

The pilot switched his headset to intercom. "Hey, Jerry," he said to the weapons system operator, "are you ready?"

"You bet," the WSO said easily. "Once Ramsey tells me, this submarine is toast."

Passing fifty feet over the surface of the river, the pilot held a steady course upriver.

"We're getting close," Ramsey said as he stared intently at the sonar screen. "Stand by. Now!"

The WSO flicked a series of switches on the weapons control panel and launched the package. The depth charge flipped over once before splashing into the water and sinking. The pilot of the P-3 slowed the airplane and loitered over the area awaiting further instructions.

Ho Pei heard the first ping on the hull of his submarine only seconds before the depth charge exploded and rocked the submarine onto its back. He just caught the terror in his wounded navigator's face before the lights inside the submarine flickered off. The mini-sub was tossed from side to side, then did a complete 360-degree roll. A seam in the underbelly of the small craft split and water began to fill the lower deck. The Plexiglas viewing port cracked and pinpoints of water shot inside the hull. Pei twisted a series of knobs to blow off ballast and allow the submarine to surface.

It was every submariners worst nightmare.

Pei felt the warm liquid flowing from his ears where his eardrums had ruptured and he touched his hands to the wetness. He stared in the black void both inside and outside the submarine.

Then very quietly he began to cry.

*   *   *

Two U.S. Navy fast-attack crafts raced up the Potomac from their base at Norfolk. Dispatched from their base an hour earlier, the boats had hit speeds of ninety miles an hour as they raced north. Passing Rock Point, they slowed as they neared the area where the charges had been dropped. Scanning the water with high-powered searchlights, they found the disabled submarine floundering on the surface.

After the submarine was lashed to the side of one of the fast-attack crafts, a line was dragged underneath and hooked to the conning tower. Using the windlass, the line was tightened until the submarine was pulled right side up. A navy officer began to pound on the hatch so it would be opened from inside. Pei couldn't hear the pounding, nor could his dying navigator. The concussion from the depth charge had destroyed their eardrums.

Ho Pei would never hear again.

The following morning General Benson was shaving in his office bathroom when the phone rang. Dressed in a sleeveless T-shirt and boxer shorts, he brushed past his uniform, neatly pressed and hanging on the door, and lifted the receiver.

"Benson."

The connection was poor, most likely due to sunspot activity affecting the satellite transmission. "This is Agent Miles, sir. I'm using a secure phone from Israel."

"I can barely hear you, Agent Miles, please speak louder," Benson said loudly.

"Very well, sir," Miles shouted. "Agent Smoot has examined some of the remains from one of the bombs. They were produced using Czechoslovakian Semtex."

"What else did you discover?" Benson asked.

"They used Chinese-manufactured blasting caps as the detonators."

"Very interesting," Benson said. "But that doesn't prove conclusively the Chinese were behind the attack."

"Not that one clue alone, sir. But we just uncovered another clue."

"What is it?" Benson said quickly.

"The threats Israel received were written on a paper that is unavailable in the Middle East," Miles said.

"Where is the nearest source for the paper?"

"Hong Kong," Miles noted.

Benson paused. "Good work, Agent Miles. Please congratulate Agent Smoot."

Hanging up the phone, Benson dressed in his uniform and called downstairs to alert his driver he was ready to leave. Squaring his shoulders, he left from his office for the short drive to the White House.

The *Carondelet* sat bobbing on the water. The agents watching from shore could see no activity on deck. The only light that was burning inside the ship was inside the pilothouse, where a single crewman was on duty. The lone crewman was assigned to monitor the radio in case the mini-sub ran into difficulties. However, since the submarine was not due back for several hours, the rest of the crew was sleeping. All hands would need to be rested by tomorrow when *Carondelet* made her way out of Chesapeake Bay and into the Atlantic Ocean.

Just upriver and out of sight from the *Carondelet* a team of men dressed in black wetsuits and carrying full combat gear rolled over the side of a black inflatable boat. They slipped below the water soundlessly, then met up underwater. The team leader glanced at a small computerized GPS plotter strapped to his wrist. Then he steered his team toward the *Carondelet*.

The Lar Mark V fully enclosed chest-mounted rebreathers and regulators the team used allowed no bubbles to rise to the surface of the water. Their approach, timed to carry them along with the current, was invisible from the surface of the water. Once the team leader located the stern of the *Carondelet* he motioned for his men to shed their fins and prepare for the assault. .

Two parties, each comprised of two men, would swim to the bow. One party of two would take the port side—the other party the starboard. At the signal from the team leader they would toss grappling hooks over the bow of the ship and hoist themselves on pulleys to the bow deck. Their mission was to secure the pilothouse.

At the same time, eight men would enter the ship from the stern. Spreading out, they would fan through the ship capturing the crew and securing the engine room. Beneath the hull of the *Carondelet* the teams hung suspended in the water like a feather floating on a breeze. They were waiting for their signal.

At exactly 12:00 A.M. the assault began.

At seven minutes after twelve in the morning, U.S. Navy SEAL Commander Warren Oakes secured his side arm and glanced across the deck of the *Carondelet*.

"All clear abovedecks," he shouted.

Chief Petty Officer Rick Chutetski walked on the deck through the pilothouse door.

"All clear belowdecks, sir."

"Did the crew have time to get off a radio call, Chutes?" Oakes asked.

"Shit no, sir," Chutetski said easily. "They never knew what hit them."

"Secure the crew in a hold belowdecks and post guards."

"What then, sir?"

"We wait for further instructions," Oakes said.

A cold front blowing in from the north brought freezing rain to the nation's capital. Inside an office in the West Wing of the White House, the National Security briefing started exactly at nine.

Robert Lakeland rose and addressed the group.

"First to speak today is General Benson of the Special Security Service," Lakeland announced.

Benson rose from his seat and walked to the podium.

"The Special Security Service division of the National Intelligence Agency believes we have linked the bombings plaguing Israel with the poisoning of the Saudi oil fields by oil-eating microbes stolen from a laboratory in Texas. Our agency is working on a comprehensive report the diplomats can take to the respective embassies listing our proof. The report is being assembled as we speak. We think the report should be completed inside an hour."

A murmur rose in the room. "Who do you believe is behind all this mayhem?" the president asked.

"The Chinese government," Benson said.

"They've never shown much strategic interest in the Middle East," Lakeland interjected.

"We believe their actions in the Middle East are tied to their recovery of what has become known as the Einstein papers."

"What's the status of these mystery papers?" Lakeland asked.

"One of our agents was shot in a gunfight last night. But we managed to recover the papers."

"Excellent," the president said. Then he looked with concern at Benson. "How did your agent fare in the gunfight, Earl?"

"He's still in surgery, sir, but the doctors believe he'll pull through. The papers will be forwarded to the Advanced Physics Laboratory in Colorado so the scientists there can attempt to decipher the formula."

"What reason could the Chinese government have for inciting the trouble in the Middle East?" Robert Lakeland asked.

Canter, the director of the CIA, spoke.

"The NSA has alerted our agency that China has been amassing troops and supplies on their eastern coast. Till now we assumed they were there for the scheduled war games." Canter scanned the notes in front of him. "Since Hong Kong reverted to the Chinese in 1997, the Chinese government has had a pool of hard currency they never had before. They have been spending the windfall on advanced military hardware. To showcase the new hardware they have been enacting quarterly war games. In addition, China has become more aggressive. We believe it is their goal to assert themselves as the dominant force in Asia as quickly as possible. The fifty-year anniversary of the founding of the People's Republic is fast approaching. Our analysts have been bracing for a hostile move from the mainland against Taiwan for some time now."

The president stopped Canter. "Is it far-fetched to believe that the Chinese wanted the Einstein papers to create a weapon that would allow them to annex all of Asia and the Middle East?"

Benson answered. "That may have been their plan. Once they had an operational weapon, the annexation plan would be possible, sir. However, right now I believe their reason for inciting conflict in the Middle East is somewhat simpler."

"And what is that, General?"

"I think Mr. Canter is right. The Chinese plan is to draw off our forces from the Asian theater so they can attack Taiwan without fear of American retaliation. Once our armed forces are diverted to the Middle East, the Chinese have the time they need to strengthen their position in Taiwan. Perhaps China attacks Korea or Japan next."

"If that occurs we could lose the world to Chinese communism," the president said slowly, "after years of fearing the Russians."

"Sounds like a distinct possibility, sir," Benson said.

"When do you expect the Chinese will move against Taiwan?" the president asked Canter.

"Like I said," Canter explained, "October 1st, the anniversary date of the formation of the People's Republic of China. That would be my guess, sir."

"That gives us five days to stop the Chinese," the president said.

The president turned to the chairman of the Joint Chiefs of Staff. "I want naval redeployment orders drafted immediately. Split your forces—send half back to Asia, leave half in the Middle East. As soon as that is done, prepare a defense plan for Taiwan if we cannot get a naval force there in time."

The chairman and his aides rushed from the room.

"Canter, have your agency get me some human intelligence data from inside China. I want to be sure this theory of yours about the date of the attack is correct."

Canter rose and walked out the door.

"NSA, DIA, NRO—I want all your agencies to go to priority-one gathering. Every agency should share *any* information they receive about anything that remotely pertains to China." The heads of the agencies made their way to the door. "I mean *anything*. I don't want to go into this thing blind," the president stressed as the intelligence officers exited.

The room was almost empty. "General Benson, I want you to spearhead the work with the Einstein papers. See if you can get me an operational weapon that will stop the Chinese within five days."

The president and Benson both rose from their chairs and walked toward the door. "Your agent pulled our feet from the fire, Earl. If the Chinese still had those papers our country would be on the defensive, not the offensive. Where's your agent undergoing surgery?"

"Bethesda Naval Hospital, sir."

"I'll call to check on him, you can count on it."

CHAPTER 43

Martinez leapt to his feet when the surgeon entered the waiting room. The doctor's hospital scrubs were spotted with blood and he removed his glasses and rubbed his eyes. "I'm Dr. Gundersen," the surgeon said, motioning to a table away from the others in the waiting room. "Let's sit over here."

Martinez's face showed his concern.

"Don't freak out on me, Agent Martinez. I just need to rest my feet. I've been up most of the night," the surgeon said as he glanced longingly at the coffee machine in one corner of the waiting room, then decided against another cup. "Your partner is going to be fine. It was a good thing you arrived on the scene just after the shooting, though. The bullet missed his heart but we would have lost him from the hemorrhaging if you hadn't applied direct pressure to the wound when you did. As it was, it was a clean shot through the shoulder that just bled like hell. We don't anticipate Agent Taft will suffer any permanent damage."

"Thanks, Dr. Gundersen, you don't know how relieved this makes me feel." Martinez sighed and settled into the chair. "John and I have been partners a few years now. Do you know how soon it will be until he can be released?"

"Hard to say. Agent Taft appears to have some pretty strong

recuperative powers. His blood pressure hardly wavered during surgery. He even came out of the anesthesia at one point and winked at a nurse."

"John's about as tough as they come," Martinez agreed. "How much blood did he lose?"

"We ended up infusing three units, but I had another standing by if we needed it," Gundersen noted.

"That's some serious blood loss," Martinez said.

Gundersen nodded and rose to his feet. "Very serious. You can go into the recovery room now if you want," Gundersen said as he started to leave.

"Which way?" Martinez asked.

Gundersen pointed down a hall. "I'm just glad it went so well. This is the first time I've had a call from the president of the United States checking on a patient of mine," he said as he walked from the room.

An early snowstorm was blanketing the grounds outside the Advanced Physics Laboratory in Boulder, Colorado. The snow piled up on the trees outside. Some of the trees were still holding the leaves of summer, and the weight of the snow sent the limbs crashing to the ground. Schoolchildren were excused from school early and tow-truck drivers were working overtime.

In a laboratory on the ground floor six archivists from the Smithsonian were preparing to separate and treat Einstein's papers. Mounted to the workbenches in the laboratory were a series of the type of lighted and magnified scanners used by fly fishermen to tie delicate flies. Chet Hammond, leader of the archivists, was a sixty-year-old man who bore a remarkable resemblance to the famous author Ernest Hemingway.

Hammond carefully removed the stack of papers from the pouch. "Tweezers," he said to his assistant.

Taking the tweezers in his hand, he delicately peeled off the first page in the stack. He turned the paper two and fro with the tweezers. "Looks like the writing is only on one side. That should help some."

Motioning for his assistant to line up a Teflon-coated tile on the workbench, Hammond carefully placed the paper on the tile with the writing side visible. Hammond used tiles because paper would not stick to the surface as it dried. Next he rolled a support frame mounted with a camera above the tile. Adjusting the focus, he snapped three photographs.

"This is what we are going to do to each page," he said to the archivists.

One of the men raised his hand.

"Yes, Andrew, a question?"

"How do you want to dry the pages?"

"We're still testing methods. For now just separate the pages and place each one on a tile. Make sure that you take three pictures of each page. As you finish a roll of film signal one of the agents over there." Hammond pointed to two NIA agents dressed in black suits who were seated in a corner of the laboratory. "Do not open the camera or handle the film. The agents will remove the film and reload the camera."

Slowly and carefully the work began.

The dampness and deterioration of the last dozen papers had slowed the restoration process but the originals were now stabilized and copied. For drying the sheets Hammond decided simply to leave the papers on the tiles, turn the heat up in the laboratory, and post a guard. Jeff Scaramelli handed one of the folders filed with the series of photographs to Choi and smiled briefly. "Let's start combining these equations with what you've already completed and see what we have."

Choi's hands trembled slightly as he took the folder. "How long do you think it will take?"

"At least a couple of days," Scaramelli said. "Don't worry, the agents will notify your wife that you need to remain at the laboratory."

"We'll work around the clock," Choi said eagerly.

"That's the idea," Scaramelli agreed.

In the recovery room at Bethesda Naval Hospital, Taft regained consciousness. He touched the stitches on his shoulder, then opened his eyes. A nurse standing at the side of the bed was recording his vital signs on a chart.

"Mr. Taft," she said, "I see you've decided to grace us with your presence."

"Where am I?"

"Bethesda Naval Hospital," replied the nurse.

"I'm thirsty," Taft said.

The curtain surrounding Taft moved.

"That's probably your partner. The doctor just went to the waiting room to update him." She walked to the slit in the curtain and opened it.

"The doctor said I could visit," Martinez said, poking his head inside.

"Come on in, Mr. Taft's awake. I'm leaving to get him some ice water. I'll be back in a few minutes," the nurse said as she walked out.

Martinez slid back the curtain and walked over to Taft's bed.

"How are you feeling?" Martinez asked.

"Not as bad as the last time I was shot. My shoulder's a little sore, though," Taft said easily.

Martinez stared down at his partner. "Your color's good."

"You always know how to flatter me."

"The doctor said you'd be fine," Martinez relayed.

"Good."

"I just called Marie. The kids were up all night worrying about you. They'll be glad to hear you're okay."

"You have good kids, Larry. Send them my love," Taft said as he wet his lips with his tongue. "I need some water."

"You must still be high from the anesthesia. The nurse just went to get you some."

Taft nodded. "So what happened to the papers?"

"We recovered them. They're already in Colorado being studied."

"Good. I hate getting shot for no reason." Taft straightened up on the bed slightly. "Explain to me everything that happened."

"When the shots rang out I ran to the river to see if you needed help."

"I don't know why I bother to tell you anything, you never listen. I thought we'd agreed you would stay and wait for help."

"If I'd listened to you I'd be talking to a tombstone now," Martinez said easily.

Taft nodded slowly. "Okay, you win that round. Just so you know, the guy in the conning tower of the mini-sub was the shooter," said Taft.

"It turns out the courier had a gun too," Martinez said. "It appears he was reaching for it when your shot hit him."

"What's his condition?"

"Your bullet took off the top of his head; he was dead before he hit the ground. The papers must have fallen at his side. You probably don't remember this but you grabbed them and clutched them to your chest."

Taft looked away. He never relished the idea of killing a man. "I was aiming for his midsection, to try to wound him," he said quietly.

"You were hit yourself, your aim was off. It couldn't be helped," Martinez said. "You didn't start this war, so don't start feeling guilty now."

Taft nodded.

"Once I saw you were hit, I started firing at the sub," Martinez said. "When I'd used up my clip I fired the rounds in your pistol."

"What happened then?"

"You were bleeding quite a bit. I thought I'd better figure out a way to stop the bleeding. I called Central Operations on my cellular phone. One of the dispatchers called for a helicopter and talked me through the first aid until the chopper arrived." Martinez paused. "The sub managed to slip below the surface but it was tracked from Potomac Beach and it was stopped at the bridge by the navy. The *Carondelet*, the ship Benson mentioned we had agents watching, was acting as the tender. She remained just off the mouth of the Potomac and was boarded by a team of Navy SEALs."

"So the Chinese have no way of knowing we have the papers?"

"That's what we think right now. The SEAL team leader reported they secured the radio before anyone could call out."

"Good." Then Taft said slowly, "You saved my life, Larry. Thanks."

"You were bleeding pretty bad. I just kept my hand over the wound until we could chopper you out. No big deal."

"It is to me," Taft said. "I owe you one."

"Not a problem," Martinez said. "That's what partners are for."

The nurse returned with a plastic cup of ice water and handed it to Taft who downed the entire contents in one gulp. He smiled at the nurse and held out the empty cup.

"When can I eat?"

"Let me check with the doctor, Mr. Taft," she said as she took back the cup. "I'll bring you some more water in a couple minutes," she said and left again.

"Is it the drugs," Taft asked, "or is that nurse gorgeous?"

"I can see you're feeling better," Martinez chuckled. "And it's not the drugs. You're thinking clearly, she's a beauty."

"So we recovered the Einstein papers. I guess this ends our involvement with this."

"Looks like it," Martinez agreed.

"When can I get out of here?"

"The doctor wasn't sure, a couple of days probably. Do you want to stay with Marie and me while you recuperate?"

"Probably not. It would be nice to just relax at home for a change. It seems like months since I've been home."

"Hard to believe you brought Choi out of China less than two weeks ago," Martinez agreed. "You probably need to rest. Do you want me to bring you anything next time I visit?"

Taft thought for a moment. "See if you can find me a biography of Albert Einstein at the bookstore. I think I'd find that interesting."

"I'll be back in a couple of hours to check on you—I'll bring it then," Martinez said as he started to leave.

"Hey, Larry," Taft said as Martinez began to walk away.

Martinez turned and looked at Taft.

"Thanks again," Taft said, grinning.

Martinez smiled, then, shaking his head, he walked from the room.

CHAPTER 44

The summer palace of King Abdullah of Saudi Arabia was on top of a small hill overlooking the town of Taif. A stone and brick structure with over 40,000 square feet of space inside, the palace was completely surrounded by a high stone wall.

Although the palace was located less than fifty miles from the Red Sea, the area around Taif was dry and desert-like.

The grounds of the palace made sharp contrast with the surrounding terrain. Tons of topsoil had been brought in when the palace was being constructed and the grounds had the appearance of an English garden. Tall trees formed a small forest and a series of hedges forming a maze sat to one side of the grounds. Water pumped from a well on the property kept the immaculately trimmed grounds green. Behind the palace, to the left, was a cricket field, and a swimming pool and tennis courts were hidden from view behind the grove of trees.

The guests arriving at the palace passed through a series of security checks, starting with the gate leading into the compound. At the gate, the identities of the drivers and their passengers were checked. Then the limousines themselves were checked with a sophisticated sniffer that could detect any trace of a bomb. Once the guests arrived at the front door, they walked through a scanner similar to an X-ray machine.

Only then were they allowed to proceed any farther.

The conference room located on the ground floor of the palace was 8,000 square feet—eighty feet wide by one hundred feet long. The floors of the conference room were finished in white Italian marble. Clustered along the walls were rows of couches. The walls were covered in a rich red brocade fabric with intricate designs of gold and silver woven into the cloth. At the end of the room was a slightly elevated couch reserved for King Abdullah.

Behind the king's couch was the door through which he entered the room. In front of the couches were low, hand-carved mahogany tables. On the tables were crystal ashtrays, silver pots containing dark Arabian coffee, along with plates of delicate pastries, figs, and dates. Rivulets of condensation rolled down the silver pitchers filled with ice water.

Once the last of the guests had arrived, the doors were shut and guards were posted outside. After a wait of several minutes the door behind King Abdullah's couch was opened by an attendant and the king entered the room. After he made his way to his couch and sat, two bulky guards took positions just behind and to each side of the couch. The guards stood with folded arms, watching the guests.

"*Inshallah,*" the king began. "Thank you all for coming here today." He paused and motioned for coffee which an attendant quickly poured and handed to him. "Most of you are unaware of the crisis that has befallen the kingdom. In the last few days a biological weapon was introduced into our oil fields, which, had we not acted in time might have wiped out our oil reserves permanently. A radical Israeli faction has claimed credit for the attack." The king sipped from his coffee, then motioned to one of his brothers sitting to the side. "You look like you have a question, Amin."

Crown Prince Amin sat upright. "As you know, I have been in Switzerland and only just returned when I was telephoned to attend this meeting. Because of that, I know little about what has transpired. My question is, how do we know the radical Israelis are actually behind the poisoning of our oil fields?"

"A letter was received at the palace in Riyadh. The letter claims the poisoning was the work of a group calling itself the Jewish Front for Recognition."

The head of intelligence for the Saudi Arabian National Guard glanced at the king and nodded.

"You wish to add something, Yousef?" the king asked.

"Yes, King Abdullah. My organization has conducted a detailed search for information about a group called the Jewish Front for Recognition but we have turned up nothing."

Crown Prince Mashoud turned to Yousef. "How many Israeli groups does your agency follow?"

"At any one time as many as two hundred," Yousef admitted.

"And new groups are constantly being formed as other groups disband, is that not true?" Mashoud said.

"That is true, Crown Prince, but it is the other research we have done that is more distressing," Yousef said.

"What might that be, Yousef?" the king asked.

"The letter bore a postmark from Egypt," Yousef noted.

Crown Prince Mashoud leaned forward, motioning with his hands. "That is easily explained. The Israelis know we search every letter or package coming from their country for messages that might incite our citizens."

"But," Yousef continued, "we tested the paper the threat was written on and found it unusual."

"What was unusual?" the king asked.

"The paper they used is unavailable in the Middle East."

"Where does the paper come from?" the king inquired.

"It took us a great deal of work but we feel we now know the answer to that question," Yousef said. "After careful analysis we found traces of rice husks in the paper. Assuming that meant the paper was from somewhere in Asia, we requested samples of paper used in conjunction with the kingdom's oil contracts."

"Did you find a match?" the king asked.

"We did," Yousef said. "The paper was a direct match to a preliminary contract that was sent to us by the Chinese government."

In the office of the Israeli prime minister, the head of the Mossad, the Israeli intelligence arm, was placing a disarmed detonator cap on the desk.

"It's definitely of Chinese manufacture, sir."

The prime minister reached for the blasting cap and turned it over in his hand. "You took this off a bomb that was disarmed before exploding?"

"The Americans found it outside their embassy and disarmed the weapon, then loaned it to me to show to you."

"What about this group called Islamic Sword?" the prime minister asked.

"We have no record of such a group," the Mossad chief noted.

"What is your current theory as to who is behind the bombings?"

"As yet we are still unsure."

"May I suggest you find out quickly?" the prime minister said. "Members of the Knesset are calling for my ouster, while my military advisors are seeking approval for a first strike against Saudi Arabia."

The head of the Mossad nodded grimly. "We will get to the bottom of this."

CHAPTER 45

Yanni Arimen downshifted his British-made Ford as he weaved his way up the asphalt road leading ever higher up the mountain. He reached over and touched the flight bag on the seat next to him, something he had done five times already since leaving his home. Rounding a tight turn, he slowed as he noticed the fence and the guard shack ahead.

Pulling to a stop, he turned the car off, set the parking brake, then climbed from the car. Strangely enough, a guard walked toward him leading a beagle. While a second guard examined his identity card, the beagle climbed inside the car and sniffed around. Finding nothing of interest, the dog climbed from Arimen's Ford, wagged its tail a few times, then sauntered over and urinated on the car's front tire.

"Everything checks out, Major Arimen. Sorry about the delay," the guard said, handing back Arimen's identification.

Arimen nodded and climbed back in the car. He started his engine and waited until the gate slid to the side, then put his car in gear and drove into the compound. Following the road, he entered an underground parking lot. When he found a parking spot, he glanced around. The lot was nearly full, something Arimen hadn't seen since the Persian Gulf War almost nine years before. Arimen had just graduated from flight school when the war ended, but he remembered studying the American air war in great detail. Decisive air power proved the key to the Gulf War, Arimen knew.

As he grabbed his flight bag from the passenger seat, he wondered if his superiors felt the same way about the coming war.

Royal Saudi Army tank driver Saud Al-Sheik peered intently through his viewer as he steered his American-made M-1 tank up a gully under a cloudy, pitch-black night. The remote camera mounted on the turret of his tank beamed an image onto a screen inside the cockpit. Since it was night, Al-Sheik had switched on the camera's night-vision capability. The terrain flashed onto the screen with an eerie green glow.

Al-Sheik's journey would eventually take him near the Saudi Arabian town of Magna, but his immediate problem was locating a tanker truck so he could refuel. The massive engines of the M-1 burned fuel like it was being poured on a fire. Al-Sheik turned to his radioman.

"Send a coded message asking for the location of the tanker trucks," he said, turning back to the viewer.

"Do you want the location by map coordinates or GPS?" the radioman asked.

"Both," Al-Sheik said. The fuel gauge was reading one-quarter, and that was beginning to make Al-Sheik nervous.

Al-Sheik continued to steer up the gully. The tank was moving at only twenty-five miles per hour to conserve fuel. On open stretches, where the fuel burn rate was not a consideration, the M-1 was easily capable of fifty. Movement at the corner of the viewer screen caught Al-Sheik's eye. Instinctively trained to fear the worst, he moved his hand atop the fire control button.

A pair of desert deer ran down the side of the ravine. They darted back and forth across the path of the tank as it drew closer. When the M-1 was almost upon them the larger of the two, the buck, broke hard to the far side of the ravine. Leaping free, it raced up the side of the ravine.

The second deer, the doe, was not so lucky. Attempting to follow her mate she leapt a second too late. Crushed under the tracks of the tank her mangled body was unceremoniously tossed from the rear of the tank.

As the tank disappeared in the distance, the buck carefully approached. His mate had been flattened. She was little more than a deerskin pelt filled with crushed bones and viscera. Later that night the hyenas would come to feast. In the morning the buzzards would come calling.

"Commander Al-Sheik, I have the coordinates for the tanker," the radioman said.

Al-Sheik scanned the terrain. Finding what he felt was a safe place to stop, he steered to the edge of the ravine. After examining the coordinates on the sheet of paper he punched the numbers into a computer. The screen lit up with a map of the sector around them as well as a suggested route to reach the tanker. The fastest route to the tanker would take them into open desert, and that bothered Al-Sheik slightly. Still, it was night. If the Israeli jets came, Al-Sheik reasoned, it would be by morning light.

Pushing forward on the throttle, he steered his tank toward the fueling station.

❖   ❖   ❖

In the headquarters of the combined Israeli military forces, the attack planning was entering its final stage. It had been decided that if an attack against Saudi Arabia was to happen, it would be best if the Israeli troops, airplanes, and armored divisions avoided crossing over Jordan on their way to Saudi Arabia.

The Royal Jordanian Air Force would certainly try to defend their airspace, and that could hamper the Israeli efforts to strike first and hard. It was rumored that most of the southern tip of Jordan was littered with defensive installations. The mountain passes were protected by artillery, in addition to being rigged with explosive charges designed to eradicate the road as well as trigger landslides.

The Israeli high command had decided that the war would be led by the air force. Every squadron that was operational would fly over the southern tip of Israel across the Red Sea, then enter Saudi airspace just south of its border with Jordan. The troops and armored divisions would be ferried by ship. An amphibious landing would be attempted below Aqaba. The Israeli goal was to gain control of Saudi Arabia from the Tropic of Cancer north, including the capital city of Riyadh, within seven days.

It was an ambitious plan.

King Abdullah pointed down at the scale model of his country the Saudi military leaders were using for war planning.

"Make sure Mecca is protected at all costs," the king said firmly. "We are the custodians of the holy site for the entire Muslim world."

Major General Mohammed Hakim grabbed a pointer from the side of the table. "We have the town ringed with antiaircraft guns. A division of troops, along with a helicopter squadron, is stationed nearby. In the desert to the north of Mecca we have just completed the placement of an extensive number of mines. Mecca will be held, no matter what."

General Ali Mustach pointed to the northern part of the country. "Our armored divisions stand ready to attack through Jordan. We believe that as a fellow Arab nation the Jordanian government will support our efforts and allow our troops passage."

"The air force is ready to assume either an offensive or defensive posture," General Sultan Saud added. "We have prepared for both."

King Abdullah raised his hand and moved it in an arc around the table. "All of you should heed what Sultan Saud has said. I want your preparations to include every possible contingency." And with that he left the room, followed by his entourage.

National Security Advisor Robert Lakeland brushed the stack of photographs back into a pile and placed them in a folder. The light in the Oval Office was dim except around the president's desk, where a lamp burned brightly.

"That's the latest intelligence?" the president asked Lakeland.

"Only a few hours old, sir," Lakeland noted.

"Troops massing at the borders. Our AWACS planes are showing greatly increased air traffic. Satellite surveillance is detecting the movement of nuclear weapons. This looks ugly," the president said.

"A war *will* happen unless we act," Lakeland said, "and act now."

"What can we do to prevent this?" the president asked.

"We need to have the Secretary of State visit each country immediately and explain to their leaders everything we know."

"That might compromise the safety of Taiwan. If news leaked out that we knew of the plans, the Chinese might move early. With our limited military presence in that area right now, Taiwan could be lost for good," the president said wisely.

"What other option do we have?" Lakeland asked.

"Brute force," the president said. "Have the chairman of the Joint Chiefs of Staff come in here."

"What's your plan?" Lakeland asked.

"I'm going to position a squadron of B-52s loaded with nuclear cruise missiles over both the Persian Gulf and the Mediterranean Sea."

"And the message?" Lakeland asked.

"One that you are going to deliver in person," the president said. "First, negotiate—tell them some of what we know. Then, if that doesn't work, explain to them that whoever attacks the other side first will suffer immediate retaliation from the United States."

Lakeland rose to leave. "I should begin packing."

"I'll have *Air Force One* made ready to transport you," the president said as he rose from his chair and looked out the window. "And one more thing, Robert. Just between you and me, I'm not bluffing. It's your job to make that clear to both sides."

"I'll do the best I can, sir."

"I just need you to buy me a few more days, Robert," the president said wearily.

As *Air Force One* streaked east, Robert Lakeland read a Defense Department report that analyzed Israeli and Saudi deployments at their borders. The border was cluttered with fighter jets, transport planes, tanks, artillery, ground troops, and missile batteries.

In the Persian Gulf and the Red Sea, both nations had their navies on alert. A pair of Israeli submarines stationed in the Persian Gulf were being quietly tracked by a Saudi AWACS jet. The plane then relayed the information to six Saudi submarine chasers that stood ready to attack the subs if ordered. Surface ships of both nations were passing close enough to one another for crew faces to be visible.

Lakeland closed the folder containing the report, then removed his reading glasses and rubbed his eyes. With his eyes still closed he leaned back in his leather seat and rubbed his stiff neck. He was trying to will his body to relax when the air force steward walked over.

"Sir, we have a bed made up in the back of the plane for you. It's nice and quiet back there."

Lakeland opened his eyes and smiled. "That sounds good, Sergeant."

"Would you care for something before you sleep? Perhaps some hot chicken broth or hot chocolate?"

Lakeland rose from the seat. "Some hot chocolate would be nice."

"If you will follow me back to your cabin," the sergeant said, "I'll get you situated, then return with the hot chocolate and some of the chef's homemade oatmeal cookies."

Lakeland followed the steward to his cabin. Fifteen minutes later, when the steward returned to remove the empty dishes, Lakeland was fast asleep atop the bed. The steward covered him with a blanket and informed the guard at the end of the passageway not to disturb him.

Air Force One was crossing into Saudi Arabian airspace before Lakeland awoke. He had just shaved and showered as the plane set down at the airport in Riyadh. As soon as *Air Force One* rolled to a stop it was directed to a giant air-conditioned hangar off to one side of the airfield.

A fleet of limousines led by a pair of Saudi military Humvees sporting flashing lights drove directly into the hangar and pulled alongside *Air Force One*. Ali Al-Sheik climbed from the backseat of the middle limousine and stood waiting as Robert Lakeland descended the stairs.

Al-Sheik was of medium height by western standards, five feet eleven inches tall, and his weight had remained a constant 180 pounds since age twenty. Educated at the University of Virginia, with a master's degree from Georgetown University, Ali Al-Sheik had been the chief advisor for King Abdullah since his reign began a year ago. Al-Sheik had jet-black hair and a thin mustache. It was his genuine smile and his warm and friendly manner that attracted people, however.

Lakeland reached the floor of the hangar and walked toward Al-Sheik with his hand extended. After shaking hands, the two men climbed into the rear of Al Sheik's limousine and made themselves comfortable. As the procession pulled from the hangar Al-Sheik reached into an ice chest built into the door of the vehicle.

"I seem to remember you favor Dr. Pepper in a bottle, Bob," Al-Sheik said as he removed the cold soft drink and handed it to Lakeland.

"Are you still drinking that ginger ale you have shipped in from South Carolina?"

"Best stuff under the sun," Al-Sheik said.

In a twist of fate that occurs in diplomacy, Lakeland and Al-Sheik were friends from their student days at the University of Virginia. They were familiar enough to be direct with one another. As the limousine pulled onto the main highway leading from the airport and accelerated, Al-Sheik began the discussion.

"It appears the United States is not interested in diplomacy—otherwise I would be entertaining the Secretary of State and not you, my friend."

"I'm afraid you've summed up the situation with your usual speed, Ali," Lakeland said quietly.

"Then you come to threaten us with force."

"If necessary," Lakeland admitted.

The limousine slowed at an intersection, then followed the Humvees as they sped west toward the king's mansion. Lakeland looked out the window at the miles of sandy wasteland broken by the black ribbon of asphalt leading to the mansion.

"As advisor to the king I should warn you he does not enjoy being threatened," Al-Sheik said. "On a personal note, as your friend, I should tell you that you will have greater success if you explain the situation calmly and clearly. King Abdullah is quite a bit smarter than your intelligence agencies report."

Rising from the desert in the distance Lakeland saw the vast walled grounds of King Abdullah's palace. Rising above the walls Lakeland could see the towers that stood at the four corners of the mansion, as well as the second floor of the palace, which faced the approaching limousine.

"What do you mean?" Lakeland asked.

"We receive a great many intelligence briefings from the major world powers. The United States intelligence community seems to think Abdullah is a benevolent but not very wise leader."

"I wouldn't say that," Lakeland lied. In fact, what Al-Sheik had just said was the general assessment of Abdullah.

"Don't make that mistake," Al-Sheik cautioned Lakeland.

Lakeland stared at his friend and silently nodded.

The limousine was pulling up to the massive gate. The Humvees stationed themselves at each side of the gate like bookends. Once the limousine carrying Lakeland and Al-Sheik pulled to a stop at the gate, several dogs brought from inside the guard post sniffed the exterior and undercarriage of the limousine. Once the limousine was approved for entry into the palace the doors swung open. As they drove down the long cobblestone driveway Lakeland stared out the window at the palace grounds.

The rich landscaping surrounding the palace was a visible legacy of the king's attempt to defy the desert sands that comprised most of his kingdom. As Lakeland glanced out the window, a pair of peacocks strutted across the road to join a flock of nearly thirty birds that were clustered around an artificial pond. Perfectly positioned palm trees, set exactly eight feet apart and six feet back from the cobblestones, lined the roadway. In the half-dozen feet between the cobblestones and the start of the palm trees, vast color-coordinated flower gardens replicated the colors of the rainbow ending in a field of deep-blue violets nearest the palace.

The limousine pulled to a stop in front of the main section of the mansion. Bought from a noble French family that had fallen on hard times, each brick of the massive sixteenth-century structure had been painstakingly disassembled and hand-numbered by a Belgian construction crew. Transported by a Boeing 747 cargo plane, the bricks were carefully reassembled around a modern steel frame, incorporating state-of-the-art heating, cooling, plumbing, and security systems. The site King Abdullah had selected for his palace was atop a small bluff overlooking the lights of Riyadh.

As soon as the door to the limousine was opened, Lakeland could feel the heat from the desert. The full effects of the heat were more obvious as Lakeland stepped from the limousine. Deep breathing was difficult and Lakeland's eye membranes dried quickly, making him feel as if he had sand in his eyes.

Lakeland and Al-Sheik followed a butler up a red carpet to the main door, a massive slab of antique wood dating back to the castle's original construction. Once the door swung silently open, they were led into a stone-floored foyer that ended in steps leading down to the main living areas. To the left was a massive carved-wood staircase that curved and rose into the second level, where eighteen bedrooms were arranged along a long hallway. Lakeland's eyes slowly scanned the opulence.

"I thought we would talk in my study," a voice broke the silence.

Lakeland glanced to the right, where King Abdullah stood framed in a doorway. Abdullah was a large man weighing nearly

270 pounds. His chest and shoulders were massive, and though he had a slight paunch he appeared reasonably fit.

Dressed in Italian trousers and silk shirt, with a pair of butter-soft Swiss-made Bally loafers on his feet, Abdullah could have blended in at a fashionable New York discotheque if not for the red-and-white checkered headdress he wore over his hair.

Lakeland followed Al-Sheik to where the king was standing. Abdullah smiled, then extended his hand toward Lakeland. His grip was cool and firm, Lakeland noted as they shook.

Lakeland detected a slight British accent when Abdullah said, "Come on inside, please."

Abdullah walked behind an antique dark mahogany desk, then motioned for his guests to be seated. After secretly pushing a button beneath his desk, he waited until a servant appeared. The walls of the study were lined with stout wooden bookcases filled with the classics on the higher shelves and popular books and novels in several languages on the lower shelves.

"We will need refreshments," he said quietly.

The servant scurried off toward the kitchen as Abdullah peered over at Lakeland. "Ali tells me you and he attended university together."

"Yes," Lakeland said. "It was years ago but it seems like it was only yesterday."

The servant reentered the study carrying a tray of finger sandwiches and two pots, the one containing hot tea, the other strong Arabian coffee. He set them down noiselessly, then stood off to the side.

"We can serve ourselves," the king said to the servant, who bowed at the waist and walked from the study, closing the door behind him. Abdullah poured a cup of the tea then added a measure of hot milk and a single lump of sugar. Carefully stirring the mixture, he set the spoon to the side and took a sip. Smiling at the taste, he addressed Lakeland.

"My ambassador to the United States seems to feel that a

visit by the president's National Security Advisor can only mean that a threat wishes to be relayed. Is that the case, Mr. Lakeland?"

Lakeland returned the smile. "What would you have us do, King Abdullah?"

"For starters you might tell me about the Chinese and what involvement they have in all this," Abdullah said as he lifted one of the trays of finger sandwiches and offered them to his guests.

Lakeland felt like he had been hit between the legs with a garden rake. He struggled to regain composure. "I'm not sure what you mean, King Abdullah."

"I'm not one for the machinations of diplomacy, so let me simply ask you, Mr. Lakeland. Were the Chinese involved in the attack on our oil reserves or not?"

Lakeland sat in stunned silence while the two men stared at him.

"Do you need to make a telephone call?" Al-Sheik asked after thirty seconds had passed.

Lakeland shifted, as if coming out of a trance. "No, I just went over it in my head. I feel I should answer this truthfully. Yes, King Abdullah, we do believe the Chinese government is involved in the attack on your oil fields."

"And the Israelis?" Abdullah asked.

"Is your country in any way involved in the bombings in Israel?" Lakeland asked Abdullah.

"Of course not."

"Since you know that to be true beyond doubt then it stands to reason the bombings also must be the work of the Chinese," Lakeland said. "Wouldn't you agree?"

"Can you tell me why the Chinese have seen fit to poison our oil and incite my country to the brink of war?"

"We believe we know the answer, King Abdullah, but we cannot disclose that information at this time."

Abdullah leaned back in his chair and stroked the hair on his chin. He slowly began to rock in his chair. Lakeland watched silently as several minutes passed.

"I will order my forces to stand down if you get the Israelis to do the same," King Abdullah said. "But on one condition."

"And the condition?" Lakeland asked.

"That you allow my country one act of retaliation against China."

"And what will that be?" Lakeland asked.

"I will determine that later," King Abdullah said.

"To agree to that I would need to talk to the president," Lakeland said quietly.

"There is a small office outside the door that my assistant sometimes uses," Abdullah said. "Please feel free to use the telephone in there. It will allow you a measure of privacy."

Ten minutes later Lakeland had an agreement between the president and King Abdullah and was back inside the limousine, heading for the airport. He turned to Al-Sheik.

"Thanks for the advice about King Abdullah."

Al-Sheik nodded.

"Can I ask what led you to suspect the Chinese?"

"You can ask," Al-Sheik said as the limousine turned off the highway onto the access road to the airport. "But that doesn't mean I'll answer."

Air Force One had received permission to fly over Jordan, making the flight time to Tel Aviv just over two hours. In the plane bound for Israel, Lakeland thought about his options. The latest intelligence information had just been sent to Lakeland over a secure fax line direct to the plane.

Lakeland could see time was of the essence.

The latest satellite photographs showed the Israel army breaking camp at their staging area near Elat. The images Lakeland viewed were so detailed they showed the tents that had housed the troops being taken down, plumes of exhaust from truck engines being started, even the boxes of supplies being loaded into the rear of the open trucks.

Lakeland was less than thirty minutes from landing when he closed the file containing the photographs and placed the magnifying glass back in the seat pouch. Turning to his side, he motioned to an air force officer.

"I need the communications officer to connect me with the president, ASAP," he said wearily.

Less than three minutes later the officer returned from the front of the plane. "The president will be on the line in two minutes, sir," the officer said, pointing to the front of the plane.

Lakeland rose from his seat and walked forward to a small room containing the communications equipment. The officer rapped on the locked door and waited until it was opened from inside. Holding the door open, he motioned for Lakeland to enter.

The communications room was small. The walls were padded to make the room soundproof. The reporters who often flew on *Air Force One* liked to hang out near the communications room in an effort to obtain information. The room was stacked floor to ceiling with electronic equipment. An air force chief master sergeant pointed to a stool, then handed Lakeland a headset that had a small microphone in front.

After a wait of twenty seconds or so, he whispered to Lakeland, "On in ten seconds."

A voice that Lakeland recognized as the president's secretary came over the headset. "Hold, please, for the president."

And then the voice of President Harper came over the headset as clearly as if they were sitting next to one another.

"What is it, Robert? It must be important."

"Have you seen the latest satellite photographs over Israel?"

"I was in a meeting with the Joint Chiefs of Staff examining them when I was told you needed to speak to me."

"I still have 20 minutes of flight time before I reach Israel, plus the time it takes to drive to the prime minister's office. I'm afraid the Israelis are going to move before I speak to the prime minister."

The telephone was silent as the president thought.

"I have no choice but to call the prime minister myself," Harper said.

"I hope it will go as smoothly for you with Israel as it did for me with Saudi Arabia, Mr. President," Lakeland said.

"Have *Air Force One* bypass Israel and set a course for home," the president said. "Even if we can avert this war in the Middle East, we still have China to contend with, and I'll need you here for that."

It took the U.S. Navy's nuclear submarine *Montana* signaling its presence in the Mediterranean Sea, a fly-over of air force fighters from Turkey, and a stern threat from the president to forestall the Israeli attack. Finally, fearing retaliation from the United States, the prime minister and the defense minister agreed to hold off any hostile actions until they met with the Secretary of State, who would arrive in seventy-two hours.

It was an uneasy truce. The distrust between the Arabs and the Jews remained, a legacy far older than the Chinese attempt to inflame the anger to action; but the threat of an immediate conflagration was defused. Both sides began to slowly withdraw their offensive troops from the borders. Three days later, after the Secretary of State met with the Israeli leaders, the situation was stabilized enough to begin the withdrawal of American forces from the region.

On the eve of September 28, the American naval battle groups in the Persian Gulf and the Red Sea were ordered to begin steaming toward the Taiwan Strait at flank speed. Even cruising at full speed, only a few of the United States Navy's faster ships could reach the area by the October 1st deadline. Luckily, the United States' nuclear submarines, the thoroughbreds of the sea, would prove to be a different story.

CHAPTER 46

"The Americans have discovered our intentions in the Middle East," Sun Tao said while slowly drawing on a cigarette.

"How can you be so sure," the Chinese prime minister asked, "that they discovered China is involved?"

"The latest from our intelligence sources suggests their naval battle groups have begun to leave the Middle East and are steaming through the Indian Ocean."

"They could simply be returning to their bases in Okinawa and the Philippines," the prime minister said as he sipped from a glass of Coca-Cola. "The English-speaking news organizations report a truce has been obtained in the Middle East."

"Don't you find it odd there is no mention in the news media about the terms of the truce or the cause of the unrest?"

"There was some attention given to that topic today," the prime minister said. "The Western media reported on both the Islamic Sword and the Front for Jewish Recognition. News reports today mention the police in both countries will be trying to find the ringleaders of both groups. That leads me to believe our cover story is still holding."

The room was silent as both men thought.

"You may be right, sir," Tao said. "But whatever the case may be, the distance the United States Navy needs to travel to provide any measurable help to Taiwan is great. Our experts estimate they cannot reach Taiwan until the 2nd or 3rd of October even if they continue to run at flank speed."

"And the Einstein papers, the key to our future power—are they safely in our grasp?" the prime minister asked.

"The *Carondelet,* the ship transporting the papers, finally left the Chesapeake Bay yesterday. All efforts to contact the ship by radio have been for naught. We believe the ship simply has communications problems. If their radios are out, the only way to reach them would be to air-drop them a new radio."

"Is the *Carondelet* headed south toward Cuba as planned?"

"Yes, they appear to be on a direct course. In addition the *Carondelet* is following the original plan precisely. We have had Chinese agents positioned in a fishing trawler offshore of Norfolk. They reported that when the *Carondelet* passed their trawler it was flying the Chinese flag."

"That *was* our signal the mission was a success, was it not?" the prime minister said loudly.

"Yes. Still, the lack of radio contact bothers me," Tao said. "I would think the electricians or the radio technicians on the *Carondelet* would have the skills to repair at least one radio by now."

"The problem could be one of a hundred things, from an electrical glitch to a shipboard fire," the prime minister said confidently. "If the Americans had recovered the papers, we would have heard something about it by now. We have spies everywhere."

"Then it is your wish for us to proceed with the attack on Taiwan?"

"When is the *Carondelet* due to reach Cuba?" the prime minister asked, temporarily deflecting the question.

"The morning of October 1st," Tao answered.

"That means if we fly the papers here by fast jet we would

have them in our hands by the second day of the battle for the liberation of Taiwan."

"If all goes according to plan, yes," Tao agreed.

"Then we proceed with the attack on Taiwan as planned. The U.S. Navy was the one element that could have stopped the attack cold. It appears they will not be able to reach Taiwan in time to stop us. Later, if they decide to interfere with our plans after the initial day of battle, we will explain to their president that we have the Einstein papers and have built a weapon based on its formula."

"As a threat?" Tao asked.

"A threat with some teeth in it. Particularly once we explain the powers the formula can unleash."

"But we still aren't sure what the formula can be used for," Tao said logically.

"Neither are the Americans," the prime minister said quietly. "Neither are the Americans."

Tao sipped from a cup of green tea. "Then everything is falling perfectly into place."

"Yes," the prime minister said, smiling. "Once again we have outwitted the capitalists. To the rise of a new dynasty. One that will last ten thousand years."

Tao touched his tea cup to the prime minister's glass of cola and smiled.

Twelve miles off Cape Hatteras in the Atlantic Ocean an early fall storm was blackening the sky. Commander Oakes turned to Chief Petty Officer Chutetski.

"Have all the Chinese electronics been safely jettisoned?"

"Packed in watertight crates with locaters attached."

"Another SEAL team will retrieve them from the ocean floor within the hour. Once they are taken to the intelligence experts and analyzed, they should provide a treasure trove of information," Oakes noted.

"What will the intelligence boys be looking for?" Chutetski asked.

"Codes, how their scramblers work, communications frequencies, stuff like that," Oakes explained.

"The rest of our team seems to be handling the ship without problem. What do you want me to do?" Chutetski said.

"Start rigging the fuel lines for a fire. Once the *Carondelet* is within fifty miles of Cuba our orders are to torch it."

"Sounds like fun," Chutetski said as he began to climb down the ladder, then stopped. "Commander?"

"What, Chutes?"

"Slow burn or fast?"

"Make it medium," Oakes said.

Jeff Scaramelli slurped from a cold cup of stale coffee, then tossed his pencil in the air, sticking it in a ceiling tile. After glancing at Choi, who shrugged his shoulders, he turned in his chair.

"We've got nothing," Scaramelli said in a voice tinged by disgust.

Benson stared directly into Scaramelli's eyes. "You're sure?"

Scaramelli glanced at Choi, then slowly nodded. "I hate to be the one to tell you this, General Benson, but the formula you brought us is like a giant jigsaw puzzle of the Lincoln Memorial."

"Only with Abraham Lincoln's beard missing," Choi added.

"Son of a bitch," Benson muttered.

For two days now Benson had been patiently waiting in Boulder for the physicists to finish their work. The waiting was taking its toll on the general. "Damnit," he said bitterly. "Do you have *some* idea of what the formula contains? I would like to tell the president *something*."

Choi glanced at Scaramelli, who nodded. "We think if we

could solve the equation we might be able to explain most of the world's natural phenomena, sir."

"Could you be more specific?" Benson asked.

"Not really," Scaramelli said, staring at Choi.

"How do whales find their way underwater, why migrating birds don't become lost, maybe why mineral deposits are where they are—heck, it's still all up in the air," Choi said quietly.

"If you *could* understand this formula," Benson asked, "could you build a weapon that would stop an invading army?"

"General," Scaramelli said, "if we had the solution to these equations, I could make a waterfall flow uphill."

"You men keep working," Benson said. "Maybe something will break. I want you to understand something. The solution to these equations is the most important thing you will probably ever work on. The lives of hundreds of thousands of people hang in the balance."

Scaramelli and Choi nodded slowly, then started working again. It had been two days since either man had slept.

The relentless heat of an Indian summer gripped Washington, D.C. The sun seemed to burn with a vengeance brought about by the knowledge that winter would soon be here. In the District of Columbia ordinary citizens went about their daily rituals never suspecting a war that could envelop the world was only days away.

At a coffee shop less than a mile from the White House a clerk from the Department of Veterans Affairs dipped a toast point into his over-easy eggs, then chewed. In front of the reflecting pond on the Washington Mall a retired schoolteacher from New Zealand took a photograph of his wife for their travel album. Edging forward in thick traffic on the road from Silver Springs to the District, an accountant from the General Services Administration listened to a Spanish language tape and repeated the phrases he heard.

Special Agent John Taft awoke in his hospital bed in Bethesda. Raising the top of the bed with the electric lift, he stared out the window at the sunny day. As he waited for the nurse to arrive he took stock of his body. He was still tired and sore but his color had improved, and his appetite had returned with a vengeance.

With a little luck this would be the morning he would be returning home for the first time in what seemed like years. He had enjoyed reading the biography of Albert Einstein that Martinez had brought, but he felt strangely removed from the case at this point. Taft had been injured before in the line of duty. Once he was crushed by a truck and had nearly died. He had broken his ankle parachuting into Pakistan with a heavy pack on his back. His arm had been broken while he was being tortured in Vienna, Austria. He had even been shot once before, a round that glanced off the side of his head, opening up his scalp but causing little damage.

Each time he was badly injured he became reflective.

He felt that at his age he should already be a father. He wondered if he should return to school and make a career change. He was good at his job—one of the best in his profession—but he wondered if it was just a matter of time before fate caught up with him and he was killed in some backwater country performing a mission he doubted would hold much value for the world. Sometimes he dreamed of giving it all up—maybe returning to school for his doctorate and becoming a professor in political science—something where his experience could be used for good. Or maybe just buying a fishing boat and making his living outdoors every day trying to farm the ocean. He wondered if he shouldn't find someone to marry, then opt for an NIA office job and leave the field operations to those younger and more eager.

He was deep in thought when the nurse walked into the room.

"You rang?"

"Have you considered my offer?" Taft asked.

"Yes I have," the nurse said, smiling. "And as interesting as your offer of a full-body massage might seem, I'm afraid I have to work Friday night."

"I'd just break your heart anyway," Taft said in jest. "In that case, who do I have to kill to get breakfast around here?"

The nurse glanced at her clipboard. "This shows you filled out an order for breakfast but not for lunch."

"That's because I'm going home."

The nurse glanced at her clipboard again. "I don't see that anywhere."

"Maybe that's because I haven't told them yet," Taft said.

The nurse poked her head out the door. "The food cart is two rooms down, so your food will be here shortly. Do you want me to call the doctor for you to see about releasing you?"

"Sure, give him a call," Taft said. "But bring me my clothes just in case. If I have to escape I don't want my ass hanging out of this gown as I run out the front door."

"I don't know why, John," the nurse said, "but I think I'm going to miss having you as a patient."

"It was the sponge bath we shared," Taft said as the nurse walked out.

Twenty minutes later Taft was fully clothed and sitting in a chair in his room, finishing up the last of his breakfast.

"You really should stay here a few more days," Dr. Gundersen advised.

"Appreciate the offer, but I think I'd be happier at home."

"Let me just note on the form that I asked you to stay," Gundersen said. "Then I'll have a nurse bring up a wheelchair."

Martinez entered the room just as Taft finished slipping on his shoes.

"Will you explain to your partner he needs to ride downstairs in a wheelchair?" Gundersen said.

"Don't look at me for help. He never listens to me," Martinez said easily.

After thanking the nurses and shaking Gundersen's hand, Taft followed Martinez to the elevator and rode down. Following Martinez across the parking lot, he climbed in the passenger seat of an NIA sedan.

As they pulled out of the parking lot Taft spoke.

"I've been cooped up inside for way too long," he said easily. "Let's stop and let me get some fresh air before you take me home."

"Do you want to go downtown?"

"That's fine," Taft said, rolling down his window.

Taft was quiet as Martinez steered the sedan through light traffic and drove toward the Washington Mall. Taft watched the scene through the open window. The tourists visiting the capital in the fall were mainly older couples, seniors visiting in the off-peak season to save money. The kids who flocked to the nation's capital in summer were already back in school. Most of the citizens of the District were at work, so the area around the mall was not crowded. Taft saw a shadow pass over his arm, which was resting on the edge of the car door. He glanced up at the sky and watched a flock of birds pass overhead. Unlike ducks and geese, which attempt to maintain a formation when they fly, these birds were common wrens and their flock fluttered about as if their leader was indecisive as to direction. Taft glanced back through the windshield as Martinez slowed the sedan and turned.

Martinez pulled into a parking lot and parked the car. Walking over toward the passenger door, Martinez glanced at Taft.

"I can handle it Larry, thanks," Taft said as he swiveled to the edge of the seat, then pushed himself to standing with his good arm.

Without any words being spoken, the two men walked to the Vietnam Memorial. Stopping at the nearest end, they looked at the black marble wall of the memorial. The names of the dead were etched deeply into the stone, a silent but visible reminder of the cost of freedom. Walking a short distance away from the slab, the pair sat on a park bench and breathed in the scenery.

"You want one of these beers?" Martinez said, reaching into his jacket pocket.

"I didn't think you'd remembered my request," Taft said.

"I figured Gundersen would be pissed if I gave you one in the hospital. But I didn't forget. Ask and you shall receive—that's my motto," Martinez said, smiling.

Together the men sipped the lukewarm beer in silence.

"You okay, John? You seem a little quiet," Martinez asked.

"Ah, you know," Taft said, "just wondering about my place in all this."

"If it helps any, Jeff Scaramelli, the physicist at the Advanced Physics Lab who's been working with Choi on the Einstein papers, said to say thank you. It turns out his father was one of Einstein's drivers in college and Jeff grew up in awe of the man. He calls the papers the greatest scientific discovery of the twentieth century," Martinez said as he finished the beer and tossed the empty into a trash can next to the bench.

"Then my labors were not in vain."

"Not completely, anyway, but there is a snag. It seems that Scaramelli and Choi still can't understand what the theory is all about," Martinez said slowly. "Apparently, the last and final key to the equation was not among the papers we recovered. That was according to the last report I received, which was just before I left the office to pick you up at the hospital."

Taft sipped his beer quietly, then shook his head as if disgusted.

Martinez stared at his friend. "I'll say it again—are you all right? You've been acting strange since we left the hospital."

"Just thinking," Taft said as he straightened up on the bench. "So you're telling me we chased someone halfway across the country, plus I was nearly killed recovering these papers, and now the physicists can't figure out what the equations mean?"

"Sucks, doesn't it?" Martinez said quietly.

"I'll say," Taft said as he took another sip. "Are they going to work on the equations some more?"

"That's the word, but apparently they can already tell they won't be able to solve the final equation as it stands. The physicists all agree some important part is missing."

Taft closed his eyes and rubbed his forehead. He still felt tired and sore, and now the stitches in his shoulder were itching. And now this. Everything he had done was a giant waste of time.

Some say don't sweat the little things and the big things will take care of themselves; others believe it's all in the details. One little thing was nagging Taft. What little thing was he missing? In his mind he ran through all that had happened.

And then it hit him.

Taft's disgust gradually gave way to a thin smile and finally rolling laughter.

Martinez stared at his partner in concern. "Maybe we ought to take you home. You look like you could use some rest."

Taft shook his head at his partner. "Not quite yet," he said confidently. "We need to go back to the car now and call the general."

"What the *hell* are you talking about?" Martinez said as he rose and began to follow Taft toward the parking lot.

"The final equation," Taft said, smiling. "I know where to find it."

CHAPTER 47

At Andrews Air Force base outside Washington, D.C., a dark gray Gulfstream jet sat on the runway with its door ramp down and engines warming. Martinez drove to the side of a hangar, then parked and locked the sedan.

"You're sure you feel up to this?" he said to Taft as they walked toward the jet. "The agency has other personnel who can handle this project."

"I've gone this far," Taft said, "I want to see this through. I need to make sure I'm right."

Martinez nodded, and knowing that further argument would be futile, climbed up the ramp and made his way to the rear of the jet. Taft stopped at the door and signaled the pilot in the cockpit that they were aboard. The ramp retracted and in less than a minute the Gulfstream was taxiing toward the runway. Three minutes later they were airborne.

Flying east, Taft and Martinez arrived at the Long Island airport in early afternoon. They were met at the door of the Gulfstream by an NIA agent, who motioned to his car. Once they were seated inside they were driven toward the water. The agent followed Taft's directions, and they arrived at the marina in less than ten minutes.

"We're going to be gone a couple of hours," Taft explained to the agent. "You can leave and return later if you'd like."

Sliding the sedan into park, the agent reached under the seat and withdrew a paperback novel. "My orders are to wait here until you finish," he said, and using the novel for a writing surface, scribbled a number on a business card and handed it to Taft. "Here's my cellular number. If you need anything, just call."

As Taft and Martinez climbed from the car, the agent was already thumbing through the paperback. Stopping at the grocery store inside the marina building, Taft purchased a box of trash bags and a roll of duct tape, then walked next door to the local dive shop. Taft stared at the certifications on the wall as he waited until a compressor in the rear shut off and the owner emerged from the rear of the shop.

"Are you Walt Taylor?"

"In the flesh," the man said, smiling.

Taylor appeared near fifty years old but fit from a lifetime of outdoor activity. His skin was tanned and leathery. His graying hair was covered with a black bandanna, and a thin scar ran along the side of his face. The scar was the result of scraping his face along an iron support beam inside a shipwreck. He walked with a slight limp from suffering the bends when he stayed underwater too long. All Taylor needed was an eye patch and a parrot on his shoulder and he'd be at home in a pirate movie.

"I need to hire you for the rest of the afternoon," Taft told Taylor without preamble, "for a private charter."

"Charter to where?" Taylor asked.

"I need to dive a wreck out near Block Island."

"Are you both diving?" Taylor said, pointing to Martinez.

"No," Taft said. "I want you to dive with me. Larry here will stay topside and watch over the boat."

"I'll need to close my shop for the afternoon. I don't have anyone that can take over." Taylor turned his head sideways slightly as he sized up Taft. "I'm afraid the cost is going to be a flat five hundred dollars."

Taft smiled at Taylor. "The government is paying for this trip, so money won't be a problem."

Taylor smiled. "The boat's out back. It's already fueled but it'll take me a few minutes to load up the gear."

"We'll meet you in back in a couple of minutes," Taft said.

Taft motioned to Martinez, then walked outside to the other agent waiting in the car. "Call General Benson for me and ask him to contact the air force to see what's the fastest plane they have that will make it to Colorado without refueling. If I'm successful we'll need to transport something west ASAP."

The agent nodded. "No problem, Agent Taft."

He was reaching for his phone as Taft walked away.

Taylor had finished stowing the gear when they returned. Taft stared at the name on the stern as he and Martinez climbed aboard the dive boat. The agents cast off the lines and Taylor, seated above in the flybridge, pulled smoothly away from the dock.

The dive vessel, which was named *Sir Walter*, was new but spartan in furnishings. Designed for diving, not pleasure cruising, its catamaran hull provided a stable platform but little in the way of creature comforts—a single head below, tank racks lining the gunwales, and a pair of large portable ice chests mounted on the deck. The seating consisted of benches padded with cushions covered in beige vinyl.

As they cleared the no-wake area outside the marina the dive instructor called down to the deck from the flybridge. "You two grab a seat. I'm going to take us up to cruising speed."

Taft and Martinez settled into a bench running down the center of the boat as Taylor advanced the throttles on the pair of 250 horsepower Evinrude FITCH outboard engines. The boat immediately responded. Once at cruising speed, they made fast time to the site off Block Island where the *Deep Search* had raised the *Windforce*.

Taft directed the dive-boat owner where to anchor using a hand-held GPS unit. Once they were over the spot, Taft shouted to Martinez, who unhooked the anchor and dropped it into the water. When they were sure the anchor was set and holding, Taylor backed *Sir Walter* off a short distance and shut down the engines. Climbing down from the flybridge, he turned to Martinez.

"In case there's an emergency I left the keys in the ignition."

"Gotcha," Martinez said.

Taft removed his shirt, exposing the bandage over his shoulder wound. "Tape me up," Taft said to Martinez.

Taylor stared at the bandage, began to say something, then decided to remain silent.

Martinez wrapped Taft's shoulder then bound the area with the tape.

Once the taping was complete Taylor helped Taft pull the wet suit up over his shoulder, now wrapped in a plastic garbage sack.

Taylor couldn't help but notice as Taft winced in pain. "Are you sure you want to do this?" he asked quietly.

Taft gritted his teeth and nodded.

Martinez glanced at his partner. "Are you *sure* you'll be all right? You lost a fair amount of blood. I don't want you blacking out down there."

"This won't take long," Taft said.

Taylor and Martinez stared at one another. "Don't worry, I'll keep a close eye on him," Taylor said. "I haven't lost a diver yet, and it's too damn late in my life to start now."

Taylor quickly pulled on his wet suit, then checked both sets of gear in preparation for the descent. After being helped into his BCD, Taft slipped his fins over his feet, placed his mask over his eyes, and took a breath from his regulator. After giving a quick thumbs-up sign, he climbed onto the dive platform then stepped into the water. Taylor quickly put on his gear and followed.

Taft jerked in pain as the saltwater crept inside his wet suit and slipped under the plastic and tape. The jury-rigged waterproofing job on his shoulder had not worked. The stitches were already soaked and Dr. Gundersen would later need to replace them. Taft waited as Taylor adjusted his gear in the water and signaled all was okay.

Communicating with one another through hand signals, the two men swam to the anchor line, then began to descend slowly into the depths.

When they reached the bottom, Taft began to swim in a circle. The water was cloudy and the light he carried seemed to reflect back as much as it pierced through the murk. Taft swam slowly, his arms outstretched, feeling as well as looking. Luckily the GPS coordinates he had written down were on the money. He found the small stern piece from *Windforce* after only a short search.

Kneeling on the ocean floor, Taft motioned for Taylor, who had kneeled next to him, to help him raise the rusted stern hatch. Jamming his dive knife into a crack, Taft pried the crack wider until their hands could fit inside.

The hatch was warped and weathered from its years underwater, but it gave way slowly as the two men tugged. When the opening was large enough, Taft slid one leg into the opening. Standing on the floor of the ocean and supporting himself using Taylor's shoulder, Taft wrenched the hatch with his leg.

Once Taft had the hatch two-thirds open, he stopped to look. Several small crabs scurried from the opening as Taft shined his light inside. With his light Taft searched the area carefully while Taylor watched.

Taft found absolutely nothing. The inside was as barren as the surface of the moon.

Reaching out his gloved hand, Taft slammed the hatch closed angrily. All this work for nothing, he thought to himself. Thousands of man-hours, millions of dollars, and for what? A giant practical joke that had brought the world to the edge of annihilation?

Finally Taft had to accept harsh reality—the theory was never completed. He stood on the ocean floor and exhaled a sigh through his regulator. Shrugging his shoulders at Taylor, he willed himself to relax. It was not the end of the world—at least not yet.

He stared at the stern section in disgust.

His wrenching open of the hatch had pulled the buried stern section slightly from the silty bottom. Taft waited as the murky water was cleared by the current. He began to make out the outline of what appeared to be symbols. Taft touched the hatch and felt something whittled into the wooden surface. Moving rapidly, he tore off his gloves and traced his fingers along the etched wood.

Hands shaking from the cold, he was beginning to feel the excitement of possibly wringing victory from defeat. Taft ripped the board from its worm-eaten mounting. Bringing the board up to his face mask, he shined the dive light onto the etchings. For a few seconds he stared at the carved letters and symbols in shock. Smiling inside his mask, he motioned with his hand to Taylor that it was time to surface. Kicking with his fins, he started his ascent with the board safely in his hands.

When they broke the surface they were directly alongside the catamaran.

Taft yanked his regulator from his mouth. "Larry," he shouted, and Martinez's head appeared over the side of the *Sir Walter*. "Grab this."

Taft passed the board up to Martinez, who quickly wrapped it in a wet towel.

Swimming to the dive platform Taft climbed the ladder then stepped onto the deck of the boat and removed his gear. Walking back, he helped Taylor get inside the boat and helped him off with his tank.

Taft removed his badge from the pocket of his pants and flashed it open. Looking deep into Taylor's eyes Taft said quietly, "This is a matter of national security. It's important for you to forget this ever happened."

Taylor nodded. "What happened?"

"Thanks, Walt," Taft said as he toweled off his face. "There will be a nice bonus for a successful job."

"Works for me," Taylor said as he pulled off his wet suit. Then he walked to the bow of the *Sir Walter* and pulled the anchor. A few moments later he climbed up to the flybridge, started the engines, and set a course for Long Island.

Taft and Martinez set the board on the bench and stared at the inscriptions. With Taylor hard on the throttles, the group aboard the *Sir Walter* was back at the dock in under an hour.

CHAPTER 48

As soon as the black Sikorsky helicopter touched down at the marina on Long Island four commandos leapt from the side door and raced toward Taft and Martinez, who were seated in the rental car. Dressed entirely in black and toting black composite assault rifles, the commandos' demeanor was as serious as the situation. They quickly assumed a defensive position around the car, and Taft waited until they were in place before rolling down the window.

"I take it you're our ride," Taft said to the commando nearest the door.

"Our orders are to guard you aboard the helicopter," said the commando.

With the board clutched under his arm still wrapped in the wet towel, Taft climbed from the driver's seat. Martinez rose from the passenger seat. Surrounded by the commandos, the pair proceeded to the helicopter. Climbing through the side door, the half-dozen men quickly seated and belted themselves in place. Two minutes later the helicopter was airborne.

As the helicopter banked out over water and began to head south, the copilot turned from his seat and shouted to the rear, "Agent Taft, we have your office on a secure communications link."

The commando nearest Taft reached for a receiver on the bulkhead wall. Punching a button on the phone, he handed the unit to Taft.

"John, what have you got?" boomed the voice of Benson.

"I think I've found the missing link," Taft answered. "At least that's what it appears to be. A series of equations notched into the *Windforce's* nameplate."

"Don't try to read them over the phone," Benson said. "We can't be positive our transmissions won't be intercepted."

"Okay, boss," Taft noted, "but we may have a problem then."

"What's that?" Benson asked.

"The wood's been underwater for years. As soon as it reached surface air it began to deteriorate."

Martinez, who was seated next to Taft, gripped his arm. "I have an idea," he shouted over the din of the rotor blades.

"Hold on, sir," Taft said to Benson.

"Do you have a notebook or some paper on board?" Martinez shouted to the copilot.

Reaching into a stowage area between the seats, the copilot removed a clipboard containing a flight log and handed it back. Clipped to the top was a mechanical pencil.

"If we lay several sheets across the board we can do a tracing," Martinez said to Taft.

Taft nodded at Martinez, then spoke into the phone. "I think Larry's figured out a way to copy the equations onto paper."

"Good," Benson said, "also figure out a way to keep the wood wet."

"That I can do," said Taft.

"I'll round up something to keep it wet on the trip to Colorado and meet you when you land at Andrews," Benson said.

"Right," Taft said as he handed the phone back to the commando.

Carefully unwrapping the quickly drying towel from the board Taft carefully positioned it on his knees. Taking the paper from Martinez he placed it over the equations and began to scratch the surface with the mechanical pencil. It required three sheets to cover the entire formula.

"How do they look to you?" he said to Martinez once he was finished.

"Not bad," Martinez commented.

Taft turned toward the copilot. "Does anyone have any water on board?"

The copilot motioned to the pilot, who shook his head no. "We left as soon as we received the call," the copilot said apologetically.

Taft glanced to the commandos, who also shook their heads in the negative.

The helicopter was still seventy miles from Andrews Air Force Base when Taft unbuckled his seat belt, raised himself up, unzipped his pants, and urinated on the towel.

"Damn," Martinez said when he had finished, "I can't take you anywhere."

From the time the Air Force received Benson's call until the ESR-99, code-named *Dark Star*, landed at Andrews Air Force Base outside Washington, D.C., less than an hour had passed. Much of that hour had been used in preparing *Dark Star* for takeoff. The trip from Edwards Air Force Base in California across the country went smoothly for its pilot and copilot. The pulse engines that powered *Dark Star* operated without a hitch, and the view of the curvature of the earth from 100,000 feet was spectacular.

The pilots' space suits were functioning properly, regulating their body temperature; still, the copilot felt warm as he glanced out the tiny side window at the leading edge of the delta wing. The edge was glowing white-hot as the temperature on the edge of the wing reached nearly 1,000 degrees.

Dark Star was a unique design, borrowing the successful parts of the Stealth programs of the 1970s and eighties and combining them with the latest in artificial-intelligence and computer-aided design. The craft itself resembled a triangle when viewed from above. If viewed from the side a person could make out the flare of the fuselage which grew as you followed the lines to the rear.

Strangely enough, unlike most of the spy reconnaissance aircraft that went before her, which were a black color, the *Dark Star* was an odd metallic blue. The blue color was not a paint or coating, since nothing would stick to the skin of *Dark Star,* but rather the actual color of the metal, which was a weird alloy whose molecules were arranged in a man-made weightless environment. Stubby, retractable stabilizer fins extended from the fuselage for low-speed maneuvering, which for *Dark Star* was anything under Mach 1.

Passing 100,000 feet above Cincinnati, Ohio, the pilot radioed the tower at Andrews that they would be landing soon and to please alert security. Five minutes later, right at dusk, just north of Baltimore, a thin trail of white vapor threaded inside what appeared to be smoke rings from a giant's cigar but was in fact the exhaust trail from the *Dark Star.* The contrail quickly dissipated and the few people on the ground who witnessed it assumed it was some odd weather phenomenon.

"*Dark Star* on final approach. Is the sweeping complete?" the pilot radioed the tower.

"Affirmative, *Dark Star.* Once you're on the ground please follow the pair of air police Humvees. They will lead you to your hangar."

"Acknowledge," *Dark Star*'s pilot noted.

The pilot's inquiry about sweeping was important. The pulse

engines of *Dark Star* used tremendous volumes of air, which they sucked into rounded intakes like a vacuum. Any small parts, loose screws, rocks, or cans left on or near the runway had a good chance of being sucked up as *Dark Star* passed. The intakes were screened, but if something got past the screen it could be catastrophic for the engines, each of which cost $14 million to build.

When *Dark Star* touched down on the runway night was falling. The air police Humvees were already rolling down the asphalt at nearly sixty miles per hour. Flanking *Dark Star,* they matched her speed while the pilot engaged the braking system, a series of air jets that burst from the front of the fuselage. The bursts of air scrubbed off speed while also cleaning the runway of any debris.

It was critical that *Dark Star* get inside a hangar as soon as possible after landing. Although rumors of the plane's existence had circulated, as yet no pictures of the craft had reached the press. Taxiing faster than most planes would attempt, *Dark Star* followed the Humvees to an open hangar. Leaving the Humvees outside, the *Dark Star* pilot rolled inside at nearly thirty miles an hour. The pilot engaged the air-stop brakes once the plane was near the center of the hangar. A heavy-steel fifty-five-gallon trash drum was tossed against the side wall and partially flattened. It hung there, pressed against the wall, until *Dark Star* came to a stop and the pilot released the air brake.

Then it crashed to the floor.

The pilot and copilot slid from a small hatch at the bottom of the fuselage just as the head of security, a captain with the air police, raced over.

"I'm sure Edwards gave you orders to have everything removed from the hangar, Captain," the pilot said.

Nearly twenty special air policemen in red berets took up position around *Dark Star.* Circling the aircraft, they pointed their M-16 rifles outward.

"Yes, Colonel, those were the orders. However, we weren't alerted to your arrival until fifteen minutes ago and it was impossible to get a forklift to move that barrel in time."

The colonel nodded.

"Any idea how long we'll be on the ground?" the copilot asked.

"The last I heard, the package is due to arrive"—the captain stared at his watch—"in fifteen minutes."

"Good," the pilot said, "that gives me time for a cup of coffee."

A large Igloo cooler half-filled with liquid sloshed about on the floor of General Benson's GMC Suburban as he turned the last corner and came to a stop outside the hangar where *Dark Star* was parked. Turning off the headlights, he switched off the ignition and left the keys in place. Once he had been cleared by the air policemen, Benson removed the cooler from the Suburban and placed it on the ground. Sitting atop the cooler he waited for the helicopter carrying Taft and Martinez to land.

With the night pitch black and no moon to light the sky, the pilot of the Sikorsky carrying Taft and Martinez followed a three-ton truck with an airman in the rear bed directing the helicopter with flashlights. The truck stopped next to the hangar containing *Dark Star,* and the pilot of the Sikorsky touched down there.

Taft jumped from the helicopter and raced toward Benson, who was opening the cooler. "Set the board in here," Benson shouted over the noise of the helicopter.

"What's in there?" Taft shouted as the Sikorsky with the commandos aboard noisily took off again.

"Antifreeze and water," Benson said. "Are the tracings safe?"

"Yes, I have them right here," Martinez shouted.

"Good," Benson said, closing the lid of the cooler. "Grab a handle of this cooler and let's take it inside."

At the door of the hangar, Martinez was deemed nonessential by the air policemen and asked to remain outside. Taft and Benson entered the hangar and walked toward *Dark Star*, carrying the cooler. To the left side of the hangar, the pilot and copilot emerged from inside a small lunch room used by the mechanics.

The pilot stared at the cooler for a second. "What is it, an organ transplant for a VIP?"

"No," Benson said, "it's an old board."

"You're kidding," the copilot muttered.

"But," Taft added, "it's an old board Albert Einstein whittled on."

Dark Star lifted off from Andrews within five minutes of loading the cooler aboard. The sixteen-hundred-mile trip to Colorado took *Dark Star* just over twenty minutes. They landed at the nearest base to Boulder, the Buckley Air National Guard Base in Aurora, Colorado, where the cooler was immediately transported to a U.S. Army Huey helicopter for the rest of the trip to the Advanced Physics Laboratory. Touching down on the grounds of the laboratory, the helicopter pilot handed the cooler to two NIA agents, who carried it inside and handed it to an NIA photographer who was waiting to shoot the wooden board.

Outside the Advanced Physics Laboratory it was twilight. Behind the mountain Boulder nudged up to, the setting sun burned with an orange glow. Crickets began to chirp as night came. The wind died down to a whisper.

Scaramelli and Choi stood off to the side of their laboratory, studying the etchings Benson had faxed to them. Once the photographer had finished his work, the laboratory began to quiet as everyone except Scaramelli and Choi filtered out.

When they were alone, Scaramelli lifted the board and

rubbed his fingers over the etched symbols. He stared at Choi and smiled. "What do you think, my friend?" he said easily. "Should we see what Dr. Einstein discovered?"

Choi stared at his watch. "We might as well. General Benson called. He's taking a commercial flight here. He arrives in just over six hours on the early-morning flight."

"It would be nice if we had something to show him by then," Scaramelli said.

"That's what I was thinking," Choi agreed.

That morning brought a fierce thunderstorm that blackened the Colorado sky. High in the mountains the storm brought snow, but down in the foothills the storm was mostly wind, intermittent rain, and lightning. The storm blew over the top of the series of rocks outside Boulder known as the Flatirons, then spread out toward the eastern plains.

Loud thunder boomed in the distance followed by bolts of lightning that streaked quickly downward to the dry ground like spears from heaven. The light from the natural electrical discharges quickly disappeared into the clouds, then reappeared in seemingly random order. All at once, the skies opened up and rain and hail began to pelt the ground.

Strangely, certain parts of Boulder were bathed in sunshine.

General Earl Benson sat in the director's office of the Advanced Physics Laboratory with Scaramelli and Choi. He stared at the pair in anticipation.

Benson looked slightly haggard. Black rings formed half-circles under his eyes, and his forehead was lined with tension. Even so, he was cleanly shaven and alert, as though he refused to accept the fact he had slept less than three hours in the last twenty-four.

"Tell me what you've found," Benson said without preamble.

Scaramelli picked a piece of crust from his eye and flicked it on the floor. "To put it simply, we think we have the key to moving matter instantaneously."

Benson immediately saw the possible applications and leaned forward in astonishment. "You need to explain this to me in as simple terms as possible."

Scaramelli thought for a second before beginning. "Think of the Apollo missions. The astronauts needed to steer the craft into an exact position with the moon to be sucked in by the moon's gravitational field. Every orb has a gravitational field—and the earth is no different. But what is unusual about the earth is the presence of orbs scattered across the globe, a result of the earth's very formation. Our planet's gravitational field is unique. It is altered by the presence of so much metallic mass below the surface. The presence of metals beneath a planet's surface is unusual, and probably quite uncommon in the universe."

"Go on," Benson said.

"Okay," Scaramelli said. "Now, are you familiar with the ionosphere?"

"Yes, I remember studying it in school. It's a belt of free electrically charged particles in the earth's atmosphere from about twenty-five miles to 250 miles out. Once radio waves bounce around in it they can travel around the globe."

"It's often used by our military to send secret communications great distances," Scaramelli noted.

"So we have a spinning ball—the earth—and on that ball we have intense magnetic fields that form into bands encircling the planet. Outside the bands, suspended miles above, is the ionosphere—a band of free electrically charged particles."

"I'm following you so far," Benson said.

"May I?" Choi asked.

Scaramelli nodded.

"Let's say you had a ball bearing on the floor and you turned on a gigantic electromagnet that was mounted on the ceiling," Choi said.

"The ball bearing would be pulled to the ceiling," Benson said.

"Except if the electricity in the ionosphere prevented that," Choi said. "Then it would be drawn up until the opposing force of electricity exerted a force sufficient to offset the magnetism. If that occurred the ball bearing would hover in place."

"So you balance the forces to suspend the object?" Benson asked.

"We upset the very matter that forms the object. The combination of electricity combined with gravity and magnetism acts upon the strong and weak forces at a subatomic level. The resulting intense vibration separates the matter, so it may be drawn along through space."

"Then it is sucked along the magnetic belts that encircle the earth," Benson said logically, "in the area between earth and the outer edge of the ionosphere."

"Exactly," Scaramelli said.

"How much time does it take to move an object?" Benson asked. "And does the matter rearrange itself in the same form?"

"The speed the object would obtain is unknown," Scaramelli admitted. "Einstein's notes about the curvature of space still have me baffled. However, our preliminary tests indicate that the amount of time that would elapse would be negligible, approaching zero. As to the form of the object, that is what we will test today."

"You already have a test that can prove this?" Benson asked, incredulous.

"Einstein's final notes were the piece of the puzzle we were missing," Scaramelli said. "It explained the theory beautifully."

"Disrupting the strong and weak forces inside atoms won't result in an explosion, as we first thought?" Benson asked.

"The strong and weak forces in molecules are all around us," Scaramelli noted. "What Einstein's formula finally explained is how to unlock them."

"And how *do* you unlock them?" Benson asked.

"Seawater," Scaramelli said quietly. "We electrically charge seawater."

"So Einstein discovered an instant, invisible method of time travel," Benson said.

"Beam us up, Scotty," Choi said quietly.

Inside the Advanced Physics Laboratory, Jeff Scaramelli stood next to Li Choi at a control panel. Scaramelli looked at the group that had assembled in the laboratory.

"We're about to begin the test," he said to no one in particular.

A television camera had been installed inside the laboratory to beam the test east to the NIA office in Maryland. There, only Taft and Martinez, along with the two technicians who would record the incoming signal on tape, had been authorized by Benson to watch the results.

A separate video feed was directed to the White House. There, National Security Advisor Lakeland sat with the president. Lakeland appeared unemotional, but the president puffed a large cigar until the tip was a glowing red. The president sipped from a cup of coffee and focused his complete attention on the screen.

It was time for the big show.

In the northwest corner of the laboratory in Boulder, a bronze bust of Albert Einstein was positioned in a stainless-steel tub filled with seawater. A pair of copper wires led off to a cyclotron. The cyclotron would help propel the particles forming the bust of Einstein by alternating electrical fields in a constant magnetic field.

Scaramelli hit the switch on the control panel for the cyclotron, then turned up the current with a rheostat.

The bust began to glow as it was lit by an electromagnetic beam never before produced on earth. As though it was not of this earth, the bust began to shimmer and change into colors previously unknown to man.

Twin wind vortexes shot from the center of the bust. One rose to the ceiling while one descended to the floor, raising a cloud of dust and lint. The two video cameras that were earlier placed in the corners of the lab recorded the effects of the bizarre experiment.

As the group watched in amazement, the bust of Einstein became covered with clouds. Small bolts of electrical energy flew in a circular pattern from the bust and dissipated in the air as an unnatural storm was created.

The molecules of the bust unlocked from one another. Infinitesimally small, they became a level of matter up until now unknown. Traveling through the formed particles that made up the solid of the building, they raced through the roof of the laboratory, then up through the atmosphere and into the ionosphere.

There they remained in a suspended state, held in place by the actions of the charged electrical particles of the ionosphere combining with the gravitation of the earth and the naturally occurring magnetic belts encircling the earth. The entire process occurred quickly as the rapt audience watched.

Scaramelli stared at the ceiling, hoping to see the window that would open in the molecules, but it happened so quickly it was past the point of human awareness.

To those in the laboratory, the bust simply disappeared from view.

It grew darker in the laboratory as the storm outside the laboratory intensified. At the same time the overhead lights dimmed. A bank of computers off to one side of the laboratory shut themselves down.

Scaramelli reached over to the control panel and switched on a powerful electromagnet positioned in the far corner of the laboratory. Almost instantly an intense storm began to ravage the corner. Wind, rain, and lightning spun from the center of the clouds like a bizarre cyclonic weather system run amok. The computers restarted, and then, as if the entire series were a single machine, the monitors grew bright as a flare, then burned out. The air pressure in the room changed.

Benson opened his mouth and yawned, forcing his ears to pop.

After a tense wait of several seconds, Scaramelli clicked the electromagnet off, then carefully walked to the corner of the laboratory. He paused for a few seconds then bent over and lifted a metal blob from the floor. The bust had reappeared, all right, but in several large pieces.

Later, when the scientists weighed the balls of metal taken from the floor, it would be found that not a single atom remained in the ionosphere. Nevertheless, the atoms had not rearranged into their prior form. Scaramelli tossed the ball of bronze into the air, then turned to Benson.

The test had proved to be a failure.

The laboratory grew deadly quiet.

John Taft rose from his chair in the media control room in Bethesda and walked over to one of the technicians. "Kurt," he said casually, "can I talk to Benson at the laboratory over this feed?"

"Sure," the technician said, pointing to a stalk on the control panel. "Just flick that button on the microphone."

As Taft walked over to the microphone he watched the real-time image from the laboratory on the screen in front of the control room. He switched on the microphone and spoke.

"General Benson," he said, "this is Special Agent Taft in Maryland. May I ask Mr. Scaramelli a question?"

Benson looked at Scaramelli, who was bent over picking up pieces of bronze from the floor and hefting them in his hands.

"Might as well, John," Benson said quietly.

"Jeff, this is John Taft in Maryland. I have a question for you."

Scaramelli rose slowly and faced the camera. His face was drawn and ashen colored. He appeared stunned that the test had been a failure. A tic had formed in a corner of his left eye and his eyelid fluttered. Taft noticed Scaramelli's knees were shaking as if they might give way at any moment.

"Yeah, John," Scaramelli said haltingly.

"What's with the storm that was created?"

"We think it's a natural reaction of the atmosphere being upset," Scaramelli blurted.

"Would it be safe to say that the bigger the object moved, the bigger would be the storm?"

"I guess so," Scaramelli said.

"This is National Security Advisor Lakeland with the president at the White House," a voice boomed over the television. "Just what are you getting at, Agent Taft?"

Taft paused before answering. "If we move enough large objects into the path of the Chinese navy, the resulting storm should slow or stop the assault."

"Interesting idea," Benson said.

"Not only that," Taft said, "it would give Scaramelli and Choi another chance to perfect the use of the theory."

Choi piped into the conversation. "I believe that we are using the theory correctly—we just need to adjust the amount of electricity and gravity we use."

Scaramelli suddenly came to life. He glanced toward the camera, nodding. "That must be it—we just have the settings wrong."

"What objects do you propose we use, Mr. Taft?" the president asked.

"Since you are an old air force man, Mr. President," Taft said, "I think you'll appreciate this—we literally bomb the Chinese with aircraft. We fill the skies with a phantom force."

Lakeland interrupted. "Agent Taft, we don't have a single airplane we can spare. If we did we'd bomb the Chinese as they crossed the Taiwan Strait. The U.S. Air Force must stand ready to defend Taiwan from China's air force. In addition, we currently have a sizable number of aircraft stationed in the Middle East that cannot be moved."

"Robert," the president said, "I know Taft. He doesn't offer suggestions lightly. Please let him finish what he was going to say."

"Thanks, Mr. President," Taft said. "I think you'll like this, Mr. Lakeland. The United States has several squadrons of aircraft that we could put into service."

"And where would these phantom aircraft be located?" Lakeland asked.

"Arizona," Taft said easily.

A burst of laughter erupted over the television, then died away. "Are you talking about the planes at Davis-Monthan?" the president said.

"Exactly," Taft said slyly.

Benson looked into the camera, smiled, and nodded. "It just might work, Mr. President."

All were silent as the president thought. "Let's do it," he said seconds later. "Absolutely, let's do it."

The army helicopter had just passed over Broomfield, Colorado, when Benson placed his hand over his briefcase phone and shouted over the din of the rotor blades across the cabin to Scaramelli.

"Is there anything else you can think of that you might need?"

"No, General, that should do it."

"That's all," Benson shouted into the phone.

Scaramelli scanned the neat rows of houses below. The people who lived below would be going about their daily activities without any notion of the discovery that had just been made. It was an eerie feeling for Scaramelli to have knowledge only a handful of people in the world knew existed. Rather than reassure him or fill him with pride, it made him feel uneasy—as if he were now a target, an unworthy recipient of information beyond his scope.

"What *about* the storm?" Benson asked.

Scaramelli misunderstood Benson's question. "I'm sure in time, when we have more experience with the formula and the power needed to scramble molecules, the storm can be reduced or even eliminated," Scaramelli said wearily.

"Don't tell me that now," Benson said. "We need a major typhoon out there. You can experiment with working the bugs out after this is all over."

"Don't worry, General Benson. So far that's all we know how to do. You can rest assured that the storm that hits the Taiwan Strait will be bad," Scaramelli said. "Very bad."

CHAPTER 49

It was late when Sun Tao burst into the office of the Chinese prime minister.

"The *Carondelet* is on fire. Our agents in Cuba just flew over the ship. They report smoke billowing from the stern, and the ship is stopped dead in the water."

"How long ago did this happen?" the prime minister asked.

"I just received word," Tao said.

"Did the crew escape?"

"The agents reported several rafts in the water," said Tao.

"Good, then we still have the papers." The prime minister paused to think. "Have the crew picked up immediately. We can still tell the Americans we have the papers."

"I have already taken care of that, sir. We have a submarine on exercises off Cuba. I have ordered her to surface next to the rafts."

"Excellent," the prime minister said, glancing at his watch. "It is time you caught a flight south to help orchestrate the beginning of the assault. It will take you time to find your ship and assume command. You cannot be late—our first wave is scheduled to begin the liberation of Taiwan at exactly midnight, October 1st."

"To victory, sir," Tao said, rising to leave.

Carl Vickerson wrapped his arm tighter around his wife, Clara. At seventy-seven years of age, Carl no longer felt much need to rush. Still, the men in blue uniforms who were directing the tourists back to their buses seemed in a hurry, so he helped Clara along.

"Did they say *why* we had to leave, dear?" Clara said in a voice a few shades too loud.

Carl had broad shoulders that spoke of a lifetime of work. Dresden-blue eyes looked out from a tanned face, and the hand that clutched Clara's arm and steered her around the F-105 fighter-bomber was large and meaty.

"No, honey. But it must be something serious," Carl said as he pointed to two tanks that had roared across the desert and stopped near the fence surrounding the base.

Clara's face was taking on a red glow from the desert sun. Through her sunglasses she glanced across the hard-packed dirt and watched as several trucks stopped midway along the fence and troops climbed from the rear. The soldiers formed lines and set out down the fence line.

Carl Vickerson had spent his life in Iowa, first as a farmer, later as the owner of a feed store. His World War II service in the Army Air Corps took him the farthest he had ever gotten from home. The Vickersons were in Arizona now for a vacation and to attend a reunion of the surviving members of Carl's World War II squadron. Part of the reunion was a guided tour of the plane graveyard at Davis-Monthan Air Force Base.

Now the tour was being cut short by unknown events half a world away.

Carl and Clara didn't worry much about the shortened tour. They were tired from all the excitement of the trip and seeing Carl's old friends. By the time the tour bus left the base and was on the blacktop leading back to Tucson, the two of them were asleep, their heads resting together, Carl's arm across his wife's shoulders.

Seconds later, the plane carrying Li Choi landed at Davis-Monthan Air Force Base.

Chutetski glanced across the round Chinese rescue raft, then out the side opening in the tent top to the water beyond. Oakes was speaking into a secure satellite phone, and the part Chutetski could hear was not reassuring.

"Roger that," Oakes said as he cut the connection.

Turning to the SEAL team in the raft, Oakes smiled. "Start preparing, men. We are about to capture a Chinese submarine."

Chutetski stared at Oakes. "What could possibly happen next!"

"Don't worry, Chutes," Oakes said. "We'll have some help."

Inside the command center set up in a hangar at Davis-Monthan, Taft wiped his brow on his sleeve. The next to the last day of September 1999 was blistering hot in southern Arizona. The air conditioning inside the hangar building was working overtime. The stitches in Taft's shoulder itched, and he was reaching inside the sling to scratch them as Martinez walked toward his desk.

"Choi tells me they have finished the installation. He had the air force hook directly into a high-power transmission line, so we have plenty of juice when we need it," Martinez said.

"Good," Taft said, "our end is handled."

"Exactly," Martinez said wearily.

"It's hard to believe these planes are going to war again. Some of them were built before I was born," Taft said.

"From mothballs and parts planes to smack dab in the middle of the Taiwan Strait," Martinez said quietly. "Isn't technology amazing?"

Carl Vickerson sat on the edge of the bed in the hotel room in Tucson. He flicked through the television channels with the remote control. Landing on CNN, he watched the broadcast with interest.

"Hey, Clara," he yelled toward the bathroom, where Clara had gone as soon as they entered the room.

"Yes, dear," Clara said through the closed door.

"CNN is reporting that the navy has sent ships into the sea between Taiwan and China. They're calling it 'Showdown in the Strait.'"

"That's nice, dear," Clara noted.

"It doesn't sound so nice to me," Carl muttered.

"What, dear?" Clara asked through the door.

"Nothing, honey," Carl said.

But it was far from nothing.

The water near the rescue raft carrying the navy SEALs began to boil like a pot of water left too long on a stove. "Here they come!" Oakes shouted, peering through the canvas. "I hope your Chinese is as good as you claim, Chutes."

Chutetski glanced at his commander. "It's quite good, sir," he said easily, "as long as the crew speaks Mandarin Chinese. Otherwise, of course, we're screwed."

The conning tower of the Chinese sub broke the surface of the water, and almost instantly the hatch in the conning tower popped open.

In the city-class nuclear attack submarine *Phoenix,* Commander Eric Devers glanced to his helmsman. "Blow the tanks."

Oakes paddled the raft a few feet closer to the submarine then motioned to Chutetski, who shouted across the water.

At just that instant, below the raft in the water, Commander Steve Thompson of the ballistic missile submarine *John Paul Jones* said to his sonar man, "Ping them."

In position just behind and in back of the Chinese submarine at a depth of seventy feet, the *John Paul Jones* sounded its presence just as the conning tower of the *Phoenix* broke the surface of the water.

"We are United States Navy SEAL Team 16," Chutes shouted in Mandarin. "You are surrounded on both sides by United States Navy nuclear attack submarines. Assemble your crew on the deck. We are taking possession of your vessel."

The Chinese submarine commander noticed the *Phoenix* breaching. At that instant he received word by intercom of the detection of the *John Paul Jones* on sonar.

Glancing around for a second, he issued an order to hoist a white flag.

Forty minutes later the Chinese submarine was fully secured. After smashing the radios with their rifle butts Oakes's SEAL team fanned out in pairs, holding the crew of the Chinese submarine hostage until an American team could be flown from Florida to drive it to port.

Just before midnight, Sun Tao breathed deeply the diesel fumes that hung low over the water in the port at Xiaman. The Chinese ships that would take part in the assault bristled with weapons. They sat with their engines running, awaiting orders to cast off. They were greyhounds in the gate, and the start of the race was only minutes away.

At exactly midnight of October 1, 1999, the mainland Chinese flotilla steamed from port and started across the Strait of Taiwan. There were over sixty vessels in the assault group and they ran the gamut from destroyers to small attack crafts.

Just before 5 P.M. on September 30, on the other side of the international dateline from China, Taft spoke into a portable radio.

"Are the roads shut off?"

"The roads are secure," the ranking army security officer replied.

"Has all air traffic been halted?"

"For the next thirty minutes, sir," the officer answered. "However, at this time in the afternoon there's not a lot of air traffic anyway."

Taft looked out the window of the air traffic control tower. A series of power cables leading directly from the main power grid were attached to the planes like rows of Christmas lights. Once inside the planes, the electrical power lines were hooked to cyclotrons the Air Force had hastily scavenged from storage racks and test centers worldwide. Choi had personally supervised the installation in each of the planes and had reported to Taft less than an hour ago that he was pleased with the results.

All Taft could do now was wait.

Taft and Martinez had been ordered to take every possible step to ensure that this test of the Unified Field Theory was not observed by civilians. First, they had to clear the base. That had proved to be easier than first imagined. Arizona was currently in the throes of an Indian summer, and with the September sun beating down, the interior temperature of the mothballed aircraft at Davis-Monthan was over 100 degrees. The exterior metal that formed the skin of the aircraft was hotter still.

Then there was the problem of observation from nearby. Luckily the airplane graveyard at Davis-Monthan was far enough from developed areas and people with their prying eyes. Taft had also asked the Air Force to assign roving groups of security men in Humvees to search the nearby hills for the random hiker or four-wheel-driver.

Taft thought they could probably pull off the disappearing act without too much trouble. His primary concern now was making sure the test would work. From his control tower he scanned the area with binoculars one last time.

"Well, old buddy," he said to Martinez as he set the binoculars back on a table and nodded at the airman working in the tower, "it's about time we go see if this crazy idea works."

They took the elevator from the top of the tower to ground level, where a truck was waiting to drive them to the control center hangar to wait out the last few minutes.

On the deck of the Taiwanese naval cruiser *Lotung* a thick fall rain was falling. Scaramelli wiped the face of his watch. He glanced from the bridge of the cruiser to the deck below. Then he raised a pair of night-vision binoculars to his eyes and watched as a lone plane flew west. Benson touched his shoulder.

"Don't worry, Jeff," he said, "that plane is loaded with enough explosive power to blow a hundred-foot section out of the cable."

"My problem is that I won't know exactly where the electricity enters the water," Scaramelli said. "I would have felt more comfortable if a submersible could have set the charges in place."

"Me too," Benson said, "but there simply wasn't time."

"It will make it harder," the scientist in Scaramelli said, "for me to accurately measure this test, not knowing the precise area of the ocean that is electrified."

"Later, when the cable is repaired they can measure the exact spot where it was cut," Benson said.

The thought seemed to brighten up Scaramelli's mood considerably. "Are they ready at Davis-Monthan?"

"Yes," Benson replied.

Just then, in the far distance, the U.S. Air Force B-52 dropped the load of mixed ordnance into the ocean. The combination of bombs traveled down to the ocean floor, then exploded. The concussion from the blast sent a geyser of water several hundred feet into the air and could be felt the length of *Lotung*, and the cruiser rocked back and forth as the waves pounded her hull.

"What about at the power transmission station on Taiwan?" Scaramelli said a bit too loud because his ears were ringing.

"Yes, we just have to tell them when," Benson said, popping his ears to clear them.

Scaramelli's idea of cutting the cable had been harder to sell to the Taiwanese than first imagined. The only way to generate a large enough electrical field to attract the scrambled molecules of nearly a hundred aging aircraft from the ionosphere to the ocean's surface was to divert most of the electricity that powered Taiwan into a trans-Pacific communications cable that stretched from Taiwan to mainland China.

To do that, National Security Advisor Lakeland had to beg and cajole the Taiwanese president. Once Taiwan's power was diverted, she'd be a sitting duck—though most of the military installations had backup generators that would supply electricity to essential equipment, and they could probably continue to operate and perform their missions.

If the power diversion blew the main transmission line and the power could not be quickly restored, it would be the ordinary citizens who would suffer the most. The fans in the public air-raid shelters wouldn't work. If fires broke out, they would be impossible to fight without the electrical pumps used to move the water. Those unfortunate people in Taiwanese hospitals— and there were tens of thousands of them—would be faced with barbaric conditions that might prove life-threatening. Traffic lights would cease to work, food in refrigerators would soon spoil, and darkness would rein.

If the main power grid exploded from the surge of power being diverted into the ocean, or if the current flowed back along the cable and somehow got into Taiwan's electrical infrastructure, the country would be plunged back into the Stone Age just as the numerically superior forces from mainland China attacked.

Only a firm assurance by Lakeland to Taiwan's president That the American fleet was only days away and would enter the fight brought the needed permission.

It was just past five in the afternoon Arizona time when Taft spoke into his cellular telephone.

"It's time, Li," he said to Choi, who stood before a hastily assembled control panel. Without a word he twisted a knob and sent electricity surging to the cyclotrons.

Taft walked toward the open hangar door and glanced toward the graveyard of airplanes in the far distance. Like a mirage over a desert oasis the air surrounding the airplanes began to shimmer. A yellow-edged aura began forming in the air ten feet or so over the tops of the aircraft.

And then, all at once, the planes blinked once like a light switch had been thrown on and then they disappeared.

"Coming your way," Taft said quietly to Benson.

"Our airborne radar reports the Chinese flotilla will be able to detect us in the next few minutes," the Taiwanese admiral in command of the *Lotung* said to Benson.

"Power to the cable," Benson shouted.

Scaramelli looked through his binoculars across the water. Far in the distance he could just make out a blinking red light he had ordered attached to one of the nearly thirty metal barges that had been loaded with scrap iron and then magnetized at the docks in Kaohsiung. When that was completed, the barges had been towed into place in the Taiwan Strait and anchored. The thick copper cables that hung from the sides of the barges into the water were designed to act like lightning rods and attract the current from the cable. The electricity would increase the barges' magnetism and attract the molecules of the plane from the ionosphere.

At least that was the plan.

And then to the west, directly in the path of the Chinese flotilla, the night sky began to lighten and roil with a massive thunderstorm.

"Here comes the storm," Scaramelli shouted to Benson over the increasing noise.

Benson watched through infrared binoculars as a cloud of fog grew on the surface of the Taiwan Strait several miles away. A stiff wind arose, forming whitecaps on the water and blowing the fog toward mainland China. A roiling wall of clouds began to form. The clouds began to emit light from deep inside, yellow and orange with peach and red in the center. The outer edges turned deep purple, then black as the cloud expanded at an alarming rate. From the top of the clouds random bolts of lightning streaked downward, then all at once they linked and formed a wall of electrical energy. A loud clap akin to a gigantic sonic boom spread in all directions from the center of the cloud.

Then a hail of aircraft parts along with misshapen blobs of molten metal rained down from the skies. Parts of wings and propellers sliced through the air like a cleaver to a butcher's block. Suspended in the windstorm, they spun ever faster as the storm began to track west.

Benson managed to shield himself behind a deck gun before the boom reached the frigate and lost only his hat in the gust of wind that rocked the massive missile ship like a giant hand. The commander of the Taiwanese navy was not so lucky. Blown off his feet, he smashed his head against the deck. When the first blast abated he had to be carried to the infirmary with a mild concussion. A tornado was created in the center of the cloud. Unlike those naturally formed, which have a tendency to wander back and forth like a dog's wagging tail, this one remained centered. Less than a minute later the decks of the ships of the Taiwanese navy were covered in a rain of fish and other sea life. And still the storm grew stronger.

Minutes before, the Chinese fleet commander had stared from his command post aboard the largest destroyer in the Chinese navy as a freak storm began to form directly in front of the flotilla. Less than ten seconds after he first noticed the cloud, a fury of wind, rain, and lightning struck the fleet with an intensity he had never witnessed before.

On board the Chinese fast-attack boat *Fuzhou* the situation was turning from bad to worse. Captain Ling Chow had watched as a cloud of fog enveloped his vessel. Seconds later the steel decks of his forty-foot boat were being pelted by hail the size of tangerines. He watched from the pilothouse as the two crewmen manning the front and rear gun emplacements began to dance as if they were trapped in a swarm of bees. Stupidly, the sailor in the front emplacement sought to remove his battered combat helmet. Chow watched as the man was knocked unconscious by a flurry of hail pounding his bare head. The crewman slumped over his gun, a trickle of blood seeping from his head.

Another crewman dashed to his aid but a moment later reversed himself and began to run toward the safety of the cockpit. He was halfway to the cockpit when a ten-foot-long plate of metal appeared seemingly from out of nowhere. Cutting the crewman in two at the waist, the metal imbedded itself in the gun emplacement, the man's upper torso skewered on the metal.

Three seconds later Chow watched as a violent gust of wind sucked the lower body of the crewman, still clad in pants and shoes, into the heavens. The wind continued to suck upward until it ripped the upper half of the torso from beneath the slab of metal and flung it against the window of the cockpit.

Chow screamed as the lifeless face pressed against the window was then flung, arms askew, off the ship.

The crewman in the rear emplacement fared better, as he had left his helmet, now dented, firmly attached. His mistake, however, was to look up into the sky. A large hailstone, moving with the velocity of a baseball tossed by a major-league pitcher, smashed him squarely in the nose. Blood spurted forth from the center of his face. A second hailstone hit him in his left eye and he raised his hand to cover the wound. He jammed his feet into the emplacement to avoid being sucked out into space.

And then the tornado struck.

Chow ducked as the windows of the pilothouse were sucked outward. He jammed his leg under a table bolted to the floor and held on tight. The *Fuzhou* rocked on its end beam to the port side. Thousands of gallons of seawater flooded across the decks, then raced down an open passage toward the lower decks. Chow glanced up just as the body of the forward gunner slammed into the wall of the pilothouse. The tornado lifted him into the air, dragging his unconscious body against a sharp steel edge on the corner of the pilothouse. Chow watched in horror as the man's chest opened up like a salmon under a filet knife.

And then the crewman, his entrails trailing outside his body, was sucked upward in the funnel cloud and disappeared from view. Chow swiveled his head and glanced toward his helmsman. The helmsman's legs were being sucked out the opening where the port window had been only seconds before. Screaming at the top of his lungs for help he clutched the edge of the wheel in an attempt to keep his body from being sucked out the opening.

It was not to be.

The tip of the tornado shifted for a millisecond and he was dropped onto a large shard of broken glass that was still firmly attached to the window frame. His body was severed in half as neatly as if he had been placed under a guillotine.

Chow stared in horror as the tornado sucked the lower half of his torso into the air. In a cruel twist of fate the helmsman had managed to jam the knuckle of his left hand into a space between the wheel and the helm station. The upper half of his body remained in the pilothouse, a grisly reminder of the devastation aboard the *Fuzhou*.

Chinese Fleet Commander Zang Pochan watched in horror from the pilothouse of the *Hainan*, the largest destroyer in the Chinese navy, as his crewmen on the deck of the destroyer were decimated. He glanced out the window as part of the wing of an airplane, the engine still attached, a twenty-year-old U.S. Air Force emblem still clearly visible, landed hard on his deck, shaking the pilothouse.

With horror he could see that dozens of communication antennae, ripped from their mountings by the storm, were being flung through the air. Like spears from a long-ago war, they skewered the men on the deck before the tornado lifted them into the heavens.

Zang shouted to his radio operator to alert the other ships in his fleet to abort, but with no antennae to transmit the message it was all for naught.

And then the lightning hit.

It came not as random bolts but as a wall of electrical energy, surging from one end of the ship to the other, plunging the ship into darkness and blowing every fuse on board. The main engines continued to run but the pumps, lights, and all else electric ceased functioning.

And then the *Hainan* plowed into the *Yantai*.

At the beginning of the storm, Tsung Chan, captain of the *Yantai*, had ordered his helmsman to ring the engine room for full stop. They were sitting in the water when the *Hainan* appeared through the fog and struck them amidships. The lower holds of the *Yantai* were crammed to full capacity with artillery shells, land mines, and infantry ammunition. As the *Yantai* rolled over on her back, with timing that would be impossible to duplicate, several bolts of lightning struck the exposed ordnance and ignited a conflagration.

The *Yantai* sank almost immediately. There were no survivors.

It took the *Hainan* eighteen minutes to go down. Three hundred of the slightly more than eighteen hundred of the crew were saved.

The U.S. Air Force planes from Anderson Air Force Base on Guam met the Chinese aircraft halfway across the water. Forming a defensive wall, they diverted the Chinese planes from their course. China and the United States began a deadly game of cat and mouse played in the skies. The loser would be the first side to blink.

In Beijing, the American ambassador to China glanced at his aide, who looked up from his computer and nodded. Then he addressed his Chinese counterpart.

"Two United States Navy nuclear ICBM submarines now in the South China Sea have just completed plotting their target solutions. Their payload delivery point is there," the ambassador said, pointing out the window at the Forbidden City. "A storm has stopped your ships in the Taiwan Strait, and our air force is in a standoff with yours, as we speak."

The Chinese ambassador glanced at his aide, who had just returned from the communications room. With a nod, the aide confirmed that all the information just received was correct.

The U.S. ambassador stared across the desk. "Let's not all die this day," he said in a cold voice.

"If we withdraw will you guarantee not to attack our retreating troops?" the Chinese ambassador asked.

The American ambassador to China reached for a phone.

"We're losing it," Scaramelli shouted.

And then it was quiet.

Scaramelli crept from behind the superstructure. His hair was standing straight in the air from the electrical energy that had been generated. He glanced across the water as the fog began to dissipate. Far away on the horizon he could see the ravaged remains of the once powerful Chinese navy. Collapsing to the deck he glanced into the sky. A ring of black and purple clouds high above was collapsing in on itself as the storm imploded.

And then there was a rainbow.

EPILOGUE

FORTY-EIGHT HOURS LATER

Taiwan emerged unscathed. Only hours after the storm the main electrical feed leading into the ocean was withdrawn. By midday the power to the primary electrical grid had been restored and the country, although still on a heightened state of military alert, was almost back to normal.

The storm turned west after decimating the Chinese navy. The Taiwanese island of Quemoy, located just miles from the Chinese mainland, was hardest hit. Hurricane-force winds ripped foliage from limbs and downed trees but the Taiwanese military personnel stationed on the island were deep in their bunkers. Only three soldiers lost their lives.

In the Fujian Province of mainland China the cities of Xiamen and Zhangzhou were the hardest hit. Hard-driving rains created a flooding of the river running through Zhangzhou, where mud slides killed thousands. Xiamen was devastated by a tidal wave over twenty feet tall, and most of the buildings nearest the water were washed out to sea. A fierce hailstorm pummeled the city for forty minutes; thousands of Chinese citizens, outside when the storm struck, were either killed or maimed. It was as though the gods had been angered and were showing their ire.

In Beijing, the prime minister sat in his office in the dim light of a foggy morning. His brilliantly conceived plan was in ruins. Rebuilding the navy would take China many years and great sums of money. He now knew his dream of reuniting Taiwan with mainland China would never be realized in his lifetime.

The entire episode had turned into a humiliating failure.

For his role in the failed affair he ordered that Sun Tao be jailed. Before the soldiers could take him prisoner, however, King Abdullah sought his own justice.

A team of Saudi assassins dressed in long, flowing, hooded black robes slipped onto the floor where Sun Tao's offices were located. The floor lacked its usual complement of guards, the knowledge that Tao was a marked man having already swept through the building. No one wished to appear loyal to a man on the wrong side of the prime minister.

The man who only hours before had wielded incredible power was now a pariah.

Slipping quietly into Tao's office, two of the assassins held him in place in the chair behind his desk as the leader of the team read from a sheet of paper in Arabic. The paper contained the charges and sentence of an Islamic court. Although Tao had no idea what was being said, he understood the sentence as soon as the leader removed a large polished steel scimitar from beneath his robe and motioned for Tao's head to be placed on his desk.

Tao struggled against the hands that held him but his efforts were in vain.

With both hands firmly around the hand-tooled solid silver handle of the saber, the leader of the assassins swung the blade down with all his might.

The beheading took but one swipe of the razor-sharp blade—the scalping, one more.

When the soldiers sent by the prime minister arrived at Tao's office they were met by a grisly sight. Tao's head had been cleanly removed from his neck and the top of his skull and his scalp lopped off. The open skull that sat on his desk resembled a coconut with its top chopped off by a machete, the inside filled with tuna fish dip.

Tao's face bore an ugly grimace made all the more horrifying by the empty stare in his blank, lifeless eyes. Tao's torso, minus the head, sat upright in his chair.

When the news of Tao reached the prime minister it confirmed him in his decision.

Taking a plastic bottle from his desk drawer, he emptied a measure of white powder into a glass of plum wine, then stirred the mixture with his letter opener. Glancing out the window at the square below, he guzzled the liquid with a vengeance.

Three minutes later he took his last sleep.

Taft sat at the desk in the office at his home along the Potomac River. He was exhausted. The type of bone-weary tiredness that comes after intense, protracted stress is finally relieved. The type of melancholy and malaise that come from the burden of knowledge. It is said a person's life work molds his being, forms his backbone, drives his existence.

Taft was a man full of doubt.

He had begun his career with the NIA fresh out of the army, full of patriotic fervor and with the strong sense he was doing what was right and good. More and more, lately, he wondered if he was part of the solution or instead part of the problem. His sense of humor, one of the hallmarks of his personality, seemed to be slipping away.

After putting the finishing touches on the report he was writing, he pushed *Save* on his computer and stored the information onto a disk, then ran a program that scrubbed his hard disk clean. Then he reached for the telephone.

"This is Agent Taft," he told the switchboard operator at the NIA. "I need a secure courier for a pickup at my home."

At the NIA the operator consulted a schedule listed on the computer screen. "We'll send someone right away, Agent Taft."

"Thanks," he said as he hung up the telephone.

Taft needed to get away, to cleanse his soul, to feel the power and the beauty of nature. Sitting back in his office chair, he reached for the telephone, then hesitated. Grabbing the telephone, he dialed the number from memory.

"National Museum of American History, Kristin Fazio speaking."

"I'm sorry, I was trying to reach Quickies-R-Us," Taft said easily.

"I've quit all that," Fazio said. "It seems that every time I do that, the gentleman never calls me back."

"Sorry about that," Taft said. "Would it help if I told you I haven't called you because I was involved in a matter that threatened the very existence of the world?"

"No need to lie," Fazio said. "A simple apology would suffice."

"I'm sorry," Taft said. "What I did was inexcusable."

"That's about the tenth time, Taft," Fazio said.

"Let me take you away from all this to make it up to you," Taft said easily. "Can you take a few days off work?"

"I work for the government," Fazio said, "what do *you* think?"

"Good," Taft laughed. "Bring some sweaters—it can get cold on the water this time of year."

"I take it we're going for a cruise on *Tango*," Fazio said.

"That's the plan," Taft said. "Just come over after work. I'll provision the boat and we'll set out tonight."

"I'll need to stop by my house first," Fazio said, "so look for me about sixish."

Taft paused before speaking. "I really am sorry, Kristin."

"Don't worry," Fazio said, "I'll make you pay."

Reaching into the desk drawer, Taft removed a set of keys for his boat and tucked them in his pocket. Just then chimes rang as the sensors buried in his driveway registered a car approaching. He walked to the front door with the disk. Opening the door, he smiled at the tall young man who wore a crew cut and a serious expression.

"A car followed me up the driveway," the courier said. "My partner is questioning the driver."

Taft glanced at the mini-van parked farther down the drive. "That's my partner, Agent Martinez. He's one of us."

Martinez must have already shown his badge because he was climbing from his van. Taft slipped the disk into the silver metal pouch the courier held and sealed the opening. Signing his name across the strip, he handed it back.

"Thanks, it goes to Benson," Taft said. "Do you or your partner want a soft drink or something?"

"No sir," the courier said, "we need to get back to the office."

Tucking the pouch under his arm, the courier nodded as he passed Martinez walking up the drive. Then he slipped into the driver's seat of the NIA sedan as his partner climbed into the passenger seat and fastened his seat belt. Placing the sedan into drive he steered his way down the driveway.

"So," the partner said, "what's the legendary John Taft like?"

"He offered us a soda," the courier said.

"You mean you finally get to meet your hero and all he does is offer you a soft drink?"

"What did you expect he'd do," the courier said, "pull a rabbit out of a hat?"

"Something like that," the partner said slowly.

On the back deck of his home in Maryland, John Taft propped his feet up on a table and glanced over at Larry Martinez.

"I need to get away for a few days," Taft said quietly. "Kristin and I are going to take a cruise on *Tango*."

"Feeling blue?" Martinez asked.

"Tired of getting shot," Taft said. "Tired of feeling like I have the weight of the world on my shoulders."

"Somebody has to do it," Martinez said.

Taft nodded wearily. "The latest word is that China lost half of its fleet."

"How are Benson and Scaramelli?" Martinez asked.

"The Taiwanese cruiser they were on received little of the storm, they're fine," Taft noted. "Benson is briefing the president as we speak."

"Good thing the storm moved west as planned," Martinez said as he brushed a fly from his neck.

"I forget how Choi explained it," Taft said easily, "but the magnetic belts on the earth run a certain way, and they were pretty sure that would be the way the storm moved."

"What's the latest on Choi?" Martinez asked.

"Apparently his citizenship papers are forthcoming—he plans to work at the Advanced Physics Lab in Boulder."

"I guess it's over," Martinez said.

"For now."

"Do you ever think physicists will be able to control Einstein's theory so it can be used for good?" Martinez asked.

"Who knows," Taft said. "Whatever happens, *we* won't know about it. They slapped a circle of secrecy around this entire affair—the tightest I've ever seen."

"I know," Martinez said, "they came by my office yesterday and shredded all my reports and notes."

Taft stood up from his chair. He stared into the distance to the river running past.

"I found something inside the *Windforce* I didn't tell you about when we were in Boston," he said quietly.

"What?" Martinez asked.

"It was a chart of the stars," Taft said easily.

"Einstein must have liked to view the heavens at night," Martinez said, smiling. "Nothing unusual about that."

"You're probably right," Taft said quietly. "I kept the map. I never included it in any of my reports, so no one knows it exists. I just wanted to have something here that Einstein had touched."

"You know Benson will suspend you if he finds out," Martinez said. "He'd have to."

"Then I guess it will be our little secret," Taft said, rising.

"Where are you going?" Martinez asked.

"Come on into my office," Taft said as he opened the back door, then paused. "There's something written on the edge of the star chart. It looks like five letters."

Martinez rose from his seat and began to follow Taft. "Can you make out any of the letters?" he asked.

"The first three look like T,E,S, then something, and maybe an A," Taft said as Martinez followed him inside.

"I wonder what it means?" Martinez asked.

"I have no earthly idea," Taft said as he entered the office and handed Martinez the chart, "but I thought you could play around with it while I'm gone."

Martinez nodded. "Keep your cell phone with you. I'll call you if I find anything interesting."

"Don't you always?" Taft said as he led Martinez to the front door.